LOVERS AND NEWCOMERS

Rosie Thomas is the author of a number of celebrated novels, including the bestsellers *Sun at Midnight*, *Iris and Ruby* and *Constance*. A keen traveller, she has climbed in the Alps and the Himalayas, competed in the Peking to Paris car rally, spent time on a tiny Bulgarian research station in Antarctica and travelled the Silk Road through Asia. She lives in London.

ROSIE THOMAS

Lovers and Newcomers

HarperCollins*Publishers*

HarperCollins*Publishers*
77–85 Fulham Palace Road,
Hammersmith, London W6 8JB

www.harpercollins.co.uk

First published in Great Britain by
HarperCollins*Publishers* 2010

A catalogue record for this book
is available from the British Library

ISBN: 978 0 00 728595 2

Set in Sabon by Palimpsest Book Production Limited,
Grangemouth, Stirlingshire

Printed and bound in Great Britain by
Clays Ltd, St Ives plc

Mixed Sources

Product group from well-managed
forests and other controlled sources
www.fsc.org Cert no. SW-COC-1806
© 1996 Forest Stewardship Council

FSC

FSC is a non-profit international organisation established
to promote the responsible management of the world's forests.
Products carrying the FSC label are independently certified
to assure consumers that they come from forests that are managed
to meet the social, economic and ecological needs
of present and future generations.

Find out more about HarperCollins and the environment at
www.harpercollins.co.uk/green

To Theo

Acknowledgements

With particular thanks to Georgie Fogg.

SEPTEMBER

ONE

The old house has been cold and empty for so long, but now it's stirring. A joint of the oak stair treads releases a sudden sharp snap, a window left open for air rattles in a gust of wind, and the scent of baking rises from the kitchen.

The place is coming back to life around me.

I am making cakes for tea, and already I have looked into each of the guest rooms at least three times in order to enjoy the sight of folded towels and the little jugs of flowers placed on chests of drawers. Meadow flowers from Mead fields; oxeye daisies, and cow parsley, which has shed a faint dust of grey pollen on the waxed wood. I reach out to sweep away the powder with my little finger, before deciding that it looks pretty as it is.

Not that my old friends will be guests, of course.

They will belong here, they *do* belong here, that's why they are coming. I'm excited at the prospect, the pleasure of anticipation tautened with nerves, like a child before a birthday. This thought makes me laugh as I close the bedroom door. Childhood is a very long way off, for all of us. That's part of the story.

It's already four o'clock. A hot afternoon, for September. Only the angle of the sun, which has altered from full day to the first suggestion of evening just while I have been lingering in a doorway, suggests that autumn stalks not far off.

They'll be here soon.

As I walk down the stairs the longcase clock that stands in the hall chimes the hour, echoed today by the faint, damped note of the village church bell. You can only hear the church bell ringing when the wind blows from the south-west, Jake told me that when he first brought me here.

My late husband would be pleased with what's happening at Mead. I'm sure he would. I whisper to him in my head, as I sometimes do, in the way people who have become used to living alone conduct imaginary dialogues.

We lived our time here just the two of us, Jake, and came neither to want or need any other company. But without you there is too much time and silence. The house withers, and so do I.

From today there will be a new order, and different voices in the old rooms and outside under the heavy trees. The novelty, though, will have a retrospective glimmer that suits Mead, feeding it like wax polish on old wood. Selwyn and Amos and the others are your old friends as well as mine. Although this plan of mine will throw us all into new alignments, we have years of history between us.

In the kitchen I lift the tins out of the oven and turn out my cakes to cool on wire racks near the open window. A huge bumble bee flusters against the glass so I find a muslin-covered frame to place over them. But I find myself standing, lost in thought, my fingers still gripping the harmless frame as the bee escapes into the breeze.

I want this experiment to succeed. *I want it so much.*

From three different directions, three vehicles were converging on the old house in its cradle of fields and trees.

Selwyn Davies cursed as he ground the gears of the borrowed van yet again.

'This thing is a heap of shit. It's knackered. It's about as old as me, and just as useless.'

His partner didn't look up from the newspaper she held in

two hands, braced at chest level. *Partner* is a gruesome bloody word, Polly would say, but what are you supposed to call the person you never married but have lived with for thirty years and have three kids by?

'You're not old, or useless. Stop saying you are.'

'Is there any more tea in the flask, Poll?'

She sighed. 'Do you want to stop?'

'No. I just want some *tea*.'

'You're driving.'

'Am I? Oh, right. Thanks. Might have overlooked that if you hadn't reminded me.'

Polly smiled. 'It's not far now. I'd offer to drive, if I thought you'd agree to change over.'

'This gearbox. You wouldn't want to tangle with it, my love, believe me.'

Polly roughly folded her newspaper and rummaged in the Tesco bag at her feet. She brought out a dented Thermos flask, wedged it between her knees to remove the cup lid and unscrew the cap beneath, then poured the last dregs of beige tea. She nestled the cup in Selwyn's outstretched hand.

'Ta.' He drained the tea at a gulp, gave the cup back without looking at her. He shifted from buttock to buttock and stretched his neck in a futile attempt to ease the perennial ache in his back, then wound down the window and rested his elbow on the sill. Draught tore through the cab of the van, harrying Polly's newspaper and blowing his hair into a demented-looking crest. They reached the crown of a low hill and gathered speed. Selwyn tapped the dial and crowed, 'Look at that. Fifty mph.'

'Downhill, with a following wind,' they both added.

They often said the same things at the same time. Studying Selwyn as he drove, his teeth bared in a grimace and his fists locked on the wheel, Polly thought he looked like a pirate. She still found him attractive, even after thirty years. He made her laugh, and at other times the stab of love for him made her catch her breath.

'You know,' he said as they slowed to a crawl up the next hill, 'I never thought I'd end up going to live with her.'

'You live with *me*, Sel. Having her next door is a domestic technicality, not a contract in the biblical sense.'

He seemed to turn this over in his mind.

'It's her place. She's milady of the manor, isn't she?'

'It's our place. We're making it ours, from now on. That's the whole idea.'

'We'll see how it turns out. Anyway,' he added with a flash of a grin, 'it's too late now, eh?'

Selwyn loved the whiff of burning boats, and the wild leap for freedom out of the snapping jaws of disaster. It made him a tiring companion, but an interesting one.

'Yup.' Polly disentangled her newspaper, and seemed to concentrate on the arts pages.

In one of the two cars that were heading towards Mead, a silver Jaguar driven very confidently by her husband at unnecessarily high speed, Katherine Knight imagined how an eye in the sky might see them all. Three specks of metal, flashing an occasional point of light when chrome caught the sun, moving through a chequerboard of pasture and crops. Where they were going there was only farmland, and a scatter of villages, and then the white-laced edge of the land where it broke off into the sea. Katherine let out a small gasp, as if she were thinking so hard about what was to come that she had actually forgotten to breathe. Amos Knight glanced at her. He was wearing a blue shirt, crisply ironed, the cuffs folded back.

'Are you happy?'

It was an unusual question, for Amos. She said at once, 'Yes. Excited, too. What about you?'

He changed down with a dextrous flick and accelerated past a muck-spreader that was leaving a trail of brown clods on the crown of the road. He raised a hand, flat-palmed, in a magisterial salute as the other driver dwindled to a speck in the rear-view mirror.

6

'Good, good. That's what I like to hear.'

He concentrated on her answer and ignored the question. It had always been a trick of his to act as if he bestowed everything upon her, as if her life itself somehow flowed from its source in him and its abundance was his generous gift.

Katherine let her head fall back against the leather of the seat headrest.

It was rather impressive, in a way, that he felt he could still do this to her. Of course, she acknowledged scrupulously, in the economic sense he did provide. Amos was a barrister specializing in tax matters, whereas she was the administrator of a small medical charity. He earned per year – or rather *had* earned, she wasn't quite sure what would be happening in the future – rather more than twenty times her annual salary. That was a lot of money. He paid for their handsome house, deposits on flats for their two boys, holidays in the Caribbean or the Maldives, the various bouts of their joint entertaining, most of her clothes.

But, she had taken to telling herself, his money and recent professional status didn't mean that he owned her, nor that she had no existence apart from him. Not now, not any longer. Katherine now knew that as a person, as a good human being with solid worth, if she were somehow to be placed in the opposite pan to him on a pair of moral scales, her metal might not shine as brightly as his but she would still outweigh him.

Yes, she would.

Out of the corner of her eye Katherine looked at the chino-clad bolster of his thigh and wondered why it was that her attempts at self-affirmation never quite succeeded, even in her own estimation.

Amos was Amos, and she tended to get washed up on the granite cliffs of him like a small boat driven in a gale on to the Chilean shore.

They were driving through a village, its main street set with small grey stone terraced houses that broke up in places to reveal vistas of new bungalows set behind them. A group of resentful teenagers stared out from a glass and steel bus shelter like ruminants from a pen at the zoo. Amos patted the palms of his hands on the wheel, then brightened.

'Are you hungry?' he asked, which meant that he was.

On a corner of the long street he had spotted a teashop. He braked and the Jaguar slid in to the kerb.

'We said we'd be there for tea,' Katherine remarked. Amos got out of the car, came around and held open the door for her.

'There's no hurry. We've got a lifetime at Mead ahead of us.'

For a moment, she imagined he had said life sentence.

The teashop was cool, with a stone-flagged floor and a cluster of mismatched chairs and tables. Amos sat down at the table in the window and Katherine took her place opposite him. He chose scones and cream for both of them, and wedges of Victoria sponge and fruit cake, chatting with the waitress as she took the order. He had always had a big appetite, and lately he seemed even hungrier for food.

'We don't have to eat it all,' he laughed at her protest, 'but you know I love cake.'

Katherine acquiesced. It was restful sitting in the window of what must once have been the village shop, with the traffic trickling by outside. The country was a slower place, they would both have to learn that. Gripped by affection as well as happy anticipation, she leaned across and put her hands over Amos's.

'We're at the beginning, aren't we?' she said. 'A new place, a different way to live, but still with the benefit of everything we have learned. That's all right, isn't it?' Then, knowing that what they both knew really couldn't be construed as all right, she added hastily, 'Remember what we were like, all of us, when we met?'

'Only vaguely, thank God.'

He withdrew one hand, then the other, and as soon as the waitress put the plate in front of them he started work on the scones. He began to talk about their rather famous architect.

The woman had promised to send a revised set of drawings for part of their magnificent new house, to be built at Mead on a plot of land purchased from Miranda, but had failed to do so before they left for this inaugural weekend.

The teenagers had broken out of the corral of the bus shelter. Now they lurched up the street in a mob, arms and legs shooting out of the central mass. They enveloped Amos's glimmering silver Jaguar and one of them tweaked the nearside wing mirror, which instantly lent the car a comical lop-eared appearance. Amos was concentrating on loading jam onto the second half of scone and didn't see what was happening, but Katherine watched. Without feeling much concern for the car, she hoped that they would move on before her husband noticed the assault on his property and caused a scene.

One of the bigger boys glanced up and caught her eye. He bounded across the pavement and pressed himself up against the café window. He had a broad red face, hummocked with pimples, which he brought up against the glass, misting it with his breath. His mouth opened wider and suckered itself to the glass, lips paling as his tongue licked a trail through the dust in a lingering smooch. Katherine gazed with interest at this spectacle as Amos bit into his scone. Behind the window boy, the rest of the group were pulling the wipers of the car to the vertical, rocking on the rear bumper and trying to prise open the doors.

She coughed slightly as the boy doing the kissing formed a tube with the fingers and thumb of his right hand and waggled it at her.

Amos did look around now. The boy immediately detached himself and ran, leaving a wet smear on the window like the trail of a giant mollusc.

'Bloody feral kids, same everywhere,' Amos growled, through crumbs and jam. The other boys dashed after their leader, hooting as they went.

'Christ, look what they've done,' Amos roared, suddenly noticing.

Katherine tucked away a smile as she looked at the car, wing mirrors drooping and wipers standing erect.

'More tea?' she asked.

Selwyn negotiated a lane lined with trees that looked leaned-upon by the wind. He swung the wheel sharply and steered the van through a pair of lichenous gateposts topped with stone balls twice the size of a man's head.

The drive curved under more trees, then straightened, and Mead revealed itself against its ancient green backdrop. At its heart was an old flint building with bigger Georgian windows than the original farmhouse construction had featured, which gave it a slightly startled aspect. A modest porte cochère, also a later addition to the fabric, framed the double front door. The plaster was falling in chunks from the bases of the fluted pillars. On either side of the original house, short, unmatching wings had been added at later dates, partly in reddish-orange brick and partly in flint. The overall effect was harmonious but not at all grand, as if the house had quietly expanded according to requirements over several hundred years without any particular design having been set or followed.

The van coasted over the gravel and came to rest at a tangent to the circular flowerbed that formed the centrepiece of the front courtyard. The scent of lavender flooded the cab.

Polly looked through the insect-spotted windscreen at the russet and grey façade of the house. There was moss growing beneath broken sections of lead guttering, and the paintwork of the front door was faded, but the size of it and the almost magical seclusion of the setting never failed to impress her. Mead was a beautiful place to end up, she reflected. If ending up was actually what was happening.

In the front doorway, framed by the pillars, Miranda Meadowe appeared. She held open her arms.

Selwyn vaulted out of the van and trampled through lavender and leggy roses. He wrapped his arms around Miranda's narrow torso and swung her off her feet, laughing and kissing her neck.

'Babs, darling Barb, we thought we'd never get here.' He took in a great breath of air, 'Ah, smell that countryside, will you? It's ripe with pure cow. Or is it sheep? Now we *are* here we're never going to leave. Are we, Poll? So you'd better get used to it. I hope it isn't all a mistake, is it, Barb? You haven't changed your mind?'

Polly followed behind him, skirting the flowerbed. Her hips and buttocks and breasts made a series of globes, tending towards one circular impression as she moved.

'Put me down, Sel,' Miranda protested. 'No, of course I haven't changed my mind. Hello, Polly, love. Welcome to Mead. Welcome *home*.'

The two women kissed each other, hands patting each other's upper arms where the flesh was soft.

'Thanks, Miranda,' Polly murmured. 'Here we are. I'm very glad.'

Selwyn called Miranda Barbara mainly because he could. They had known each other since their first term at university, the almost prehistoric time when Miranda had still been Barbara Huggett, fresh from her divorced mother's semi in Wolverhampton. When Barbara took the part of Miranda in the University Players' production of *The Tempest*, in which Selwyn played Trinculo, she decided that as a name for a black-haired siren with a future in theatre, Miranda had a lot more going for it than Barbara ever would.

It was a considerable number of years after that that she finally met and married Jacob Meadowe, farmer and landowner.

'Come on in,' Miranda beamed.

She danced her way through the house, past the handsome staircase and the doors opening to the drawing room, and a shuttered dining room where the table was already laid with six places for dinner.

'When are the others getting here?' Selwyn called, peering in at the glimmer of silver candlesticks.

The final establishment of the new households would take some more time, but with her developed sense of theatre

11

Miranda had decreed that there should be a weekend gathering to mark the beginning of their new association.

'Now,' Miranda said, with her wide smile. It was nearly five o'clock.

This was the weekend.

The kitchen was warm, with one of the solid fuel ranges that Polly thought a country living cliché and quite impossible to cook on, and which Miranda claimed to love like a dear friend. The floor was red quarry tiles, starred and pocked with a history of dropped saucepans and tracked with the passage of generations. There was a built-in dresser running the length of one wall, its shelves crowded with mismatched china, and a scrubbed table in the centre. Polly lowered herself into a Windsor chair painted some shade of English Heritage blue to match the legs of the table.

'Tea coming up,' Miranda said happily. She brought the kettle back to the boil, poured and stirred, and then began to slice sponge cake.

'Just a small bit for me,' Polly murmured.

'Oh, come on. I made it.'

Selwyn had bounded straight to the back door. He unlatched it and stood on the threshold, rocking gently on the balls of his feet and staring out into the cobbled back courtyard. Chickweed sprouted between the stones and clumps of nettles grew against the flint walls. There were two short wings projecting from the rear of the main house as well as from the front, giving it the profile of a broad but stumpy and irregular H. These two wings were smaller and more dilapidated than the forward-facing pair, having been used in the past partly as barns for the farming that no longer happened at Mead, and partly as garaging for long-vanished cars. The right-hand wing had been converted years before for holiday lettings, but now stood empty and waiting. The left-hand one was much more tumbledown. A section of the roof stood open to the rafters, the panes in some of the windows were broken and patched with cardboard, and a barn-sized door hung open and let in the weather.

It was this most sorry portion of the old house that Selwyn and Polly had recently bought from Miranda, using quite a large slice of the capital that remained from selling their own house and paying off accumulated debts. Despite her unworldly air, Miranda – or her financial advisors – had driven a hard bargain.

'We should get some of our stuff unloaded,' Selwyn said. 'Set up camp. Polly?'

He vibrated with so much eagerness and seemingly innocent energy that the natural response would have been to go along with whatever he suggested. The two women knew him better, and gazed back at him.

'We've only been here ten minutes,' Polly observed.

'Camp? What do you mean? You can't be thinking of sleeping across there tonight?' Miranda wailed. 'Have a rest first.'

Selwyn rubbed his hands. They were big, broad, and scarred.

'Rest? Rest from what? There's a lot to do out there. We want to get started, Poll, don't we?'

Polly looked from one to the other.

'Tomorrow,' she said.

The Jaguar purred between the gateposts, accelerated past the bend in the driveway and came to a halt beside the abandoned white van.

Amos nodded at it. 'That'll be Selwyn's.'

He and Katherine sat in the quiet and looked across at the front of the house.

'I always forget. It's lovely,' Katherine breathed.

'It's falling down.'

'That, too.'

'Come on. Let's go inside and at least get ourselves a drink before the place collapses.'

Amos sprang out and immediately buried his head in the Jaguar's limited boot space, then emerged with a box in his arms. The evening air was rich with the scent of lavender and agriculture. Miranda appeared once more in the doorway, framed by the pillars. Burdened with his case of champagne

13

Amos could only boom a greeting at her, but Miranda and Katherine embraced.

'You look well,' Miranda murmured in Katherine's ear, as if she had been expecting otherwise.

'I *am* well. You know.'

'We'll talk. Amos, give me a kiss.'

He leaned over the box and kissed the cheek that she turned to him.

It was Amos who led the way inside. Katherine pulled down the ribbing of her heather-coloured cardigan and followed, carefully placing her feet on the uneven paving. Miranda came behind, light on her feet in her worn ballet flats.

The kitchen boiled with noisy greetings.

'*Bollinger?* Amos, you're still a flash fucker.'

'Right, you'll be sticking to tea, then,' Amos grinned as he dropped a weighty arm on Selwyn's shoulder. 'Mirry, glasses for the rest of us. We'll drink a toast to the new order.'

'Ah, Katherine, come here. Your husband's a prat, but you are gorgeous. And you smell divine.'

'Do I? It's Jo Malone. I thought it might be a bit young for me . . .'

'Now, listen. I don't want to hear the *y* word, not from any of us, now or for the rest of our years at Mead. Or the *o* word, either. Definitely not that one.'

'Shouldn't we wait for Colin?'

Everyone was talking at once. Miranda moved happily between them.

Colin was the sixth member of their group. 'He'll be here in a minute, I'm sure.'

'Polly, my darling. How do you bear living with this man?'

'How do I? You're going to find out, aren't you?'

'Christ. Yes. What have we all let ourselves in for?'

'I don't seem to have any champagne glasses. Or not matching ones. Not much call for them lately.'

'It doesn't matter about matching. Any glasses will do. Just don't give Amos the biggest one. Here, let's use these.'

14

Selwyn applied strong thumbs and the first cork popped. Miranda swooped a glass and caught the plume of silver froth. The five of them stood in a smiling circle, between the dresser and the scrubbed table with its litter of mugs and cake crumbs.

'A toast,' Amos proposed. 'Here's to Mead, and to Miranda, and the future.'

'Here's to all of us,' Miranda answered. 'Long life and . . .' she searched for the appropriate word, then it floated into her head, 'harmony.'

'Harmony. To all of us,' they echoed.

The words came easily enough. They had known each other for the best part of forty years. For some of those decades the friendships had seemed consigned to the past, but now there was this late and intriguing regrowth.

Polly put down her empty champagne glass. 'Where *is* Colin?' she asked.

The third vehicle, a small German-made saloon, had reached Meddlett village. It passed the church and the general store-cum-post office on the corner, and skirted the village green. It had passed the pub too, where the lights were coming on as the daylight faded, but then the driver braked quite sharply. A car following behind hooted and accelerated past with another angry blast on the horn. The first car reversed a few yards, then made a dart into the pub car park.

The bar was yellow-lit. It had been slightly modernized, which meant that the horse brasses, patterned carpet and tankards had been removed and replaced by stripped wood. Various jovially phrased notices warned against hiking boots, work clothing and requests for credit. A list of darts fixtures was pinned to the wall next to a cratered dartboard. The window table was occupied by a young couple with a dog seated on the bench between them. They each had an arm wrapped around the dog, and over its smooth black head they were talking heatedly in low voices. An old man in corduroy trousers sat on a stool at the bar, and two younger men stood next to him with pints in their hands. Their conversation halted as their heads turned towards the door. Colin ducked to miss the low beams and made his way to the bar. The barman put down a cloth and rested his weight on his knuckles.

'Evening,' he said.

Colin smiled. He felt about as at home in this place as he would have done in the scrum of a rugby international, and wondered why only a minute ago it had seemed like such an excellent idea to call in for a solitary, sharpening drink before turning up at Mead.

'Evening. I'll have . . .' A cranberry martini? A pink champagne cocktail? He ran his eye along the labelled pumps. '. . . ah, a pint of Adnam's.'

'Coming up,' the barman nodded. The conversation to Colin's left resumed, being something to do with reality television.

'If they will pick monkeys, they'll get gibberish, won't they?' the older man observed.

'Do better yourself, Ken, could you?' one of the others laughed.

'I could,' Ken said flatly. He drank, then stuck out his lower lip and removed a margin of beer froth from the underside of his moustache.

Colin carried his drink to a table facing the dartboard. He centred the straight glass on a circular beer mat, drew out a chair and sat down. He was very tired, not just because of the drive to Meddlett. He resisted the urge to tip his head back against the dado rail and close his eyes on the saloon bar. Instead he took a mouthful of beer. A man in checkered trousers, white jacket and neckerchief looked in through the door. He was dark, eastern European, perhaps Turkish, Colin guessed. The chef briefly met his eye, then withdrew.

There was a laminated menu slotted into a small wooden block on the table in front of him. Colin studied it.

'Why not try our delicious smoked haddock hotpot?' it queried. 'Served with chips and salad.'

He wondered, if he were going to eat here, whether he would

choose the hotpot over the Moroccan-style lamb tagine or the hot and spicy Thai noodles. There wasn't much hope of getting away from the chips. He wondered how life would be if he didn't move forwards or backwards but took a room right here at the Griffin, eavesdropping on the conversations of strangers and submerging himself in a lake of Adnam's.

Miranda and Polly and the others would come looking for him. However he tried to evade them they would search him out and take him by the arm, kindly but unstoppably, and lead him to Mead. In his present directionless state this thought was vaguely comforting. He didn't want not to be at Mead any more strongly than he wanted not to be anywhere else. He would occupy one of Miranda's several spare bedrooms, listen to the conversations of his old friends, and his external inertia would secretly mirror the other lack of function that he had yet to come to terms with.

Miranda had been a bright, unsteady flame when he first knew her.

He could see her as she had been, as vividly as if that early version of her had just danced into the room. She wore her black hair in thick ropes, pinned up anyhow, and the tangled, reckless volume of it made her thin arms and legs and narrow waist seem all the more elegantly fragile. She had appeared like some newborn quadruped, all unsteady limbs and wet eyelashes, but with a healthy young animal's instinctive hold on life. Miranda had been at all the parties, all the Hunger Lunches and demos and concerts and poetry readings, dressed in her tiny skirts and suede jerkins and velvet cloaks and dippy hats. He didn't think she had been to all that many lectures, but that wouldn't have mattered because Miranda was going to be an actress. She had scaled the university's various social ladders, hand over hand, and perched near the top rung of all of them. She had been, decidedly, a success.

Colin was almost sure that he could remember the actual party where they had all joked about their commune-to-be.

There had been a small room, probably somewhere up

Divinity Road, every wall and hard surface painted purple, filled with mattresses and candles and joss sticks, the reek of joints and half-cured Afghan coats.

Amos had definitely been there. Amos was a somewhat marginal figure in those days. He had been to a public school, while the rest of them took pride in the fact that they had not. He played rugby and would disappear slightly shame-facedly on weekday afternoons to train at the university sports ground, often vanishing on Saturdays as well to play in college matches. Like the rest of them he wore loons and tie-dyed vests, but his hair never seemed to grow quite long enough to eradicate the school prefect's neat side-parting and razor-clipped neck. Amos was loudly a member of the University Communist Club. When he got drunk he liked to link arms with his friends and zigzag home chanting 'Ho, Ho, Ho Chi Minh'.

Selwyn had been there too, laughing and skinning up, all red mouth and lean, flat belly. Selwyn's little jumpers and shrunken vests tended to ride up and away from the tops of his velvet pants to expose disconcerting, lickable expanses of his smooth skin. It was Selwyn who would have been responsible for the music, most probably at that time precisely on the groovy cusp between the Yardbirds and Led Zeppelin. Colin acknowledged to himself that he had no real idea; even in those days he had preferred Verdi. But Selwyn would have known. Selwyn ran a mobile disco called Blue Peony out of his Dormobile van. He often played at student balls and big parties, standing at the decks in headphones, dappled by the bloom of strobe lights and enclosed within a three-deep ring of girls.

Polly had been there too, talking hard and gesticulating and prodding the air to make a point. Not Katherine, though. Katherine came along later.

And Miranda of course. Wherever Selwyn was, in those days, Miranda went. Miranda had got up to dance between the tangle of legs. She made vine-tendril twisting motions with her small white hands, swaying with her eyes closed, hair falling down her back in a thick dark river. Colin watched Selwyn who

18

watched Miranda who was wandering happily in her own universe.

'It's not going to happen,' Polly said. 'Not to us. Never. We've got the Pill now, they'll have developed a magic medicine bullet by the time we're fifty. We'll all take it, we're going to stay young and beautiful.'

'If you want to be loved,' Colin hummed, but nobody heard him.

'That's rubbish,' Amos scoffed. 'Medical and technological advances haven't quite got to the point where they can stop you hitting fifty, Polly, and then sixty and seventy, and then you'll die. But we're young now, that's what counts. We're going to start making a difference as soon as we can.'

'What difference?' someone yawned.

'We'll bring down the old order, establish the new. Attack the morbid old institutions, the BBC, the party political system, the monarchy . . .'

This was not a previously unheard speech of Amos's.

'The class system, the public schools . . .' Polly patiently and amusedly listed for him.

Colin stirred himself. He had smoked enough of Amos's hash to realize that he knew secrets and understood mysteries, and should concentrate on those insights instead of dissipating precious energy on worrying about his clothes and the exams.

'Listen, man. Before long, Americans will be standing on the moon. Think of that. Why can't there be a cure for old age?'

'There is. It's called *death*,' Amos snapped.

Miranda had gyrated to the window. She leaned her hot forehead against the cool glass and then gave a little cry.

'Look. Oh, look. Everyone.'

Heads turned. The moon was a pale, perfect disc sailing through streamers of cloud.

Miranda breathed, 'Imagine it. Men on the moon. How . . . beautiful. Their footprints will be up there in the dust, you know, for ever and ever. I'm envious. I'd like that to be *my* epitaph.'

'If Polly and Colin are right, you won't be needing an epitaph. You'll still be here, cluttering the place up.'

'Oh, I don't think I want that at all. What I'd like when the time comes is to be a magnificent old lady. With a brilliant, scandalous history. Frail of course, rather grand, *greatly* loved. Deeply mourned, when I go.' She lifted her arm, the trumpet sleeve of her velvet dress falling back to leave her wrist bare. 'You know what? I've got the most amazing idea. When we are all old, if it *has* to happen, we should live together in a fabulous, outrageous commune. We should all come back together again, at the other end of our lives, when we've achieved everything we want to, and just refuse to do what old people do.'

'Old people being like my gran, you mean?' a boy interrupted. 'She sits in a chair all day waiting to be taken to the toilet, and begs for her cup of tea because she can't remember she had it five minutes ago?'

Miranda looked on him with pity. 'It won't be like that. Not for us,' she said. 'Polly's talking about it all being different by then, not about actual immortality.'

'Christ,' Amos said. 'What is all this? There's so much to be done *now*. Why are we talking about what's going to happen to us in a hundred years time?'

'I like my idea,' Miranda insisted.

Selwyn stirred himself. He reached up to grasp Miranda's wrist, and drew her back into the circle. She had stuck sequins along her cheekbones and they flashed in the candlelight.

'Then you shall have what you want,' he told her. Most of them laughed. Selwyn was joking, but the joke was in part a reference to his acknowledged supremacy and power in the group. What Selwyn decided usually came to pass.

Silence had fallen after that. In their different ways they were all thinking about the conversation and peering, into the chinks between the phrases, at the remote and chilly landscape of their old age. It had seemed no less distant than the moon.

Or perhaps it was just me who was contemplating it, Colin thought now.

Maybe the others were all far too preoccupied with the constant murmur of sex. Or the roar of sedition, in Amos's case.

'He's mine, for fuck's sake. You're not having him, whatever you say.'

The sudden shout made Colin jump. The young couple who had been sitting in the window were now on their feet and measuring up to each other as if they were about to trade blows. The dog jumped off the bench and whimpered and the boy grabbed at the lead clipped to its collar. The girl reached to snatch at the lead too. In doing so she lost her footing and overbalanced against Colin's table. It tilted sharply and his glass slid off and smashed on the floor. Beer and shards splashed over his shoe and sock.

'Shit, Jessie,' the boy hissed.

The girl turned to look at what she had done, but she didn't miss the opportunity to grab the lead out of the boy's hand first.

'Bugger off,' she told him.

The boy was scarlet in the face and everyone in the room was looking at him. Beer dripped off the leg of Colin's trousers.

'You're a cow,' the boy told the girl. He banged past the table and marched out of the bar. The dog whined again, and then consoled itself by lapping at the puddle of spilled beer.

'Mind the *glass*, Raff,' the girl screeched. She jerked on the lead to haul the animal out of danger, and anchored him to the leg of a heavier table. She and Colin stooped together and began to gather up the shards of broken glass.

'I'm really, really sorry,' the girl muttered. 'He wanted to take my dog, you know?'

'Watch out,' the barman said, arriving with a cloth and a dustpan. The girl mopped up the puddle as he swept the debris away. Colin ruefully examined his wet ankle, shaking off the tinkly remnants of broken glass.

'Shall I, like, mop you up as well?' She made some flapping

21

movements with the dingy cloth. Colin took a folded white handkerchief out of his pocket and did the job for himself.

'It's all right. No permanent damage,' he said, sounding pompous in his own ears.

'Really? You'd better let me buy you another drink, though, since the last one went in your shoe.'

Colin sat upright and looked at her. She was no more than eighteen, with a pretty, monkeyish face. Her open top showed the upper tendrils of a tattoo extending above her right breast. She smiled suddenly at him, and Colin smiled back.

'Just a half,' he said.

'Right. What was it?'

'That one,' he pointed. The dog watched with its ears pricked as she bought two halves and carried them back to the table.

'There you go. Can I join you? Just split with my bloke, haven't I? Mind you, that's no great loss. He's a disaster. This is Rafferty, by the way.' The dog's tongue fell out of its mouth. 'And I'm Jessie.'

'Colin,' Colin said. 'Sorry about the boyfriend.'

'Uh, well. There's not a lot of choice round here, that's the thing. It's make the best of what there is or DIY, if you get me.'

Colin laughed.

'So, you on holiday?'

'Not exactly,' Colin said.

Jessie took a packet of Golden Virginia and some Rizlas out of her pocket and began to construct a roll-up. 'It's all *right*,' she pre-empted the barman's protest. 'There's no law against making a fag, is there? I'm not going to *smoke* it in here.'

She turned her attention back to Colin. 'So?'

'I have a friend, some friends, who live near here. I'm just visiting. For a few days, maybe longer.'

'Where's that, then?'

'Mead House. Do you know it?'

Jessie turned down the corners of her expressive mouth and wagged her head from side to side.

'La-di-dah.'

22

'*Is* it?'

'Yeah, it's posh for this part of the world.' She gave a quick cough of laughter, and at the same time checked out Colin's shoes and watch. 'Dead posh. You should see the places that aren't. Open your eyes a bit, that would.'

'Do you live in, uh, Meddlett?'

'Yup. Born and bred. And Damon.'

'Damon?'

'Him.' She jerked her head to the door.

'Why was he trying to take your dog?'

'He *did* belong to both of us. Me and Damon're living together, right? Rented a place off this bloke who was going abroad, and we got the dog as well, the same time, from a dogs' home. Made us seem like a family. But the bottom line is he's mine. Raff knows it, Damon knows it. He was trying it on, just now, that's all.'

Jessie raised her chin, but Colin could see that she was on the verge of tears. Rafferty pulled himself forward almost to throttling point in order to rest his jaw on the corner of her knee. He rolled his eyes upwards and Jessie stroked his head.

'Can't stay with us, Raff, can he? He'll have to find himself somewhere else to live. *Fucking* loser,' she muttered.

'What do you do, Jessie? Have you got a job?'

She sniffed. 'Yeah. Course. I'm not one of those scroungers. I've been on the casual all summer, since I left sixth-form college. Cleaning. You know, holiday lets and that. End of the season, now, though. I could go on the agricultural, but that's mostly for the foreigners. Have to think about uni, won't I, next year? Now me and Damon are finished.'

'That sounds to me like a good idea.'

He was becoming quite the embodiment of pomposity, Colin thought. He glanced at his watch. Somehow it was now twenty minutes to nine. They had finished their drinks while they were talking.

'Yeah, I gotta go too,' Jessie said at once. She stood up abruptly and detached Rafferty's lead. 'Night all,' she called loudly to the other customers. Four pairs of eyes watched them as they filed out.

In the car park, Colin took a deep breath and gave thanks for the fact that he hadn't tried to buy them both another drink. It was a long time since he had consumed even two pints of beer.

'Nice talking to you,' Jessie muttered.

He noticed that there was a full moon behind the tall trees that lined the car park wall, a pale disc floating behind branches and stirring up memories.

'Can I give you a lift anywhere?'

Jessie was grinning as she considered him. 'We-ell. Don't suppose you're going to *jump* on me, are you?'

'No.' Not you, or anyone else.

'All right. It's the same way you're going, anyway.'

Jessie sat beside him with the dog pressed between her knees. They drove in silence, down an empty road turned pewter by the moonlight.

'Just in here,' she said abruptly, after a mile. The car nosed into a break in the hedgerow barred by a lopsided gate.

'Know your way from here, do you? It's another mile, then stone gateposts on the right.'

'Yes. I've been there before.'

'See you around, Col.'

The dog bounded out, followed by the girl. Jessie vaulted the gate, the dog squeezed between the lower bars, and they both vanished into the darkness.

When he turned the corner in the drive, Mead was a blazing patchwork of light that dimmed the moon. Colin sat for a few minutes and stared at the yellow windows, watching as figures passed back and forth inside. It had turned cold under the crackling stars and he shivered.

Miranda was standing outside the dining-room door as he slipped into the house. She wore her hair in a neat silvery bob but now there were strands sticking out all over her head, and she had the look of just having recovered from laughing very hard.

'Here you are at last,' she exclaimed to him. 'Thank goodness. Why's your phone turned off? We were about to send out a search party.'

'I guessed you might,' Colin said.

She kissed him, her mouth rubbing against his, her hands cupping his face.

'Darling, you're freezing. Come on, come and get warm. Have you eaten? Amos wanted us all to play Sardines. For a moment it looked as though we might have to, but things have moved on.'

'I was held up, sorry I'm late. What's going on?'

'Fun.' Miranda tilted her head back so that she could look squarely at him. Her eyes were brilliant. 'It is, you know. Remember? I didn't expect getting together to be quite so lively.'

'Good,' he said simply. 'That's a really good start.'

She took his hand, lacing her fingers through his, and drew him into the dining room.

'He's finally arrived.'

Four faces turned at once. Colin had the momentary, disconcerting sense of having slipped back into another time.

These people were not the same age as he felt; they were not medically ravaged or disappointed in love or grown cynical in the wake of too much compromise. They were students, sprawled and giggly and careless. He blinked. The difference was that the empty bottles on the table had held champagne, the crumbs scattered between the place settings were Stilton and oatcakes and the smoke was from Amos's cigar. But there was a glitter in the air that was even more startling, a mineral sparkle that was nothing to do with the candlelight or Katherine's earrings. Dust was not settling; currents of anticipation set the motes whirling. The room felt charged, as if a single spark might ignite a blaze.

Selwyn leaped up and spread his arms out wide.

'Never trust anyone over seventy, Col.'

Polly left her seat and came to Colin's side, wrapping an arm around him and dropping her head on his shoulder.

'Don't listen to him. We were just talking about the old days. How are you feeling? Are you well?'

Polly always emanated warmth and ease, not just because of her rounded haunches and broad, well-fleshed back, or her apparent happy security within the solid defences of her body. Unusually, and unlike Amos, her cleverness didn't make her impatient. She listened and remembered and so her sympathy could be depended on, but she was also clear-sighted and wasn't afraid to be brisk, or even truthful. She was the member of the group with whom Colin felt most comfortable. If he loved anyone, in the objective and unspoken and theoretical manner that was all that was left to him nowadays, it was Polly Ettridge.

'I feel fine.'

Looking from Polly down the length of the table, to the faces and the backdrop of old furniture and folded dim curtains, he realized that he really did feel fine. Now that he had actually arrived at Mead.

He found his way to a place at the table end. Miranda placed a dish of blackberry tart with ivory clots of thick cream in front of him, with a wineglass of champagne. Colin had a sweet tooth. He attacked the pudding and then took a swig of champagne. He brandished the glass.

'Here's to the big Mead adventure.'

'Jake would have enjoyed this, wouldn't he?' Miranda said.

In their different ways, in the small pool of silence that followed, each of them acknowledged his absence. The scale of it, the absolute way that Jake had left them, had gone and *died*, was made harder to contemplate because they were so alive tonight.

After a moment Colin asked deliberately, 'What stage are the plans at now? Fill me in.'

Amos sat back in his chair. He described how the new house would rise on a sloping plot of land hidden by a belt of trees to the south-west of the house. It was to be uncompromisingly modern with impeccable green credentials. The last adjustments to the plans, to meet the requirements of the local authority planning committee, were now in progress. Building work, Amos announced, would soon be starting. In the meantime, once the move up here was completed, he and Katherine were going to make a temporary home in the one-time holiday wing at the back of Mead.

'We need to be right here. Keep an eye on the contractors,' Amos said.

There was a collective shifting in seats, another change in the glittering currents of air as no one mentioned the real reason why Amos was leaving London and his chambers.

Katherine thoughtfully broke off a piece of oatcake and bit it in half. She was the only one who had changed before dinner, into an amethyst silk shift dress. Anything that plain and unadorned, Miranda reckoned, must have cost well into four figures.

'We're looking forward to it. Living in a holiday cottage will be like being on holiday,' Katherine laughed.

Selwyn nodded. 'Maybe it will.'

Miranda listened to his deep voice rather than the actual words. She knew what Selwyn's plans were. From now on Polly and he would be living here too. They were going to do most of the work on the derelict wing themselves. She didn't doubt Selwyn's ability to tackle the job, or Polly's willingness to assist him.

Selwyn had read medicine at university, but he had never completed his clinical practice. He had moved to Somerset instead, to a ramshackle cottage, where he set up a business buying, restoring and reselling antique furniture. Over the years, as the supply of undervalued old gems in need of a French polish seemed to dwindle, he had gone into buying timber and making furniture himself, and once Polly had given up academia and joined him they had run the business together. Polly wrote historical biographies in the short hours that were left to her between the furniture business and bringing up three children.

Miranda never knew precisely how successful or otherwise their enterprises had been, but it was no secret that they had never had any money to spare. The Somerset house and the workshops had finally been sold, and they had bought their piece of Mead from her.

Selwyn flexed his chisel-scarred fingers and grinned. 'I'm busting to get started.'

That was obvious enough. The undischarged electricity that flickered in the room seemed to crackle about him, just as it had done when they were young.

Miranda looked across at Colin, inviting him to take his turn.

'I'll monitor progress and supply strong drink when required. When I'm not working I'll stay if and when Miranda lets me.'

Colin was a theatre set designer. Mostly he worked in London, but sometimes a job took him to Italy or New York. Unlike the others he was not planning to move to Mead for good. Miranda leaned over and covered his hand with hers.

'There are nine bedrooms in this house. Be here with us as much as you can,' she implored.

Colin needed to be with somebody, after everything he had been through. They all thought that, not just Miranda. And if not with them, then whom?

'Thanks, Miranda. Here I am.'

Selwyn had fidgeted and twitched through all the talking. Now he tipped back half a glass of red wine and jumped to his feet.

'Sitting for hours makes my back ache. Where's the music, Mirry?'

'Next door.'

He bounded through a set of double doors, dragging the white loops of earphones and a black iPod out of his pocket. Ten seconds later music crashed out of the speakers.

'C'mon, let's dance,' Selwyn hollered.

They groaned, but left their seats. It was 'Baba O'Reilly'.

Selwyn kicked back a rug to expose dusty oak floorboards.

They launched into the dance, laughing and kicking out their arms and legs and swinging their buttocks, without the embarrassed scorn of the Knight boys or Selwyn and Polly's son and twin daughters to inhibit them. The Who were succeeded by Pink Floyd.

'Haven't you heard of the Arctic Monkeys, Selwyn?' Amos shouted.

'No, and neither have you.'

Katherine, flushed and beaming, was jiving with Colin. As always Amos missed every beat but made up for it with general enthusiasm.

Watching the dancing, her nervous anticipation melted into delight at the success of the first evening, Miranda noticed that there was no wine left on the table. She thought of the remaining bottles of Bollinger in the fridge in the pantry and slipped out into the hall to collect one or two of them. A narrow passage behind the stairs, lined with coats and cluttered with wellingtons, provided a short cut directly to the pantry. She didn't need to switch on the lights, she knew every creak underfoot and every draught on her cheek, so she swore softly when her ankle connected sharply with a suitcase that Amos had brought in and left there. As she stopped to let the pain subside there was a rustle and a darker shape moved against the darkness.

It was Selwyn. She knew the scent of him before he reached for her, before his lips touched her ear.

'You are beautiful, Barb. You're so fucking gorgeous tonight, I don't know where to put myself.'

'And you're pissed, Sel.'

'No, I'm not.'

Even though it was pitch dark Miranda could see the lines of his profile. Through the muffle of waxed jackets and tweed caps she could hear pairs of feet thudding to the beat.

'You didn't always think I was gorgeous.'

There was a ripple of amusement in her voice.

'Oceans of water have flowed under more bridges than there are in Venice, since those days,' he protested.

He kissed her and she responded with a sharp intake of breath that seemed to catch in his throat.

'Stop it,' Miranda breathed, but they still hung together. He ran his fingers over her throat, down to the open buttons of her top.

She did move then, forcing herself to duck under his arm and skip away to the kitchen. He followed her, into the bright lights and the debris of cooking.

'Take a couple of those bottles through for me?'

'Amos has had quite enough already.'

'So have you,' she countered.

In the drawing room they were still dancing. Miranda was relieved that no one had missed them, even though all that had happened was a kiss exchanged by friends at the end of a long evening.

Everyone is asleep.

I could just hear the low rumble of Amos talking to Katherine as they undressed, but that stopped a while ago. Selwyn and Polly will be under the bedcovers, oblivious too. I imagine them spooned together, breathing in unison, Selwyn's dark face crumpled up against her dimpled shoulder.

Amos will be wearing pyjamas, Katherine a nightie, but Polly and Sel will sleep naked. I remember what that felt like, the safety of interlocked bodies, the balm of skin against skin.

None of my business.

I hope Colin is sleeping too. He looks brittle with illness and exhaustion. Maybe Mead will soothe him, if he will allow it to.

These thoughts dance a gavotte around the other. How long since I was kissed, like Selwyn kissed me tonight?

A long, long time.

The lingering heat of that kiss makes me restless.

I cross the room, lean on the windowsill and gaze out. The moon has gone but over the crowns of oak and beech I can see stars. Tomorrow will be another warm day.

The house settles around me. No – around *us*.

As my mother encouraged me to do, I reckon up my blessings. This is what I have.

Mead, my husband's house, now mine. I love it as if it were a living thing, even its dilapidation, multiplying outbreaks of decay, creeping damp and splintering bones.

Now friends have arrived bringing our cargo of history, jokes, secrets. Beyond price. A future will unfold here on these acres of Jake's, shared by people he loved. We have different, complicated reasons, each of us, for investing ourselves and our hopes in Mead for this new beginning, but I believe the outcome will be shared happiness, and security, for all of us. Why not? Age at least brings the benefits of wisdom, mutual tolerance, which we did not possess when we were nineteen, for all our beauty and optimism.

But I'm getting sentimental.

That's new, as is the realization that I can't drink the way I used to.

The two things are, of course, quite closely connected.

My feet are as cold as ice.

I wish my bed were not empty.

TWO

Rain came sweeping across from the North Sea, borne on flat-bottomed bolsters of cloud that released a steady grey downpour as they slid over the land.

Miranda was down at the site with Amos, who was marching up and down in his wellingtons, waving his arms and chopping the air with his hands as he fumed about delays to his project.

The foundations of his house-to-be were now marked out across the churned-up meadow with pegs and tape, and as their boots slithered in the mud he reminded her of exactly where the terraces would be, where and how huge windows would slide up and down, and the ingenious way that doors would fold out onto the land.

She was as stirred and excited by the prospect as Amos himself. Almost anywhere on earth this building would be a thrilling expression of modernity, and she loved the idea of it being set right here against the old grey bones of Mead.

Amos never tired of telling anyone who would listen about his systems for storing heat and generating energy, the layers of insulation that would reduce thermal loss almost to zero, the waste water recycling technology, all the other innovations that he had planned with such glee, with a rich man's confident relish for the latest and best. Dreamily, Miranda envisaged how the house would look, tethered here on its vantage point like a squared-off soap bubble, the planes of glass reflecting the leaves and the clouds.

The land fell away on three sides of the site, offering views for miles over the farmlands and copses, with a thin crescent of old deciduous woodland at the back of it in which the oak and horse chestnut leaves were just beginning to turn. The little wood offered protection from the winds off the sea that sometimes battered Mead itself.

The situation was perfect, as if the grand design had always been for people to build here, but its rightness had been overlooked until now. Miranda was proud of the potential, as though she had some hand in establishing it.

Amos swung to face her, oblivious to the rain, gouging up a little ruff of muddy earth with his heel.

'Miranda, just tell me, why can't we get going? The planning bureaucracy, the endless delays. It's driving me insane. I want to see the trenches cut. I want to see my house rising out of this earth. I want it badly enough to get down on my knees right now and start digging at it with these.'

He waved his hands in front of her. She thought he might flop down in his corduroys and start burrowing at the flat grass like some immense sandy mole.

'It's not long now. Monday.'

'That is long. One hundred and twelve hours . . .' he glanced at his watch '. . . precisely.'

Miranda laughed. 'It will be worth waiting for.' Rain was dripping off the brim of her hat. 'Let's go back to the house. There's nothing to be done out here.'

The Knights had now completed the move to Mead. Katherine had confided to Miranda that Amos had resigned from his chambers, and Miranda could see how restless he was without the demands of work to distract him. He didn't want to go back to the sheltered confinement of Mead's holiday wing and sit there looking out at the rain. He stuck his hands in his pockets instead and stared hungrily at the blue Portakabin that had been brought in the week before on a low-loader and lifted into place in a cradle of chains. There was a caravan waiting to one side with a yellow JCB parked next to it.

'Come on, come on,' he muttered and paced, as if the machinery might shudder into life under the force of his will.

'Amos. I'm getting wet. I want a cup of coffee.'

He stopped. 'What? Oh. Apologies in order. I'm being thoughtless.' Then he sighed. 'Standing here staring at some string and a digger's not helping my blood pressure, in any case.'

They turned away on the caterpillar-tracked dirt road that would be the Knights' driveway. It curved past the belt of trees and joined the main drive to the house a few yards from the gate.

Automatically, because none of them now used the front, Amos and Miranda headed for the back door into the house, crossing the wet glimmering cobbles of the yard. The holiday wing looked demurely occupied, with laundered curtains at the windows and even some pots of herbs placed by Katherine beside the doorstep. Across from this statement of domestic order sat the reverse of a mirror image – a picture of destruction.

Polly and Selwyn's barn now had no windows, no door, no interior walls, and only a few gaunt beams for a roof. There came a series of thuds and the powdery splinter and crash of falling plaster and masonry. Amos raised his eyebrows at Miranda and a second later a figure appeared in the jagged hole that had once been a window. His hair, clothes and skin were thick with dust, and clods of ancient plaster clung to his shoulders. In this grey mask Selwyn's mouth appeared shockingly red. Miranda caught the inside of her lip between her teeth and forced herself to look elsewhere. It was more difficult to have him so close, his physical presence always nudging into sight and from there marching into her private thoughts, than she had bargained for.

'Hey, come and take a look,' he yelled, brandishing his sledgehammer.

They ventured obediently to the doorway and peered through

the hanging veil of dust. The floor was heaped with broken brick and laths and roughly swept-up piles of rubble. In the far corner, under the only remaining fragment of roof, a tarpaulin shelter had been rigged up, the corner looped back to reveal a camping mattress with folded sleeping bags and pillows all exposed to the dust. A primus burner on an improvised trestle table stood next to a tap that sagged away from the wall on a length of crusted pipe.

'Just look at it,' Amos muttered. The derision in his voice might have masked a tremor of reluctant awe.

Miranda stared at the tarp shelter. The whole scene was strongly reminiscent of the dwellings of primitive people, possibly hunter-gatherers huddled in caves, protected only by animal skins and a low fire. It was obvious that Selwyn adored descending to this level. Pitting himself against the weather, pulling his hut dwelling apart with his bare hands in order to rebuild something better for his woman and himself, he probably felt the very embodiment of primitive Man.

It was a joyous spectacle, as well as a sexy one. Miranda propped herself against a shaky wall to enjoy it.

'Excuse me? What's funny?' Selwyn swung the sledgehammer in a small arc. He looked offended.

Amos coughed and slapped his hands together to shake off the dust and grit.

'You see,' Selwyn added, vaguely indicating a slice of rubbled floor, 'this is where the snooker table will be.'

'But you don't *play* snooker,' said Amos.

'You always were a literal-minded person,' Selwyn sighed.

Amos looked about. Small scraping and collapsing sounds came as the latest demolition area settled. 'You've got quite a lot to do, haven't you?'

'It'll be done before yours, mate. And anyway there's no hurry. This place is fine as it is.'

'Does Polly think so?'

Apart from the first, Selwyn had slept every night since their arrival at Mead under his own potential roof. Miranda guessed that he wanted to distance himself from the soft option, to demonstrate that he needed nothing from anybody, least of all creature comforts. Polly sometimes slept in their bedroom in the house, sometimes in the barn with him.

Miranda tried not to notice which, or when.

But she did notice. She couldn't help it.

For the new residents at Mead the kitchen in the old house had become a kind of common room. It was where people congregated if they were not working or keeping to their own quarters, and it was big enough and already shabby enough to absorb the influx without looking much different. Today there was an earthenware jug of ragged crimson dahlias on the table, with a heap of magazines and envelopes drifting over an open laptop.

Miranda and Amos came in from the rain and tramped through to the passage beneath the stairs to leave their coats. Their boots left gritty prints on the tiles.

Colin was resting next to the Rayburn, in the Windsor armchair that had been favoured by Miranda's late cat, and Polly was reading out to him the lonely hearts ads from a newspaper. Katherine had just arrived back from two days at her charity's offices in London and her Burberry and briefcase were deposited on another chair. When Amos returned, padding in his socks and with what was left of his hair sticking up after he had rubbed it dry, he kissed her absently and patted her shoulder.

'Meeting go off all right, darling?'

'Yes. I . . .'

'We've just been down to the site, Mirry and me. I'll walk back down there with you, if you like.'

'Has anything new happened?'

'No.'

Katherine said, 'Then I think I'll go into the village with Polly and Colin. We were just talking about it. The rain is going to stop in a minute.'

36

He looked at her in surprise. 'You've only just got back from town.'

Polly glanced up from her place at the table.

'Yes, that's right,' Katherine agreed.

Amos hesitated, then nodded vaguely. 'Right. Mirry, let's have that coffee, then.'

Miranda straightened her back.

'Yes, let's. Black for me. Thanks.'

There was a small silence in the wake of her words. Amos seemed to become aware of four pairs of eyes on him.

'What's this? What are you all looking at?'

The reverberations of Selwyn's sledgehammering made the cups on the dresser tinkle.

Polly murmured, 'What do you mean, looking at?'

Amos puffed out his red cheeks but didn't pursue the question. He lumbered about the kitchen collecting up the coffee pot and rummaging in the cupboards for coffee beans. Once he had located the jar he experienced a moment's difficulty with fitting the lid on the grinder, then pressed the button as gingerly as if he expected the machine to detonate.

Polly read out over the clatter, 'Erasmian fool, M 37, seeks warm-hearted man, London or Cambridge, to explore gravity and grace. Downhill skiing champion preferred.' Colin shuddered. Amos stared briefly at them over his shoulder.

'Is there any milk?' he asked Miranda.

'Have a look in the fridge.'

By the time he had produced two cups of coffee and set one down in front of Miranda, the other three had got up and were preparing to leave.

'Might have a drink at the pub,' Colin said, winding a scarf of Indian silk around his neck.

The kitchen was quiet after they had gone.

'Why do I suddenly feel like the butt of some incomprehensible joke?' Amos said abruptly into the silence.

Miranda thoughtfully drank some coffee, then replaced the cup in its saucer.

'Do you?'

'It reminds me of when we were students. It's all coming back to me. I was forever arriving a crucial minute too late, after the decision had been made or the punch line delievered. Have I spent getting on for *forty years* demonstrating that I am not some egregious hanger-on, only to step back into a room with all of you in it to feel a callow nineteen all over again?'

The corners of Miranda's mouth lifted. 'I don't know. But isn't it rather good, in its way? Rather rejuvenating?'

He stared at her, trying to work out whether he was being teased.

'No, I don't think so.'

Miranda made herself be serious. 'You're not going to regret moving up here, Amos, are you?' She didn't want any of them to regret the decision, not even for a moment.

'Katherine loves it.' Amos's expertise in deflecting questions was considerable. 'Even in the car when we were driving up, I noticed how gleeful she was. She likes the life here better than living with me in London, that's quite obvious. She seems happier now than at any time since the boys left home.' He added, 'Of course, I'm glad about that.' His big hands, lightly clasped, rested on the table.

Miranda stood up and came to him. She put her arm over his shoulders and Amos flinched, just perceptibly, as if he feared what might happen next.

'What about *you*?' she murmured.

'I want to get my house built.'

'Yes. But what do you feel about being here at Mead, with the rest of us? We did all that talking about money and business and land and security and contracts, but I don't think we – or you – did much more than mention the communal aspects.'

'It's a business arrangement, isn't it?' Amos said briskly. He ducked his head from beneath Miranda's chin.

Miranda stood upright. Her expressive face showed the depth of her conviction. 'But I want it to be *more* than that. For me, for Mead, for all of us. I want it to be about faith, and friendship, and the way that those values outlast, survive longer than marriage. Children grow up and go. Partners die, or leave, or whatever they do. What have you got left that means more than what we have here, the six of us?'

'How about work? Call it achievement, if you prefer. Hindsight, that's always a gift. Wealth, even, if you like. Quite a number of significant things, anyway.'

She slid her narrow hands into the back pockets of her trousers and paced away to the dresser.

'I was thinking more emotionally.'

He widened his eyes in a show of amazement. 'Really? You were, Mirry, of all people?'

'Stop it, Amos. You said a minute ago that you felt unnerved by being with us again. That's an emotional response. It's an acknowledgement that we do have something significant here, between us all, old friends.'

Her eyes met his. The lids drooped and there were fans of wrinkles at the corners but otherwise her face was not much altered by the years. Miranda had always been a beauty. As far as Amos was concerned she was one of those women who ought to come stamped with a warning notice. Luckily, he might have added, she was not his cup of tea.

He said, 'What we've got here is Selwyn going berserk, Polly being exaggeratedly patient with him, my wife suddenly as happy as Larry in spite of our various not insignificant problems, Colin who is clearly ill, you being your mystical self, and me, waiting for the bloody builders to come and start building my *house*.'

Miranda saw that Katherine had been right, the rain had stopped and a dilute sun now shone in on them.

Amos muttered, 'But, even so, I'm moderately pleased to find myself here.'

Her smile reflected the sun. She skipped back to his side, kissed the top of his head and flattened his upstanding hair.

'Oh, that's *good*. Very good.'

'I don't know how it will turn out, though,' he warned her. 'I bought into a plot of rural land for development, at a good price, thank you, not into a new-age nest of nightmares.'

'Sweet dreams,' Miranda laughed.

Colin and Polly and Katherine took the footpath that skirted a series of fields on the way to Meddlett. The sky to the west was the blue of a bird's egg, and the yellow leaves in the hedges hung luminous in the oblique light. Polly led the way, brushing through soaking long grass and tramping down the arms of brambles so that the others could pass. She walked briskly, and soon drew ahead. Katherine found that she was breathing hard, and looked back to see whether Colin wanted to overtake her. But he was strolling with his hands in his pockets, apparently studying the edge of the rain clouds where a bright rim of liquid gold shone against the grey.

The clean, damp air swelled her lungs. She liked the gleam of the wet leaves, and the iridescent trails of slugs glossing the stones.

Katherine was unused to country walking. She had grown up in Hampstead, and Sunday walks on the Heath with her parents had marked the limits of rural exploration. She had lived all her married life with Amos in London, and apart from occasional games of tennis and some gentle skiing there had been no call to exert herself. In his forties Amos had taken to going on trekking holidays, but always with male friends and colleagues. The idea of leaving the boys and accompanying him to Nepal had seemed so far-fetched to her in those days that it had never even been discussed. Nowadays Amos was too heavy for the mountains, and preferred a tropical beach.

Polly sat down on a stile and waited for her to catch up.

'Am I going too fast?' she asked.

'Yes, but I like it. You know the way?'

'Sel and I walked along here the other night.'

'Did you? Going to the village?'

Polly shook her head. 'Just having a walk together. He can't work every minute of the day and night, but he gets so rest-less.' She picked off a yellow leaf that was blotched with dark spots like skin growths, and twirled it in her fingers.

'I noticed that,' Katherine said.

'I wish he'd relax more,' Polly murmured.

'Why does he drive himself so hard?'

Amos had driven himself too, especially in his early years at the Bar, but he always claimed that it was work undertaken ultimately to generate the time and money that would allow him to enjoy himself. A simple equation, Katherine reflected. And of course, as it was her habit to acknowledge, he had always been generous with the money.

Buying you off? A voice that she didn't recognize startlingly murmured inside her head. She ignored it, and concentrated her attention on Polly.

'Because he thinks he has fucked up,' Polly answered in a level voice. 'He thinks that he's failed with everything else in his life, therefore he's trying to compensate by building us a new home overnight, using his bare hands. We're totally broke, you know. We had to sell the house, finally, to pay off the debts, and we've put just about everything that was left into the Mead barn.'

'I didn't know.'

'No one does, really. Don't tell Amos, will you? He and Sel are so competitive.'

'He'd probably try to give you some money.'

'Exactly,' Polly smiled, without much humour.

'What are you going to do?'

'I'll have to get a job.'

'In the furniture business again?'

'No. I'm sick to death of wood and patina and British brown.'

'Writing more books, then?'

'I don't think so, no. That's the kind of work that you have to demonstrate some continuity in. I'm not sure if any publisher these days would be interested in me popping up with a proposal for a new life of Mary Seacole or someone. I mean a *job* job.'

41

'I see,' Katherine nodded.

'Wish I did. But I'll think of something.'

'Of course you will.'

'Do you need an assistant at the charity?'

'No.' Katherine was slightly in awe, even after so many years, of Polly's academic and literary achievements. Polly would never make a belittling or even clever rejoinder if you made a mistake or revealed your ignorance in some way, she was far too gentle for that, but that didn't mean she couldn't if the circumstances were different. Katherine didn't think that someone with opinions as definite as Polly's would fit particularly easily into their quiet offices.

'Oh, well.' Polly sprang off the stile. Her bulk didn't seem to impede her movements in the least. Polly raised her voice and called, 'Colin, what are you looking at?'

'I was just thinking that it's a very painterly light.'

The answer came quickly enough, but it was obvious to both of them that this wasn't at all what had been in his mind.

'Shall we walk on?' he smoothly suggested.

They followed the path for another half-mile until the fine tower of St Andrew's, Meddlett came into view between the trees. The footpath joined the minor road into the village just at the sign displaying its name. With a black aerosol spray, someone had rather neatly deleted the *ett* of Meddlett and added *-ing twatz*.

'Not everyone's mad about village life,' Colin observed.

The road led past the churchyard gate. There were quiet rows of gravestones. The church itself, Perpendicular with great arched windows, rose like a grey ship out of a smooth green sea.

In the distance, a man with a dog at his heels strolled on the other side of the road, raising his hand to a car as it crept by, and a woman in a green padded coat towed a wheeled shopper. The village street was otherwise deserted, yet they had the sense that they were being watched. The cottages enclosing the central green had low, deep-set windows. There was a pond in the centre of the green, and several ducks pottered on the bank under the willow branches. A bus stop, a post box and a red telephone kiosk stood in a line. The door of the combined general store and post office was open and there were bundles of kindling and logs stacked beside tilted boxes of tired-looking cauliflowers and onions.

Colin went inside to buy a newspaper, but came out without one.

'You have to order the *Guardian*,' he remarked.

Katherine was reminded of the village where she and Amos had stopped for tea on their drive up, and warily looked about her for the gang of teenagers. The fact that there was no one actually in sight under fifty meant that the three of them ought to have blended in perfectly. But they did not. She felt conspicuous, the precise opposite of being in London where the expected blanket of invisibility had indeed fallen around her at some point in her mid forties.

'Let's have this drink,' Colin said.

He steered them past the pond and another row of flint cottages with tiny front gardens until they reached the Griffin. In the bar two silent couples were finishing their food but the table in the window, the one that had been occupied on Colin's first visit by Jessie and Damon and the dog, was now empty. The same barman was in his place behind the pumps.

'Afternoon,' he said, after a pause.

'Hello, again,' Colin answered, with slight emphasis. 'It's pretty quiet this afternoon.'

'That's Meddlett for you,' the man replied, slowly, as if they were foreign enough for him to be doubtful about their levels of English comprehension.

They chose glasses of wine from the options chalked up on a blackboard. Polly was already telling the barman that no, they were not passing through. They had come to live here. A flicker of interest animated his face.

'Is that so? At Mead, is it? I'd heard about that. Planning issues, weren't there, to do with building a new house?'

'All sorted out now. Aren't they, Katherine?'

43

'It's my husband's house.'

Why not say it's yours too? The discordant new voice niggled in her head.

Colouring slightly she added, 'Work's about to start. It's very secluded. It's not going to spoil anyone's view or anything like that.'

'No? Well. Live and let live, I say, in any case.' Three glasses of wine were passed over the bar. 'I'm Vin, by the way.'

They introduced themselves. Polly took the glasses of wine and put them on the window table.

'We don't see much of Mrs Meadowe,' Vin remarked. 'Her late husband used to come in, after I took this place on. He always said I'd made big improvements. It was a proper dump before that, the old Griffin.' He was leaning on the bar now, settling in for a talk.

'We are all old friends of Miranda's and Jake's,' Polly said.

Katherine understood that unlike herself or Colin she was used to the rhythms of country pubs. She knew how much chat to exchange and when to make a cheery move aside. Polly steered them to their table now, closing a deft bracket on the conversation.

The window gave an oblique view of the green. Cars and passers-by in the middle distance now seemed to move very slowly, as in a film playing at the wrong speed.

Polly took a satisfied swallow of her wine.

'Look at you,' she said to Katherine.

'What?'

'You look beautiful.'

Katherine was startled. After their damp walk she knew exactly how her hair would be frizzing and her nose shining like a fog lamp. Instinctively she put up her hand to fluff out a chunk of hair over one ear.

'She does,' Colin agreed. 'You do.'

Katherine heard a *click*, like the shutter of a camera. She wished that she might have a picture of this moment, if a camera could have captured the surge of warmth that ran

44

through her blood and loosened her muscles, the unlooked-for buzz of pleasure at finding herself drinking wine in the afternoon with Polly and Colin for company, with a view through the window of amber and crimson leaves, and a word like beautiful in her ears. She couldn't remember anyone having applied it to her, ever, not even Amos.

How disconnected have you been? the voice chimed in.

'I don't think so,' she began to murmur, but Polly leaned forward and briefly covered Katherine's hand with hers.

'It's all right, you know. You can be beautiful, it's allowed. You don't need Amos's permission. Does she, Colin?'

'No,' he agreed.

Katherine thought for a moment. Her instinct was to deflect the compliment, but then, why? She sat forwards, smiling, her fingers lacing around her glass of pub merlot with the chain of purple bubbles at the meniscus.

Everything is going to change.

What did that mean? She was taken aback by the idea.

A burst of loud music suddenly poured through the pendant strings of brown plastic beads and bamboo tubules that separated the back of the bar from the kitchen. *Thank you for the music,* a woman's voice warbled.

'Oi, Jess,' Vin called over the din. 'Turn that down, customers can't hear themselves think.'

There was quite a long interval, and then the volume diminished a little.

One of the pale couples was leaving. A girl appeared in the doorway, where Colin had previously glimpsed the man in chef's clothing. She came in and gathered up the dirty plates from the vacated table.

'Hi, I was wondering if you'd be back,' she called to Colin.

'Hello Jessie,' he answered.

Polly and Katherine turned to him in surprise.

'We met the other night. I came in for a quick drink, and Jessie and her boyfriend were sitting here. We got talking.'

Jessie grinned. 'You and I did. That loser Damon had buggered off, remember, it was just me and Raff.' Her eyes flicked from Polly to Katherine. 'Your, ah, husband gave me a lift home . . . ?' She made it a pointed question.

'These are my friends, Polly and Katherine. I'm not married,' Colin explained.

Jessie glanced at the folds of Colin's scarf, and his expensive soft jacket.

'No. So you're all from Mead, then?'

She shuffled the plates into a precarious pile, scraping leftovers on to the uppermost one. 'Whoops.'

Cutlery threatened to slide out of the plate sandwich and she dipped her hips and shimmied to tilt the load the other way. She looked very young and cheerful.

'All of us,' Polly answered. 'We're old friends, we've known each other for years, and my husband and I and Katherine and hers have moved up here to be together and not to sink into a decline in our old age.'

'That's cool. So it's like, what did you call it in those days, a commune?'

'No,' they said, absolutely in unison.

Miranda was passionate about her scheme and each of the rest of them would have differently defined what they hoped Mead would become, but they had always been unanimous in declaring that it wouldn't be a commune. Amos had said that communes stood for vegetarianism and free love and bad plumbing, and he would not be interested in any of those separately, let alone in combination.

'The jury's out on number two,' Selwyn had muttered out of the corner of his mouth to Polly at the time. The memory of this made her smile. When she was amused, Polly's eyes narrowed under heavy lids and her cheeks rounded into smooth apples so that she looked like a thumbnail sketch of a Japanese lady on a packet of egg noodles.

'It's more a collaboration, I'd say,' Polly offered.

'What about you, then?' Jessie asked Colin.

'I come and go,' he told her.

'Can't see my mum doing anything like that. She lives in a bungalow,' Jessie remarked, as if this entirely defined her.

Vin leaned heavily on the bar. Jessie seemed to feel his glare on her back.

'I got a job, as you see,' she announced to Colin, rolling her eyes. She raised her voice slightly. 'Helping out in the kitchen, bit of cooking, washing up and that. There's plenty of work around here, not a problem. Are you going to have lunch? We're supposed to stop at two. Chef's off today, we're just microwaving, but I could do you lasagne and chips, or a baked and toppings if you like.'

'No, we're fine. We'll just have our wine. Thanks.'

Jessie nodded and hoisted her pile of plates. 'Nice to have met you,' she told Polly and Katherine. 'Come back one evening. We've got live music Fridays and Saturdays, not completely crap, as it goes, then quiz night's Tuesday.'

'Amos and Selwyn would love a quiz,' Katherine said.

'But they don't know anything about telly or sport or pop music,' Colin pointed out.

Jessie turned on him in indignation. 'Some of the questions are quite intellectual. You should come as well and meet Geza. He's the chef.'

'I see.'

'Sure you won't have some food?'

They assured her that they would not.

'Bye, then,' Jessie said, and danced her way back to the kitchen.

Polly gave her Japanese noodle lady smile. She leaned closer to Colin and lowered her voice. 'You've got the chance of a nice gay chef, by the sound of it.'

'I've already seen him. Not bad at all,' Colin smiled.

She tapped her hand lightly on his knee.

'No,' he said. 'Not even to please you, Polly.'

'Not yet, you mean. I know. It's all right. Shall we have another glass of wine, do you think?'

The others pretended to be shocked.

'*Two* glasses of wine?'

'In the middle of a weekday afternoon?'

And then they agreed, why not?

Amos went back across the yard to his house, saying that he had calls to make to the architect and the contractors and a mass of paperwork to deal with.

Looking around the kitchen, Miranda saw that it was in need of some attention. She put the dirty coffee cups in the dishwasher and emptied the grounds from the pot into the compost bucket. Someone – probably Amos – had been treating the bucket as a waste bin, and as she stooped down to pick out a polythene wrapper she discovered some pieces of broken plate. It was the one with ivy tendrils wreathed around the rim that she and Jake had found years ago in a junk shop in Norwich. She was sad that it was broken.

After she had disposed of the fragments, too badly smashed to be worth repairing, she wiped the table and picked up a few shed dahlia petals. From this angle it was apparent that the dresser was dusty, so she cleared a clutter of bowls and papers and searched in a drawer for a cloth and a tin of polish. Wadding the cloth up in her fist she pressed the tip of it into the brown ooze of polish, then began to work it in smooth strokes into the grain of the wood. She extended her arm in wide arcs, rubbing hard, enjoying these ministrations to her house.

In the days and weeks after Jake died I used to wake in the night and howl, letting the sobs rip out of me because I couldn't think how to stop, even though I was frightening myself. Nothing will ever be as bad as that, and I know that I have done enough crying. More than enough to last what remains of a lifetime.

I look up from my polishing, and remind myself again of what I have.

Here is Mead, this lovely place where I belong.

There are no more Meadowes, Jake was the last of the line

and I am the last to bear his family name, but thanks to my friends there are voices and laughter again in these rooms. Sometimes when we sit around the table it is as though we are not six, but a dozen or more – here are the earlier versions of each of us, gathered behind the chairs, leaning over one another's shoulders to interject or contradict, phantoms of teenagers and young parents and errant mid-lifers, all these faces vivid in memory's snapshots with the attitudes and dreams of *then*, half or more of which are now forgotten.

With this much familiarity between us, when I single out our older faces from the crowd, I have come to imagine that I can read off the latest bargains we are striking with ourselves, with each other, and – with whom?

If I believed in God, I would say so.

With fate, then.

If we can stay alive a few years longer, be healthy, live just a little more, maybe experience something new that will make us feel that everything that is passionate, breathtaking, surprising is not already behind us. If we can be fractionally careless, and just frivolous enough, amongst our old friends. If we can be not lonely, and only sometimes afraid: that will be enough.

These are selfish desires, of course. We are a selfish generation, we post-war babies, for whom everything has been butter and orange juice and free speech and free love.

But even with all our privileges, we have made mistakes.

Whereas if I thought about personal fallibility at all when I was young, it was just one more thing to laugh at.

And now I look up, and see Selwyn coming across the yard to the back door. The latch rattles, and he tramples his feet on the doormat to shake some of the plaster dust off his boots.

'Hi. There you are. Where's everyone?' he asks.

'Gone for a walk.' I bend deliberately over the polishing cloth, making long sweeps over the dresser top.

'Barb?' He comes across and stands much too close to me, just six inches away. I can smell dust and sweat. 'What's the matter? You're crying, aren't you?'

He doesn't touch me, but he picks up the tin of polish instead as if this is the closest connection he dares to make. He screws the lid in place and I study his notched and grimy hands and the rinds of dirt clinging to the cuticles.

The polishing slows down, my reach diminishing, until it gradually stops altogether.

'No. I was just thinking sombre thoughts.'

He does touch me now, the fingers of his right hand just coming lightly to rest on the point of my shoulder. We look into each other's eyes.

'About the other night . . .' he begins.

'It's all right. Don't. No need to. You were a bit drunk. Me too. Two glasses of wine, nowadays, and I'm . . .'

He stops me.

'I wasn't drunk, and I don't believe you were either. I meant it. You are so beautiful, and necessary to me. I'm numb these days, I'm like a log of dead bloody wood, totally inert except for the termites of anxiety gnawing away, but when I look at you it's like the log's being doused in petrol and set alight. I can't stop it. I don't *want* to stop it, because it's being alive.'

'Don't say these things, Selwyn. You shouldn't, and I shouldn't listen.'

'I'm bursting into flames, look.'

His index finger moves to my bare neck, slides down to the hollow of my collarbone.

I step backwards, out of his reach, skirting the corner of the dresser.

'Polly,' I manage to say. 'Polly, Polly, Polly, *Polly*. Partner. Mother of three children. Your partner. Your children.'

'You are not telling me anything I don't already know,' Selwyn says reasonably.

It was Miranda who had very nearly become Selwyn's wife.

After they left the university they had drifted to London where Miranda found herself an agent and spent her days going to auditions, hitching up her skirt in front of a series of directors and chain-smoking afterwards while she waited for the phone to ring.

Selwyn was in the first year of his clinical training, and finding that he hated the sadistic rituals of medical memory tests and group diagnostic humiliations. At the time Miranda had a room in a shared flat in Tufnell Park and more often than not Selwyn stayed there with her, huddling in her single bed or crouching in the armchair amongst discarded clothes, a textbook on his lap and the apparatus for fixing another joint spread on the arm.

He claimed later, with reason, that this was the lowest period of his life. He knew that he wasn't going to qualify as a doctor, but had no idea what else he might do with himself. Startlingly, he was also discovering that he was no longer the centre of attention. Amos and Polly and Colin and all their other friends had set off in different directions. It seemed that Miranda, with her jittery determination to be an actress, was the only thing he had left to hold on to.

He held on hard.

One night, lying ribcage to ribcage in her bed and listening to the cats squalling in the dank garden backed by a railway line, he said, 'Let's get married.'

They could at least then get a flat on their own together. There would be regular cooking, laundry would somehow get done, life would be legitimized.

Miranda said, 'Yes.'

They went to Portobello Road the next Saturday afternoon and chose a ring, a Victorian garnet band that Selwyn couldn't afford. Plans were made for a registry office ceremony at Camden Town Hall, to be followed by a restaurant lunch for Miranda's mother and Selwyn's parents and brother. In the evening there was to be a catered party in a room over a pub, at which a revived Blue Peony would be the disco. Weddings in those days were deliberately stripped of all tradition. Miranda hooted with laughter at the idea of a church, or a bridal gown, and a honeymoon involving anything more than a few days in a borrowed cottage in Somerset was out of the question in any case.

One weekend Miranda's mother came down from Wolverhampton. Selwyn was banished to his rented room near the hospital. Joyce Huggett was in her forties, a normally outspoken and opinionated woman who was uncomfortable in London, which she hardly knew. She was also a little uncertain of her own daughter these days, because Miranda had gone to an ancient university and had acquired sophisticated friends, and was – or was about to become – an actress.

'Couldn't you at least wear white, Barbara? It needn't be anything bridal. Just a little dress and coat, maybe. I'm thinking of the photographs.'

In Joyce's own wedding picture, dating from the same month as Princess Elizabeth's, Joyce was wearing a dress made from a peculiarly unfluid length of cream satin, with her mother's lace veil. By her side, Miranda's handsome father smiled in a suit with noticeably uneven lapels. The marriage lasted nine years before he left his wife and daughter for a cinema projectionist.

'I'm not a virgin, Mum,' Miranda said.

Mrs Huggett frowned. 'You're a modern young woman, I'm well aware of that, thank you. But this will be your wedding day. Don't you want to look special?'

'I know what I want,' Miranda said calmly.

They went together to Feathers boutique in Knightsbridge and chose an Ossie Clark maxi dress, a swirling print of burgundy and cream and russet and rose pink that fell in panels from a tight ribboned bodice. Joyce paid for it and Miranda hugged her in real, unforced, delighted gratitude.

'It's perfect,' she said. She agreed with her mother's plea for her at least to wear a hat, and they chose a floppy-brimmed felt in dusty pink, from Biba.

'You look a picture. I hope you'll be happy, love,' Joyce murmured.

Selwyn was very quiet. He slept a lot, as if he were clinging to every possible moment of oblivion. Without telling Miranda, he stopped going to lectures and practicals, and he smoked even more dope. Instead of balancing his life out, as he had hoped it would, impending marriage was destabilizing it even further. As soon as she became a bride-to-be, Miranda seemed to slip out of his grasp and turn into someone less compliant, less adoring, much less in his thrall than she had ever been before. She was often irritable with him, and he felt so limp and so hopeless that he knew she could hardly be blamed for that. His only responsibility before the wedding, apart from taking his velvet suit to the cleaners, was to find a flat that they could afford to move into together. He did drag himself out to look at two or three places, but the sheer effort of the process exhausted him, and he was shocked to discover that he couldn't imagine living in these rooms with Miranda as his wife. He never even suggested that they might visit one of the rickety attics or basements together.

One week before the wedding, he got up very early in the morning and left his fiancée sleeping. From Euston he caught a train to Wolverhampton and then took a taxi to Joyce's.

When she opened the door to him Joyce thought he had come to tell her that Miranda was ill, or dead. She snatched at his wrists, shouting in panic.

'Where is she? What's happened to her?'

'Let me in,' he begged. 'She's all right, it's me that's wrong.'

In the narrow hallway, with bright wallpaper pressing in on him, Selwyn blurted out that he couldn't marry Miranda after all. In her relief that her daughter wasn't dead or dying, Joyce turned cold and glittery with anger.

'Does she know?'

'No. I've come to tell you first.'

'My God. You cowardly, selfish, pathetic creature.'

'Yes,' Selwyn miserably agreed. He didn't need Joyce to tell him what he was. 'It isn't right to marry her. I won't make her happy.'

Joyce looked him up and down. 'No. You would not. Right. Now you've told me, bugger off out of here. I don't want to look at your face. And leave my daughter alone, do you hear? We'll be all right, we always have been, Barbara and me. Just don't mess up her life any more than you've done already.'

'I won't do that,' Selwyn promised.

He was true to his word. He gave up his medical studies, left London, and went to stay with the friends in Somerset who had been going to lend the happy couple their cottage for the honeymoon. He started work with a local carpenter, discovered that he had a talent for woodworking, and in between fitting staircases and kitchen cupboards he began to buy, restore and sell furniture.

Miranda recovered, helped by a rebound affair with an actor.

Seven years later, when Amos Knight married the quiet, pretty girl called Katherine whom he had met at the house of one of the other young barristers in his chambers, Miranda wore to their wedding the Ossie Clark dress and the Biba hat. The outfit was by then grotesquely out of fashion, but Miranda carried it off. She was on the brink of making a small name for herself as an actress.

I can't stop myself. Instead of walking out of the kitchen I lift my head, and our eyes meet. Selwyn's eyelashes and hair are coated with grey dust, as if he's made up to play an old man on some amateur stage. He doesn't try to reach out for me again, and I'm sharply aware that this is disappointing. My heart's banging against my ribs, surely loud enough for him to hear, and my mouth is so dry that I don't think I can speak.

Why now? Why, after all these years, is this happening again?

The answer comes to me: it's precisely because of now.

We're not young any longer, there's no network of pathways branching invitingly ahead of us. No personae to be tried on for size. We're what, and who, we are.

But we're not yet ready to be old.

We stand in the silent kitchen, speechless and gaping like adolescents, but both of us realizing that through decades of duty and habit we've somehow forgotten about the thrill of choice:

oh God, the breathtaking drama of *sexual choice*. The cliché that swims into my head might have been made for this instant. I *do* feel weak at the knees. I'm not sure that my legs will hold me upright.

When I don't say anything, Selwyn sighs. He brushes his hand through his hair and a shower of splinters and plaster particles fall like snow.

'Would it be all right for me to have a bath?' he asks.

'You don't have to ask permission. You live here.' My voice comes out in a croak, sounding as if I've borrowed it from someone else.

'Thank you,' he says.

I listen to his steps as he goes upstairs, the familiar creak of the oak boards, the clink of the bathroom latch somewhere overhead.

Without giving myself time to think, I run after him.

From the linen cupboard opposite my bedroom door I snatch up an armful of fresh towels. I race along the landing and push at the bathroom door. Not locked. It swings inwards.

The taps are full on and the room is already cloudy with steam.

Selwyn's barefoot. He's taken off his filthy sweater and shirt and dropped them on the floor. As soon as he sees me he nudges the clothes gently aside with his bare foot, clearing a space. He holds out his arms.

What I feel is an extraordinary lightening, giddiness, swirling of blood; it's like being very drunk but with all my senses cleansed and heightened.

'I've brought you some clean towels.'

'No, you haven't.'

He snatches the towels and drops them on top of the clothes.

It's me who takes the last step.

Our mouths meet. Immediately we begin to consume each other, as if we're starving, with the steam billowing in clouds around us. Out of the corner of my eye, as Selwyn twists off my jersey, I see that the bath is almost overflowing.

Once we're started, rediscovering the inches of skin and the declivities and shadows of a pair of bodies that were once familiar territory (only yesterday, as it now seems), it's impossible to stop.

Selwyn fumbles to his knees, drawing me down with him, wrestling to extricate me from absurd layers of vest and straps. Towels coiled with clothes and grit mound beneath us. Water laps at the very rim of the bath.

I hear myself gasping with laughter. 'There's going to be a flood.'

'Fuck it.'

He drags me with him as he strains to reach the taps and stem the tide.

In the quiet that follows, there's the sound of voices.

'Oh, sweet Jesus.' Selwyn slumps back against the side of the bath.

I'm already on my feet, spitting building rubble out of my mouth and frantically raking fingers through my hair. I pull my clothes into a sort of order and plunge out of the bathroom.

Colin and Katherine and Polly are all in the hall below. They're laughing and exclaiming and apparently having some difficulty in taking off their boots and coats.

Polly glances up and sees me on the landing.

'Colin's been getting the eye from a nice young chef,' she calls.

'I had to carry these two home, just about,' Colin says drily. The hall clock chimes. It's four o'clock in the afternoon.

Luckily, they're all too busy and happy to notice anything.

I run down the stairs, relief all but cancelling out guilt.

Ben and Nicola

The boy climbed the flight of stairs that led straight up from the street door. With the usual smell of warm grease from the café following him, he leaned briefly against the thin ply of the flat door and juggled a bunch of flowers, a brown takeaway bag and a carton of milk. He twisted a key in the Yale and the door sighed open. He nudged it further with his hip and wriggled into the dark, confined space beyond.

'Nic? 'S me.'

No answer came but he shouldered his way cheerfully onwards past the coat pegs and the parked Hoover and a stack of cardboard boxes. The light in the main body of the flat was slightly brighter. There was only one room, L-shaped, with a kitchenette and a partitioned bathroom that would not have passed a health and safety inspection with flying colours. To excuse this Nicola's Greek landlord told her that he was not making formal rental, no, more like place for his own family, and cheap for now while he wait for his cousin to come and fix up.

Nicola was sitting in the armchair at the end of the room farthest from the unmade bed, next to a window overlooking a row of lock-ups and the fading leaves of a plane tree. Her knees were drawn up to her chest. Ben saw that she was wearing her grey holey jersey and leggings, for about the fourth day running, but she had pulled a little skirt on over the leggings and her hair was freshly washed.

'Hi, babe, you OK? Look, I got you these.' He held out the flowers, yellow and white daisies that he had chosen from a green enamel bucket outside the grocer's at the end of the road. 'And some soup as well, properly healthy, bean and something. It might have got a bit cold but I can heat it up again, easy. Or would you rather have a cup of tea? There's milk.'

Nicola gazed up at him, her wide eyes expressionless. He was uneasily conscious of wanting to placate her, although he didn't know why she should need this treatment. She had been a bit off, lately. He kept looking up and finding that she was staring at him. When he responded with his wide, frank smile she'd blink, and quickly look away again.

'Not bad out,' he went on. He put down the takeaway bag, and the milk and flowers.

Nic stirred, unwinding her legs and biting off a yawn. 'How was work?'

'Yeah. It was good. You know, average.'

'Did you speak to him?'

'He' was the editor and manager of the local listings and events magazine where Ben worked part time. Ben wanted to be a writer, like his mother had once been, and even though what he mostly did was go out to the post office or ring venues to check the times of the week's gigs, he insisted that this was the perfect pathway to literary success. Ben had been saying for a couple of weeks now that he only had to ask and he'd get a proper slot, like a column of his own or something.

'No. Didn't get a chance. It was mental there today.'

'Right.'

Nic stood up. Her shoulders dropped and she reached out an arm and hooked it around him.

'Thanks for the flowers.'

'OK. I wish . . .' Ben hesitated, lost as he often was for words to express his desire for all to be well, for there to be a safe enclosure for himself and Nic within the only slightly enticing chaos and mystery that the adult world seemed to present. Best of all would have been a house in the country, with a wilderness garden, the sort of place where he and his sisters had been lucky enough to grow up. 'Well, you know.'

They stood close together, with Ben's chin resting on Nicola's head.

'Are you hungry?' he asked gently.

'No. What time have you got to go out?'

Ben earned some extra money from working in the set-up and take-down crew of a smart party organizer. The hours were awkward, but the pay was better than bar work.

''Bout four?'

She moved away from him and twisted the daisies out of their paper. There wasn't a vase, so she splayed them out in a plastic jug and put them on the table.

'Gina wants me to babysit later.'

Nic worked three days and occasional evenings as nanny to the two small children of a GP, and the other two days she went to college to train in alternative beauty therapies. Their various different commitments meant that Ben and Nic sometimes only saw each other for a few hours a week.

'D'you want to go out for a walk?'

'I don't know. No, not really.'

Ben followed her from the table to the armchair, his movements unconsciously mirroring hers. He was two years younger, but it could seem like much more. Nic sighed.

'Maybe we could just go to bed for an hour.'

He grinned at that. 'Maybe. Or, I dunno, perhaps we should do the washing up instead?'

Nic's fugitive smile flashed at him, making her look like the girl he had first caught sight of at an unlikely party. 'Hey. Watch it.'

She padded across to the bed as he unlaced his Converse and took off his jeans. Nic lay down just as she was, balling up her small fists inside the sleeves of her jumper. Ben stretched out half on top of her, his hands sliding up her ribcage, but she turned her face away to avoid his mouth.

'No, Ben, wait a minute, can't you? Let's just have a cuddle.'

'After,' he muttered, trying to press his knee between hers. His mobile began to ring in the pocket of his jeans. 'Shit. Better get that.'

He reached a long arm for the phone and studied the display. Then he turned it off. 'My sister,' he yawned. He rolled back against Nic but she was lying on her back now, her chin lifted and her eyes fixed on the ceiling.

'I'm pregnant,' she said.

Shadows of the plane tree branches moved on the ceiling. 'What?'

'Pregnant. In the club. Up the duff. Expecting. Bun in the . . .'

'Shit,' he said again. And then, on a long breath, 'No.'

Ben shook his head, trying somehow to dislodge this enormous notion before it could settle on him. 'How?'

'Oh God, Ben, don't make this so hard. Can't you ever meet me halfway? How do you *think*?'

'But we always use . . . well, I know, not every time, but . . .'

'There you are,' Nic said coldly.

'How do you know? Are you sure?'

'I got a tester thing. I did it two days ago, and again this morning. You pee on a stick.'

'And?'

'It's positive.' She spaced out the words, speaking as if to a child.

Ben fell back now and they lay side by side. Then he reached out and found her hand. He laced his fingers with hers, trying to radiate reassurance.

'It's all right, baby.'

Nic writhed away from him. 'Don't call me that. Just don't, do you hear?'

There was a choke in her voice that he had never heard before.

'I'm sorry. Listen. We'll sort it out. You know, you can get a . . .'

'An abortion,' Nic said. 'That's what it's called.'

'Yeah, that's right. I know what it's called. You could maybe ask Gina what we should do.'

'No *way*. She's so fucking brisk and tidy and sorted, she's the last person I'd ask.'

'OK, OK. But there are people. Agencies, and clinics and things. There's my mum, as well, if it comes to that.'

'Your mum?'

Nic suddenly began to cry, quite noisily, with her mouth open and tears sliding out of the corners of her eyes. Unable to bear this, Ben hoisted himself on to his knees and knelt over her, gripping her arms.

'Nic, don't cry. Please don't cry. We'll fix it, we'll do it together. I'm here, look.'

She looked into his eyes. 'Will we?'

'Yes. Of course we will. It happens.'

'Promise?'

'Yes. Cross my heart.'

'I feel so bad. Like it's a bad thing, a really black wicked thing we've done, and we shouldn't have and everything will be wrong now . . .'

'Hush. It won't. It's going to be all right, Nic. I promise.'

Ben leaned down and kissed her, tasting the salt on her cold mouth, and it was long seconds before she yielded and wound her arms around his neck.

'I promise,' he repeated.

Alpha and Omega

Alexandra Davies rummaged in her bag to retrieve her mobile phone, wedged it precariously between her left ear and her shoulder, and with her right index finger jabbed the button of the stop request at the traffic lights.

'Yeah, Omie? Hi?'

'God, what's that racket? Listen, have you heard from Mum?'

'No,' Alexandra told her sister. A bendy bus swished by and then a high-sided truck that rocked her with a blast of turbulence.

Olivia's voice rose slightly.

'Alph? Are you there?'

'Yeah. It's traffic. I'm out.'

'What d'you think they're doing?'

The lights refused to change but the stream of vehicles briefly slowed and Alexandra took the opportunity to dash across the first three lanes. It was coming on to rain, and she had no hood or umbrella with her.

'Who?'

'Our *parents*.'

'Omie, you know as well as I do what they're up to. They have moved further out to the sticks, they're doing up some wreck of a house on Miranda Meadowe's estate, Dad's full of wild schemes, Mum's going along with it. What's new?'

Olivia sighed, and her sister could hear her settling herself for a long talk. 'Nothing, I suppose, when you put it like that. I'm worried about them, though. They don't call, do they? And when I call them, they're always busy. Ben says the same, you know.'

'I don't think it's a cause for worry, is it? They've got a life. We've got a life. Even Ben has. We're a success story, the Davies family.'

From the safety of the central island Alexandra weighed up her chances of survival if she darted onwards against the lights.

Olivia said, 'Is that what you call it? Growing up felt more like a car crash, most of the time.'

'Success against the odds. Have you talked to Sam or Toby about it? It must be the same for them.'

'No, it isn't. The Knights were at boarding school and always moving anyway. Hampstead, Islington, Richmond, one of those places. But I *so* miss our old house, you know? Don't you? I have these dreams about it, all the time. It's where we grew up. It's got all our *history* locked in it.'

'I know, I feel the same. But at the end of the day it's only bricks and mortar, isn't it? The house had to go, they needed the money, that's that, and what matters is we've all got each other. Even Mum and Dad are still around for us, you know, even though they're not right here.'

'You're right, Alph, 'course you are. I just feel a bit, what, lost? Abandoned. Is that totally weird at our age?'

'You mean, Parents Leave Girl Twins, Twenty-five, All Alone in World. Social Services Intervene?'

They made the humming noise that was their shorthand for laughter. 'OK, so I'm a freak.'

'No, you're not. Mum's always been right beside us. So has Dad, even, in his own way. Now they've sold our house and gone to live somewhere we don't know at all with what might seem to be a random new family made up of friends of theirs from a hundred years ago, and they're suddenly quite busy with stuff that doesn't seem to concern us. It's bound to be strange, isn't it? But isn't this what happens to all families, in the end? We were never going to be at home in the kitchen with Mum for ever and ever with Ben in his highchair and us two making jam tarts. At least they're not divorced, like most people's p's.'

Alexandra ran, and successfully completed the crossing. Fat raindrops landed on the pavement, the same size as the blobs of discarded gum already speckling it. She transferred her mobile to the other ear, wedged it in place again and fished in her bag for her purse. She calculated that there was just time to run into Pret and pick up a coffee before going back to work.

'Yeah. It is what happens. Anyway.' Olivia sighed. The conversation had followed a familiar pattern, with her own anxieties temporarily allayed by Alexandra's reassurances. 'I forget what you're doing tonight?'

'Meeting Cam and Laure. Might go out after. You?'

'Film, something foreign, can't remember what it's called. Tom wants to see it.'

'Speak later, then?'

'Yeah. Thanks, Alph.'

'Love you. I've got to go now. Bye, sis.'

'Me too. Bye. Wait – I'll give Ben a call, shall I? I don't know what he and Nic are doing. I haven't seen them, either.'

'Do that. Bye.'

Alexandra crammed her phone into the pocket of her black jeans and slid through the queue at the coffee counter. She had seven minutes of her lunch hour left. She would talk to Olivia at least once more, perhaps twice, before bedtime.

The Davies girls were monozygotic, or identical, twins.

At their birth their father had exclaimed in rapture, holding the squalling crimson scraps against his heart, 'These two are my world, from this day onwards. They are my Alpha and my Omega.'

The family story went that Selwyn had tried to insist that

64

the babies should be christened accordingly, but Polly firmly opted for what she called nice, normal names.

Polly's mother had agreed. 'Lovely. Not letters, or Zebedee or Dusk or Cowslip, or whatever poor little children seem to get landed with nowadays.'

It made no difference though. To their family, their baby brother Ben, and most of their friends, the twins for ever bracketed the Greek alphabet between them. To each other and to the rest of the world apart from employers, airlines and the DVLC, they were Alph and Omie. Two halves of a whole, one another's best and closest ally.

Not that they were all that much alike, at twenty-five, even to look at. From their Facebook profiles, it would have been difficult to deduce a relationship. Alexandra worked in retail marketing, and lived alone in a rented glass and steel studio flat near Bethnal Green. She wore monochrome clothes with a decidedly Japanese influence, and intended to set up her own company within five years. Olivia lived with her boyfriend in his chaotic flat off Shepherd's Bush Road. She was a freelance illustrator, working from home, and was usually dressed in a picturesque scramble of rainbow knits and tie-dye.

Because they lived at opposite ends of town, the two girls didn't see each other all that often, not more than twice or even once a week. The principal link between them, as vital as their umbilical cord had once been, was their pair of mobile phones. They always had exactly the same make and model. It was really weird, Omie said, but she had lost hers one night because it had fallen out of her pocket and dropped down the toilet when she was at a club, and she had been *way* too grossed out to reach down and fish it out again. But then less than twelve hours later, Alph had had her bag with her phone inside it stolen from beneath her desk by a sneak thief who had slipped into her office while she was down the corridor talking to her boss and everyone else was out at lunch.

The twins consulted each other, and then agreed on the new model.

They talked or texted each other all the time, the little chirrup of a ringtone or bleep of an arriving message so familiar that they presented no barrier to the seamless dialogue between them.

OCTOBER

THREE

The digger driver reversed smartly away from the trench. A flock of gulls rose from the raw earth and banked over the ochre tree tops, wheeling back as the machine trundled off to dump its hopper-load of soil and flints on a swelling mound. It was a soft, windless morning. The grinding of the digger and the cries of the gulls carried a long way in the still air.

Two workmen towed a heavy roll of polythene sheeting from the back of a truck whilst the site manager in a fluorescent jacket and hard hat talked on his mobile at the door of the Portakabin office. On the lip of the trench a young man in a helmet was standing alone with his hands in his pockets. He studied the loads of earth as they were sliced and scooped away, from time to time glancing over at the contractor or his client. He was the first person at the site to notice two women and a tall, thin man strolling towards them from the direction of the main house. He sighed to himself. They were entitled to be here, of course, but in his experience visitors at an excavation meant nothing but delays and questions. He didn't know Mrs Meadowe personally, but he came from Meddlett where she had the reputation of being unfriendly. He stuck his hands deeper in his pockets and concentrated on the digging.

Amos was also watching the work. He was in an excellent humour. Something that was ingenious, fitting and intricately designed was going to be created here out of nothing, on the rim of a field in an attentive landscape. Satisfaction that construction was at last under way spilled all through him. His sense of happy anticipation even increased when the digger momentarily halted and he caught the sound of laughter and raised voices close at hand. As soon as he saw Katherine he raised his arm and waved, beckoning the visitors across. Miranda and Colin followed her, picking their way past the contractors.

'We thought we'd come and see what's happening,' Miranda called to him.

'Progress,' he shouted back.

The three of them scuttled towards him, bundling out of the path of the digger and gathering to inspect the work.

Amos put a proprietorial arm around his wife's shoulders.

In the course of their married life Katherine and he had lived in a dozen houses, from the first cramped terrace to the latest sprawling mansion in half an acre of suburban garden. He thought of all the different property viewings, the potential homes with actual merits to be decoded from the hyperbole of various estate agents, the subsequent measurings and deliberations, and the final compromises that had to be made in order to fit a family within a set of walls, like a crab into a pre-existing shell, with the boys arguing over who was to have the bigger room and Katherine saying that really she was going to miss the old house. Now for the first time his family would have a home designed around it, not the other way around. Not that they were any longer precisely a family, of course; Sam and Toby had their own places, he had seen to that. But they would still come. Children took a long time to detach themselves nowadays, he had noticed, if they ever really did so.

Now his wife turned her head and remarked to Colin and Miranda that she couldn't imagine what their home was going to be like when it was finally built.

'There's so much space, and air and sunshine. It's hard to picture what a house will look like plonked down here.'

Amos frowned. Her vagueness as well as her choice of words irritated him.

'Darling, you've seen all the plans a thousand times. Drawings, computer simulations, every single stage of the process.'

She only shook her head, and laughed.

'I know. Weird, isn't it?'

Miranda had brought a basket. 'I thought we should have a celebration,' she announced, to cover the momentary awkwardness. She led the way to a vantage point under the trees and unpacked a bottle of champagne and a carton of orange juice. Amos waved to the workmen and followed the others.

Miranda had found a reason for a celebration almost every other day at Mead. It was as if she were the entertainments secretary and they were freshmen newly arrived at university, needing scheduled social events and copious supplies of drink to kick-start their friendships. Four days ago Selwyn had announced that a major phase of his demolition work was complete, and they had gathered between the ceiling props and barrows of rubble to admire the open space and to drink wine poured into the plastic mugs that were all Polly had been able to muster. It was two in the morning before they finally dispersed to bed. Amos had joked that he wasn't sure he could stand the pace and Selwyn countered that he couldn't see why not, since they had little else that was significant to occupy them these days. At that point Polly took his arm and guided him off to bed in the tarp shelter.

Miranda threw herself into all these events, carrying the others on the tide of her high spirits. She was already screwing the plastic feet into a set of picnic wineglasses as they sat down in a row on the dry turf. Colin leaned back against a tree trunk. He was tired, but he raised his glass when Miranda handed it to him.

'Here's to the perfect house. May you live like a king, Amos. A solar-heated, green-spirited monarch.'

'What about me?' Katherine demanded. They all turned to look at her.

71

'And a queen, K, of course,' Colin added.

They sipped champagne and watched the digger as it rolled to and fro like a sturdy toy. The sun rose higher above the trees, but the outlines of the copses and field crests in the distance were blurred by mist, suggesting a cold night to come. The digger came up with another hopper full of earth, and they heard the note of the engine change as the driver backed up a short distance.

He jumped from the cab and walked across to look down into the trench. At the same time, the young man who had been watching slid his hands out of his pockets and walked briskly to the edge.

Amos was leaning on one elbow. He propped himself a little higher to see what was going on.

The digger driver returned to his seat and Amos nodded his approval, but then the man turned off the engine, dismounted once more and hurried away towards the site office. The other workmen stopped what they were doing.

'What now?' Amos groaned.

'Maybe he's found some buried treasure,' Miranda teased, but she sat up straighter too. 'After I've gone and sold the land to you, as well.'

'It's some bloody annoying thing. I just know it.'

The site manager left the Portakabin. There was now a cluster of hi-vis jackets and helmets gathered about the raw slit in the ground. Amos launched himself to his feet. He charged off with his head down and his elbows jutting at an angle. His trousers rippled over his broad shanks. Rather uncertainly, Katherine got up and followed him.

'Better take a look?' Colin murmured to Miranda. She was already on her feet.

A line of gulls settled on the roof of the stationary digger. They rotated their heads as if they were waiting for a curtain to go up. A sharp smell of sour earth and torn roots hung in the air.

A few inches below the surface the cut edges of turf, roots

and a few inches of topsoil gave way to dense earth, packed with stones. Protruding from the bottom of the trench, where a band of earth seemed to be darker than elsewhere, Miranda saw what appeared to be a long piece of flint. It was grey, clogged with dirt, and splintered where the sharp edge of the digger blade had smashed into it. The young man ignored her, and everyone else. He knelt to examine the find.

'Just caught my eye, didn't it?' the digger driver was saying to the other workmen. He was big with a red face, his yellow helmet perched above it looking much too small for his head.

'Right you are, Alan. Let's take a look,' the site boss said. He vaulted into the trench, but the young man snatched at the collar of his jacket and pulled him back.

'Wait there,' he snapped, with surprising authority. 'Everyone, just stand where you are.'

Silence fell over the little group. Even Amos hesitated.

The young man slid down into the trench. With his right thumb he rubbed the earth from the protruding flint, stroking it as if it were a baby's fist. Then he took out a tiny trowel, and with infinite care began to scoop the debris from around it.

'Who is he?' Colin murmured.

'The archaeologist,' Amos said curtly.

'The *what*?'

'Oh, for Christ's sake. It's the planning regulations. One of the hoops you have to jump through to get anything done. The county bloody archaeologist assessed the site, told me and the architect that there was a minimal chance of there actually being any old bits of Roman pottery or anything else buried here, but he was sending someone in on a watching brief just in case. Someone *I* end up paying for, naturally. That's him.'

It was obvious to Miranda now that what was protruding from the ground was not a flint but a broken bone. She watched intently, only half hearing Amos's tirade.

The archaeologist gently worked the bone free. He placed it in a bag, carefully labelled the exterior, and laid it on the lip of the trench.

'Right, then. Let's get going again,' Amos called.

The men shuffled, and the archaeologist continued to ignore them all. He was kneeling again and scraping at the earth. A moment later he came up with a smaller bone. He cupped it in his palm and brushed away the dirt.

Amos trampled forwards. Miranda wanted to restrain him, and when she caught Katherine's eye she knew she felt the same.

Amos called, 'Look. I know you've got a job to do. But I can't allow the remains of some animal to hold up the work of an entire site crew for half a morning.'

The second bone went into a separate bag.

Amos raised his voice. 'It's a dead . . .' there was a second's hesitation while he searched his mind for a farm animal, any animal '. . . *cow*.'

The archaeologist did look up now. Beneath the plastic peak of his helmet his face looked startlingly young, almost unformed. To Colin, standing beside Miranda at the end of the trench, his features seemed vaguely familiar. Until recently he would have searched his memory for where and when, and what they might have done together.

'These are human remains,' the young man said.

A deeper pool of silence collected. Bowing his head, one of the workmen took off his helmet and held it awkwardly across his chest. Shocked, Miranda gazed down into the freshly sliced earth at the bottom of the trench, and then at the labelled bags. Who was it, buried here in this peaceful place? Who, and when?

Amos broke in again, 'This is my land. We have all the necessary permissions in place to build a house right here, and that's what you are delaying.'

Katherine put her hand on his arm. 'Amos, please.' But he shook it off. He marched to Alan's side and tried to nudge him backwards towards the digger. The two of them performed a tiny dance with their chests puffed out. The gulls rose in unison from their perch, their wingbeats loud in the stillness. Alan scratched the back of his head under his hard hat and retreated a couple of reluctant steps, followed by the site manager making pacifying gestures. Miranda reached for Colin's hand and held it, but her eyes were still fixed on the disturbed ground. Amos measured up to the contractor and Alan, as if he were going to manhandle them back to work. His face was red and he was puffing slightly. Amos was not used to having his orders ignored. For a moment it looked as if he might win, as Alan placed his boot on the step of the machine and prepared to climb up.

The archaeologist put down his trowel. He stood in front of the digger with his hand raised.

'Work at this site is temporarily suspended,' he said, 'pending further investigation.'

'On whose authority?' Amos demanded.

'On my own, for the time being,' the young man answered. 'I am just going to notify the police, and the coroner's office.'

'The police? The *police*?' Amos came to a standstill, his arms flopping to his sides.

Katherine looked at her husband, then turned away from him.

'What is it? Who was it?' Miranda murmured.

The workmen were already filing cheerfully in the direction of their caravan, pulling off their helmets as they went.

'I'm sorry,' the young archaeologist said to Miranda and Amos and the others. He had a stud in his nose, and ropes of hair pulled back and buried under the loose collar of his plaid flannel shirt. His hands, heavy with dirt, hung loose at his sides. Colin tried to recall where he had seen him before.

'I can't say for certain, not immediately, but I'm fairly sure, based on what I can see, that this is not a recent interment. But I've got to act by the book.'

Miranda lifted her head. Her face was white. 'Recent? What does that mean? I've lived here for more than twenty years. It's my home. This was my husband's land, he grew up here. Who would be buried in a spot like this?'

'Are you sure these are human bones?' Colin asked.

'Yes, I am. There is part of a femur, and a patella.' He tried to sound authoritative but a flush coloured his face, showing up the scattered pocks of healed acne. He was probably in his early twenties. Hardly a match for Amos, Colin thought, the poor kid.

The archaeologist continued, speaking directly and gently to Miranda because of the shock in her eyes. 'The way the thigh and the knee were uncovered makes me think that the corpse may have been buried in a semi-crouching position. The remainder of the skeleton will be there, almost definitely.' He raised his hand and pointed to the wall of the trench. Grass roots and a few bruised daisies overhung it.

'How long ago?' Miranda asked.

'I'll really have to check with my field supervisor. I'm not all that experienced.' His colour deepened. 'There are tests, of course. But he's probably prehistoric. That would be my guess. Bronze Age, or Iron Age. Something like two thousand years old.'

'Two thousand?' Amos muttered, in spite of himself.

They looked out over the plateau of grass and the sweep of farmland and dappled country beyond it.

The regular perspective tilted, and swung out of alignment. Miranda steadied herself against Colin's arm. She and the others had been thinking about their present concerns, she realized, and speculating only about the new house and next month and next year, but now their attention was forcibly dragged back through the centuries. Under the thin skin of earth, hardly more than two spade-depths below the grass, lay history. Silently she wondered what this landscape had looked like so long ago, and who it was who had come out of the opaque past to be uncovered in front of them.

Miranda found that she was shivering.

Amos recovered himself first. 'The local CID are going to be most helpful with that, then.'

'It's a formality, sir. But this is a human body.'

'How long is all this going to take? As a formality, of course?'

The archaeologist met his eye. 'I don't know,' he said.

'Let's find out, shall we?'

Amos went to the site manager's Portakabin and Miranda could see him vigorously making his points while the builder shook his head and fended him off with raised hands. Then Amos took out his mobile phone. Colin walked away and stood at a little distance, apparently contemplating the view. Katherine and Miranda were left at the side of the trench.

Seeing Miranda's pallor Katherine asked, 'Are you all right?'

Almost to herself Miranda said, 'I can't say I've ever thought about it before, but bones are so intimate when you'd really expect them to be quite dry and inanimate, wouldn't you? It's so apparent that once there was flesh and sinews and smooth skin. We were looking at a person's leg, part of the body of a real person who lived and breathed, and then you have to take in the fact that they've been lying there in the ground for thousands of years. Jake and I used to come here sometimes and have a picnic, looking out over this view. It rather changes the picture, doesn't it?'

Katherine touched her arm. 'Do you want to go back to the house?'

Miranda was grateful for her concern. Realizing that she was still holding her picnic glass, she tipped the residue of her drink into the grass. The plastic was smeared and there was a scum of orange pulp sticking to the sides.

'No, I want to see what's going to happen. Champagne seems suddenly a bit off key, though, doesn't it? Shall we go back and just sit down for a bit?'

They could hear Amos still shouting on the telephone. The archaeologist had made some calls too, and now he took out a camera and started snapping the open trench from various angles. The workmen were gathered around the caravan with their sandwiches and copies of the *Sun*.

The two women went back to their vantage point and sat down. Miranda dropped the empty champagne bottle into her basket and unscrewed the foot of her glass. It was becoming clear that they were going to have to wait some time for any developments. Miranda rested her chin on her knees. She had been thinking about Jake, and the quiet graveyard of Meddlett church where he was buried. Then her thoughts switched to Colin as she watched him strolling down to the distant fence marking the boundary of what had once been Miranda's land and was now Amos's.

She asked suddenly, 'K? Do you think Colin is any happier living here with us, or is he just going through the motions?'

'Of living, or trying to be happy?'

'Doing one, while feeling obliged to attempt the other. There's a glass wall around him, don't you think? Ever since Stephen was killed. It's as if he's here because of not knowing where else to be? Although, come to think of it, maybe he's not alone in that. Do you remember the times when we *all* used to live our lives, not just inhabit a corner of them?'

Katherine turned to look at Miranda's face. After a moment she answered, 'I don't know what it must be like for Colin. Polly may know more, with her and Colin being so close, but probably none of us can do more than imagine. But, yes. He has put up barriers. Do you remember how exuberant he used to be?'

'I do. The Ibiza trip?'

Laughter chased the sadness out of Miranda's eyes as they acknowledged the memory.

In the mid-1970s, when Amos was insisting to Katherine that he was going to marry her so she had better get to know and like his friends, he had rented a holiday villa near San Antonio and invited a dozen people for a summer holiday. In the party were Miranda and the actor she was at that time considering as a potential husband, and Colin and the man with whom he had recently fallen in love.

Stephen was five years older than Colin. He was a compact, rather unsmiling businessman who didn't try very hard to integrate himself into the group. He didn't particularly enjoy the island nightlife, he didn't take any drugs or even drink very much, and it was obvious that he had only come on the holiday because he wanted to be with beautiful and extrovert Colin, whatever that might take.

It was a big enough group to absorb his differences without them seeming particularly noticeable, Miranda recalled, and in any case it was the time when Amos was remodelling himself as a traditionalist barrister and upholder of family values, which was much more remarkable and amusing to them all.

One day, when most of them were too sunburned and hungover to do anything but lie in the shade beyond the pool, Colin and Stephen whiled away the siesta hour by dressing up.

Miranda remembered waking up from a nap. Done up as Carmen Miranda, 'As a tribute to you, of course,' he had told her, Colin was kneeling precariously on a lilo in the middle of the pool. He was wearing a flamenco skirt, a bra top, gold hoop earrings, full make-up and a hat made out of a laden fruit bowl topped with a crest of bananas. He wobbled to his feet and began to strum a guitar. He managed a passable samba rhythm and a warble of 'Bananas is My Business.' But even with this apparition in front of them, it was Stephen they were all gaping at. He was arranged on a second lilo, two legs crammed into one leg of a pair of lime green trousers and two feet into a single swimming flipper. He was slowly combing the strands of a very old and matted long blonde wig to tumble over his hairy chest and looking at Colin with a parody of adoration that very clearly had real devotion embedded in it.

That was the first inkling that Miranda or any of Colin's friends had of the extreme contradictions in Stephen's nature. There were, they understood, all kinds of warring elements concealed under the solid exterior. It suddenly became much less surprising that Colin found him so interesting.

It was only a few seconds before Carmen Miranda very slowly and with great dignity tilted sideways into the water. Stephen neatly caught the guitar as it fell past him. Miranda's actor cine-filmed the whole sequence.

'I wish I had that film,' Miranda sighed. 'I'd give anything to see it again.'

'Do you ever see whatshisname? The actor?' Katherine wondered.

'No. What *was* his name? Although in fact, I did see him about three years ago. In an episode of *Holby City*.'

'Any good?'

Miranda laughed delightedly. 'As a psychopathic father on the run while his teenaged daughter haemorrhaged in casualty? Absolutely excellent. I've probably got some photographs of the Carmen Miranda event in a box somewhere.'

'We should get the old pictures out.'

'Maybe.'

Katherine said, 'It's good to have these shared memories. It's historic glue.'

Miranda considered for a moment, and then asked, 'Do you ever feel that you're only inhabiting *your* life, K?'

Katherine studied the patch of turf framed by her knees. There were ants busy between the blades of grass. Then she lifted her head. The archaeologist had descended into the trench once again.

'I did. Sometimes. I think being here has changed that.'

'Has it?' Miranda was pleased. 'Has it really?' She seized on any confirmation that the Mead collaboration was working as she hoped.

Katherine said quickly, 'Of course, I had Amos and the boys, and work, and people coming to dinner, all those things, so I wasn't exactly lonely, but I did feel that I was sort of watching from the sidelines rather than pitching into the scrum myself. And I *would* use a bloody rugby metaphor, wouldn't I, as if even the language for framing my own experiences has to be borrowed from my menfolk?'

She attempted a laugh at this, while Miranda only raised her eyebrows.

'But I feel different here, being with you and Colin and Selwyn and Polly. It's old ground, yet new at the same time. There's a sense of anticipation, definitely hopeful anticipation. It's not all to do with the glass house, although of course that's exciting.' She made this dutiful nod out of habit, and consideration to Amos and Miranda herself. 'It's almost a rebirth, isn't it? A completely different way of living, and that leads to general crazy optimism, which is rather at odds with the reality as far as Amos and I are concerned.'

There was a pause. This was quite a long speech, for Katherine.

'Any news about that?' Miranda asked, treading carefully.

The reason for Amos's departure from London and the law wasn't discussed at Mead, although everyone knew that everyone else knew about it. She was relieved when Katherine answered matter-of-factly.

'About whether the young woman is finally going to press charges? The most recent notion is that she won't. I think she may be on dangerous ground because she almost certainly reciprocated some of Amos's attentions, at least to begin with. Then she probably withdrew, and he naturally refused to accept her withdrawal, and then he would have crossed the line between pursuit and harassment somewhere along the way. I imagine that would all be rather delicate to prove in court, don't you? Particularly against an adversary like Amos.'

Katherine picked a blade of grass and thoughtfully chewed on it.

'Now he's left the chambers that may be enough to satisfy her. I don't know if he'll go back to the Bar some day. If he'll need to, that is. I don't mean for the money, God knows he's got enough of that piled up, but just to stay the Amos he is, in his own estimation. That's why this new house, seeing it take shape here, is so important. It gives him a reason for being. He's not the kind of man who retires to the golf course, particularly against his will. He's been bored, lately, and it makes him more difficult.'

There were opposing notes of sympathy and of dismissal in her words, chiming together, that took both women a little by surprise.

'Yes, I can see that,' Miranda agreed.

*　　*　　*

81

Colin turned back from the boundary fence. He walked slowly, on a wide arc, but he was drawn steadily back to the trench. The young archaeologist was still on all fours, gently scraping with his trowel. He was so absorbed in what he was doing that he didn't hear Colin's approach, and it was the shadow falling across his work that made him jump. He jerked upright on his knees but his expression relaxed as soon as he saw that it wasn't Amos.

'Sorry,' he muttered.

'Why? You're doing your job.'

The boy wasn't looking at him. His gaze was fixed on the earth.

'There's something here.' He knew he should keep the discovery to himself, maintain a professional detachment, but he couldn't help blurting it out. His fist closed tightly on the handle of his trowel and it was all he could do to stop himself in his eagerness from lunging back at the find and gouging at the remains.

Colin heard how his voice shook.

'What? What is it?'

The boy glanced quickly past him. Miranda and Katherine sat a way off, talking. Amos was still telephoning, the site crew lounged in the sunshine.

'Look.' He pointed downwards.

Out of the earth close to the edge of the trench, the rim of something smooth and curved now protruded. Crusted with dirt, it might have been taken for a large piece of broken glass or pottery, but the archaeologist had already rubbed an inch of it clean. The sun struck a dull gleam out of precious metal.

'Good God,' Colin said.

'Yeah. And a bit,' the boy agreed.

'What happens now?'

'Well, it doesn't happen every day, does it? It's killing me but I've got to wait for my field supervisor to show up. I don't know much, but I'm pretty sure this is big.'

In the middle distance, a car drew up at the point where

Amos's driveway would one day meet the curving route to the main house. A uniformed policeman got out and opened the gate, then the patrol car bumped slowly over the builders' track to the site.

'Christ, now here's the cops. I hoped the boss would get here first,' the boy sighed.

'You can handle it,' Colin told him. The boy's resemblance to someone he knew was no longer troubling. It came to him that this wasn't actually Jessie's boyfriend from the first evening in the pub, the one she had squabbled with about ownership of the dog, but the two of them were certainly sufficiently alike to be mistaken for one another.

A second solid policeman emerged from the car. Amos made straight for the pair of them, with the site manager bobbing at his side.

'Here we go then,' said the archaeologist as he climbed reluctantly out of the trench.

Across the field, alerted by the sighting of police in the driveway of the house, Selwyn was hurrying towards them with Polly moving more slowly in his wake.

'Has there been a murder?' Selwyn asked.

'Not recently, by the look of it,' Colin told him. 'Although I think Amos would prefer it to be a straightforward drug-related shooting. History may take longer to unravel.'

Amos said, surveying his site later that afternoon: 'So, the monkeys have taken over the zoo.'

A van arrived, with 'Anglian Archaeological Services' painted on the sides. Several archaeologists of various degrees of seniority climbed out, donned helmets and fluorescent jackets with AAS printed on the back, fanned out and began measuring, pegging lines and scribbling on clipboards. The field supervisor, a lean bearded man in his forties, made a series of urgent calls. A frame tent was brought out and quickly erected over the trench, and the white nylon fabric sucked and billowed in a rising wind. The policemen conferred with the supervisor, the intermittent crackle of voices from their radios carrying across to where Selwyn stood joking about how English Heritage and the county archaeologist would never let Amos dig the channels in the earth for his futuristic ground exchange heating now that there was known to be treasure beneath.

'Buried gold,' Selwyn murmured. 'Who knows, Amos, you might just have got even richer.'

'Probably not, under the 1996 Treasure Act,' Amos retorted. But that they should be even discussing this sharpened the sense that an unwelcome change was coming to Mead.

Another car wound its way towards them and yet another archaeologist emerged, bearing a licence from the Ministry of Justice to allow the human remains to be excavated. A copy of it was formally pinned to the door of the Portakabin. Amos read the licence and gave a curt, unwilling nod to acknowledge that, for now at least, he would have to agree to a suspension of work. It was clear that there would be no more progress on the site for the time being, so the builders packed up and went home. The police lingered long enough for the osteologist who had arrived in the van to assure them personally that the uncovered bones were hundreds of years old, then they folded their double bulk back into their patrol car and drove away.

The bearded field supervisor introduced himself as Christopher Carr. He promised that as soon as his team had had a chance to make a first assessment of the finds, Mr Knight would be informed. In the meantime, it was important that the excavation be conducted methodically in order that no vital information or clues were lost in the process, and they would understand that, wouldn't they? His young assistant, Kieran, had acted correctly in calling a temporary halt to the site work. He thanked Amos for his cooperation.

'When can we have a look?' Katherine asked him, then glanced away, as if she suspected it had been in some way wrong of her to ask.

'As soon as there is anything interesting to see,' Christopher told her. 'But I would be grateful if for the time being you wouldn't mention the find to anyone at all outside this group. Sightseers and the press are never helpful on the scene until we are ready for them.'

Amos struck his forehead quite hard with the heel of his hand.

Katherine and Polly left the site to go back to the house and make sandwiches, but Miranda found that she couldn't leave the site while so much of Mead's unimagined history was being uncovered. The archaeologists moved in and out of their tent, watched by Miranda and the others from their picnic place. They could hear the metallic clink of trowels. Bags and buckets filled with spoil were brought out, and a young woman with dreadlocks longer than Kieran's knelt to sift the loose earth through a sieve.

Amos ate smoked salmon sandwiches and loudly fumed about the delay, until Miranda snapped at him.

'It's my land too. My home for twenty years, Jake was born here. Can't you acknowledge that whatever is lying in that trench might have at least a comparable importance to your *house*?'

At once Amos put his big hand on hers. 'Of course, Mirry. I do apologize. How thrilling for Mead if this does turn out to be a major discovery. But I don't think you've quite got the hang of what a disruption it may turn out to be.'

'Let's wait and see, shall we?' Miranda said quietly. Colin lay back and seemed to fall asleep.

At the end of the afternoon, Kieran came out of the tent and crossed to where they still waited. His face was flushed under the faint pockmarks.

'Would you like to come and take a look?'

They got to their feet and followed him.

Within the white tent, sheltered from the wind that had got up, it was warmer and surprisingly still. The fabric rippled and snapped with small popping sounds. The pleasantly diffused light coupled with the strong scent of trampled grass was reminiscent of a garden fête or agricultural show. The archaeologists were lined up beside their trench, mostly with their hands folded, looking downwards like proud but modest exhibitors. A photographer's tripod and camera stood in place at one end of the tent.

Miranda looked down and caught her breath.

The earth had been cleared partially to expose the skeleton. It was dark, discoloured and broken, but still shockingly human. It lay on its left side, the legs bent up towards the chest and the forearms extended. Earth filled the collapsed ribcage and crusted the pelvic bowl. The skull was tilted at an angle, the eye sockets blinded with dirt and the jaw with a rim of teeth seeming to grin into infinity.

Two feet away from it lay a second skull, much smaller, and the ribs of a young child.

Only when she had taken this in did she see that resting between the jaw of the larger skeleton and the framework of its ribcage lay a band that once would have circled the neck. To the side of the body, the curved edge of metal that Colin had glimpsed had been further exposed. It looked like the edge of a large plate. A raised pattern that might have been part of a scroll or leaf design was just visible.

Stillness spread outwards and seemed to press against the nylon walls and roof of the tent, where the wind chafed.

At Miranda's side, Colin remembered Stephen's funeral in the village on the edge of the Yorkshire moorland, and the priest and the mourners gathered at the edge of the open grave as handfuls of earth thudded on to the coffin lid. He raised his head now in an attempt to blot out the memory, searching along the line of silent people as if he hoped to see a priest amongst them.

He was not a religious man, but he would have liked to hear some words of blessing or a simple prayer spoken over these bones.

The first person to break the silence was Christopher Carr. His voice was low and they had to listen to catch his words.

'This is an important discovery,' he said. 'Perhaps very important. We have a rich burial here, probably dating from the later
Iron Age. We may be looking at a prince, a tribal leader at
least, who was buried with his symbols of rank and power and
provisions for the afterlife.'

'What about the child?' Katherine asked. This time she looked
directly at Chris. He nodded sympathy at her.

'We can't tell yet. Perhaps it was an attendant, maybe even
a human sacrifice as part of the funeral ritual. Our osteologist,
that's David over there, may well be able to establish the cause
of death.'

David was a small man with glasses. He smiled and then
suppressed it, all the time looking as if he couldn't wait to start
handling the bones. The atmosphere was slowly lightening. The
archaeologists began quietly to stack their tools. Kieran ducked
out of the entrance with one more yellow plastic bucketful of
loose earth.

One by one, the Mead people turned away from the trench
and its contents. As the shock of staring death in the face
subsided, they became aware that these relics were from a time
so distant that they could hardly connect with it.

Chris said, 'There's one more thing. We'll be leaving a security guard here overnight. The site will have to be protected
until the artefacts have been removed to a safe place.'

Miranda demanded 'Why? This is a private estate. No one
comes here.'

'Forgive me, Mrs Meadowe. We don't know yet what these
grave goods are, or what else we might find. If they should
turn out to be alloys of precious metals, or even solid gold,
imagine what the material alone might be worth, without adding
up the historical value.'

Amos began to say something, then stopped himself.

'I see,' Miranda said, although she was only just beginning
to. This discovery was going to change the delicate balance of
life at Mead, the life she had wanted for them all, that much
was already clear.

Chris continued, 'With your help, we'll keep this discovery quiet for as long as possible. But in my experience news inevitably leaks out sooner or later, and you'd be surprised at the nighthawks who will turn up looking for a piece of treasure to keep for themselves.'

Outside the tent it had grown chilly and the sky was overcast. Another van had arrived, this one marked 'Lockyer Security'. A very large shaven-headed man sat in the driver's seat, frowning over a print-out.

Amos stood in front of Chris. 'Can you give me any idea of how long?' he asked yet again.

'How much time my team will be granted to complete the excavation is the decision of the county archaeologist, and that depends on how important he judges the findings to be, in terms of local and national history.'

Amos's lower jaw was protruding now, a dangerous sign. 'And so?'

The archaeologist sighed. 'If I have to put a frame on it I'd say something more than a few days, but not as long as several months. We'll do the job as quickly as we can.'

'Thank you,' Amos said, as if he were dismissing the most unreliable of witnesses.

Chris turned to Katherine, who stood a yard behind her husband. 'I'm sorry,' he told her.

Katherine's smile was transforming. Miranda saw it, and so did Polly, although Amos wasn't looking at her. 'Please don't be,' she said. 'There's no need.'

As he passed Kieran, Colin asked him, 'Did I meet your brother, at the Griffin in Meddlett, with a girl called Jessie and a dog?'

'Yeah, that'll be him. Damon.'

'I thought so. You're very alike.'

'Not really,' Kieran frowned.

The security guard lumbered out of the shelter of his van, and Amos made his comment about monkeys and the zoo.

*   *   *

They sat in the kitchen, over the remains of dinner. Selwyn had taken the blue chair next to the range and he balanced it on two legs and drank whisky as he surveyed the room. They had been talking all evening about the day's discovery. Amos insisted that he was no expert on the exact terms of the Treasure law, whilst leaving no doubt at all that he knew far more than the rest of them. He explained that if they fell within the definition of treasure, the finds would belong to the Crown. If they turned out to be spectacular, or historically significant, they would probably be bought by a museum. There might be a reward for the landowner.

'The best reward I can think of would be to get my house built,' he growled.

The others sighed. They had heard this enough times already. Miranda cupped her chin in her hands and looked at Amos.

'Jake would have loved the Warrior Prince of Mead.'

'The Warrior Prince?' Selwyn tried out the sound of it, dangerously tipping his chair and steadying himself with one hand burrowed amongst the tea towels and laundry hanging from the bar at the front of the range. 'This could make us as famous as Sutton Hoo. English Heritage will come and put up a tearoom. There will be boxed fudge, and a coach park.'

'No, there will not,' Miranda said sharply.

'Amos might decide otherwise. He owns the land, I believe.' Whisky made Selwyn malicious.

'Shut up, Sel,' Polly advised.

Amos got up from his chair and crossed to Miranda's side of the table. He hovered behind her chair, not quite able to do what he wanted, which was to hug her.

'Mirry, let's promise each other this minute in front of witnesses that whatever happens, this land business and prince business and the skulls and archaeology drama will not compromise our friendship. I solemnly promise there will be no tearoom, and certainly no fudge. Can you forgive me for happening to own the little acreage under which the bones have turned up?'

Miranda had never been immune to the force of his deliberate charm.

She answered solemnly, 'I promise, too. And there's nothing to forgive. The prince belongs to Mead itself, regardless of whose bit of turf he's lying beneath. That's what Jake would say.'

'I wish he were here, too,' Amos said. He sketched a sort of kiss in her direction and went back to his seat. Smiling dangerously over the rim of his glass, Selwyn studied him.

Polly's mobile rang. She took it out and inspected the display. 'Omie, hello darling. Are you all right?'

'Doesn't anyone else want another drink?' Selwyn called out.

'Yes, that's Dad.' Polly glanced up. 'Sorry, all. *No*, Omie, that's not what I meant. Of course I'm not apologizing to anyone for you ringing me. What's the matter? Wait a minute.' She got up and went out into the hall. They could hear her talking, and then she moved further away. Selwyn let his chair crash forward on to all four legs.

Katherine carried dishes to the sink, then leaned to look out into the yard. It was raining hard, and puddles glimmered in the porch light from their wing. Polly and Selwyn's side was a darker slab of darkness.

'Pretty bleak for the guard,' she said. 'I wouldn't like to be out there with only the dead for company, would you?'

'They're not going to come back,' Colin said.

Miranda broke in, 'No. Except, in a way they have, haven't they? We're thinking about them, peering down the centuries, dressing them in our minds in their necklaces and attaching stories to their lives and deaths. I can't get that child's skull and ribs out of my head.'

Amos took Katherine's arm. 'Come on, old girl. History's all bones. We're going to bed now.'

The Knights went out into the yard. Colin collected up his book and laptop, and said goodnight. Selwyn and Miranda were left alone.

'Barb,' Selwyn began softly, in the voice that he used only for her.

'No.'

His mouth curled, making him look dangerous again. 'Is that no generally, as a blanket edict, or in relation to something specific?'

Since the bathroom day, Miranda had avoided being alone with him. Now the possibility that Polly might step back into the room at any moment held her in a bubble of tension. Each of her senses was amplified. Miranda could imagine so vividly what it would be like if he left his chair, took her in his arms and put his mouth to the hollow formed by her collarbone, that it was as if he had actually done it. She swallowed, her mouth dry.

'Just no,' she whispered.

'I want to touch you.'

'I know.'

They listened to the rain.

'What shall we do?' he asked, as much of himself as to her.

'We'll live here at Mead, value our friendships, and get old together.'

There was a shocking crash as Selwyn's glass hit the red tiles at his feet and smashed into fragments. Neither of them could have said for certain whether he had thrown it or accidentally let it fall.

'I don't want to get old.'

There was so much vehemence and bitterness in his voice that it frightened her. 'I don't want to hear any more about death. Jake's dead, Stephen's dead. There are skeletons at the bottom of the fucking garden. What happened to the fairies, then? I want to live now, Mirry. I want *you*.'

'I know,' she whispered again.

If Polly hadn't come in at that moment, she would have gone to him.

'That was Omie,' Polly said. She flipped her phone shut.

'Was it?' Selwyn sounded dazed.

'I just said it was. There's broken glass all over the floor.'

He sighed. 'I dropped my drink.'

91

'Probably just as well.' Polly had already gone for the dustpan. He took it from her and roughly swept up the broken pieces. Miranda stood up, very stiffly, as if all her joints hurt.

'It's been an interesting day, hasn't it? I'm going to bed. Sleep well, you two,' she said.

Polly and Selwyn lay on their bed under the tarpaulin. Water dripped steadily above their heads and ran off into an enamel bowl. The various drips into various receptacles around the room sounded like an elaborate piano exercise.

'Are you ready?' Selwyn asked.

'Yes.'

He leaned up on one elbow, his shadow looming grotesquely on the opposite wall. He fiddled for a moment with the knob and then turned out the gas lamp. The mantle glowed red for two seconds and then they were in darkness.

'Were you and Miranda arguing?' Polly asked.

'No.'

She waited, but he didn't add anything.

She was intensely conscious of her heavy thigh and the six inches that separated their two bodies. If Selwyn and Miranda hadn't been arguing there was something else going on, and that possibility worried her much more than routine squabbling. History meant that there was always a buried connection between the two of them, but Polly was beginning to realize that she had underestimated the pull of it. Living here as closely as they did, seeing each other constantly, was disinterring the ancient foundations.

The dripping seemed to grow louder, as if the drops were hitting her skull.

'I'm concerned about Omie,' she said at length, casting her fears in a less threatening mould.

Selwyn gave an impatient twitch. 'That's nothing very new. What is it this time?'

'She's angry with us. We've sold their home, moved up here. She says it's as if we've abandoned them.'

92

There were five drips, then six. Three of them came very close together, almost as one.

'Poll, our children are all adults. We've brought them to this point, healthy and educated and relatively normal. Or you have, mostly, I'm not claiming any particular glory for it. But we've got to let them live their own lives, now, and in the future. You can't be their guardian and safety net for ever. Even you can't do that.'

'I could. Isn't that what parents are meant to do?'

'No, I don't think so.'

'Omie says she thinks there's something up with Ben. Alph does, as well.'

Despite her anxiety, Polly felt drowsiness beginning to smother her. She was always tired, these days. She knew that her voice had taken on a meandering quality.

As if from a long way off she heard Selwyn say, in an impatient mutter, 'If there's something up with Ben, as Omie says, then we'll hear about it.'

'Yes,' Polly finally agreed. She turned on to her side, away from him.

Selwyn lay on his back, unmoving.

FOUR

Gardening makes me think of Jake.

He's here in all the stones and shadows of Mead – or rather his absence is, because rational recall often fails me and I look up expecting to see him, only to experience all over again a miniaturized spasm of shock and loss – but it is the garden that contains the most vivid memories.

The first time he brought me here, when we were newly in love and I could still hardly believe that there were no obstacles to our being together for ever, we sat against the wall of the house, over there on the wrought-iron bench where my discarded jacket and gardening apron now lie. It was the end of May, and the bricks were warm with the day's sunshine. There were sprays of thick cream roses arching off the walls, and wood pigeons noisy in the trees.

'Could you live here?' Jake asked me.

It was like being asked if I thought I could endure Paradise.

'You're an urban woman,' he said, when I asked why he doubted it. 'You might get bored here with me. You might feel isolated from London, from acting and all the people you know and the life you're used to.'

I told him that I loved him, and the only life I wanted was with him, and that was the truth.

I was turning forty and Jake was already sixty. I had had a

modest success as a stage actress, but I knew that I was never going to be as good as a dozen of my contemporaries. Hollywood casting directors were never going to come calling. I had had numerous boyfriends and lovers after my first and only fiancé, Selwyn, but this sense of rightness with a man, of there being nothing to qualify or redeem in our relationship, was absolutely new to me.

Jake had been briefly married in his thirties but there had been no children, and his wife seemed to have made little impression on the house or indeed on him. After that, I assumed, there would have been girlfriends; after all I had met Jake at that most unpromising of romantic opportunities for a single woman, a dinner party given by a couple I had met on holiday. He had singled me out, and the next evening we went out to dinner on our own. It was hardly likely that I was the first to receive this sort of attention from him, but I believed him when he promised me that I would be the last.

Although he didn't bring me here immediately I learned very quickly, just from the way he talked about it, that Jake was inseparable from Mead. And as soon as he did invite me and I began to know the place, I understood why.

He was offering me himself, and he didn't do it lightly.

We sat on the wrought-iron bench and listened to the birds. The sun slowly sank, the bricks glowed as if they radiated their own light, and Jake turned to me.

'Could you be a country wife, do you think?'

Yes, I told him.

It was not an isolated existence, in any case. My old friends and their children came to visit us. Even my mother came from time to time. She liked staying at Mead, and she and Jake got on well together even though she tended to make barbed remarks on the lines of some people not knowing they were born, and how iniquitous it was that ninety per cent of the land in this country belonged to less than ten per cent of the people.

Jake was more than equal to her. 'Quite agree with you,

Joyce,' he used to nod. 'It's a lousy system. Getting rid of land, that's what the Meadowes have been about for the last hundred and fifty years.'

She would laugh, impatient but disarmed.

I didn't exactly choose not to involve myself in village affairs, but that was what happened. As Jake's wife and the chatelaine of Mead I was in any case outside the circle of Meddlett women who gossiped about local events at a level of detail I couldn't be bothered to absorb. Inevitably there were the sly hints and whispers about Jake, too, and his local affairs before we met. I didn't want to hear any of these.

The women probably thought I was standoffish; it was true that I found the coffee mornings and book groups tedious and repetitive. There were a few county couples with whom we had dinner, but I didn't play tennis or ride horses and so those women soon overlooked me. Jake also had his own circle of friends, mostly men of his own age who enjoyed fishing and bird-watching and were interested in land management and country politics, and he continued to involve himself with the parish council and the village church.

I found that I was happy and entirely fulfilled in the peaceful world Jake and I inhabited together. If I wanted a change of scenery I went to London, to the theatre or shopping, or just to gossip with Katherine or Colin or any one of a dozen other friends. Sometimes I even felt resentful when local commitments took up too much of Jake's time. He did say he wished I would participate more, and so for several years we hosted Meddlett's November the Fifth party until the annual bacchanalia finally got out of hand.

While I reflect on all this I have been wielding the shears in snapping bursts, within a thicket of honeysuckle growth that is blocking the light into the dining-room window.

I lean back to judge the effect and out of the corner of my eye see a figure coming towards me. Once again memory plays its trick of elision and I think it is Jake in his old tweed coat.

A companionable greeting, nothing as formal as a word, takes shape in my head, and then the nudge of reality makes me blink and duck.

'Let me go up the ladder and do the top bit for you,' Colin says.

An ache has developed between my shoulder blades so I hand him the shears in silence and wipe my forehead with the back of my gardening glove.

Colin works more methodically, disentangling the excess growth before clipping it back. I hold the stepladder with one hand, and listen to the rooks in the trees along the drive. Very quickly the top of the shrub looks disciplined while the sides that I have butchered bristle with snapped twigs and dying tendrils. He dismounts and touches my shoulder.

'Don't you have anyone to come in and do this for you?'

'Am I so bad at it?' I smile.

'It's a lot of work.'

I glance about trying to see the house and its setting through his eyes.

The roses and lavender need attention, it's true, and there are weeds sprouting between broken stone slabs. Jake was a knowledgeable gardener, whereas I am only trying to keep the place looking cared for. I don't employ a regular handyman, even for a few hours a week. This is partly because of the money, but mostly because I don't want anyone else working amongst Jake's flowers. Gardeners have strong ideas of their own. I might come out one evening and find the old roses replaced with those variegated evergreens, the kind that look like shiny oilcloth splashed with bleach.

There *are* days when Mead is too much, even though looking after it is my only job. Sometimes I count up and there are half a dozen light bulbs waiting to be replaced in three different rooms. Blocked gutters are sending rainwater chutes down the old walls, and doors have warped in the winter's damp so they no longer close properly.

Sell up, demon voices immediately whisper in my ear. *Move to a modern apartment, somewhere with underfloor heating and windows that don't rattle.*

I shan't do that, of course.

At other times, much more consistently, I know that I can – and will – do anything to keep it going.

The idea of having Colin and the others to live here with me is part of that process of preservation. They choose to see it as a more emotional matter, Mirry gathering everyone together in her old hippy way, and it has that element of course. Who else can we look to, now that we have reached this time of our lives?

But I am more practical than my old friends give me credit for.

Colin leans the stepladder against the wall of the house. The exertion has brought some colour to his face, but I notice how thin he is. We all know that he has, or has had, prostate cancer, but I don't think even Polly knows much more than that bald fact. Colin talks so little about himself.

'Shall we go in and have a sandwich?' I suggest.

I want to feed him up, to mother him, but the idea of Colin, the most self-contained of men, welcoming any maternal attention from me is comical enough to make me smile.

He looks up at the sky. It's pale and luminous. Two days of rain and wind following the discovery of the burial site have now given way to a warm, damp stillness. The air smells of ploughed earth and leaf mould, and it's hard to believe that the bracing sea is only six miles away.

'I think I'd rather go for a walk. Indoors is a bit claustrophobic on a day like this.'

I put away the ladder and the tools. Nowadays before we can set off on even a short impromptu walk we have to change our shoes and put on different jackets and Colin finds a flat tweed cap to cover his thinning hair. I note these signs of elderly caution only in passing, because I am getting used to them. We all display them, except for Selwyn. Selwyn, I think, would still set out for Tibet at an hour's notice without a backwards glance, and in the clothes he stood up in.

Colin and I head down the drive together, tacitly steering away from the track that leads to the site. Earlier today Amos got in his Jaguar and raced off to protest the delay to his project at a meeting with the contractors, his architect, and the various senior representatives of the county authorities. He asked me if I would like to join them, but I assured him that I'd be quite happy to hear everything from him. The idea of sitting through a meeting with Amos on the boil and a row of local authority archaeological experts was not enticing.

He's not back yet.

Katherine is in London, at the charity, and Polly and Selwyn are working on their house. There's a cement mixer parked in the yard.

Colin takes my arm. He has long legs, but he shortens his stride to match mine.

'Where are we going?'

I don't want to walk into Meddlett. If we did we'd bump into people I know and for now I want Colin to myself.

'Along the footpath and up the hill. We can look back at the house and the digging.'

'Why don't you tell me some more of the history of this place?' he says as we negotiate the path.

I'm used to thinking of Mead's story as Jake told it to me in our early days together. Now, unsettlingly but intriguingly, it has acquired an Iron-Age dimension. The past five hundred years once seemed time and depth enough, yet now they are foreshortened. I wonder if this is a diminishment, but what has been disinterred can't be buried and forgotten all over again. I begin the story anyway, with the part I know.

Jake's ancestors were farmers in this part of the county, in a small way, from the time when records began. At the beginning of the fifteenth century we know there was a house on the site of this present one, probably no more than a huddle of stone walls and a couple of barns, because parish records detail the modest holding of land and the number of individuals who lived and worked there. A hundred years later, a record from the county assizes showed that one of the sons of the family had been imprisoned for thieving from travellers passing along the highway to Norwich.

Jake was always greatly pleased with this detail of his ancestry.

'I am descended from highwayman's stock,' he boasted.

The upturn in the family fortunes came a hundred years later, when the wife and children of a wealthy London silk importer moved out of the city to escape the plague, arriving to stay with a sister who had married into a local landowning family. The silk merchant had no sons, and the current heir to Mead wooed and married the eldest daughter, a Miss Howe. With Miss Howe's fortune, Jake's ancestor bought hundreds of acres of adjoining land and began the informal enlargement of his farmhouse. The family name became Mead Howe, and eventually Meadowe.

Over the next hundred years there was a slow ascent into the ranks of the gentry. The family acquired indoor servants, a coach was kept, and the horses stabled where Selwyn is now busy mixing concrete. Then came a pair of Victorian gamblers, father and son, who accelerated the decline of the family fortunes as much of the land was lost or sold to settle debts. By the time Jake's amusing, cynical and profoundly lazy father died, there was nothing left but the house itself, the outbuildings and a modest acreage.

Jake was the last of the Meadowes, and I inherited the estate from him. The remaining acres of land, apart from the portion I sold to Amos, are rented to a local farmer.

Seeing the house and its setting, the more unworldly of my theatrical friends who came to stay assumed that I had married money, but that really was not the case. Jake made a modest income from farming and writing on country topics for rural interest magazines. I contributed a small amount from converting a couple of barns to make the holiday cottages where Amos and Katherine are now staying, and we were deeply content together. What I did marry was a much more primitive connection to the land and to a place that became unexpectedly important to me.

Jake's uncomplicated theory was that it *was* that much more

100

important to me partly because I had so determinedly sidestepped the connection to my own history – if you can use the term to relate to a Midlands semi that my mother unsentimentally got rid of when I was in my early twenties. I was always welcome in her various flats after that, but none of them had any pretensions to being home, the way Mead became almost from the moment I set eyes on it.

Jake wasn't implying that I was an *arriviste* (although in Meddlett terms I most certainly am); he was just pleased and interested that I fell so much in love with his life and background, as well as with him. I didn't have the outward appearance of a country wife and I don't think he had been expecting anything of the kind.

Colin walks with his shoulders slightly hunched, his hands in his pockets, listening.

'Roulette, or cards? Or the horses?' he asks when I come to the bit about the gamblers.

'I'm not sure. All three, perhaps.'

He says wonderingly, 'You know, I never really asked Jake about his family history. He wouldn't have volunteered it, would he? It's a major trajectory, over six centuries. That's a long time to be able to trace your forebears.'

'Jake took it for granted. It's the likes of you and me who find it so remarkable.'

'Two generations, that's how far back my family acquaintanceship goes.'

Colin's parents were Yorkshire schoolteachers, very proud and slightly respectful of their talented son. I remember them coming to see Colin receive his degree, and him posing afterwards in his gown and mortarboard, flanked by his smiling mother and father. I took the photograph with the camera his father handed to me.

They acknowledged but never fully accepted that Colin was gay, and they died within a year of each other when he was still in his thirties.

'Mine too,' I say.

I never saw my father after he left home.

'That useless bugger? Don't waste your wishing on him, love. He doesn't deserve it,' was my mother's usual response to my questions.

In the end, since he never tried to contact her or me, I took her advice.

I knew her parents, my Nanny and Gamps, as tidy old people who sometimes looked after me for weekends, or whole weeks of the school holidays, in their miniature and sepulchrally quiet house in a village in Warwickshire. They liked *Sunday Night at the London Palladium*, and sitting in deckchairs in their back garden on fine afternoons. I loved them, in the undemonstrative way they favoured (they didn't hold with kissing and hugging. That was for other folk, the sort who liked to make a show of things), but staying with them was boring.

At home with my working mother I got fish fingers and tinned spaghetti on toast, which was what I liked to eat, but at Nanny and Gamps's there was bright yellow haddock disgustingly cooked in milk, complete with skin and brackish foam, and mystifying lemon curd tart instead of Wagon Wheels or mini swiss rolls in red and silver foil.

At my grandparents' I coiled myself up and concentrated even harder on growing up as quickly as possible, in order to make my escape into a more glamorous world. I never doubted that I would do it. I must have been an unrewarding grandchild for them.

Colin says, 'We find Jake's pedigree remarkable now. We didn't back then, did we? Who cared about Amos's background except as a good joke, or anything about that etiolated guy who lived on his staircase who was the grandson of a duke? None of us was interested in what had been or what had made us, except maybe in working out how to overthrow it. What was important was what we were going to make happen. That was the gift of our generation. The absolute conviction that we could change the world.'

'Yes. It's only since we failed to do that and then discovered that we were going to get old as well that we've started to be hungry for history.'

'And that'll be a tenner in the box, please,' Colin says.

'Damn.'

What started out as a joke between Selwyn and Amos has gathered momentum at the New Mead (spoken within the same quotation marks that we now employ for New Labour).

Whenever any of us remarks that we are old, or mentions something that we did when we were young but can no longer enjoy or endorse, a fine is levied. It started at a pound, but that turned out not to be a sufficiently serious deterrent. There are plans to use the accumulated fund for the most unlikely group outing any of us can come up with. The current front-runner is a weekend's extreme snowboarding in St Anton.

'Jake never had any illusions about changing the world. He believed in micro initiatives like selling the estate cottages, so the people who lived in them and worked on the land could own their homes. He never went on a demo in his life. He poked fun at me about my agitprop days.'

'Jake wasn't a Boomer, he belonged to the previous gener-ation. I bet he'd have gone on the countryside march, though.'

I smile. 'Yeah, he would. I went on it for him.'

We cross the Meddlett road and climb a low hill crowned with a line of crooked oak trees. They are still holding on to their dun and yellow leaves, but through the thinning screen I can see the dense nodes of mistletoe. From the windows of Mead these trees are familiar sentries on the skyline.

We turn to look back the way we have come. Colin is out of breath.

'Look,' I say unnecessarily.

The land dips to the road, then unrolls all the way in front of us. There is the small natural plateau and vantage point that now belongs to Amos, and the fence that marks his boundary and mine. I have always known that it was a commanding spot. It seems obvious, now, that ancient people would have chosen it for the same reason.

In the shelter of the trees Colin sits down to rest on the step of a stile.

We can see the white tent, and people processing in and out of it. Without binoculars I can't be sure but I assume the two figures who seem to be kneeling in prayer are in fact still patiently sieving earth from the grave. There are a couple of parked vans and a car, but no sign of any of Amos's contractors.

'And now six hundred years seems relatively modern. A mere interlude,' Colin murmurs.

This chimes precisely with my own thoughts.

'All that time, while the land was being settled and farmed, then bought and sold, plague coming and going, the crops growing, cattle grazing, Jake's highwayman ancestor sticking his pistols in his belt and galloping off on his black stallion, those two were lying there. Ancient, invisible.'

'Even though we've dug them up again they are still inscrutable,' he says.

'I expect the osteologist and the Iron-Age man from Oxford will soon be able to tell us everything about them,' I sigh.

Colin glances at me.

'Do you mind that?'

'Not exactly. It's more on their behalf that I regret the disturbance. Two thousand years of unbroken peace, then along comes Amos with his ground source heating system.'

'From my own completely detached and therefore selfish point of view,' Colin offers, 'I rather appreciate the contrast of scale. Looking back a couple of millennia does put one's personal, short-term problems into perspective.'

I turn my head to look at him. Polly and Katherine and I, now that we are living so closely together, have taken to describing versions of our problems to one another. But it's unusual for Colin to touch even this lightly on his feelings.

I say, 'Talking your problems over with your friends might achieve the same result, without the archaeological intervention.'

Unfortunately this comes out sounding like a criticism, which I didn't intend at all.

'Mirry, you're a sympathetic ear, I know that. But I'm not much good at soul-baring. What can you really say to anyone, even your closest friends, about personal loss? Or about the individual slow decline, or sudden end, that's lying in wait for us all?'

I blurt out, 'Because that is part of the human condition. And to share the grief and the fear, those things we've all known by the time we get to our age, as well as the picnics and birthdays, isn't that what we're put here for? At the very least, to ease each other's loneliness?'

He says very gently, 'I've no idea why we're put here. To me there seems less of a reason for our existence than there probably did to the Warrior Prince and his cup-bearer over there.'

Across the fields and floating tree tops we watch a sudden flurry of activity on the site. A large open crate is borne out of the tent and laid on the grass, and every one of the distant figures lays down their tools and crowds around to look. Colin stands up, brushing leaves and moss from his coat.

'What's happening, I wonder?'

I can't help reflecting aloud, 'Wouldn't Jake have been fascinated?'

'He would.' Colin puts his arms around me and holds me close against him. He has always found non-sexual touching easy and natural, unlike a straight man.

Jake died after only a short illness, here at Mead, with me beside him. He was twenty years older than me; I can't even say that he was snatched away before his time. Not like Colin's Stephen, who was murdered. Almost casually, for money for a fix, by a boy he had taken up with after he and Colin broke up. Without it ever having been discussed, I know that Colin blames himself. If he and Stephen had still been together there would have been no casual sex with dangerous young men.

I'm trying to find a way to acknowledge that my loss is painful to a lesser degree than his, but it's too clumsy a sentiment to put into words. Colin probably reads my mind in any case. I ask abruptly, 'Tell me, how are you? What about the illness?'

To my surprise he laughs. 'Polly wants me to get off with the luscious chef at the Griffin.'

'Well, why not?'

It's nice being held by Colin. I'm not cold, but the warmth our bodies hatches between us is welcome. Not for the first time I reflect what a shame it is that he's not interested in women.

'Dearest. I don't need a chef in my life.'

'*I* wouldn't mind one.'

'You could cope with it, Mirry. More than cope. Look at you.'

He strokes my hair back from my face. 'Listen. I had the radiation therapy. I chose that rather than surgery, and it works in quite a high percentage of cases, but not in mine. It's testosterone that fuels the cancer growth, did you know that? Mine's an aggressive one. *Mucho macho*. When I first met my specialist I thought he was a patronizing little fart, excuse me, but I've warmed to him lately. He tells it straight. The radiation treatment didn't do the trick. I can still opt for surgical removal of the tumour, but it's in a ticklish spot. There is the risk of a little slip with the blade, can you imagine? Whoops, I'm suddenly incontinent. Rubber knickers, absorbent pads, worrying about how strongly I might smell of piss when I'm sitting in the theatre.'

'No. Don't do that.'

'Exactly. So instead of going under the knife, my friend the specialist gives me injections of female hormone. It works, but there's a payoff. It makes me completely impotent. However much I might want to, these days I couldn't get it up for a whole chorus line of chefs. Not even individually basted in virgin olive oil and served with side dishes of oysters and rhino horn.'

'I see. That's difficult.'

'In a way it is. But, you know, it's not the worst thing in

106

the world. Thirty years ago, even ten years ago, it definitely would have been.'

'Does Polly know?' I ask.

'Yes, she does. She came to some of the treatments with me.'

Polly would never betray a confidence. She is the most discreet person in the world. Thinking about Polly's goodness makes me feel ashamed to have been the one who was grappling with her husband between the coats and on the bathroom floor, for all the world like a pair of pensionable teenagers at a party.

'So, why's she . . . ?'

'Promoting the chef?' Colin laughs again. 'Because she's like you, and like all women. You and Polly would both say, wouldn't you, that there's more to sex than in and out? There's kissing, touching, holding. There's intimacy.'

'Yes.'

'Exactly. You're not men. And you don't know anything at all about gay sex.'

I slide my elbows under his jacket and lock my arms around him. Beneath his ribs I can feel his heart thumping.

'Poor Colin. I'm sorry.'

'Thanks. But I am managing. And for touching and holding I've got you, haven't I?'

I can't look at him, because there are tears in my eyes.

I don't want to think that he might die: there has been more than enough death already, it's as though the Iron-Age skeletons are there to remind us of what waits around every corner. And then my thoughts fly onwards in an urgent arc to Selwyn, as if there is only a whisker between contemplating death and wanting sex.

Now, without a second's warning, sexual longing floods through me. The heat and urgency of it take me utterly by surprise. It is all wrong to be clinging to Colin, and I disentangle myself and hastily step aside.

He looks curiously at me. 'Are you all right?'

I straighten my hair, pull my collar up around my throat, and I can feel the blood pulsing in my face and throat.

What's happening to us all?

The quick surge of lust is like helium in my lungs. It makes me feel light, disconnected, as if I might bob into the air and sail away over the trees.

Down in the field, the archaeologists have turned back to their prayerful work.

To anchor myself to the ground I take Colin's hand and turn him to face back down the hill. I have to move, to disperse the pressure.

'Come on,' I call out.

Towing Colin behind me I set off down the slope, moving faster until we have to let go of each other and start running. We gallop all the way down to the end of the path, where it emerges on the bend of the Meddlett road. As we come out of the trees, panting and elated, the sun suddenly appears from behind thin, high cloud.

Out of the corner of my eye I catch a brief glimpse of erratic movement, two blurred patches of it, then comes the blare of a car horn. Colin shouts a warning.

The cyclist swerved on to the verge to avoid an oncoming car and toppled into the grass. A dog started yapping and bounding in circles around the tangle of limbs and turning wheels.

A girl's voice yelled, 'Fuck you! Stupid fucker!'

The Jaguar had stopped, half on and half off the road.

Amos leaped out and strode back to where the cyclist lay.

To his relief the girl reared up. 'You could have killed me,' she screamed.

Amos's shock and relief discharged themselves as anger. 'You were in the middle of the bloody road. And your damn dog ran straight in front of me.'

'Rafferty, be quiet.' The dog subsided a little. 'You come around the corner doing ninety in your big old car, and you expect everyone else to take avoiding action, don't you? People like you don't own the world, whatever you might think.'

'If I hadn't been the one to take avoiding action, I'd have hit either you or the dog.'

As he calmed down Amos suddenly became aware of Colin and Miranda.

'What are you doing here?'

'Having a walk,' Colin said. 'You know. Travelling on foot?'

The girl struggled with her bike. It was a very old, rickety one. She glowered up at Colin.

'Are you stalking me or something?'

It turned out that the bike's front wheel was too buckled for the girl – Colin introduced her as Jessie – to ride it any further. She had grazed one hand in the roadside grit and after inspecting it Miranda told her that Amos could either drive her home now, or she could come back to Mead where Miranda would clean up her injury and then take her home.

The girl grinned. 'I'll come back to yours. Ta very much.' The dog was still barking and waving its tongue and tail. 'Shut *up*, Raff. Count yourself lucky you're not dead in the ditch.'

Colin wheeled the bike behind the hedge. He and Miranda squeezed into the cramped leather scoops in the back of the Jag and Jessie sat up front with the dog between her knees. She leaned forward to run her finger along the walnut dashboard, then rocked backwards in the leather embrace of her seat.

'I don't blame you, really. If I had a car like this I'd probably drive it at ninety and scare the shit out of the plebs as well,' she said to Amos.

'I was doing thirty-five, if that.'

He looked sideways at her, his gaze settling for half a second too long. He saw a good-looking young woman, pierced and tattooed, in ripped jeans and a band T-shirt stretched tightly over healthy breasts. He had to swerve again, this time to miss a tractor and trailer loaded with muck coming around the last bend before Mead. Miranda recognized a farming neighbour and sank lower in her seat, as if anyone could spot her in the back of a speeding car.

'Yeah. And that was David Furnish driving the tractor,' Jessie sniffed.

'Who is David Furnish, may I ask?'

Colin leaned forward. 'He is a homosexual, m'Lud, who is married to Mr Elton John, a popular singer.'

'I don't imagine he's interested in the speed limit on rural roads, is he?' Amos said pleasantly.

The car turned in at the stone gateposts and bowled up the drive to the house.

Miranda took Jessie up to the bathroom and sponged the grit out of her grazes, then dabbed them with antiseptic.

'Ow. That hurts.'

'It won't last long.'

The girl looked about her with interest.

'This is a nice house. Really old, but still nice.'

'Thank you. It was my husband's, but he died a couple of years ago. Where do you live, Jessie?'

'Rented place. It would look like a bit of a dump to you, but it's not that bad. Between here and Meddlett.'

'Are you from around here?'

'Yeah. 'Course. I wouldn't *be* here otherwise. I've not met you before, though, have I? I remember Mr Meadowe, of course,' she added rather hastily, 'from the church fête and that. Was he really your husband?'

'Yes, really. Are your parents in Meddlett?'

She looked at Miranda. 'My mum.'

'Would you like a plaster on this?'

Giggling, Jessie withdrew her hand. 'No. It's all right. I'm grown up now.'

In the kitchen, they found Amos sitting over his laptop and Colin making tea.

'Two months suspension of work, they've asked for. To conduct a full and proper investigation,' Amos snorted. 'It's a farce.' He leaned back and tilted the lid of the machine to hide the screen from Jessie's glance.

Rafferty was slobbering up water from an enamel pie dish

placed on the floor next to the range. As soon as he saw Jessie he leaped at her, dragging the cable connection out of the computer.

'I wish I had run over that dog,' Amos muttered and then he caught Jessie's eye. There was no rancour in the exchange of looks. In fact they seemed to recognize each other. Colin put four mugs of tea on the table.

'Cheers,' Jessie said. She spooned sugar into hers. 'Get down, you.' Rafferty slouched off, his toenails clicking on the tiles. He flopped on the floor with his spine close up against the warmth of the range.

'Damon didn't get his half of him, then?' Colin said, nodding at the recumbent animal.

'Of course not, the loser.'

'Damon's my ex,' Jessie explained to Amos and Miranda.

'And also the brother of . . .' Colin stopped himself.

Like some adolescent whose nose had been put out of joint he wanted to counter Amos's casual appropriation of Jessie by demonstrating his local knowledge, and by doing so he'd almost given away the secret of the excavation. He frowned at himself.

'Dame's brother is Kieran. How do you know him, then?' Jessie asked smartly.

'I just met him,' Colin said. 'They're very alike.'

'Not if you know them, they aren't. Kieran's got a job, for a start. He's an assistant archaeologist. Dead keen on it, he is.' Jessie tilted her head. 'He's working on a big job somewhere around here, actually. He won't say anything about it though, even to his mum. I saw her in the shop, picking up her paper, and she told me. Did he mention that to you, at all, when you just met him?'

She was very quick, Colin thought ruefully. Too quick for him.

'No.'

There was a small silence.

'I think there is some cake. Would anyone like a piece?' Miranda asked.

'Yes please,' Amos called.

Miranda went to the larder for the cake tin. On her way back she glanced out of the window and saw two men picking their way across the yard. They were Chris, the bearded field supervisor, and Kieran himself. An AAS Land Rover was parked close to the gate at the far end. The men were carrying a crate between them, as gently as if it contained nitroglycerine.

Selwyn emerged from the barn in his ragged coveralls and work boots. He headed off the archaeologists and peered down into the crate. Chris seemed to warn him, but Selwyn tweaked a cloth covering off whatever lay within.

She saw how Selwyn straightened up and gazed in astonishment. He called over his shoulder and Polly came out to join them. Her hair was wrapped in a scarf and she pulled a dust mask from over her mouth. Polly's reaction was the same.

'Where's that cake?' Amos asked.

'We've got visitors,' Miranda said.

It was too late to head them off. Selwyn rushed in first, tramping the dust off his boots, then Chris and Kieran with the crate, followed by Polly unwinding the scarf from her head.

'Just look at this,' Selwyn cried.

Kieran stopped short when he saw Jessie, colour flooding his face.

'Jess? What you doing here?'

'Nice to see you too, mate,' she said loudly. 'Hi,' she nodded to Polly. 'It *is* a commune, this place, isn't it?'

Chris placed the crate at the opposite end of the table, and tucked the cover more closely over its contents.

'Mr Knight?' he said. 'Maybe we could have a few moments in private?'

'Certainly.' Amos got to his feet.

'This the big job your mum was telling me about, is it?' Jessie asked Kieran.

'Shut up, Jess, will you? I dunno what you're doing here.'

'Knocked off my bike, wasn't I?' She waved her grazed hand at him.

112

Amos interjected, 'You were not. You fell off your bicycle when your dog almost caused a serious accident. Mrs Meadowe brought you back here to patch you up.'

Jessie nodded. 'Yeah. She's been really nice.' She grinned at Amos as she spoke then darted a last look at the crate. 'Anyway. Looks like I'd better make myself scarce, doesn't it? Only I haven't got my bike, that's the problem.'

Kieran glanced at his boss, and stepped forward. 'My van's here. I can give you a ride.'

Jessie whistled and Rafferty lurched to his feet.

'Cheers. Bye then, everybody. Thanks for the tea and medical aid, Mrs Meadowe.' She bestowed another of her smiles upon Colin as she passed by. 'Be seeing *you* around again, no doubt.'

The rest of them waited until the back door was closed and Jessie and Kieran with the dog at their heels had passed out of the yard gate.

'Quite a self-possessed young person,' Amos said. He turned back to Chris. 'So, what have you got there?'

'Show them,' Selwyn urged.

The archaeologist wouldn't be hurried, Miranda noticed. If you were used to measuring time in thousands of years you were unlikely to be moved by the various urgencies specific to Amos or even Selwyn.

Chris explained, 'We thought you might want to see what we have found, before the items go to our finds specialist for preliminary examination.'

'Yes please,' Amos prompted.

'Isn't Mrs Knight here?'

Amos stared at him. 'No. She's in London. Why?'

'She would be interested to see our discovery too, I imagine.'

Amos had the grace to look slightly discomfited by this.

Chris finally lifted the folded cloth. He gave it a magician's flourish. Miranda warmed to him. He probably did have a sense of humour, buried like his artefacts.

They crowded around the crate.

In a nest of newspaper and bubble-wrap lay an elongated,

curved oval of dark brownish-gold metal. The shield was less than three feet long. Standing proud of the curved surface they could distinguish three circular bosses of elaborate scrollwork. Some of the circles within the fluid arabesques were set with stones. Even though the piece was discoloured, dented and still crusted with earth, it was beautiful. Miranda longed to pick it up and trace the curves with the tips of her fingers. She was amazed that this exquisite object had emerged from the ground here, at Mead.

'And there's this too,' Chris added.

He unwrapped another piece of cloth and placed what lay within it on the table.

It was the dark band that they had last seen in its resting place between the skeletal jaw and ribcage, an almost solid chunk of earth and metal. A short section of it had been cleaned of dirt, to reveal a heavy twisted strand that was itself made up of several smaller twisted strands. The metal was brighter than that of the shield, with a seductive glimmer to it.

There was a collective gasp.

'My God,' Miranda breathed. 'Treasure.'

'Yes. Very significant treasure,' Chris agreed. 'This is a pure gold torc, one of the finest I have ever seen. I've never come upon a find like this, not in twenty years. I know it happens, of course, but this is the first time I've seen it with my own eyes. I can't quite believe my luck.'

There was an awed silence as they studied it, measuring the tiny neck span with their eyes.

'It looks so heavy,' Polly murmured. Chris nodded his permission and she picked it up at once, unable to keep her hands off it.

Chris said, 'One thing we do know already. You met David, our bones expert?'

The small, eager man with thick glasses.

'He says that our prince is almost certainly a princess.'

Miranda clapped her hands in delight.

Polly touched a finger to the metal coils, following the twists within the twist. Dust fell out of the seams of her overall and powdered the red tiles.

'The Warrior *Princess?*' she repeated. 'How very, very satisfying.'

'And the child?' Colin asked.

'A boy, probably, aged about seven. From the damage to the skull, we can see that he died from a crushing blow to the back of the head. It was so severe that he could not have survived it.'

They took that in in silence. The princess had been accompanied on her final journey by a sacrificial victim.

Chris explained that the excavation would continue under careful direction. There would probably be more grave goods, possibly other bodies to uncover.

It would take time to do the job properly, but there would be no unnecessary delays. He hoped that the significance of the discovery would be some compensation to Mr Knight for the frustrating interruption to his project.

'Not the right kind of compensation unfortunately,' Amos said.

Chris seemed to accept with equanimity that Amos and he were unlikely to be friends. He took a card from his wallet, and instead of handing it to Amos he put it on a corner of the dresser.

'If Mrs Knight would like to see the finds, I can arrange that for her. And if I might just remind you once more, please don't mention any of these discoveries outside the immediate circle.'

He took the torc back from Polly, who yielded it with reluctance. Then he said a pleasant goodnight. He carried the precious crate across the yard to the Land Rover and drove away.

Selwyn strode back to his trenches, saying that he couldn't sit around all afternoon drinking tea. Amos gathered up the archaeologist's card, his papers and the laptop and headed out to the cottage. Colin went upstairs, planning to sleep. He slept heavily at Mead, eagerly sinking into afternoon naps and giving himself up to long nights from which he remembered no dreams.

Left alone together Miranda and Polly performed a kitchen two-step involving the dishwasher, the cake tin, earth and dust on the floor and crumbs on the table.

'That was extraordinary,' Miranda breathed.

'It was,' Polly agreed.

When the room was in order again Polly paused at the sink with its view of the back yard and the open doors of the barn.

'I should go back to work,' she said.

Reluctance dragged at her. She didn't mind a level of discomfort but she was coming close to hating the squalor of their quarters, and the damp, and the insidious cold. It might be a warm, sunny autumn afternoon outside, but indoors they worked in shadowy gloom and kept warm by layering plaster-caked jumpers under their overalls. She was starting to dream about warmth at the touch of a switch, and hot running water in her own home seemed as much of a remote luxury as piped asses' milk, or peeled pomegranates brought to her on a silver salver.

She was getting old, she acknowledged. She was not as hardy as she used to be.

Selwyn wanted to lay the drains and complete the sub-floor so the bricklayer and the electrician could come in. He insisted he could manage the plumbing and roofing and the plastering himself, but at least he had conceded that he wasn't qualified to do the wiring. He had even agreed, reluctantly, that it would be quicker and cheaper in the long run to employ a brickie. It had taken hours of exhausting haggling with him to achieve even this much.

In all his projects over the years, Selwyn had been single-minded. It was single-mindedness that had been his major failing, Polly reflected, because he was both physically and mentally incapable of standing back and contemplating the margins of whichever picture he was myopically painting.

The pattern was a familiar one. When he had decided that as well as making and restoring furniture he was going to grow and sell vegetables for profit, he had spent weeks double-digging the beds and carting in tons of manure. He had planted and mulched and weeded in every spare moment but when the tomatoes ripened all at once, the runners sank under the weight of beans, and lettuces bolted as soon as he turned aside from their luxurious beds, he lost all patience. The creation of the garden and bringing the crops to fruit had taken up his supply of love and attention. It was left to Polly to pick and pack the results, to drive them to farmers' markets and implore women who had arrived in mud-free 4x4s to buy them, and finally to help Selwyn acknowledge that in order to turn a profit these would have to be the most highly-priced blowsy lettuces and oversized beans in the country.

There had been further skirmishes over the years with free-range chickens, rare breed pigs, and – worst of all – a business dedicated to sourcing country artefacts and selling them on-line to people who lived in Shoreditch.

Polly had been his ally in all these experiments and she had never had to make herself forgive him for the failures, because she loved him as he was. He was like a river in flood, the torrent of his enthusiasm carrying with it whatever lay in his path. He had never bored her, never in all their years together, and the quickness of Polly's mind meant that she was quite easily bored.

None of these earlier projects had sucked him in like the black hole of the Mead barn, however. She had never seen him as fierce as this.

As soon as he woke up he was rolling out of his sleeping bag and hefting a sledgehammer. He worked for as long as he could keep on going, standing up to eat a sandwich or drain a mug of tea, and Polly did her best to keep up with him and restrain him. So far, between them they seemed to have achieved more destruction than progress.

In two, maybe three days' time, he kept assuring her, they would turn the corner. Then she would notice the difference, just wait and see.

In the evenings, when she threatened him with violence if

he didn't stop, he turned to whisky, sitting and dangerously rocking the chair next to Miranda's country kitchen range.

Polly understood that Selwyn saw the barn as his last chance to make good, after too many failed efforts.

He wanted her to have a comfortable home, he wanted to have the same himself, but the core need was to prove that he could provide one – created with bare hands, with minimal cash, at speed and in an incandescent blaze of finely focused energy. He wanted to prove this to Miranda and the Knights and Colin, because they were so close at hand, as well as to herself and their children, and all the time it was obvious that the demonstration by these means mattered hardly at all to anyone except Selwyn himself.

She loved him as always, but now there was an exasperated tenderness in it, as if he were her wayward child rather than her husband.

There was another difference to contend with, too.

Miranda's intention, Polly knew, was that Mead would provide insulation for all of them. Living together here would help to counteract the void left by children no longer needing them, the loneliness that followed the death of friends, and the stealthy approach of old age. What Polly hadn't allowed for, in accepting Miranda's proposition, was that Selwyn's preoccupation, his mental absence from her, in their tarp tent, under conditions of such strenuous intimacy, would actually make her feel loneliness as sharp as pain. With Miranda always so close at hand, with the stirrings of jealousy that she knew she ought to be able to dismiss but somehow could not, Polly's bruised love for Selwyn was expanding until it seemed as fragile as bread dough rising beneath a cloth.

Polly became aware now that Miranda was hesitating behind her in the warm and humming kitchen.

They had spent more time together in the last weeks than they had done since student days. They had always been friends, in the way that opposites can appreciate each other, whilst

Katherine bridged the gulf between them, but lately a definite constraint had separated them.

Polly wasn't cynical. She had invested the same hope and belief in Mead as Miranda herself, but now she was wondering whether she had been naive to do so.

She turned slowly from the window, and was not surprised to find that Miranda's eyes had been resting on her back.

'Don't go straight back to the barn. Stay here for half an hour and talk to me,' Miranda implored. She went to the larder and came back with a basket of vegetables.

The sight of the neat wicker and the burnished onions and carrots laid within ignited a blaze of irrational fury that burned behind Polly's eyes. Under her hair the nape of her neck prickled with sweat. It was hot in the room, not merely warm. It was too organized and photogenic, an untruth like a magazine picture. No muck, no puddles of cold water, no Selwyn creating one vortex of disorder before moving on to create another in a different place.

She was suddenly jointly enraged by the thought of him and by the spectacle of Miranda serene in the heart of her house.

Miranda laid out the pretty onions and a Sabatier knife on her big chopping board on the scrubbed table.

She was saying, 'I thought of roasting some veg for dinner. These beets look nice. We'll all have supper together, shall we? We need to celebrate the treasure. The find's even bigger than we thought, isn't it?'

The knife sliced through white onion flesh. Miranda chopped and sniffed as the fumes rose. 'Unless you and Sel have got a different plan for later?'

'There'll be a little soufflé for us, probably. I should think Selwyn's lighting the gas burner this very minute,' Polly snapped. 'Miranda, tell me. What's it *like* being Lady Bountiful all the time?'

The knife dropped with a little clatter. Miranda's eyes opened wider. 'I don't mean it to seem that way.'

Polly's fury faded as quickly as it had blazed up, leaving an empty grey space. She muttered, 'Sorry. That was rude of me.'

'No. *I'm* sorry. I really am. Forgive me.'

The apology was in the wrong place. Polly frowned as she tried to position it. She flopped down at the table opposite the chopping board.

'Mirry, I don't know why you're asking me to forgive you. I'm bad-tempered. I'm exhausted, Selwyn's driving me crazy, I hate that barn, I'm worried about the kids. None of which gives me any right to take it out on you. You're generous and I should be grateful.'

Miranda said, 'Gratitude doesn't make either the giver or the recipient feel all that comfortable, does it? This set-up's supposed to be cooperative. I sold the buildings and the land, you and Selwyn and Amos and Katherine bought them. I don't want to be the lady of the manor. It was Jake's house, and only mine because he died.'

She went to the fridge and took out a half-full bottle of wine. She sloshed the contents into two glasses.

'Do you really hate the barn?'

Polly drank. 'I hate the way Selwyn's going at it.'

'Why is he?'

'Because of the way he is. Because we've got no money.'

'I know, but . . .'

'You don't know. Listen. There is. No. Money. None at all.'

'Do you want . . . ?'

'*No*, Miranda. Thanks, but no. Not from you, or Amos, or anyone else. I want to help Selwyn to make the place habitable. Just on the margins will do. Nothing fancy. I'm not imagining limed oak or recessed downlighters. Running water, flushing lavatory, watertight roof and walls. That will discharge some of his rage at himself. He'll be able to take a breath, but not before that. You of all people should know the way he is.'

'Yes.' Miranda's eyes didn't meet hers.

'After that I'll get a job. Selwyn can finish the house in his own time. And all will be well,' Polly concluded.

Miranda sliced carrots. She tipped the glowing vegetables

120

into an earthenware dish, dripped olive oil over them and rubbed sea salt between the palms of her hands.

'Why are you worried about the children?'

'Ah, it's general, not localized. They're not ill or addicts or in trouble, as far as I know. They think we've gone off and left them, at least according to Omie they do. Selwyn says that's absurd, of course. This drink's just what I needed, by the way.'

Miranda said hesitantly, 'Why don't you both move into the house? Only for as long as it takes to do what you need to in the barn. You'll be warm, the work will seem easier. Ask Omie and Alpha and Ben to come and stay whenever you want. Won't you think about it, at least?'

Polly shook her head. 'Selwyn can't. Not won't, *can't*.'

The dishwasher settled into a churning rhythm. Water trickled in the pipes in the scullery. The layered sounds of the house seemed to emphasize the gulf that lay between it and the barn.

However, Polly's face was now rounding into the noodle-lady smile. She was recovering herself. 'It's way beyond pride with him, it's an act of faith. This is the way he wants to do it, therefore it's the only way that it can be done. I left him to it for a couple of nights, didn't I, that first week, and he made no objection, absolutely none, but I felt as though I was betraying him. He can be impossible, but we're in this together, me and Sel. We've worked it out between us before, and we'll do it this time too.'

Carefully Miranda nodded.

'We'll come over tonight and eat, though,' Polly said.

'That's good.'

Polly drank more wine and sat back in her chair. That was enough of talking about Selwyn to Miranda. She changed the subject. 'What about it turning out to be a princess, then?'

Miranda dusted the salt off the palms of her hands with a flourish. Here was an unequivocal symbol for both of them.

'I love it. Don't you? I *love* her. Look how she was buried in solemn state. Decked out in her gold ornaments ready for the life to come, her weapons at her side, her page to accompany

121

her. How powerful and how revered she must have been. *There's the lady of the manor, if you want one.'*

Polly thumped her fist so that the knives rattled.

'Exactly. She's what we need to have in mind. An Iron-Age role model. A powerful woman, the leader of her tribe, vanquished only in death. Modestly veiled by antiquity, as well. No political or despotic overtones to trouble us, except for the unfortunate page, and that was probably done by her priests.' She brandished her glass. 'Here's to the Warrior Princess of Mead, rest her glorious bones.'

They drank the toast. Polly got up, and Miranda awkwardly put out her hand.

'We've got what it takes, as well,' Miranda said.

'I know we have,' Polly agreed.

Remembering the ten pound penalty they didn't give voice to it, but they were thinking the same thing.

It has been a long way. Women, and daughters, and friends. Mothers or not, wives or otherwise. We'll go on, wherever the road takes us.

'I feel quite emotional,' Polly confessed. 'Quite teary-eyed.'

'It's the onions,' Miranda smiled.

The talk of the princess had emphasized a bond between them, one which circumstances might otherwise have led them to overlook.

Alpha, Omega and Ben

The three Davies children had arranged to meet in a bar close to the offices of Ben's listings magazine.

Alexandra arrived first. She sat down at a corner table with a glass of wine and the newspaper. Olivia called her just as she took the first mouthful of her drink, and Alpha told her twin that she had only just got here and there was no sign of Ben anyway, surprise surprise, so she needn't run all the way from the Tube station.

Five minutes later Omega burst through the door. Her hair was long whereas Alpha wore hers cropped asymmetrically short, and today Omega favoured pink tights with ribbon shoelaces and fingerless knitted gloves while Alpha was in a black skirt and a grey jersey.

Omega burst out, '*Why* didn't you ask him to come tonight? I've got to meet him, haven't I?'

'That was never going to happen, Omie. Whatever Ben's asked us here for is about him, and dropping Jaime into it as well would be a major complication. Wouldn't it?'

It wasn't only their profiles that suddenly gave away the closeness of their connection, appearing like a single face and its reflection in a mirror as they briefly kissed, but also the way they resumed a conversation apparently in mid-sentence.

Alpha gathered up the contents of Omega's bag as they spilled

123

out on the table and stowed them safely away for her while Omega scanned the drinks menu and tried to decide what to order.

'Well, but, you've been seeing him for three weeks and I haven't even met him yet. What's that you're drinking?'

'House white. You'll meet him, OK? I hardly know him myself yet.'

'I'll have the same. Do you want olives or anything? I really want to get to know him, Alph.'

'You will. Exactly the way I know Tom. OK?'

'Tom's been around for ever, you must be able to tell the difference, it's not like *wooooh*, suddenly there's this person in my life that you've never even seen yet.'

'It will be the same in the end. That's just what it will be. Anyway it's really early days, Omie. He's great, that's all I do know.'

Omie's frown melted. She smiled fondly at her sister. 'It's so good to hear you say that. I'm really happy for you. Just don't keep me in suspense for too long, all right?'

They subsided with their drinks in front of them, gazing out in relaxed harmony at the after-work crowds swirling past the window.

'Where *is* Ben? Don't tell me he's not going to show up?'

'He'll get here, but why is he always, inevitably, boringly, infuriatingly half an hour late for every single occasion in his life?'

'Could it be because he's Dad's son?'

Omie said, 'I spoke to Mum. Did I tell you?'

'Yes. I did, as well.'

They watched the passers-by for another moment. 'You're right about them, Alph. They've got lives, haven't they? We can't look through the prism of them being our parents for ever.'

'No. Although they will *be* our parents for ever, won't they?'

'They've resigned all their responsibilities and become this eccentric pair of barn-dwellers. Like two old owls on a perch.'

As soon as he came through the door Ben caught sight of his sisters dissolving into laughter. It was a familiar sight that seemed to exclude him now and always, and his gloom deepened.

'Here he is.'

'Benj, it may never happen.'

He sighed. He put down his cycling helmet, his rucksack, his gloves and Day-Glo anorak.

'I am afraid that it already has.'

Alpha found him a chair as Omega pushed through the crowds at the bar to buy him a drink. Ben sat down and ate a couple of olives, spitting the pits into the palm of his hand then shaking his fist as though he were rattling dice. With his sisters' attention fully on him he unbent enough to offer them a ghost of his winning but slightly unfocused smile. The twins had their own version of Selwyn's features and colouring, whereas Ben looked more like Polly but without the foxy spark of cleverness that sharpened their mother's eyes.

The girls leaned forward. 'What's wrong?'

It was uncharacteristic of Ben to do anything as specific as ask to see them both and even to suggest a place and a time. He was more likely to agree vaguely to turn up at family gatherings and then find at the last moment that he couldn't actually make it.

He touched his fist to his forehead. They waited, doing him the favour of not laughing at him.

'It's Nic.'

They didn't look particularly surprised.

Ben went on, almost wailing, 'She's disappeared. She's moved out of her place. I went around there with some stuff for her, used the key she gave me to get in, and her things have all gone. The Greek landlord told me she packed up and went.'

'That's not disappearing, really. Not tell-the-police disappearing. It's more like escaping. Did you two have a row? Have you tried to call her?' Omie wondered.

'No, not a row. Of course I've tried calling, about seven

125

hundred times. I've texted her, and left messages, but she's not picking up. She's not been on Facebook. She hasn't been at Gina's, either. Gina's mad with her, she said to tell her that she can forget the job.'

The bar was packed now, and noisy. Ben stared around him, amazed to see so many people apparently relaxing and enjoying themselves when his own life was so taxing.

'Don't worry just yet. She'll call you. Nic's unpredictable, but you'll hear from her when she's ready,' Alpha soothed.

Ben sucked in a lungful of air and closed his eyes very tightly as if he were about to bungee off a high bridge.

'She's pregnant.'

The girls looked at each other. Ben opened his eyes again, finding that after all he was not plummeting earthwards.

'*Ben*. Didn't you . . . ?'

'Didn't she . . . ?'

'Not always,' he said.

They drew closer together around the table, shutting off some of the hubbub of the bar by leaning forwards so that their three heads almost touched.

'Maybe she's gone home?' Omie suggested.

'She doesn't get on with her mother. I don't think she's seen her more than twice in all the time we've known each other. She even came to ours for Christmas, didn't she? What would you two do if you were her?' he asked.

Perhaps his sisters could give him an insight into the extravagant mystery of women's responses. Ben quite often found other people's behaviour unfathomable, when he chose to think about it, whereas his own always seemed perfectly rational.

'How pregnant is she?' Omega asked.

'I don't know. Either you are or you aren't, isn't that it?'

'I think if I was her, I'd be looking into the possibility of getting a termination,' Alpha said with some caution.

Immediately Ben's tragic expression brightened a little.

'Exactly. That's what I said to her. I told her to ask Gina

what to do, I said we could get things fixed up, all that. But she just rolled over on her side and cried and wouldn't speak to me. I hugged her, talked to her, and in the end after hours and hours she cheered up enough to eat some soup, but she wouldn't say much about it afterwards. I thought she'd be thinking about it, you know, making a decision, and so I didn't keep on about it. I just tried to be really loving and helpful, and I even turned down a couple of nights' work so I could keep her company. Then four days afterwards, she's gone. I mean, what could I do?'

'Ben, what do you want to happen?' Alpha asked him.

'I want everything to be like it was. I want Nic and me to be happy together. I'm really worried about her.'

He sat back, breaking the circle.

For Ben, saying what he wanted was easily confused with getting what he wanted.

Omega went to buy another round of drinks. When she came back they talked some more about Nic and where she might be and how they might find her. Both girls predicted that she would reappear once she was no longer pregnant, but they didn't share Ben's certainty that he and she could then pick up from where they had left off. Wherever she had gone, Nic was probably making an enforced step into maturity, whilst Ben was still stuck somewhere in his late teens.

After half an hour Ben said he would have to go because he was working on a late shift, clearing up after a party. He put on his anorak and reached for his helmet.

'I haven't asked about either of you,' he said with an air of baffled regret.

'Alpha's mystery man is still very much on the scene,' Omega said.

'Jaime's not a mystery,' Alpha said. Her face glowed. She looked like a woman in love and Omega felt the twist of pain with pleasure that always came when her sister experienced something wonderful that she couldn't share.

'That's cool,' Ben muttered.

He kissed them both and thanked them for their support and advice, although he was still wearing his tragic expression.

'Have you told Mum?' Omega wondered.

'No. Don't say anything. It's just more proof of how hopeless I am.' Ben said this as if it was accepted fact. He went on his way and they watched through the window as he cycled away into the glare of traffic.

'Did you notice that he had no notion that it would be his baby, as well as Nic's?' Omega mused.

'Ben's own inner child cries with a far louder voice,' Alpha answered.

FIVE

Chris led the way down a neon-lit corridor, opened a door and stood aside to let Katherine pass through.

'I'm delighted you could come in and see for yourself,' he said.

They were now standing between rows of floor-to-ceiling metal shelving, the shelves stacked with brown cardboard boxes, each with a serial number and letters written on the front. Katherine considered his use of the word *delighted*. It was not effusive, she decided. That would contradict the rather marked impression his dry but also humorous manner had already made on her. Dr Christopher Carr would employ a scientific precision when it came to language. If he said he was delighted, then that would be the truth.

She looked around. It wasn't difficult to decipher the legends on the boxes. Apart from the serial numbers there were dates, some abbreviations like *Bm Mkt*, which she guessed were site names, and *Hum F, complete*. These were rows of human bones. Storage for skeletons. The strip lighting hummed overhead.

'It's this way,' Chris said. His outstretched hand almost touched her elbow. Katherine jumped.

'Does this trouble you?' He indicated the boxes.

'No. But it's impossible not to make the comparison, isn't it?' She meant *them, dead. Us, alive.*

In fact she felt almost supernaturally alive. The crepitation within her own ears sounded like snapping twigs, the whorls of skin at her finger ends seemed so sensitive that they tingled.

He looked at her. 'In this job our aliveness, and the short span of our lives, confront us all the time.'

At the far end of the avenue of bones they came into a small room. A man was concentrating at a desk in front of a window.

Chris said, 'Here's Mrs Knight.'

'It's Katherine,' she said.

The osteologist stood up, taking off his thick glasses. He was wearing thin surgical gloves; he didn't try to shake her hand.

'Here she is,' he said, indicating what lay on his desk.

The bones had been cleaned and set in their proper sequence. Katherine studied the skull's blank eye sockets, the hanging jaw with its stubborn teeth, the jagged break in the femur, the small bones of the feet and hands.

'You're certain of the sex now?'

'There is never absolute certainty, but the signs are here.'

He took up the skull and the jawbone, and, placing them together, showed her how in a male the chin would have been more prominent. He ran his fingers over the cranium, indicating the smoother brow ridges. Then he exchanged the skull for two sections of the pelvis.

'A female pelvis tends to be broader, like this one.'

Katherine gazed at the shallow cradle of bone.

'How old was she? Did she have children?'

'I'd say maybe thirty. Not a bad age, for the time. I don't know about children. I'd expect to see some ridges or scars on the bone, here, but there are none. It's not very easy to tell from skeletal remains.'

'And the other one?'

David drew a box towards him and took off the lid. He showed her the child's skull again and the splintered crater at the back of it.

'He could have been her son?'

'Perhaps, but given the massive head wound I think much

130

more likely to have been an attendant or a slave. A ritual sacrifice, as we said, to accompany her into the afterlife. More clues may turn up as the excavation proceeds.'

Chris made a gesture of apology. 'The local people were the Iceni. This site appears to be a Late Iron-Age rectangular enclosure with a dedicated ritual or funerary function. The richness of the grave goods suggests an important burial, and so it's likely the associated settlement was a major tribal centre. Archaeologists have particular enthusiasms. It's fascinating for us, but I do appreciate that for you and your husband the entire discovery may be more infuriating than exciting.'

Katherine followed the information through in her mind. 'So where are the remains of this local settlement likely to be?'

'We have some aerial photographs showing crop-marks that indicate earthworks to the north-east of your site. These may well have performed a defensive role around an early area of settlement, and it's because of them that the county archaeologist ordered a watching brief as a condition of granting your planning permission. We were there to fulfil that brief when the digging began, and you know the rest of the story. But to answer your question, a little later on, which is when our burial seems to date from, that's in the half-century or so before the Romans came, domestic sites in this area tended not to be enclosed by defences and so they don't show up on the ground or from the air. But looking at the general topography, I'd guess that if there is an Iceni village settlement the remains would lie beneath the present house and its immediate surroundings.'

How far beneath our feet? Katherine wondered.

Chris's dry, academic explanation contained no hint of fantasy but it still sliced the solid ground away from her. She thought of Mead: Miranda's cushions and velvet curtains, the cement mixer, her clothes and Amos's laptop, their books and bottles of wine and casual detritus now seemed perched only precariously on countless layers of remains. Broken pots, rotted fence posts, ashes, axe heads and hearth stones. Their own traces would decompose in their turn.

131

David had sat down and resumed his work. He used a paintbrush to clean dirt particles from the broken chain of vertebrae.

He explained, 'I've removed a rib and sent it for radiocarbon dating. I hope that will give us a more precise date for when she lived. Chemical analysis of the bones will tell us about her diet, even the water she drank. Animal remains from the burial will indicate what herds were kept. Even the minute traces of pollen from the flowers that were buried with her will give us clues about the crops they grew. It adds up to a picture. Quite a vivid picture.' He coughed, as if fearing that *vivid* might be judged too flowery in the context.

'That's extremely interesting,' she said, in what she hoped was a suitably measured tone.

'Katherine has come in to look at the treasure,' Chris remarked. 'She hasn't seen it yet.'

She very much liked the way he pronounced her name, giving each syllable equal weight.

'Of course,' David nodded, politely but clearly conveying his opinion that the bones were the real treasure.

They said goodnight to him and went on into Chris's office. It was tidy, with no personal possessions on view, although she checked for photographs. He unlocked a safe and took out the two pieces, unwrapped them and laid them out for Katherine to examine.

After a long moment she managed to say, 'Yes. Yes, I do see.'

These ancient treasures were so brazenly beautiful. There was raw power in every twist of the ancient metal. The scale of the Mead discovery struck home to her as it hadn't done before. Their house, Amos's house, shrank by comparison to a bundle of tawdry steel and glass slabs.

Chris picked up the torc and held it out.

Katherine touched the golden twists and the elaborate ring terminals, but didn't dare to take it from him. It was Chris who raised it to her throat, waiting until she nodded her head and then angling the weighty ornament to encircle her neck. It lay at the base of her throat, heavy and cold in contrast to the warmth of his hands.

Chris stood back and gazed at her.

'Is it all right for me to have done that?' In a much lower voice he added, 'I so much wanted to.'

She stood up straight. The gold weighed her down, but she felt her bones spreading, her shoulders broadening and her head lifting as if it would float off the pivot of her spine. She caught sight of her reflection in the darkened window. Her eyes were wide.

With the great torc around her neck she looked primitive, like a barbarian.

In the reflected pane her eyes met Christopher Carr's. He picked up the shield and gave her that too. There must have been a leather strap by which to hold it but that had long ago rotted away. She grasped the rim instead and held the piece before her, the oval of her pale face a smaller repeat of the shield's smooth glimmer.

A shiver passed through her. She was conscious of Chris standing close, so close that the air-conditioned space between them seemed charged with electricity.

She laid the shield aside. She lifted her hands to the spirals of gold and twisted her neck free of its weight.

'What will happen to these things?' she asked.

Chris folded them in their wrappings once again. 'They'll be extensively studied. The academic archaeologists from Oxford are coming tomorrow to have a preliminary look, and then the specialist from the British Museum arrives. There will be papers prepared, lectures given. A big find like this is an opportunity for everybody. The excavation itself is only the beginning.'

'And after that? Where will they end up?'

'Well. The county authorities will try to acquire the treasure for the museum here. More probably they'll go on national display at the British Museum. You and Mr Knight don't have a claim on the actual pieces in law, but as the landowners you'll get an appropriate payment.'

She lifted her head.

The shield and the torc were back in the safe and Chris stood in front of her, his hands loose at his sides. His expression was serious, but the air of dry detachment was gone. In fact he looked hesitant, uncertain of himself.

Out of the blue, she suddenly thought that he might be going to *kiss her*.

The notion was so startling, so completely foreign and unlikely, that she started to laugh.

Of course he wasn't going to kiss her, what was she thinking of?

She started talking to head off the interior laughter, then under the pressure of too much to be said that was normally left unspoken she found herself unable to stop.

'As for payment, I can't speak for Amos, he would probably say different, but the money really doesn't matter. The pieces belong to Mead. The history matters, the Warrior Princess, but not the money. There's too much of that already. I often wonder what it would have been like for us if Amos hadn't made such a lot of it. Better, probably. We'd have had to invest more in each other.'

She did stop at that, and they listened to the echo of her gabbled words.

Chris fumbled with his cuff and looked at his watch.

'I wonder, would you like to come and have a drink with me?'

'Now?'

'That's what I was hoping.'

'I would like to. Yes. I would *love* to.'

Amos stood alone in the middle of the yard. A fine, soft rain was falling out of a black sky, and he took pleasure in ignoring it. A gust of wind blew fallen leaves over his ankles. The lights were on in the Mead kitchen, shining on the comfortable clutter of the dresser shelves, but he could see that the room was empty. Miranda would be reading in her drawing room, sitting on the sofa with her knees folded beneath her. She read a lot.

Amos hadn't quite got used to the communal aspects of their life here, the way they all knew what each of the others did with their days, when for so many years only Katherine had had even a partial knowledge of his comings and goings. In the past, on the very rare evenings when she had gone out without him, he would have been content with the television or the latest political biography. Now solitude coupled with the proximity of company made him restless. He had been drawn out of the neat cottage and into the rain, just to see what might be going on.

There was a pale light showing in the barn windows, and the scrape and rattle of a shovel carried across to him. A silvery film of rain droplets glimmered in the fibres of his sweater. Amos ducked the few yards to Selwyn and Polly's door and banged on the warped planks.

Selwyn bellowed, 'Yeah, c'mon in,' without stopping work.

An extension cable now snaked across the dirt-caked floor, and a naked bulb in a wire cage swung from a beam.

In the trenches lay new piping for drains. Copper standpipes rose where sinks and basins would finally be positioned. Selwyn was waist-deep in the trench at the point where the water company would bestow the mains feed. He threw aside a shovel and waved his fist in the air.

'Amos. Check out my sewage outlets. Poetry, eh?'

Amos gritted his teeth.

It was almost unbearable, in fact actually intolerable, to witness the rapid progress that Selwyn was making while his own works were at a standstill.

'Don't you ever stop?' he demanded.

'Occasionally. But I have to force myself. I'm loving it.' Selwyn insisted. He was enjoying the contrast in their situations, that was certain.

'Bastard archaeologists,' Amos muttered.

Selwyn stooped down and extracted something from the

135

trench. He rubbed a thumb over it, squinted at the edge that was exposed and flung it aside. It fell with a faint clink. Selwyn levered himself out of the hole and arched to ease his back.

'Right. Well, since you're here, what about a beer?'

Amos would have preferred whisky, but he took the bottle that Selwyn passed to him. The ambient temperature in the barn kept the beer desirably chilled. They sat down at a trestle table pushed out of the way against an exposed stone wall.

'Where's Polly?'

'Gone to the pub with Colin.'

'They're close, those two.'

Selwyn rubbed his stubbled chin. 'They are. It's good for them both. They talk a lot. You know, liberal use of the f-word.'

Amos raised an eyebrow.

'Feelings.'

Both men laughed.

'Katherine?'

'Stopped off on her way back from London to look at the shield and the torc, curses be upon the things. A bloody long look, it turns out.'

'What's up? No dinner?'

'I can cook a meal for myself,' Amos said.

'Sure.' Selwyn shrugged. He delved in a carton and took out two foil trays, shook an old sheet off a box-shape that turned out to be a microwave oven balanced on a stool, slid in the trays and pressed the buttons. Like the light cable, the power for the oven also coiled over the floor, both of them connected via a hefty socket bar to a hole in the barn wall.

'All mod cons, eh? Personally I rather liked the camping gas, but Polly wasn't having any of it. So we're on Miranda's power for now, and the electrician's coming next week to connect us to the mains. Serious progress.'

'When do you expect to finish?'

The microwave pinged. Selwyn placed one tray and a fork in front of Amos and took the other for himself. Amos

136

inspected the fork, wiped it on his handkerchief and began to eat the curry. He was hungry, and the truth was that although the fridge in the cottage had looked well stocked, he hadn't immediately seen the ingredients that would add up to the sort of meal that Katherine would cook.

'It's the second week in October now. It'll be looking a lot different in a couple of months' time. By Christmas, anyway. Not the frills, maybe.'

'Flush lavatories? Or do those count as frills?'

Selwyn snorted between mouthfuls of curry. 'There's nothing wrong with old Chemical Ali as far as I'm concerned.' He nodded towards the chemical toilet that was decently housed behind closed doors in what had once been a feed store. 'But Polly regards an operating flush as mandatory. She tends to go in the house, for the time being.'

'You'd be happy with a shovel in the woods,' Amos observed.

He was thinking how the picture summed up Selwyn. Whatever might go wrong, and often did, Selwyn could convince people that the life he happened to be living was enviable because he was living it. It was a simple investment of self-confidence that Amos had never been able to achieve. Amos had been an eminent barrister, had grown rich, had an amiable wife and two sons who looked set to match his success, yet around Selwyn he still felt thwarted, as though there were some inner VIP room in life to which he had failed to gain admittance. He envied his old friend just as deeply and silently as he had done when Selwyn pranced in his velvet trousers at the Blue Peony decks, with a three-deep ring of girls surrounding him.

Selwyn leaned forward. 'Whereas you couldn't think of anything worse, eh? How long have we known each other?'

'Um, forty years? Can that be right?'

'Yes, and in all that time have you noticed that you've been getting more like yourself, while I've become a more pronounced version of me? That's what happens to people. Forty years ago, did you expect that our tastes and inclinations were going to converge?'

Amos considered this proposition. 'When you're twenty, you think all people in their fifties look and behave the same. The old are grey, baggy, uninteresting and largely indistinguishable. So yes, I suppose I did.'

'Nope. It was never going to happen, my friend. This is an age conversation. Twenty quid in the box.'

'To hell with the bloody box.'

'All right. I won't tell if you don't. Do you want another beer?' They had devoured the food.

'Haven't you got any scotch?'

'No.' Selwyn was rolling himself a thin, whiskery cigarette. Amos had stopped smoking on doctor's orders, even his good cigars, but he would have liked one now.

'I'll go and get mine.'

The rain had stopped, the house lights glowed in the empty kitchen, and Katherine still wasn't home. Amos tried her mobile, but it was turned off. He hoisted the scotch bottle off the polished drinks tray and walked back across the yard. Selwyn had left the table and was trundling a wheelbarrow towards a mound of rubble. The bare light bulb cast his oversized shadow up the wall.

'I thought we were going to have a drink,' Amos said, exasperated.

Over his shoulder Selwyn answered, 'We are. But since there are two of us, I want to shift a couple of barrow loads into the skip. It's too much for Polly. Do you want to shovel or barrow?'

The skip was stationed outside the barn door, with a rather steeply inclined plank leading up to the lip.

'Shovel.'

Amos trod over the piece of rubble that Selwyn had tossed out of the drain trench. It lay in a small heap of similar fragments, and he bent down to pick one up. It was a mud-caked chunk of dark brown earthenware. Selwyn saw him examining it.

'What was the actual deal with the planning department for your work, by the way?' Amos asked.

138

Selwyn did an elaborate yawn. 'No deal. Application for conversion of outbuilding for domestic use, plans and drawings submitted, permission granted.'

'Straightforward.'

'It was, yes.'

Amos leaned on the shovel and the two men looked at each other. There were two shadows looming on the wall. Selwyn finished his cigarette and threw away the tiny butt, and the shadow of his arm swiped over the shadow of Amos's head. 'What's the latest on your site? The princess and all her finery, and so on?'

Amos turned the fragment over and over in his fingers. He looked more closely, and saw a suggestion of a pattern pierced on one corner of it.

'I'm waiting. That beardy digger and his cohorts have been formally granted a month's suspension of work in the immediate area, to enable a properly structured excavation and study to take place. Nothing can happen in the meantime. *Nothing*. Zero. My contractor insists that it's not worth trying to work around the edges, which means of course that they've got another job that will fit in nicely.'

In that time, Selwyn's house would have floors and walls. Maybe even glass in the windows.

Selwyn put a hand on Amos's shoulder. 'That's rough,' he said, and it was clear that he meant it. 'But in the great scheme of life, a few weeks isn't so long.'

Amos considered a retort along the lines of it being plenty long enough to test his own sanity, whereas Selwyn would already have been carted away in a straitjacket. But Selwyn's commiseration was genuine, and in any case there would only be temporary satisfaction in punching him in the jaw. He threw away the piece of pot and it landed somewhere in the shadows.

'Let's get on with it,' Amos shouted.

They set to work.

* * *

Katherine and Chris were in a pub five minutes' walk from his office. When they arrived it had been full of groups of noisy young people, probably estate agents – the windows of most of the adjacent shops were full of pictures of cottages – but now the crowd was thinning. Chris had found a table in the angle of a high-backed bench where they were screened from the remaining drinkers at the bar.

They had been talking for quite a long time.

Chris told her more about the excavation, tracing out the shape of the grave enclosure on the table top and explaining that it was unlikely that the shield and the torc would be the only finds to emerge.

'There will be more?'

'Those two pieces are so special, I'd expect there to be more ornaments, pottery, maybe coins. We have to excavate very carefully, so as not to destroy any remains. The smallest details can often be the most telling. Merely knowing what a person ate reveals a whole culture. Animal fats mean relative prosperity, a stew made of weeds abject poverty. Our princess may have been at the head of several villages made up of family groups. She'd have been their symbolic defender, or maybe she actually went to war against tribal enemies, like Boudicca. She may have been the daughter or the widow of a chieftain, or perhaps an exceptionally powerful or charismatic leader in her own right. Having been buried with a neck ornament and a shield like that, I do know that she was somebody of great note.'

She liked the way he talked about the princess and her people as though he knew them, as though they were living at a distance from where he and Katherine were sitting, but not so far away as to be inaccessible. In the end he interrupted himself.

'I'm sorry. Archaeologists can get wildly over-enthusiastic and don't notice that they're boring the company.'

'I'm interested.'

He grinned. His dark beard made his smile bright. 'I've been

140

accused of obsession. Preferring the company of the long-ago dead to the living and breathing. Not always unjustifiably.'

Katherine could see that he might be guilty of this, but it wasn't the worst fault she could think of. It depended on who the living and breathing actually were.

'If your work is about past lives, I can see it must sometimes be quite difficult to drag yourself into the present.'

His eyes were on her face. 'Yes. It can be. What about you, Katherine?'

Their glasses were empty. Katherine knew she couldn't have another drink, she had to drive all the way home to Meddlett, but she very much wanted to go on sitting here talking to Dr Christopher Carr. It was an ordinary after-work pub with a fruit machine flashing in a corner, yet she was feeling the same warmth and the desire somehow to capture the moment that she had experienced in the Griffin with Polly and Colin. What is it, she wondered, that was all of a sudden making her pub-prone? Another of those awkward developments peculiar to women of late middle age?

'Me?' she asked.

Chris glanced about. 'I can't see anyone else I might be directing the question at. I have been talking interminably about grave enclosures and linear earthworks, and now I'd like to hear something about you. Do you live in the present, for example?'

Katherine reached for her glass before remembering it was empty.

He read her thoughts. 'You could have something different. It doesn't have to be alcohol.'

'Fruit juice, then.'

He came back with orange juice for her, another beer for himself. 'I take the bus. Or walk. It's only a couple of miles. Go on. What about you?'

It was probably at least thirty years since Amos had been on a bus.

Katherine considered. 'Living in the present or in the past?

141

You're the second person this week to ask me a version of that question. Do I look displaced? No, maybe don't answer that.'

'You look wonderful, as a matter of fact.'

She discovered she had no idea how to deal with such a direct compliment. The only option seemed to ignore it, in case it had been a joke. Perhaps he would assume she was deaf.

He was leaning towards her, his hands on the table. They were good hands, square and capable. It would have been easy to reach out and grasp them.

Quickly she said, 'I'm not certain I've lived at all. That is, I've done the usual things in the usual way, and mostly as well as I could, but I'm not convinced that that's *living*. I mean, some people take risks, don't they? They make sacrifices for the sake of others. They pioneer, or they make discoveries, or they overcome obstacles. I'm not saying that I wouldn't have done those things if circumstances had been different, but as it turned out the demands have never been placed on me. I can't look back and say, that was difficult, it was a challenge and I rose to it and I'm proud of myself.

'So what *have* I done? I've been a reasonably good wife and mother. My sons are in their twenties. They're endowed with the usual healthy male quotient of self-interest and ambition. I do love them. Looking back, I see that I've been protected and kept in comfortable prosperity. I know how fortunate I am, compared with what a lot of women have to endure. It's rather old-fashioned. Does all this sound ridiculous?'

'Not ridiculous, no. I think you could be less dismissive of yourself.'

Could I? she wondered.

'Are you married, Chris?'

'I was. For twelve years. Sarah and I split up about four years ago and she's now remarried to one of her colleagues. We have two daughters. They live with their mother and they stay with me most weekends. Daisy still loves that but nowadays Gemma doesn't always want to come, she'd rather be with her mates. That's normal, isn't it? It's all quite civilized,

Mal – that's the husband – and I even have a pint together from time to time. That's not to say that I didn't want to tear him apart when she left me. For the first year or so I could quite easily have killed and dismembered him. My daughters were asleep in his house, my wife was in his bed. Did they do the same things that she and I used to? I'd stumble around our place, remembering how it used to be when we were all together, and I was mad enough to hammer the walls with my fists until the bloke next door started hammering back. But now I see the two of them together, I can't recall precisely what it felt like when she was married to me and not him. Occasionally I even wish I had the anguish back, at least that would be a validation. But not all that often.'

'What about girlfriends?' she ventured.

He said, 'A couple. There's no one at the moment.' Then he added in a lower voice, 'It doesn't happen more than once or twice in a lifetime. You look at someone and you think, "Yes, of course, it's you. *There* you are".'

The bar was filling up again. These were different people, older and less exuberant than the young office workers. They were the ones who had gone home or somewhere else to eat a meal, and were now intending to drink away what was left of the evening. In any case, as far as Katherine and Chris were concerned the pub and the street and the whole city were deserted but for themselves.

Chris touched the back of her hand. 'You've stayed married. Don't dismiss that as an achievement. I expect it involved plenty of sacrifices and demands. Probably some pioneering.'

Katherine realized that he had not only listened to what she said to him, but had remembered it. How very unlike Amos that was.

Perhaps he was now hoping or even expecting that she might make some parallel admissions about her own marriage. But she had already been disloyal enough. The details she could at least keep to herself.

'I suppose it would be an unusual marriage if it hadn't.'

Chris nodded, looking away from her. He was lonely, she thought. Not in an odd or remotely threatening sense, but just in the way of a warm, affectionate man who wanted someone to be with.

'You'll marry again. You'll probably have a second family. That's what happens, isn't it?'

His momentarily assumed expression of mock horror made her laugh.

'Small children? All over again? At my age?'

'Are you so very ancient?'

They told each other their ages. Katherine was the older by nine years. She was nearly relieved it was that much. They might divert themselves by paying compliments, but she thought that on the whole men didn't take a serious interest in women who were their senior by almost a decade.

But at the same time she felt a sharp and quite precise pang of disappointment. Dr Christopher Carr was an attractive man. Or – she made the effort to be honest with herself – she found him attractive, decidedly so. And how long was it since she had thought anything of the kind, about any man?

Decades, probably.

She drank the last of her orange juice, now warm and sticky, and wished it were gin. Luckily, the lights were dim and so probably Chris couldn't see her pink face.

A silence developed between them. Katherine played with the idea of breaking it by suggesting they go to a hotel together, just to see how he would extricate himself.

'Well. Look at the time,' he said. He was grinning now. His confidence had returned.

'Yes, I'd better get back. Amos will be wondering where I've got to.'

A cold wind drove spitting rain down the cobbled street outside the pub and Katherine pulled her coat tighter. Chris insisted on walking back with her to her car, parked further from his office than it need have been because she was un-familiar with the town's one-way system. They strode at quite a pace past the estate agents' windows, apologizing when they accidentally bumped shoulders at a crossing.

'Here we are,' she said when they reached her Audi. He took her bag and placed it on the back seat for her, and held open the door. She hesitated. Nine years was nothing, she thought. She had never taken the sexual initiative, not once in her life; was *that* why she found herself gabbling about never having lived? Soon, *very* soon, it would be too late.

'Can we see each other again?' she asked.

'Of course we can.'

She almost reeled with shock.

He leaned down and kissed her, on the corner of her mouth, firmly enough to leave her in no doubt that there was more to come. He stepped back afterwards, which was probably just as well, she thought, or she'd have been standing there snogging him in the street like a teenager.

He was wearing a North Face anorak, the sort of garment that Amos would sneer at. He patted a pocket and brought out his mobile.

'May I use the number you called me on?'

My God, Katherine thought. So this is how it happens.

'Yes.'

What the hell.

She got into the car. The window slid down like a barrier dissolving between them.

'I'll call you,' he promised. 'Goodnight, Katherine.'

As she drove away, she saw in the rear-view mirror that he watched until she turned the corner at the end of the road. It took a prolonged negotiation with the one-way system to find her way out to the ring road, but Katherine didn't care. She felt sufficiently in control of her own destiny to have driven all the way to the North Pole.

Out in the countryside there were no lights and almost no traffic. The black tarmac unravelled between high hedges, and once in a while the eyes of a cat out hunting, or maybe a fox, glimmered at her from the depths. She felt that she had entered a foreign country, a territory that was as yet unmapped, and full of secrets.

She was sorry when she finally reached the mossy stone gateposts at Mead. She had enjoyed being out in the night, alone with her thoughts.

The trees that knitted their branches over the Mead driveway were bare of leaves except for a few tatters. The car's headlights passed over the opening to the track that forked down to the site, where the guard would be ensconced in his caravan, and she rounded the last bend to the house. All the windows were dark, and in a haphazard row in the courtyard the cars were drawn up, the Jaguar, Polly and Selwyn's dented Nissan, Miranda's and Colin's tidy German vehicles.

All are safely gathered in, she thought, except for me.

Katherine trod softly around the side of the house. The wind was loud in the trees. There was a wan light showing in the barn, and in the cottage a chink glowed between the bedroom curtains. She let herself in and padded up the stairs.

Amos was asleep in their bed, propped on pillows, his book fallen to his chest and his glasses slipped down his nose. When she leaned over him to take the book and spectacles, his eyes opened.

'I'm sorry to wake you,' she murmured.

'Where have you been?'

Into her head came the memory of all the nights in their marriage when he had come home from heaven knows where, and she had tried not to ask that very question.

'I went to see the treasure, I told you that. And I had a drink afterwards with Chris Carr.'

'Who?'

'The archaeologist.'

She went into the bathroom and put on her nightdress. When she came back she expected to find him asleep again, but he turned over on his side and watched her.

'I had a microwaved curry and a couple of scotches with Selwyn.'

146

'Did you?'

Katherine got into bed. Amos's weight depressed the mattress, but if she held herself rigid she didn't roll towards him. This was holiday cottage furniture.

Most of their own stuff was in storage and so far she had missed none of it, but it would be a relief to get her own bed back. She wondered when that might be, and realized that it would all depend on Chris and the princess's treasures, and the schedule of his excavation.

She had stopped herself from asking questions about Amos's whereabouts because she feared the answers.

Amos didn't ask for more details about her evening because he wasn't interested, or because the idea that she might have been doing anything out of order with a bearded man who wore a North Face anorak was simply too ludicrous to contemplate.

Oh, Amos.

In the Portakabin overlooking the site, the guard yawned over his paperback. He liked Dan Brown and this one was the best he'd read, but at two o'clock in the morning it was hard to stay awake. He got up and clicked the switch of the kettle. He'd do a round of the trench and the diggings and walk up as far as the trees, log his hourly report to the control centre, then make a brew and eat his sandwiches. He took his torch and went outside.

The white forensic tent had been removed. Now there were rough canvas awnings over the various holes in the ground. These strained and sucked in the wind, grey shape-shifters against the black meadow, but they were all secure. The guard shone his torch into the biggest hole. Under a skein of tapes it was empty, the sides made of layered earth and stones. This was the first time, he thought, that he had been sent out to guard thin air. A big building site with plenty of designer taps and electrical goods and copper piping lying loose, or a bonded warehouse, he could understand villains wanting a piece of those, but there was nothing here except grass and stones. Not even the tools that were locked up overnight were worth nicking, just a few old shovels and buckets and some miniature trowels. He flashed the torch into the smaller pits.

Wet grass swished over his toecaps as he tramped across to the copse, turned and listened. He swung his torch in an arc. A second ago he thought he was hearing the slow approach of a vehicle, but now there was only the creak and rustle of the rural night. He didn't care for these country places. How could people live out here, in the middle of nowhere?

He walked back to the cabin, listened again, and went inside. He used his phone to call control and made an all-clear report. It was Polish Jerzy on the desk tonight. That was a boring job, if ever there was one. At least he was out here, not just sitting in a stuffy room waiting for a series of guys to ring in and tell him nothing was happening.

The guard picked up his tea-stained mug, dropped a teabag into it, brought the kettle to the boil again. He was standing with his back to the door. When it crashed open he half-turned, but the two hooded men were on to him. They pulled a bag over his head, tied his knees and ankles and wrists, and tipped him on to the floor. He shouted as loudly as he could through the folds of the bag, but they pushed the mouldy fabric into his mouth and twisted a gag between his teeth. He stopped the noise then, because he was afraid that he would choke.

He heard them blunder out of the door and turn the key in the lock.

SIX

Miranda woke up to hear a police siren.

The noise stopped as soon as she came to full consciousness but she knew it was real, not the soundtrack of a dream. She ran to the window but could see nothing. When she stepped out on to the landing a darker shadow shifted against darkness and a shock of fear froze her before Colin clicked on the light.

'It's all right,' he said.

'You scared me. What is it?'

'I don't know. Something's happening. I'm going to look.'

'I'm coming with you.'

Outside in the yard, treading their feet into wellingtons seized from beside the back door, they hesitated in silence and blackness before the blare of another siren sounded from the drive.

'It's the site,' Colin muttered. He fumbled with a torch and began to run.

Miranda stumbled after him. 'Should we call Selwyn?'

'Because we'll need a big strong man with us? Why not Amos in that case?'

Colin could run surprisingly fast, she realized. She concentrated on keeping pace with him.

They raced through the copse, ploughing into thick drifts of fallen leaves that mounded the path. The torch beam swayed over tree trunks and knotted roots. Miranda knew every inch of the way but darkness changed all the familiar dimensions.

Colin was ten yards ahead of her as she panted out into the meadow. Two police cars with headlights on full beam bracketed the contractor's cabin, and a policeman flashing a heavy torch was already heading towards them.

Inside the hut the security guard was propped in a chair. He held a dressing pressed to his head and there was blood on his cheek and collar. Miranda made to go to him but their escort signalled her back.

'Are you all right?' she called.

He put his other hand up to his forehead. 'I didn't see them, no more than a glimpse. There were more than two, I know that much. I heard them outside.'

His face was as white as the bandage, but he was doing his best to answer the police questions. He had been tied up for almost two hours. After he failed to make his next scheduled call to control, the supervisor tried several times to reach him. He heard his phone as he lay trussed up on the hut floor, and from outside the urgent ping of metal detectors and the thud of shovels. Eventually the security company had reported his prolonged silence to the police.

By the time the first patrol car arrived the intruders had gone, but the guard reckoned they had had at least ninety undisturbed minutes in which to ransack the site.

Colin and Miranda were escorted to the workmen's caravan. Passing the trench, they looked down. The canvas awnings had been torn away, and the archaeologists' markers and tapes. The walls and floor of the half excavated grave were a ruined mass of dug earth and stones.

'This way,' the policeman told them.

'Is the guard badly hurt?' Miranda asked.

'He hit his head when he was knocked down.'

The caravan smelled strongly of sweaty work clothes. It wasn't easy to prove their identities wearing only coats over their dressing gowns and unmatched boots. When Colin pointed out that their outfits and behaviour made them unlikely suspects, the irritable copper only snapped that he would be the judge of what was or was not likely. Miranda shivered in the cold. At length the policeman agreed to accompany them back to the house. As they emerged an ambulance came swaying down the rutted track.

The guard was led into the ambulance and the door closed on him.

In the Mead kitchen, the officer took Colin's and Miranda's statements. They were in agreement. They had heard nothing, seen nothing, until the siren woke them up.

The policeman eventually left, promising that he would be back first thing in the morning to interview the others. Miranda showed him that the cottage and the barn were still in darkness, which meant everyone was asleep and almost certainly had been throughout the night.

'We'll do our job, ma'am,' he said.

'What do you think?' she asked Colin, as soon as they were alone.

'Whatever else was buried there with the princess is now in the back of a van.'

The first spasm of outrage passed through Miranda. The princess, her treasure, whatever else had lain in the earth at her side, this was part of Mead as much as the house and the trees. The robbery was an assault on Mead itself.

'Who did this?'

'It was someone who knew what might be there, and the probable value of it. Someone who was probably told by someone else.'

They pondered the possibilities. Colin counted them off on his fingers. It could only be one of themselves, one of the archaeologists, an employee of the security company, or Jessie.

'None of us. Surely not even Amos would think of pulling something like this?' Miranda said.

Nothing was quite certain, though.

They exchanged a glance, then looked through the window

151

at the black night. To Miranda the darkness seemed solid, exerting an inwards physical pressure that made the old window frames creak.

Colin said, 'I can't quite see how robbing his own site could work to Amos's advantage and the only way Selwyn might be involved would be as a gross practical joke which seriously misfired. A man was injured, after all. I'd be prepared to bet that it's not one of us, unless it was by mentioning it inadvertently to some outsider.'

Miranda looked angry and baffled now as well as shocked. Colin crossed to where she was huddled against the incubator warmth of the range. She uncurled her fists and let him rub her fingers.

She shook her head. 'Of course it's not one of us. That still leaves quite a lot of people who have been here, doesn't it? If not one of them directly, it would only take one of their wives, staff, drivers, whoever, to mention the discovery in the wrong place. How much must that brutal gold neckpiece alone be worth?'

'For the metal, maybe a few thousand? For what it is, what it represents, probably an incalculable amount. The theft is going to cause quite a stir once the news gets out. And it *will* get out.'

Miranda hadn't even considered this aspect. The appearance of the Warrior Princess at Mead was turning out to be less magical than it had seemed. The insinuations of prehistory and the demands of the present day were working together like the bony fingers of two hands, prising their way between the cracks of her shuttered privacy in this house, where she had planned to make herself secure with her old friends and her memories of Jake.

She gripped Colin's hands so hard that her nails dug into his palms.

'Why is it so *dark*? Is it never going to get light again?'

It was four in the morning.

He said, 'Come on. It's time to go back to bed.'

There was nothing more they could do tonight, Miranda had to agree.

Outside her bedroom door, he saw that she hesitated and forced herself to look into the shadows in the stairwell. She was still shivering.

'Thieves take more than loot, don't they? How can they have made off with my ease in my own house?' She tried to laugh.

'They must be miles away by now, Mirry. Would you like me to come and sleep with you?'

'A belated offer, I must say. But I appreciate it even more for that.'

She did manage a laugh now, a quick delighted wheeze of mirth that made Colin laugh too. They tottered in each other's arms on the creaking landing.

'I couldn't deliver in the technical sense, remember.'

'I'd prefer your company tonight to the hottest stud in the county, Col.'

Miranda crawled under the covers and Colin lay on top of them, wrapped in a quilt. They spooned together, listening to the wind, as warmth spread between them. It was the first time that Miranda had shared a bed since Jake's death. She had almost, but not quite, forgotten the comfort it provided.

Colin stroked her hair. 'Go to sleep,' he murmured.

She did as she was told.

They slept until early morning, when the telephone started ringing.

A journalist from the local paper was first, quickly followed by two local radio stations and a reporter from the area television news. Dissatisfied with the stonewalling answers they received from Miranda on the phone, the reporters soon started to arrive in person. Amos opened the door of the cottage to a young woman who, he claimed later, doorstepped him with a radio mike. His comments, with the more intemperate sections edited out, made the lunchtime bulletin on the county station. Complaining about vandalism and citing property rights he

153

sounded, as he put it himself later, like a puce-faced rural grandee whose croquet lawn had been trampled in the course of an audacious raid on his wine cellar.

'Why didn't you stop me making an arse of myself?' he raged to Katherine.

'When?' she asked gently, but he wasn't waiting for her answer.

Miranda telephoned the hospital. She was told that the security guard was severely shocked, but stable, and would be kept under observation for another night.

A pair of policemen interviewed Selwyn and Polly and Amos and Katherine, but all four of them had slept from bedtime to breakfast and had heard nothing.

'Missed all the drama,' Selwyn complained. 'Why didn't you wake us, Barb?'

The archaeologists returned to their ravaged dig, but it was cordoned off and guarded while the uniformed branch waited for the arrival of the forensic investigator and the CID. The neat sections of the grave's walls and floor were a trodden pit of raw earth and heaped spoil, turning to mud as the day's steady rain trickled through the hastily re-erected canvas shelters.

As Colin had predicted, outside interest in the story quickly gathered momentum.

The first local stringer for a national newspaper turned up, and several photographers lurked in the drive and on the field margins. The broadcast bulletins started mentioning Boudicca, and speculating about the glorious treasures the thieves might have spirited away. From being mentioned as a possibility, within hours it became accepted fact that the grave had contained the remains of a magnificent horse-drawn chariot complete with harness pieces and decorated terret rings, a series of iron weapons, gold and electrum torcs and arm rings, and a hoard of gold coins of the Iceni tribe. A well-known television archaeologist gave an impromptu telephone interview, widely quoted in all the subsequent bulletins, in which he offered the opinion that the stolen Meddlett treasure could well represent one of the greatest Iron-Age discoveries ever made, and that the loss of it was nothing less than a national tragedy.

The next day's newspapers would be full of the Warrior Princess, and what was missing in hard fact would no doubt be supplied by imagination.

Amos declined any further contact with the press, although several reporters were eager for some more of the lively performance he had given on the radio. He left Katherine to answer the callers while he talked to the police. The most senior officer he could pin down, who despite all Amos's insistence was several rungs on the ladder below the Chief Constable, smoothly assured him that every effort was being made to investigate the crime and apprehend those responsible. Amos also spoke to the managing director of the security company, who told him that all the guidelines had been followed and the guard on duty at Mead had been one of their best. He thanked Amos for his concern for the injured man.

Polly, Colin and Miranda drifted in and out of the kitchen. They answered the house telephone and listened with amusement or disbelief to the different versions of the radio news. Selwyn was mixing concrete out in the yard. He kicked the rubble of broken pot into the trenches where it disappeared between the piping. A grey river of concrete flowed on top of it.

The Griffin had been busy at lunchtime with a stream of locals who had looked in to trade the latest rumours with Vin. Several of the news reporters had called in too, asking questions of the pub regulars and keeping Geza busy in the kitchen. Jessie silently served them with ploughman's or dishes of braised lamb shank.

A freelance photographer asked her what time she was going to finish work.

'Not in your lifetime,' she said, sweeping away his empty plate.

Some of the archaeologists came in too but they disconsolately took a corner table and talked in low voices, ignored by the reporters. Kieran was not amongst them.

By afternoon closing time all the outsiders had taken themselves off.

When Vin opened up again at half past five, the evening was turning cold and damp enough for him to kick some logs together in the open fireplace and coax a fire into life. Outside the kitchen door Jessie and Geza pulled up their hoods and smoked before the start of their shift.

'It is a great shame to lose items that have history from the place where they should stay,' Geza remarked, coughing tragically as he exhaled a grey cloud. 'These thieves have done more than a crime like supermarket grab. It is bad for your country.'

'Yeah,' Jessie agreed, staring into the rain.

Two customers sat in the bar, one on either side of the fire. One of them was the local builder, the other was churchwarden and president of the bowls club.

The builder said, 'They belong to this village by rights, all them necklaces and horse ornaments and the gold coins, don't they? They was here long before the big estates and landowners taking over the country for themselves. The ancient peoples, these Iceni, they were our forebears. Right here in Meddlett, that's where this treasure should be kept. Not in some museum the other side of the county, nor in the pocket of a rich bloke from London who's got nothing to do with this place except he happens to be the new owner of an acre of land.'

Vin loomed over the pumps. 'They haven't ended up in either place, Stan, have they? Some nighthawk with his metal detector's got the blooming lot. All our heritage'll be going overseas, sold to some foreign collector for a fortune no doubt. I'm not all that chuffed about what's happened, either. Even though it's that lawyer who's been robbed, which is what I call justice, for once. A bit more local history in Meddlett, not just the Fifth, that'd bring in a few visitors instead of them all going straight up to the coast. We had a good lunchtime with the journalists and that today, but it's not going to last, is it?'

'It'll be them lot that's took it, like they take everything else,' Stan muttered, nodding in the vague direction of the kitchen curtain and Geza behind it.

This was by no means a new theme of his, and the other two ignored him.

'That's Mead land, where they found the treasure. Has been for centuries,' the churchwarden put in. 'Mrs Meadowe only sold it a few months ago to the barrister chap who was on the radio.'

Vin nodded. 'She ought to involve herself a bit more in the village. I said as much to some of those newcomers who are living up there, they come in here once in a while for their glass of *waite waine*, but I didn't get much of an answer.'

'I expect she's got her reasons,' the churchwarden said.

'And now the Fifth's coming up again,' Stan observed.

Everyone nodded.

The Fifth of November was a big night in the Meddlett calendar. It was the occasion for a costumed pageant with a huge bonfire.

In the early years of Jake and Miranda's marriage the bonfire and the pageant were staged on one of the Mead fields, but one year there had been a drunken brawl and three men had been arrested. Nowadays the bonfire was built in the church field and the landlord of the Griffin laid on a hog-roast for the village. The Meddlett children regarded the present-day event as a second crack at Hallowe'en, for which the preceding week was only the warm-up.

'My older one's leading the Mauby procession this year. The vicar's never been that keen on any of it,' the churchwarden said.

'Is he? Good lad. Vicar's only been here five minutes himself, what's it got to do with him?' Stan answered. 'Give us another one in there, Vin.'

Katherine kept her mobile phone close at hand all day, but there was no call from Chris. As the day began to fade into twilight she couldn't stay in the house any longer.

Amos was in the second bedroom, which did duty as his study. He didn't look up from his computer screen when she put her head around the door.

'I'm just going for a little walk,' she told the back of his head.

Selwyn was cleaning splashes of concrete off the cobbles, swishing the hosepipe behind him like a satanic tail. She pulled up her collar and found a pair of gloves in the pocket of her coat. The gate latch clinked as she gently closed it, and a shower of heavier drops from the branches of a tree fell on her face as she passed beneath. The air smelled cold and dense with moisture, but she was pleased to be out of the cottage. From the window it had looked almost dark outside, but now she was immersed in it the clouds to the west still swelled with greenish light and the wet boles of the trees looked like gleaming pillars in a dim, free-form cathedral. Raindrops steadily dripped on the path.

The police had warned them to keep away from the site, but she could see no reason why she should not take a stroll through the copse.

In the centre, where the trees were thickest, the last of the light was almost blocked out. She looked up once to see the fading glimmer of sky through the lattice of branches, and nearly tripped. Putting out her hand to the nearest tree to steady herself she heard feet swishing in the fallen leaves, and then saw him coming towards her. The hood of the North Face anorak was pulled down to keep off the rain, but she knew immediately that it was Chris.

He stopped, pushed back the hood to see her more clearly, then put his hands to her shoulders. He held on firmly, as if to stop her slipping out of his grasp. Even in the dim light, she could see how miserable he was.

'Have they taken everything?' she asked.

'It looks like it.'

He lifted one hand off her shoulder and slid it into his pocket. He held up a small polythene bag. Inside she could just make out an irregular flat disc of metal.

'A single coin of Icenian silver,' Chris murmured.

He let go of her, rummaged again in a pocket and produced a small torch.

He focused the beam and through the bag Katherine saw on one side of the coin a human profile and on the other the primitive but unmistakable outline of a horse.

She would have liked to weigh the coin in the palm of her hand, then close her fist on it to keep it safe.

'It's Face-Horse type, quite a common early variety Icenian issue. The thieves must have dropped it, the police found it lying between the trench and the hut.'

'And what about the rest? There would have been more, wouldn't there?'

'Yes, definitely. All gone.'

He clicked off the torch. The darkness intensified.

'I'm so sorry,' Katherine whispered. His dejection touched her. She was aware of the small distance that separated them, and of the rain, and the avenues between the trees, radiating from the point where they were standing like spokes from a hub.

'I was just coming across to tell you and your husband and Mrs Meadowe the news.'

'Thank you. Don't worry about us.'

'I didn't call you. It's been a very bad day.'

'I understand.'

'The television people were here to record an interview. I don't know how to do these things. I'm an archaeologist, not Andrew Marr.'

'They wouldn't have been expecting otherwise.'

He said, 'So I thought about you. Thinking about you made the difference, Katherine. It was like opening a window and seeing a new view, with a river and some hills and a glimpse of the sea in the distance. Do you mind me saying that? I'm sorry if you do. I don't know how to go about any of this, except by being honest. I could try to pretend that what seems to be happening here *isn't*, if that would be better?'

'Perhaps we should stop apologizing to each other,' she said.

A life in waiting, she was thinking. She didn't want to wait any longer for she didn't know what.

The distance between them somehow diminished and then disappeared altogether, and she found herself in Chris's arms. The wet creases of his anorak rustled as he kissed her. It was strange to kiss a man with a beard; rough and silky at the same time. It was strange to kiss any man other than Amos, and she couldn't even remember when Amos had last kissed her properly, with attention, the way this man was now doing.

'I'm not sorry,' Chris said, at length.

'Me neither,' she whispered. Maybe later, she temporized. Sorry, or guilty, or remorseful, maybe. But not now. Christopher Carr and she recognized a need in each other. She wasn't going to deny that there was neediness.

'Where were you going?'

'I'm there. Here,' she told him.

He kissed her some more.

Rain smeared her cheeks and blotted her eyes, and ran down their necks once it had soaked into their hair. Finally they acknowledged that they had better continue through the woods to the house. There would be a time and a place. It seemed now that they were both sure of that. He took her hand and drew her after him, but as they came out of the trees and the lights of Mead shone through the drizzle he squeezed her fingers and released them.

Katherine hesitated on her own doorstep. She twisted the ends of her hair and rubbed her fingers under her eyes to remove smudged eye make-up. Thinking about it later, she wasn't sure how she had managed to look and sound like her ordinary self in the awkward half-hour that followed, but Amos didn't give her more than a glance so she supposed she must have done.

They were in the sitting room at the cottage. It wasn't a large room, and the possessions that they had brought with them from London crowded alongside Miranda's holiday-home furnishings. There were framed graduation photographs of Sam and Toby, and even one of her wedding day. She was wearing a long dress and a short veil, and Amos was in morning dress. Trying to see it through Chris's eyes she thought how conventional it must all look, and how deeply, deeply married. Prickles of discomfort and giddy anticipation ran up and down her spine. She was looking at her wedding-day self as if at someone she had once talked to at a party and discovered she had little in common with.

Amos drank a gin and tonic. Chris refused a beer or even a cup of tea. He apologized to Amos for the loss of the rest of the treasure. He said that it was very difficult to keep big discoveries like this one secret. There were always collectors who were avid for antiquities and criminals who were ready to steal to supply them.

He added that there was a glimmer of good news, at least for the Knights and their house. The grave had been so comprehensively ransacked and vandalized, there was little point in making a more detailed archaeological study. It was possible that the county archaeologist might order some further ground sampling across the wider site, but Chris and he were in agreement that the burial enclosure was likely to have been at a little distance from the main settlement and so it was unlikely that any more significant finds would be made.

He spoke quietly, unlike Amos.

Amos was still smarting from the showing he had made in the radio interview, but he was the opposite of subdued. He demanded to know why and how the news of the discovery had leaked out, and insisted that he was holding Dr Carr personally responsible.

'As site director I am personally responsible, yes. But I think I can reassure you that none of our people leaked the information.'

Amos's face reddened. 'Are you implying that it might have been *me*? Or my wife, or any of us here? If you are drawing any such inference, I would advise you to be very careful of what you do say and to be quite certain that you could fully substantiate any such accusation.'

Katherine couldn't look at him. Her feelings were in turmoil, but there was a level voice in her ear that she had heard before.

Do you admire your husband's determination, or do you actually hate him?

Since they had come to live at Mead and she had been seeing him alongside Miranda and Selwyn and the others, she had felt a space opening between them. Amos's energy was prodigious, yes, but it took no account of her or anyone else. He could be the living embodiment of selfishness, yet his drive to get what he wanted could still impress her. She was churned in his wake, taking her chances in the currents that swirled around him, but it took so much of her energy to keep their marriage above water. She was tired of all the effort involved. With a new detachment, she found herself wondering whether his girlfriends came to feel the same about him, or whether his force field of personal vigour was what attracted and held them. Maybe the latest one, or more correctly the one who had resisted him and caused all the trouble, possessed some equal but contradictory determination of her own.

She must do, Katherine decided. In the abstract, she could almost admire her.

'I am not suggesting that at all,' Chris was saying. His voice was still low.

He reminded them that the police were making their enquiries, and it wasn't impossible that they might find whoever was responsible and eventually recover the treasure. He didn't add that even that eventuality could not restore the archaeological context that was so important to him.

Katherine wished that Amos could be even faintly aware of the dimensions of anyone else's loss, or of any concerns but his own.

'I have been speaking to the senior police officer involved,' Amos said, importantly. 'I have asked him for information about what happens next.'

Chris was gathering himself to leave. Don't go, Katherine longed to say, even though she also wanted nothing more than for this excruciating meeting to be over.

'Once the police have finished their investigation, we'll probably only need a few more days, a week at the most, on the site. You'll want to let your contractor know about that,' Chris said as he stood up.

'If I can get them to bloody well come back again this side of Christmas,' Amos rejoined.

She shook hands with Chris. 'See you again, Mrs Knight,' he smiled at her.

While Amos was hustling their visitor to the door, the phone rang.

'K, it's Mirry. Come over later and watch the news? We're on, apparently. Unless anything bigger than the stolen treasure of Mead happens in the meantime.'

'All right,' Katherine said.

Amos tramped in again. 'Christ Almighty. When is this ever going to end?'

He poured himself another drink and sat down.

After dinner the six of them gathered in front of Miranda's television. Colin had made an omelette and a salad for himself and Miranda, Polly and Selwyn had eaten a microwaved meal from the stock of them laid on in the barn, while Katherine had silently cooked a pork fillet with braised fennel for Amos, followed by a rather good piece of Ticklemore cheese.

'Aren't you eating?' he had asked, glancing across at her empty plate.

'I'm not very hungry.'

There wasn't quite enough room for them all to sit. Selwyn arranged himself on the floor, resting his back against Miranda's shins. She could see the grey hairs spiralling from the crown of his head, sprinkled in with the black.

'Do you remember how we used to watch *Top of the Pops*, every week, without fail?' Polly laughed. It had been a regular television date. They crammed into someone's room and shook the static out of a portable aerial to discover which record was that week's number one.

'Babs was the real number one,' Selwyn sighed.

'The number one what?'

'Pan's Person,' Amos and Selwyn chorused.

After the main news came the point where the newsreader twinkled, 'Time to join our news teams where *you* are.'

'Get on with it,' Selwyn shouted at the screen.

'Stop talking, I can't hear,' Katherine said. In a minute Chris might appear on the screen and she didn't want to miss one tenth of a second of him.

The third item in the regional bulletin was the Meddlett story. A young woman in a trench coat, standing with the screened excavation and the copse in the background, was urgently describing to camera how the Iron-Age burial site had been uncovered in the course of construction work.

'Look, it's our field,' Miranda exclaimed, sitting further forward.

'So it is. Not Peru at all,' Colin teased.

'Please, hush,' Katherine begged.

The reporter announced that last night thieves armed with metal detectors had attacked this secret location ('Not that secret any longer, is it?' Amos snorted), overpowered a guard, and made off with a major haul of gold and other priceless archaeological remains.

Then Chris appeared.

Katherine leaned forward, causing Polly, who was squeezed on the sofa next to her, to give her a curious glance.

'This is a serious loss,' Chris said. His face filled the screen.

He described how the rare quality of the two pieces already recovered indicated that this was the grave of a great tribal leader. Even if the stolen items were recovered, he said, the opportunity to learn about the history of the burial, and the life of the people who had committed their chief and her treasure to the ground, was now lost for ever. They all listened. Neither Amos nor Selwyn attempted a dismissive joke.

Katherine settled very slowly back against the cushions. She realized that the tight feeling in her chest, the sensation of breathlessness, was *pride*.

'He did that well,' Miranda said as the news anchor replaced Chris. Her face creased with vivid concern. 'I wish those pieces hadn't been taken from here. Now no one knows where they'll end up. Philadelphia, or Munich, or just a bank vault. It's a violation.'

'Maybe it will all be recovered,' Katherine said quietly.

The phone rang yet again. Colin was nearest. 'Shall I?' he asked Miranda.

'Another journalist?' she wondered.

'Mead House. Hello, *Joyce*? Is that you? How good to hear you. Yes, yes, this is Colin. I'm well, thank you. Yes. I know, we've just been watching it. Of course, yes, she's right here. Hold on.'

He held out the receiver to Miranda.

'Your mother.'

'Oh, holy moly, I know I should have called her,' Miranda murmured as she took it. 'Mum? Mum, hello? Listen, I *am* speaking up. Are you all right? What's happened? I was going to call you in the morning, I thought this would be too late for you.'

Joyce Huggett, on the other hand, was audible to all of them. She must have been shouting at the top of her voice. 'Too late? It's ten thirty-five, Barbara. I'm eighty-six, not six.'

Selwyn laughed. 'Joyce, you're going to see us all off,' he called out.

'You've got Selwyn with you. I can hear his voice. What's happening down there? You're not back with him again?'

She had forgiven him, in the end, for jilting her only child. Over the years Joyce had shown more interest in Selwyn's doings than in any of Miranda's other friends, even her eventual husband.

Three of them snuffled with laughter. Miranda frowned at them.

'Mum, you've forgotten. Polly and Selwyn live here now-adays. In the barn.'

'The barn? How uncomfortable. Won't you let them in the house?'

'Of course they come in the house. They're here right now.'

Joyce's confusion could be selective. Certainly her deafness was. Whatever the case Miranda tried never to argue with or even contradict her mother, not any longer. That had been the pattern for too many years. She hurried on, 'Are you all right? Are you taking your pills?'

Joyce ignored her. 'Susan Palmer rang me, five minutes ago. You remember Susan?'

'I'm not sure.'

'Yes, you do. She married my cousin who died of an asthma attack before he turned forty. After Kenneth died she had a terrible time. Luckily for her she took up with a dentist in the end, and they moved to King's Lynn. He's retired now, of course.'

'What did she call you about?' Miranda asked patiently.

'Who?'

'Susan Palmer.'

'I'm about to tell you, Barbara. Don't rush me. She rang to say she heard something about Mead on her local news. What's going on?'

'You might have told me,' Joyce complained, as soon as Miranda finished telling her.

Joyce still lived alone, near to where she had grown up and spent most of her life, in a small block of council sheltered accommodation. She had refused many times to move closer to Mead, although she sometimes agreed to a visit. Her dogged independence, as her old friends and her health and memory slowly deserted her, was what she clung to.

'I know, Mum. I'm sorry. It's been a stupid day. Shall I drive up and see you? I could come tomorrow.'

'I've my chiropody appointment tomorrow.'

'Well, the day after? Or why don't you come here and stay? I could easily pick you up and bring you over.'

The others were leaving. As always, when Selwyn left the room he seemed to take some of the light and warmth with him. Katherine went quietly in Amos's wake. Colin remained, sitting at one end of the sofa watching *Newsnight* with the volume off.

Miranda could clearly see her mother as she would be now, in her small living room with her large telly dominating the stuffy space, a cup of milky tea with biscuit crumbs in the saucer, her potted plants on the windowsill and the newspaper folded on the tablecloth. As a result she felt the usual awkward weight of guilty sympathy, and a prickly, inarticulate love that seemed to have revealed itself too late and was too unwieldy to admit.

'I don't know. I don't feel like making plans,' Joyce was mumbling.

She could swing in seconds from irritability to what sounded in Miranda's ears like something close to despair.

'All right, Mum,' Miranda soothed.

Joyce agreed that she might think of a visit to Mead, maybe in a week or so when her feet weren't hurting so much.

'That's good,' Miranda said. 'I'll call you tomorrow, after the chiropodist's been. Are you going to bed now?'

'Bed? Why? What time is it?'

'Don't worry.'

'Say hello to Selwyn from me,' Joyce shouted, before she hung up.

Colin held out his arms. Miranda folded herself beside him and he rested his chin on her hair.

'Old age is horrible,' Miranda murmured.

They were not old, not yet, and the towering confidence of their generation had been such that they had not expected the indignity to befall them. Gathering at Mead, occupying them-selves with their houses, and their changing relationships to one another and the world, was an act of defiance. But across a gulf of time, the Warrior Princess and Joyce Huggett both demonstrated the futility of that defiance.

*   *   *

In the Griffin, the last of the evening's handful of customers were filtering away. Kieran sat in the window with the remains of a pint of cider, while Vin collected dirty glasses. Kieran had only slipped in in time for last orders, to avoid making himself the target of any more village questioning. He was finding it difficult to steer a course between his professional obligations, which he took seriously, and having been born and brought up in Meddlett. Even his own mother had been on at him all evening, trying to get him to tell her what was really going on with the treasure up at Mead. He had said he only knew what was on the news, which was a lie evident to both of them. Luckily his brother Damon was nowhere to be seen. The only person he really had to see was Jessie, which was why he was here.

She came in from the kitchen, in her black work top and trousers, now covered by a stained apron. She carried an aerosol spray and a cloth with her and she began spritzing and shining the tables. She ignored him until all the other tables were done. He lifted his now empty glass, to indicate that she could do this one too.

'Where's Damon?' he asked.

'How should I know?'

'You haven't seen him?'

Jessie turned the shocking voltage of her glare on him. Her lower lip stuck out, ripe and shiny.

'We split, remember. That's that. Good riddance, as far as I'm concerned.'

'That's not answering the question.'

'What are you, fucking CID all of a sudden? I haven't got to answer your questions, Kieran Kennedy.'

Geza looked in, wearing a khaki camouflage parka over bleached jeans.

'I am going now. I will be in the caravan if you want something,' he told her, frowning at Kieran. Geza lived in a static caravan parked on a field past the council houses, far enough from the picturesque end of Meddlett.

'Yeah. I'm all right, mate. See you, Geza'.

'Not him as well?' Kieran muttered.

She looked on him with scorn. 'He's *gay*, you knob.'

'*Have* you seen Damon? I want to know exactly what you told him about Mead and the princess. After I gave you a lift and told you to keep it to yourself, and everything. What have you done?'

Jessie lifted her head. 'Princess?'

'Haven't you seen the news?'

'Listen, geek boy. I've been working all day, or else I've been at my place listening to my music and having a well-earned kip. There's been a load of people in here, and a lot of talk about stuff being nicked off your secret excavation. What else should I know?'

He gestured in disbelief. 'The burial site. She's a tribal chieftain of the Iceni. We found the skeleton. *I* did, in fact.' He couldn't resist trying to impress her with that, which was a joke, Jessie of all people. 'She was buried with ceremonial goods, gold and coins, an amazing shield, and someone heard about it and came last night and ripped off everything we hadn't already recovered. How can that be, Jessie? Why don't you tell me how?'

Jessie undid her apron and dropped it on the table. She was smiling now, a dazzling slice of lips and teeth that utterly transformed her. 'A princess, eh?'

Kieran didn't look at the low scoop of her T-shirt, or the exposed fronds of her tattoo.

Jessie waltzed in a slow circle. 'Ah, I love the sound of that. A proper role model, as they say. We could do with one, around here. Who was she, archaeology man? What was she like?'

He was annoyed by her failure to grasp the significance of the loss. He felt it as deeply as if that stupendous torc and the coins and the imagined splendour of the lost goods had all belonged to him personally, and as if they had been snatched out of his reverent hands and the gold and the precious shreds of prehistory carelessly thrown to the four winds. Fury blazed up in him. He grabbed her wrist, above the hygiene dressing she was obliged to wear for work.

'What have you done?' he demanded.

Jessie's smile instantly turned to a scowl. She snatched her hand back and hit him full in the face. He gasped with the pain and the indignity.

'Don't touch me. You and your stupid dig and your degree, pissy prehistory and geeky job, and poncing around the place like the batty professor. Damon is worth ten of you, and he's a useless piece of shit. Now fuck off. You *and* your brother.'

She stormed out of the bar. Out in the pub yard she let Rafferty out of the store shed where the dog had spent the evening lying on a pile of flatpack boxes. They disappeared into the night.

Kieran sat nursing his pride and his stinging face. Vin appeared through the bead curtain separating the bar from the kitchen.

'Still here, are you? Haven't you got no home to go to?'

NOVEMBER

SEVEN

The last few days of October trickled away, the nights lengthening dramatically and the light even at midday seeming as grey and filmy as old cobwebs. Rooks noisily debated in the bare trees.

The police withdrew from the site, leaving a sea of mud. The archaeologists returned and sadly picked over what remained. Another handful of coins was uncovered, fused amongst the fragments of the earthenware jar that had once contained them, but the meagreness of this remaining hoard only emphasized the imagined lustre of what was missing.

Katherine was in her office in London when Chris called her. He was in London too, he told her, showing the torc and the shield to interested experts. They agreed to meet for dinner that evening in an Italian restaurant. She shielded the phone handset as they spoke, conscious of her colleagues at the adjacent desks, surprised to find herself making these furtive arrangements even though she had longed for his call.

She hurried home first, to the small flat in Bloomsbury she and Amos had bought as a pied-à-terre following the move to Mead. She stood for a long time looking at herself in the bathroom mirror, wondering how a woman in the second half of her fifties prepared for an evening like this one. Her dating days had been short-lived, and were decades in the past. Her drawers

173

and cupboards contained what now looked like expensive camouflage – clothes to conceal ripples and bulges, to present a modest face to the world, to hide within. Plenty of taupe and black. Nothing gaudy or flamboyant or, God forbid, sexy. For a moment she played with the idea of calling Miranda for advice. But she already knew what Miranda would say.

'No, K, not a little black dress. Much too obvious.'

She opened her lingerie drawer, then catching on to the sub-text of her own imagining she slammed it shut again with her cheeks burning. This was all racing ahead of her, too fast, too eagerly. She should call him now and cancel. Definitely. She looked for her mobile.

Hesitating, with the phone in her hand, she thought a little harder.

It was unlikely that Chris would take very precise note of what she was wearing, given that he didn't seem to worry too much about his own clothes (North Face). It was only a dinner, and no promises had been made. Underwear was not yet and might never be relevant, so the absence of Agent Provocateur was not a crucial factor.

Besides, whatever she wore it would not make her beautiful, or sexy. Clothes were just clothing. She *felt* sexy tonight, there-fore she was. This last wanton thought made her smile, an unaccustomed slow beat of private amusement.

She put on scent, trousers, heels, a cashmere sweater. She was just doing up her coat (camel, MaxMara) when her phone rang. She reached for it. It would be him, of course. She hadn't changed her mind; he had.

'Hi, Mum.'

It was Sam, her elder son. He was the one who resembled her, whereas Toby took after Amos. She was close to both her boys, but they seemed lately to have floated off into a universe of work, peopled by friends she had never met, and sub-cultures and private languages that in no way touched on the family world.

'Dad told me you're down here. I thought you might like a drink or the cinema?'

'I would have done. But I'm having dinner with a friend.'

'Where are you meeting her?'

An obvious assumption. Katherine thought quickly. She'd better not mention the restaurant in case Sam breezily suggested looking in on them. Her mind went blank of any other of a million possible venues.

'Mum?'

She mumbled that they were meeting first at the British Museum (this coming to mind because Chris had told her it was where he would be this afternoon), and then they planned to find somewhere nearby.

'Are you all right?' Sam asked, after a pause.

It had been one tiny lie, but delivered with massive ineptitude. She was no good at this, she realized.

'Of course I am. Just in a hurry, darling. Shall I call you tomorrow?'

She was on her way. Katherine finished doing up her coat, walked out into the street and hailed a taxi. She felt that she might as well have been wearing a sign around her neck. A Woman on the Brink of Adultery.

Mead was a good winter house. With its low-set windows and thick walls it could be dark in summer, but as the year's sun and warmth sank away it seemed to settle on its haunches and happily turn inwards. Fires warmed the old chimney breasts, wood ash powdered the stone hearths, pools of yellow lamp light glowed in the rooms. Miranda always relished the point at which autumn dipped into winter. She ordered books from Amazon, piled up the cushions on her sofas and drew the curtains, preparing for her own version of hibernation.

'Are we Green or Mauby in this household?' Selwyn demanded on the same evening that Katherine and Chris met for dinner.

'*What?*'

A couple of days before, Selwyn and Polly had been talking to Vin Clarke in the Griffin.

He had told them the long history of the Fifth of November festival in Meddlett. Under Elizabeth I the area surrounding the village had been home to a number of devout Catholic families. The Lord Chamberlain at the time of Guy Fawkes had also been a local man, and following the discovery of the Catesby plotters in November 1605, fighting had broken out between the Lord Chamberlain's estate workers and supporters, and the sons and servants of Catholic families. One man from each side had been killed. Their names were Green and Mauby, and in the modern commemoration of the events, two men from the village, dressed up as their historic counterparts, took their places at the head of two ragged troops of followers and led them through the streets by a traditional route, rapping on doors as they passed to call out more followers.

Each year, by the time they reached the blazing bonfire most of the village and dozens of people from beyond would be dancing and singing in one or other of the groups. The mock battle that followed was supposed to be genteelly choreographed, but had occasionally been known to develop into something closer to a real fight. Over the years, the ferocity depended on which villagers and outside factions were currently opposing each other and how much drink they had consumed.

'Which one?' Selwyn repeated now. Polly looked up from her book. The three of them were sitting by the fire in Miranda's drawing room. Colin was away.

'Neither,' Miranda snapped.

'Must be one or the other,' Selwyn said reasonably. 'According to Vin in the pub, everyone around Meddlett knows which side they belong on. Like Montague and Capulet, Rangers or Celtic. You can't just pick a team, you have to have it in your blood.'

Polly's imagination had been caught by the publican's story, so she had looked up the background history. 'Rangers and Celtic is a better analogy because it was a religious divide,' she said. 'James the First's Lord Chamberlain of the time, the Earl of Suffolk, was one of the men who discovered the kegs of

176

gunpowder beneath the Palace of Westminster on the fifth of November.'

'Yes, that's right. Lockington was one of the earl's family estates,' Miranda put in.

Lockington was a nearby hamlet, no more than a cluster of estate cottages dominated by a fine hall rebuilt in the eighteenth century and now owned by the National Trust. The grounds were used for vintage car rallies and, unpopularly, for model aircraft flying days. The gnat's whine of circling models in still weather was sometimes audible at Mead.

Miranda knew the stories too. She folded her knees beneath her on the battered sofa.

'When the news of the conspiracy reached Norfolk, the Lockington men poured out of the fields, led by a man called Robert Green who was the earl's land manager and a fierce anti-Papist. The mob took their pikestaffs and converged on the homes of several known Catholic recusant families. They beat on the doors with their sticks until they either opened up or were broken down. Green's idea was to march all the Catholics to the green in Meddlett and force them to watch burning effigies of the Pope and Guy Fawkes and the conspirators, but the Catholics fought back. Women and children ran out to hide in the fields and hedges, the men blackened their faces and wrapped themselves in their cloaks so that neighbour couldn't recognize neighbour.'

Selwyn leaned across and lifted a log from the basket on the hearth.

Miranda drank some of her wine. 'There was a night of hand-to-hand fighting in the Meddlett lanes and alleyways. As the story goes, under cover of all this Green's son William was caught hiding in a hay barn with the daughter of John Mauby, a Catholic. She might have been with William by choice or under duress, but in any case the boy was dragged away and butchered. Before morning Mauby was dead too, murdered in retaliation.

'In the aftermath some of the Catholics fled the area

altogether, others went into hiding. The bitterness lasted for centuries. It's still with us, in one disguise or another, and the violence that bubbles up from time to time around here reflects that.'

Polly said, 'Ah, so there is a Montague and Capulet dimension as well. It's a bloodthirsty tale.'

Selwyn had listened to all this, lying back and tilting the red wine in his glass to catch the firelight glimmer.

'Jake's family, where did they stand? Pikestaffs or home guard?' he asked.

'The Meads were yeomen in those days, and converts to Anglicanism under Elizabeth. Always an eye to the main chance, Jake used to say.'

The log collapsed in the grate. Sparks flew up the chimney.

'Greens, then. Pity, in a way. I'd been drawn to the other side. Still, history dictates.'

Miranda raised an eyebrow at him.

'Tell me you're not planning to get involved in any of this.'

'I can't, because I am. More than that, I'd say it's absolutely not to be missed. From Vin's description.'

'But it's *horrible*. Dozens of boozed-up kids roaming the streets breaking windows and scratching cars, a kind of politically correct hog-roast parish fun unsuccessfully imposed on centuries of hatred and prejudice, police pretending to enter into the spirit of the night, and fireworks going off around your ankles. Vin Clarke's a publican, he sells beer. He's not going to tell you to stay at home, is he?'

Selwyn grinned in his piratical way. 'What's not to like?'

'Believe me. Lock the doors.'

'Mirry, why do you loathe this picturesque commemoration of our local history with such a passion?'

He sat up, bringing his face closer to her cheek, angling himself so that his knees nudged hers. Miranda immediately shifted away from him.

With her book resting on her lap, Polly watched the two of them. Selwyn was making up to Miranda, that would have been obvious to a blind man. What was in question was whether or not Miranda took him seriously. Polly knew him intimately and understood in detail how Selwyn was always grappling with his inborn twin demons of frustration and disillusionment. He leaped at any opportunity to divert himself. Miranda was one area of interest, naturally, and of course he was also going to enjoy a night of village anarchy. Even more so if it could be coupled with some mild teasing in the run-up. She turned her gaze to the fire.

She knew him and loved him because she did know him so well, everything about him, even his demons. Tonight she envisaged her love as something like a block of marble, too heavy to shift, impermeable, smooth and dense and veined with the compacted traces of shared experience. Even Miranda didn't know that. She wouldn't understand how complicated and weighty and yet how finely balanced her relationship with Selwyn was, and his with her.

No one could, who was not one of the two of them.

Miranda said composedly, 'I don't loathe it. It's an aspect of Meddlett that doesn't appeal, that's all. I love Mead, I don't have to be in love with its entire context.'

'I see,' Selwyn said.

Katherine didn't order a pudding; normally she liked puddings, the creamier the better, but this evening she was having difficulty in eating anything at all. She listened to what Chris said, or answered his questions, whilst her knife and fork lay forgotten. The waiter took away her main course almost untouched.

She drank instead. They finished a bottle of red wine between them and when the coffee arrived – she never usually drank coffee in the evening – she let Chris refill her glass from a second bottle. Wine made her talkative, in what she hoped was a good way. It wasn't turning out to be an unburdening sort of conversation – to her relief he didn't seem interested in trading the particulars of his marriage for hers,

179

or in touching on other disappointments – but rather a meandering process of discovering their affinities. She liked the way he described ordinary things. He told her about the corner shop where he had had his hair cut in preparation for this evening by an elderly Turkish man. As the barber trimmed and snipped he conversed gravely about world affairs, and when the time came to take Chris's money he accepted a five-pound note with a shrug and a tiny sigh, signifying that they were men, men of the world with serious matters to discuss, and the transfer of money was an unfortunate detail that they should not allow to interfere with their regard for each other.

Chris was an unaffected mimic. He made this small exchange come instantly to life.

'I really liked him. I want to go back and we'll put the Middle East to rights together. Maybe I'll get him to give me a hot-towel shave.'

'Don't do that,' Katherine said. 'I like the beard.'

He looked surprised, and then pleased. She didn't think he was used to women commenting on his appearance.

In exchange, she told him about the gay man who had been colouring her hair for the last fifteen years, and how even though she had never seen him outside the salon she probably knew more about the serial escapades and disasters in his life than she did about many of her friends'.

'The crimper's confessional,' Chris laughed. 'Sarah used to tell me about that.'

It was the only time he mentioned his ex-wife.

He poured more wine. They were bobbing along now on a gently alcoholic tide.

'I don't know why I'm telling you about my hairdresser,' Katherine smiled.

She was discovering that she could talk to him about anything and he would listen to her. The need to protect or present herself in any particular way melted, leaving her exposed. She recognized the exposure. She even welcomed it.

'I think I'm a bit drunk. Maybe that's the intention?' she asked slyly.

His intention or hers, it didn't seem necessary to specify which.

He took her hands in his, and turned them palms up.

If he tries to read my fortune or makes a joke about a bearded stranger I can still get my coat and leave, she told herself.

He didn't say anything, though. He was studying the inside of her wrists. With the shimmering confidence of tipsiness, she experienced a moment of undiluted happiness. The equilibrium was, as yet, perfect. She hadn't dangerously abandoned her inhibitions but she had forgotten her age, the necessity of guilt, and the problem of their uncertain intentions.

It felt delicious, to be sitting here, in the candlelight, with Chris holding her hands. She wondered if the waiters or the other diners could mistake them for a married couple.

No. Definitely not.

They smiled at each other through the nimbus of the candle flame. The restaurant was almost empty.

'Where now, Katherine?' he asked. 'I've enjoyed this evening. I feel like a child at the end of a birthday. I don't want it to be over.'

'Neither do I.'

Let's see, she thought. My place? Oh God, no, not back to the flat. New carpets, curtains, lampshades, all chosen and ordered and arranged by a *wife*. The domain of married people, even more so than in the cottage at Mead.

How *does* this all work? She had no idea. Surely Chris ought to have the next move planned, if anything more was going to happen? Amos would – of course Amos would, he'd had enough practice over the years. Yet she was sitting here holding hands with Christopher Carr precisely because he was so different from Amos. She couldn't have it both ways.

'Where are you staying?' she asked.

'With a friend. We were at university together, he's an archaeologist too. He's an unconventional person. I'm not sure I could wish Gerry's set-up on anyone, let alone you.'

181

Katherine imagined that Gerry would be a very late developer. Chris would sleep on the sofa bed in his living room and the place would be festooned with male clothing and sports equipment, something like Sam and Toby's flats in their middle student period.

They were new in this together, the two of them. She could take the initiative, if she wanted to, but when she tried out the words in her head she found that she still wasn't barefaced enough to suggest a hotel.

'Tell me, and I'll take you anywhere you like. Sailing down the Danube? Breakfast in Manhattan? The moon? Just say the word.' He seemed perfectly serious.

'None of those.' She drew in a breath. What the hell, again. 'We could go and have a last drink at our flat. It's near here.'

Our flat, that was the right touch. One glass of whisky, and she could still extricate herself by sending him back to Gerry's.

He pretended to consider, letting her know that it was only a pretence. 'I think that's a good idea. It's more accessible than the moon. I can make sure you're safely home, you can tell me to leave as soon after that as you want.'

The close echo of her thoughts made her blush and then laugh. He leaned across the table so their faces almost touched. 'I love your smile.'

He was unaffected enough to make this unambitious compliment sound like Shakespeare.

Katherine knew that Chris meant what he said. He was honest, and it was his honesty that made her open up to him like a cupboard that had been locked for years. I love *you*, she almost blurted, but she stopped herself in time.

It was a short cab ride. Seconds later, it seemed, she was fumbling with her key outside the flat. The cold air outside the restaurant had acted rather disconcertingly on her balance.

'There. Done it,' she murmured, as the door opened and they stepped inside.

What she was doing now was strange enough, and exciting enough, to switch off the stream of detached observations that

182

usually ran in her head. There was no lapse between thinking and doing.

Chris unbuttoned her coat, and she shed it. They negotiated two more steps along the hallway, and she kicked off a shoe with each. Kitchen to the left, living room to the right. He took her hand. It was as if they were dancing a slow waltz, utterly absorbed in the music. The streetlight shone as it always did through the living-room window, illuminating the lower half of the small but fine Howard Hodgkin that Amos had given her for her fiftieth birthday.

Damn. No more light. Keep the room in shadow. Better to inhabit a no-man's-land.

Two more steps. The cushions of the sofa pressed against her calves. It was easy to sit, imperative to continue this kiss.

They lay back. There was a slither of hands and skin, the various obstacles of buttons and folded cloth. Behind her head, on the sofa table between the lamp and the ivory statue of the Buddha that Amos had brought back from one of his Himalayan holidays, the telephone began to ring.

Chris lifted his head.

'I'm not going to answer it,' Katherine said.

The ringing seemed to go on for hours. At last the machine took it. After the message, Toby's voice filled the room.

'Mum, are you back yet? Your phone's off, and Sam said you sounded a bit weird. Pick up, Mum, if you're there, will you?'

Three or four seconds of silence followed.

'If we can't reach you, Mum, I'm going to come over.'

After another looming silence, her son hung up.

Katherine became aware of an undignified tangle of straps and rucked clothing. The weight of her sons' concern lay on her frontal lobes, gathering pressure like a headache. She shifted and Chris sat up at once. She saw his silhouette against the streetlamp.

'Excuse me,' he murmured.

He got up and went into the kitchen. She heard him running a tap and filling the kettle. She ran her fingers through her hair, straightened her clothing and stood up. She found Chris leaning thoughtfully against the sink. He had taken two mugs and placed them beside the kettle.

'You're married,' he said. There were layers of implication beneath the bare statement.

'I am married,' she agreed. The difference now was that up until a few days ago it hadn't been necessary to remark on it. It would have been like saying that the sea was watery.

The kettle boiled. She watched him as he found a teabag, opened the fridge for milk, made one mug of tea and left the other standing empty. He put the full mug carefully down on the counter nearest to her. Then he came and kissed her, to one side of her mouth.

'Call your son,' he said.

'I will.'

He stood back.

'I'll talk to you in a day or so. I enjoyed tonight more than any evening I can remember.'

That, too, she accepted as the truth.

'So did I.'

After he had gone she locked the front door and sat down with the mug of tea. The homeliness of it made a welcome link to him. She dialled Toby's number. He picked up on the first ring.

'Mum, you *are* there. What's going on?'

The anxiety in his voice cut into her. 'I was out having dinner, and now I'm back. I'm sorry you were worried about me, darling. There was no need to be. I'm quite safe.'

Already she was straying out of the territory of truth, and that was not with a stranger but her much loved son. Avenues of guilt yawned ahead, but she closed her mind to them for the time being. She heard herself saying yes, it had been a good meal. She was tired now, that was all.

Toby was reassured, although clearly puzzled by the tone of her voice.

'Yeah. Well, all right, if you're sure you're OK. 'Night, then.'

Katherine made a similar uncomfortable call to Sam.

Finally she switched on her mobile and glanced at the display. There were several missed calls from her sons, nothing else. The effect of the wine was rapidly wearing off. She would not, she told herself, most definitely *not*, be sending Chris a goodnight text. Suddenly, unexpectedly, she was laughing at herself. How old was she, fifty-something or fifteen? How good was it, to feel this young and silly?

The voice in her ear insisted, *You see? You are a person. You are not anyone's good or chattel.*

Still smiling, Katherine left her coat and shoes on the hall floor and went into her bedroom. Glancing at her open jewellery box, scent bottles, framed photographs, the door to the dressing room standing ajar, the gleam of polished wood, she thought vaguely that there was so much *stuff* here. The idea of the impending house was still more crowding. The as-yet theoretical granite and glass and polished concrete structure was waiting to be made solid, and then the further spaces within that unwelcome solidity that would have to be filled with interesting modernist furniture and judiciously chosen art, only to obliterate the patch of ground where ancient people had once buried their tribal leader.

'Bloody house,' she muttered. 'What do I want a new house for?'

She didn't want it. She would have to tell Amos so. In the morning, though. It could all wait until morning.

She tipped forwards on to the bed. The pillows were soft, and she was tired so she closed her eyes. Katherine fell asleep without cleansing her face, for the first time in at least thirty years.

'I'm going to London in the morning, remember. I'll need to take the car,' Polly said to Selwyn.

She had already told him that she was making a quick trip to see Ben. Alpha and Omega had both said that they were worried about their brother. There was never a shortage of

185

problems in Ben's life and it was not his way to make light of them, but the current crisis was a genuine one. His girlfriend Nicola had not only left him, but had physically disappeared. He had been crying so much when he explained this on the phone to his mother that he had had to stumble out of the magazine offices and stand in a doorway to talk.

Polly piled the supper dishes in a washing-up bowl. She had a bigger trestle table for a kitchen now, and there was a cold-water standpipe with a tap where the sink would eventually be. The rate of progress was rapid in the barn.

'Of course, take the car,' Selwyn said. He was on his knees measuring and marking lengths of planking salvaged from a demolition site. The waiting planks stood on end against one wall, like a haphazard shelter within their own not much more substantial house.

Selwyn was exhausted, Polly could tell that from the way his shoulders sagged. She wanted to kneel down and fold her arms around him but he wouldn't welcome that while he was working. She said on impulse, 'Won't you come with me? Ben needs a bit of sorting out. We could all of us have a couple of evenings together. Go to see a film and have a pizza, something cosy like that.'

Selwyn shook his head. 'Poll, I can't. I've got to get on with this. Why don't you bring Ben back with you for a few days? Miranda won't mind.'

Polly put down a handful of cutlery. It clattered faintly on top of the tools left on the trestle table. 'Why would Miranda mind? This is our house. We can do what we like in it.'

He didn't look up. 'I know that. What's the matter?'

'Nothing.'

'When will you be back?'

'I don't know yet. Two, three days, perhaps?'

She scooped up the cutlery once more and carefully dried it, then stowed it piece by piece in a clean jam jar. Selwyn finished his measuring and stood upright, hands pressed flat to the small of his back.

'That long? You'll miss the Fifth.'

'I'd like to be there. I expect it will be the same next year, though, and plenty of years to come.' The way he stood turned aside, not looking at her, ignited a spark of jealous irritation in Polly. She said in a sharp voice that was unlike her, 'Anyway, you'll be able to go with Miranda, won't you?'

Selwyn let his steel measuring tape snap back into its casing. He didn't say anything.

The evening of the Fifth was overcast, damp and chill with spits of rain in the air. In Meddlett village the foggy air was thick with the sulphurous smell of gunpowder and the acrid stink of burning car tyres.

Miranda was sitting at the kitchen table reading the newspaper. Engrossed, she shouted, 'Come in,' when someone banged on the back door. When she did look up she screamed.

'Good, eh?' Selwyn said.

He was dressed up in a rough hooded cloak made from a couple of the sacks that Miranda's logs were delivered in. His face was blackened.

'For God's sake. What's that on your face?'

'Burned cork. It's called entering into the spirit of things. Come on, aren't you ready?' Selwyn shook the leather pouch that hung from a strap across his chest. 'I've got Chinese firecrackers. Very unhealthy and totally unsafe. A bloke was selling them out of his van in the Griffin car park. Roaring trade. I was lucky to get these.'

'You are insane,' Miranda said. The face blacking made his eyes and teeth glimmer at her. She wanted to kiss him, as if that would enable her to absorb some of his wild vitality.

Selwyn went to look at himself in the mirror in the downstairs lavatory, then came back again.

'Where the hell's Amos? Let's go.'

'I'm not coming. Which part of that don't you understand?' She was laughing in spite of herself.

There was more thudding on the back door. Miranda sighed.

Amos was wearing a black ski parka with the hood up. He was carrying a fence pole.

'I thought this would do as a pikestaff. Are we ready?'

Selwyn took the newspaper from Miranda and laid it aside. He put his hands to her elbows and helped her to her feet. He murmured in her ear.

'Please come, Barb. Vin told me, only people who live in the parish can officially walk in one or other of the processions. And if you can, you should, don't you think? If Amos and I, even you, don't identify ourselves with the place we'll never belong to it.'

Amos was surprised. 'And I thought it was just about letting off a few fireworks.'

'I've been here for twenty years. I don't have to bend over backwards to belong,' she protested.

But then Miranda looked into Selwyn's eyes. He had already won her over. She wanted that sense of belonging here to be branded right through him. 'All right. Just for an hour.'

The car park at the Griffin was crammed, and the green was a surging mass of people, most of them in costume. Police cars were parked at both ends of the street and several grimly smiling policemen threaded through the mob.

A hot dog stand and a fish and chip van competed against each other via the sweat-scent of fried onions and the greasy stench of boiling fat. Smoke billowed overhead and rockets shrieked skywards, shooting powdery trails of sparks into the air. Screaming children in toyshop masks ran between people's legs. Surges of singing and taunting swept through the Green and Mauby contingents massed on opposite sides of the duck pond.

The Greens swelled around their figurehead, a fat man dressed in breeches and a jerkin. Their pikestaffs bristled through the smoke like a forest of ravaged trees. They were chanting, *Here's health to our King, boys, for he shall not be forgot*. Amos and Selwyn skirted the edge of the pond to join them, slithering in the scum of weed, mud and greasy chip papers. Miranda pulled her hat over her ears and shrank backwards against the sheltering wall of the Griffin.

The Mauby crowd massed around a younger, thinner man. His white shirt stood out in contrast to his thoroughly blackened face and throat. His supporters yelled out, *Poor Guy went to the wall, the wrong house but the right idea to end the Commons brawl.* Miranda remembered these were the words to a Jethro Tull song. This was a new addition to the rituals of the Fifth.

A huge rocket screamed from the car park and exploded into a canopy of stars and coloured balls. It was the signal for the Greens and the Maubys to begin their separate winding routes through the village streets. The singing grew louder and the crowd jostled to watch as the hooded men streamed away. Amos tugged at Selwyn's sleeve.

'See that?' he shouted.

There was a third, smaller group gathered at the far end of the pond, framed by the bare trailing arms of weeping willows. A full-sized Hallowe'en skeleton was hoisted on a pole and its plastic bones did a macabre dance as torches wove a skein of lights around it. Banners and placards waved in the air.

The Meddlett People's Princess, they declared. *Save our Heritage, Honour our History. No to the Grave Robbers and No to the BM.*

Two or three of these people were dressed in what passed for prehistoric garb, mostly tattered skirts and throws held together with rope and leather belts. Selwyn's teeth glimmered in a wide grin. He turned to look for Miranda, and caught sight of the pale half-moon of her face. She too was staring across at the skeleton.

Ahead of the Green men a sudden fusillade of firecrackers spat and zigzagged scarlet through the darkness like a dozen demented snakes. The column of men zigzagged too, banging on the locked and bolted doors of every weekend cottage lining the lane.

189

'Open up in the King's name,' they shouted. 'Here's health to our King, boys, for he shall not be forgot.'

Amos and Selwyn had joined the rush of men.

'This is utterly mad,' Amos yelled, jumping away from a rogue snake as it fizzled over his boots. Selwyn was groping in the recesses of his leather bag. He pulled out a firecracker and lit it.

Miranda realized that there was no possibility of going home yet – the green and the roads leading to it were now so packed that it was impossible to move. She watched the princess people and their skeleton's marionette dance. They were handing out leaflets to the largely uninterested crowd and she wondered uneasily if the protestors might turn up at Mead and picket Amos's house. There wouldn't be much point, she decided with a renewed flash of outrage at the theft, since there was nothing left there. They might as well go and demonstrate outside the police station for the rapid return of the stolen goods, or picket Christopher Carr's offices until he handed them back the torc and the shield. Perhaps then they could put them on display in the shop, would that be local enough?

Through the windows of the pub she could see Vin Clarke passing a steady stream of sloppy pints over the bar. Out here there were a lot of young people, hooded and studded, with a touch of the Goth about them. They were drinking cider, jeering at their friends and letting off bangers. Cigarette smoke hung around them in a heavy pall, mingling with the chip fat and fried onions.

A hand descended on her arm.

'Good evening, Miranda.'

She turned to see the vicar. He was a patient, pedestrian man who had long ago stopped saying that he hoped to see her in church next Sunday. They exchanged shouted pleasantries about the size of the crowd and the progress of the processions. A scuffle amongst the Goth teenagers sent several of them cannoning backwards, crashing into Miranda and colliding with the vicar.

'Steady on,' he remonstrated. He took Miranda's arm. 'Come on down to the barbecue field with me.'

Miranda hesitated. If she went down to the barbecue field that would give her the best chance of meeting up with Selwyn again, since the procession routes ended there.

Over their heads another huge firework exploded in a chrysanthemum of falling fire. Fundraising for the Fifth celebrations went on all year round in Meddlett. Miranda always sent a cheque.

'Yes, of course I'll walk down with you,' she said.

He beamed at her. 'Good, good. Well done.'

They struck out together through the swaying mass.

One of Meddlett's back lanes was no more than a cobbled passage that threaded between overhanging walls. As they surged through this stone bottleneck the Green men began to run in earnest, rattling their sticks on the walls. Amos was carried forwards, breaking into a trot with all the others because he was afraid that otherwise he might stumble and be trampled underfoot. As he hurtled past a cottage window he glimpsed three young children, half hidden by the folds of a curtain, staring out at the procession that had now become a mob. The village's past, hunters and hunted, seemed trapped in the alley too, thick as the smoke. Down here the original Green and his men would have rampaged, watched by terrified women and children. He felt their presence all around him.

Selwyn had let off one gratifying firecracker but he had quickly seen that it was too dangerous in the confined space between the stone cottages. He put his head down, secured the leather strap of his bag across his chest, and concentrated on keeping his footing on the uneven cobbles. There was a street-light on the corner of the alley and the beam shone briefly on his face as he passed beneath it. To his relief they soon swung out into a wider road. Here was a broad grass verge and the fences and hedges of a row of gardens. Spectators were milling on either side as the costumed men poured past with their staves held aloft.

One group was a little detached from the others. They had staked out a redoubt under the twisted branches of a big old oak tree. They were young, and like the Goths outside the Griffin they had bottles of cider and cans of beer. They were laughing at the procession as it slowed up and spread across the road. Traditional taunts were exchanged and a black dog yelped hysterically from the kerb.

Selwyn couldn't see Amos anywhere. The dog was barking at his knee.

The Hallowe'en skeleton danced on its pole a few yards away. The small group of protesters, most of them now visible as middle-aged women or elderly men, had taken a shorter route towards the church field and were emerging into the road at an angle to the Greens' progress.

'Look at them lot,' a voice jeered.

'Fuckin' ridiculous,' someone else called.

'Let 'em off, Damesy. Let 'em 'ave it.'

Selwyn heard that. Seconds later there was a hiss and a banshee wail, then a crackle of fire as several fireworks exploded from beside the oak tree. The dog howled and a boy yelled, 'Shut up, Raff. It's *fireworks*.'

'*No to the grave robbers. No to the BM.* And no to all fuckin' losers and their sad little signs,' a boy guffawed from inside a hoodie.

Headed by the sprightly skeleton, the third procession was heading away. Selwyn glimpsed substantial backsides, sober anoraks, even a knitted bobble hat or two. He half-turned to the fireworks crew, feeling more solidarity with their noise and jeering and intending to give them a thumbs' up, or something of the kind.

The next thing he knew was a point of red light, some confused shouting, then a rush of heat and stink of gunpowder. He had a split-second's certainty that he had been shot. Sparks fizzled and there was a sickening *whoosh* as his head seemed to catch fire. He collapsed to his knees, hands up to the hood of his makeshift cloak. There was a hideous smell of singeing hair.

Selwyn slapped at his head with his bare hands. The smell and the red glare of the rocket branded into his retinas convinced him that he was ablaze. He needed to beat out the flames, so he threw himself to the ground. His next thought was for the heavy bag, slung from his shoulder, the strap threatening to choke him. He wrestled it off and hurled it away from him, filled with terror at the idea of twenty cheap Chinese fire-crackers exploding next to his chest. Hearing his own thin wail of terror, he rolled over and over in the dank grass.

He closed his dazzled eyes, saw a fierce crimson star, opened them again on revolving, greenish darkness. There was no burning, no expected rush of pain. He lay absolutely still, like a dead man.

His vision slowly returned. Three or four pairs of legs appeared in his line of sight. Two pairs concertinaed as the owners crouched down beside him. Hands descended on his shoulders, pulled at the charred remains of the hood.

'He's all right, I think.'

'Can you sit up for me, dear?'

Selwyn let them hoist him into a sitting position. His right temple and his ear began to throb dangerously.

Amos reached the gate to the church field in the vanguard of the Green men. The tail end of the Mauby contingent was dawdling in, and the two streams mingled, teasing and jostling each other. He stepped to one side, wishing that Selwyn would catch up so he might joke with him about the smoke in the alley, and a momentary, clearly mentally deranged impression he had had of terrified hidden watchers behind the windows of the old houses, and throngs of other silent figures mingling in their procession.

He was rather sharply aware that there was no one else except Selwyn for him to look out for. In the weeks he had lived here he hadn't met anyone who actually came from Meddlett.

There was a bonfire in the middle of the field, a sheet of brisk flames with the dark figure of a guy collapsing into its heart. People eddied around it, driven into a circle by the glaring heat. On the left against the hedge stood a row of tented booths selling food and drink, in the farthest corner a huge barbecue pit and a roast pig's carcass was tended by professional caterers, and the thick crowds of people in between occupied themselves with paper plates heaped with food, and plastic beakers of drink. Pushchairs contained sleeping toddlers. Bigger children on the brink of exhausted tantrums ran about while their parents sat down to eat and drink on hay bales arranged in sociable groups.

Amos felt rather out of it. He couldn't remember what Miranda had said she was going to do. He decided to see if there was anything half decent to eat or drink. Katherine was away, so he might as well forage for some dinner here. He parked his fence pole against the hedge, beside some of the makeshift banners saying *No*.

The first tent was an outpost of the Griffin. At the doorway he looked again for Selwyn. A pair of hands clapped over his eyes.

'Hi,' a girl's voice said in his ear. A pair of breasts nudged against his back, which cancelled out his irritation at being forcibly blindfolded.

'Who is this?'

She had slim wrists and small, strong hands, whoever she was. He lifted them away from his face and turned to see.

'Hi?' she said, somewhat less confidently. 'You knocked me off my bike. I'd have thought you'd remember that.'

He did have one acquaintance in Meddlett, he remembered.

'I didn't knock you off your bike. I swerved to avoid you, thus in all probability saving you from serious injury.'

Jessie snorted. 'I've never ever met a person who really, actually in the flesh, uses words like *thus*.'

'You lead quite a restricted life, then.'

She grinned up at him. Under a short dark-coloured coat she was wearing several haphazard layers of clothing that gaped open to reveal the rather substantial cleavage and a few fronds of the evidently much larger tattoo. He wondered what the complete design might be.

'I bloody well do. D'you want to buy me a drink, Amos?'

He was flattered that she remembered his name. She had already had several drinks, that was quite clear, but he let her take his arm and draw him into the grassy hum of the pub tent. He bought her a vodka with Red Bull, whatever that was, and a large whisky for himself.

'Ta,' Jessie said. She drank half of hers at a gulp, then stood on tiptoe to give him a voluptuous kiss on the lips. He was quite sorry when it ended. She downed the remainder of her vodka and stroked the corner of her mouth with the back of her hand.

'I really liked your car. I thought it was beautiful. Will you take me for a proper ride in it?'

'Do you want another of those? Is that an, um, professional question?'

'You're *fucking* rude. Are you trying to suggest I'm a prozzer?'

He said cautiously, 'No, just aiming to establish the parameters.'

Now her eyes rolled. 'Here we go again. Parameters? I'll have that other drink, though. Cheers.'

They took their plastic beakers outside and found themselves a hay bale in the sheltering darkness. The bonfire was big enough to give the illusion if not the reality of warmth. Amos felt that the unpromising evening was looking up dramatically. Jessie hooked up her knees, rested her chin on them and scanned the crowd.

She told him that she had just worked a ten-hour shift at the Griffin, straight through lunch to dinner orders, and finally that slave-driver Vin Clarke had said she could go at nine o'clock. So she had come down here because her ex – that world-class wanker, by the way – had promised he'd bring the dog down here and hand him over, after he'd kept him quiet indoors while all the fireworks were going off.

'He bloody hates fireworks, Raff does. He goes mental.'

'I'm waiting for my friend Selwyn. We got separated in the procession.'

'Is he one of you lot from the commune?'

'Do I look as if I live in a commune?'

She rolled her head sideways and assessed him.

'When were they in? You look and talk like you live in the century *before* last, if you really want to know.'

Amos laughed. The girl's company was invigorating. She was very young and careless, and that appealed to him.

Jessie was a lively talker. From their vantage point on the hay bale she identified the people who shuffled into the tent and came out again with their liberal supply of drinks. Some of them she greeted, mostly with a jerk of the chin and a muttered, 'All right?' Then, out of the side of her mouth, she gave Amos the details. One balding man had had a series of Brazilian girlfriends, all of them met on the internet and brought over, as Jessie put it, scratching her index fingers in the air, as 'servants slash sex toys'. A woman in a green Husky had had a 'big ruck' with her neighbour over a boundary dispute, and had ended up pouring a gallon of petrol into the neighbour's garden shed and then setting fire to it. The house itself had almost gone up in flames.

'Two fire engines,' Jessie grinned. 'And Mrs Hayes was arrested.'

This woman now shared a probation officer with a boy Jessie used to go out with before Damon, who had sold a bit of weed, the odd wrap, nothing too ambitious; the trouble was he was just too thick to avoid getting caught. She knew a load of other people who were bigger time, and they never got any bother.

Amos said in surprise, 'And I thought it was so quiet here. As if nothing ever happens except harvest festival.'

There was a band set up on a hay wagon and people were beginning to dance, Greens with Maubys. He was thoroughly enjoying these new perspectives on Meddlett, which had up until now seemed a rather dull place for country bumpkins.

Jessie jerked her chin. 'You incomers always think the same. As if it's all green fields and divine views and bollocks like that. But people live their lives here, all kinds of lives, same as anywhere else. There are safe ones, and there are totally crap individuals. The only difference is we don't have much choice about being here. We have to get on with it. We can't go off and get ourselves a weekend cottage in Notting Hill, can we?'

Amos saw the yearning behind her narrowed eyes.

'Don't you have a choice, Jessie?'

'Oh, yeah.' She sat up straighter, rejecting his sympathy.

A pair of jeans topped by a cagoule stopped in front of them. Jessie said coldly, raising her voice over the blare of distorted music, 'You again? What do you want? Can't you see I'm talking to someone?'

The wearer obviously could see, but came another step closer just the same. Amos recognized the junior archaeologist with the dreadlocks and difficult skin who had been so officious on the site. Remembering names tended to be a problem nowadays, but somehow he dredged this one up. Kieran, that was it. The boy nodded an anxious greeting at him. To Jessie he muttered, 'Can we have a word? I've got a bone to pick with you.'

'Ha ha. Is that your little archaeology joke?'

'You know what it's about. It's why you've been avoiding me, isn't it?'

'You can find me in the bloody Griffin, any time you want.'

In an undertone Kieran said, 'I'm not dragging all this out in the pub. But I want to know once and for all. It *was* you, wasn't it?'

Amos was interested. Unfortunately, good manners got the better of him. 'I'll go and find myself another drink,' he said.

As he stood up, he saw Miranda.

She was ten yards away, closer to the bonfire, penned in by

197

a knot of princess protesters. Her hands were dug in her pockets and her shoulders were defensively hunched.

'Is there a problem?' he murmured in her ear, as soon as he reached her.

'This is Mr Knight. He's the owner of the site,' she told them. 'Thank God you're here,' she whispered back.

He listened. These earnest people seemed to think that he and Miranda were to blame for the loss of the princess's remains, first of all to the faceless bureaucracy of the museums, as they put it, and then for the theft by vandals of what remained.

Amos towered over them. He began, magisterially, to explain the planning and treasure laws.

Confused shouting interrupted him, followed by a scream rising over the music. Amos turned to see what was going on.

Jessie was at the heart of a scrum of people. The girl was definitely trouble. She was kneeling with her arms around her black dog. The animal was shaking and whimpering, its black coat drenched with sweat as she stroked it and whispered in its ear.

Over and around her three men were scuffling, dragging and pulling at each other's clothes, swinging wild punches and tripping over their feet and the hay bale. Another girl was hauling at the nearest man, trying to pull him away. She was tiny, and when he lunged forwards she sailed with him, her feet bumping like a rag doll's.

One of the men was Kieran, and he was clearly outnumbered. He raised his arms to protect his face as punches rained on his head. Amos broke away from Miranda and the protesters. Onlookers were now tentatively trying to break up the fight.

'He's got a knife,' the girl shrieked. Several people swerved aside. At the outer margins parents hustled their children away.

Jessie jumped up. She held the dog on a short leash. She swung her free arm in a wide arc, smacking one of the other two men. She kicked the second for good measure. To the third, Kieran, she bellowed, 'Go on, piss off out of here while you can walk.'

Amos reached them. He hauled Kieran aside and interposed himself between the others.

Amos said quietly, 'If anyone's carrying a knife, I advise you to get away from here right now and dispose of it.'

He must have summoned the right blend of threat and authority, because the two men and the girl immediately slipped past the onlookers and vanished into the dark. To Kieran, Jessie hissed, 'And you. You better stay at your mum's tonight.'

Amos released him. Kieran walked quickly in the opposite direction from the others, looking at no one.

'That's it. All over,' Amos announced to the spectators. The alarm was rapidly mutating into excitement and curiosity. People shuffled into buzzing groups. The music throbbed more wildly as the band attempted 'Mustang Sally'.

Jessie returned to soothing her shivering dog.

'You were pretty good,' she conceded to Amos.

'You were better. I wouldn't like to go fifteen rounds with you,' he replied. He was impressed by her courage. Jessie was trouble, but interesting trouble.

Miranda reached Amos's side. Her eyes were dark hollows of alarm in her white face.

'Are you all right? Both of you?'

'Damon took my dog out in the fireworks. Look at him,' Jessie cried to her.

Amos and Miranda exchanged a look.

'Is that what it was all about?' Amos asked. 'One of those two was your ex-boyfriend?'

Jessie frowned. She was a small, dark, spiky bundle.

'Never mind,' she spat out. 'Here, Rafferty. Come on, Raff.' She nuzzled her face against his soaking flank.

The princess protesters had gathered in Miranda's wake. Two wilting No placards stuck out at angles, and they seemed to have acquired the vicar as an extra. One of the costumed men strode forward, twitching his skins and hemp skirts around his mud-caked calves as the vicar peeled away and began benignly to circulate amidst his parishioners.

'I take your point,' the Iron-Age tribesman continued to Amos, as if they were sitting in some committee room. 'However, the fact is that these remains historically belong to the people of Meddlett. There are precedents, if I may draw your attention . . .'

He became aware that he didn't have Amos's full attention, or Miranda's.

Across the grass, passing the bonfire that was sinking into a mass of embers, came Selwyn. One side of his head was covered by a huge sterile dressing, held in place by a white turban bandage.

EIGHT

Polly sat on the modishly battered brown leather sofa at Alpha's east London flat, watching her two girls prepare supper. They were waiting for Ben to turn up. He had told his mother that he really, really needed to see her, because talking on the phone just wouldn't be good enough, yet he hadn't quite managed to get there at the time he had suggested.

Alpha and Omega sidestepped between the sink and the fridge, like one individual with four hands, wordlessly passing the chopping knife or the colander. In the big kitchen of their old house Polly had taught them how to bake and make casseroles, and now their enthusiasm for cooking outstripped hers. The girls usually gave her chefs' glossy hardback books for birthday and Christmas presents, but Polly didn't read recipes in bed these days. Even if there had been a decent light to see by, she would have been too tired to keep her eyes open.

Omega was complaining that she still hadn't met Jaime, Alpha's new boyfriend, and did Polly think it might be because Alph was trying to *shield* him from her family in some weird way?

'It's so not right to keep us in the dark. I mean, where is he tonight?'

'He's working. You'll meet him soon,' Alpha said, not rising to the bait. 'Tonight's about Ben, anyway.'

The girls exchanged glances. Ben had insisted that he wanted to tell his mother the news himself.

Polly tried to concentrate on what the twins were saying. The flat overlooked a busy road, and the room densely contained the noise of traffic. The oversized plasma screen on one wall silently flashed *EastEnders*, and some repetitive music chipped out of hidden speakers. In the end Selwyn had needed the car to pick up some tiles, so she had made a difficult train journey that involved a bus link to circumnavigate emergency works, and then a rush-hour transfer from the main line station to the Tube station nearest to Alpha's flat, which wasn't all that near.

When the doors opened and the mass of people spilled on to the platform, Polly was carried off the Tube, struggling with her shoulder bag and overnight case, her scalp damp and itching. People jostled at her back and she heard their sighs and clicks of irritation at the impediment. She had experienced a moment of pure panic. She had become too slow, too heavy and altogether too weary to cope with this city.

All her life, Polly had been used to speed: to thinking quickly, moving faster than her children, and manoeuvring Selwyn without letting on that she was doing so. Yet now, having once been the fertile source of so much energy, her body seemed to be solidifying into a block of dimpled lard. The bones that had once been hard under layers of plump satiny skin now seemed to be melting away. All that was left was fat. Her breasts stuck out painfully and she hunched her shoulders to protect them.

At the barrier she was trapped again, the pressure building at her back as she searched her pockets for her ticket. Her overnight bag was kicked sideways by flying people diverting past her into the snapping jaws of adjacent gates. As she stooped to retrieve it she briefly entered a nightmarish subworld of legs and skidding feet, sodden newsprint, stabbing heels. Finally, the ticket located, she bundled her new bruises and her luggage through the barrier and out into the street. Damp softened the dazzle of shops and traffic, splintered reflections shone out of puddled gutters. The air out here was mercifully cold and Polly sucked it into her lungs. She rested against the window of a tobacconist's shop.

She felt lost in the welter of traffic and careless passers-by. Apparently she couldn't hold her own any longer in London, and at the same time she felt crowded out of Mead. Selwyn's obsession with the building work, and Miranda's passion for the place coupled with her grand scheme for their life there combined to diminish Polly's own stake in it.

Miranda won't mind. Selwyn's unthinking words about their children coming to visit chafed her even now. She wanted to feel at home at Mead: she had embraced the idea of the move, even encouraged Selwyn to see it as a solution to their money problems, but already the ideal of companionship and support was mutating into a much lonelier, less utopian reality.

In the old days she had been at the centre of a small world. She felt a spasm of extreme longing for her old house in Somerset, and with it sadness for the loss of her children's youth.

All that's *gone*, she told herself briskly. Moreover, the same thing happens to every mother. Maybe not the part about being broke and having to sell up, but moving from the centre to the margins of a family, that was a voyage more inevitable than any physical retreat from the shelter of four beloved walls.

We have to find a new way to live, and that's exactly what Sel and I are in the process of doing, she continued. We have chosen Mead, and we will make it work.

A man came out of the shop, stripping the cellophane off a pack of cigarettes and glancing curiously at her as he did so. Polly immediately collected herself. She picked up her bags and began to walk slowly, against the gritty flow of traffic, towards Alpha's.

Now she was here she perched on the squeaky leather sofa, drinking wine too quickly, resisting the urge to let her head fall back against the cushions. She would have given anything to close her eyes for a few minutes.

'Mum?'

Alpha and Omega were staring at her.

Polly glanced down and noted splinters of wood trapped in the fuzzy fibres of her grey jumper. She picked at them, but they were embedded. This morning, rummaging in the half-light amongst her belongings, she had pulled out a pair of black boots that she had judged quite serviceable for two days in London. Now she saw that the leather was cracked and the uppers were rimmed in mud.

'What?'

'Mum, you look really tired.'

The entryphone gave its double chime.

'Here's Ben, at last,' Alpha said.

Polly brushed aside their double concern. 'I'm fine. The barn's turning out to be a bigger job than I expected, that's all.'

Ben came in, the picture of gloom, burdened with a bicycle wheel and two panniers. He shed a helmet and a pump and peeled off his anorak with reflector stripes. Polly heaved herself to her feet and Ben tramped across to her, the cleats of his cycle shoes rattling on Alpha's wooden floor. He had stopped shaving and his face was fluffed with fronds of hair. He submitted to his mother's embrace.

'How are you, Benjy? Have you heard from Nic yet?'

'Yeah. A text.'

'Thank goodness. How is she?'

Ben held up his hand to his sisters. 'Mum, it's not that simple.'

Polly stared at him. As soon as the suspicion entered her mind it smouldered and then blazed into certainty.

'She's pregnant, isn't she?'

Ben gave a gusty sigh and collapsed on the sofa. His jaw descended on to his chest.

'She was. I don't know if she still is or not. I don't even know where she is, she won't tell me. Mum, how am I supposed to cope with potentially being a dad if she won't have anything to do with me?'

Over his head Polly glanced at Alpha and Omega. They gave her the old what-shall-we-do-with-Ben look, only now with less amusement and a sharper edge of adult concern.

204

A baby?

Polly admired what she had seen of Nicola. She seemed a calm, rather self-contained girl, necessarily independent because she was effectively motherless. She might well have decided to keep her baby, Polly guessed, and her disappearance seemed to accord with that. She could understand her wanting to remove herself from Ben's orbit while she took stock of her situation.

A *baby* . . .

It would be Ben's child, as well as Nic's. The dawning realization forced a change of perspective, from yearning for the past to looking into the future, and it braced Polly. Often enough she had imagined her twins becoming mothers, Omie with her reliable Tom, even Alph, for all her colourful love life about which Polly suspected she heard only a fraction. But not Ben, her own baby.

She reached for his hand and squeezed it.

'I can understand why you're worried. But you know, I think if Nic has decided to keep the baby, she'll want to involve you in the end.'

He sighed again. 'Will she? I mean, what will I have to *do*?'

'I don't know. That depends on Nic,' she told him. 'But one thing I do know, whatever it is we'll deal with it.'

Ben looked a little more cheerful. 'Thanks, Mum.'

'Can I tell Dad about this?'

He twitched one shoulder. 'S'pose so,' he muttered.

Polly didn't think that Selwyn would welcome the immediate prospect of becoming a grandfather. It would make him feel old.

'I'm so glad I've told you,' Ben added, brightening. 'I made Alph and Omie promise not to breathe a word until I got the chance. I've been really bugged about what you might say.'

'We told him you'd be totally understanding, Mum,' Alpha put in.

'And they were right, you're as good as you always are. I do love you,' Ben said sweetly. He wound an arm around Polly's neck and kissed her, just like he used to do when he was a toddler.

Alph and Omie put the food on the table and they sat down to eat. Polly wished that Selwyn had come to London with her, so that he could have shared this family meal. She covered up for his absence by telling the three of them about his furious progress in the barn, making it comical, making them laugh.

As soon as they had eaten, Ben announced that he was going to have to dash. His editor had asked him to write up a gig for the review page of the magazine.

'Do you really have to?' Polly asked.

'Yeah. It's a nu-rave night,' he added helpfully. 'Two hundred words. That's good, isn't it?'

'Well done,' agreed Polly.

She walked with him to the doors of the lift. Longing to talk some more about Nic and the baby, she asked if he could perhaps meet her for lunch. Ben looked perplexed, but then agreed vaguely that yes, tomorrow, maybe that would be a good plan.

Polly helped the twins to clear the dinner plates. The bike wheel had left a black smudge on the white wall.

'Are you really all right, Mum? You do look a bit sad,' Omie said. 'Is it because of Benj?'

Polly wondered how much to admit to. She didn't want to burden them with her dim, pessimistic misgivings about Mead.

She smiled. 'I'm fine. But it's a bombshell, Ben's news, isn't it? Thinking about a baby makes me miss the days when you were little.' This was an elision, but it contained a seam of truth.

Alpha clapped her hands. 'I know, let's look at the photos.'

'What, now?' Polly wasn't sure whether she wanted to suffer the pain-pricks of a trip down memory lane. Omega seized on the idea, however.

'Oh, *yes*. When we were little.'

The intimation of another generation affected them, too. They weren't quite ready, yet, to say goodbye to their own childhood.

Alpha fetched her iBook. Characteristically she had digital-ized the Davies photo archive so it was available at a click.

206

Equally characteristically Omega kept her pictures pasted between the floral covers of a Cath Kidston album.

They settled at the screen, their heads close together. Their mingled scent was of sweet perfumes, hair products, a faint hint of smoke.

They looked at the pictures of sandy children shivering and grinning underneath towels and beside windbreaks. There were tents pitched in the field behind the old house, reminders of games of cricket, picnics, birthday parties, dogs and kittens, adults asleep on sofas on Christmas afternoons, gappy smiles followed by versions in which new teeth appeared too large for childish faces. There were teenagers with attitude in every line of their bodies and outfits, gap-year hobos, and graduation portraits. Mostly, the pictures could have belonged to any family of a certain type in the last quarter of the twentieth century.

Polly noted that their lives as captured seemed to have been one long celebration.

Missing altogether were any of the darker moments, including the successive deaths of four grandparents. The appearances of the older generation simply grew less frequent and then one by one petered out altogether, as if they were still absent-mindedly loitering just out of shot instead of having made their final departure. The past was preserved as a hymn to conventional happiness and it was left to the observer to murmur the counterpoint.

For this reason one picture caught Polly's attention.

She put her fingers on Alpha's wrist, delaying the next click of the mouse.

Their first summer in the house, Selwyn hammered together a rough timber arbour in the garden and Polly planted a golden hop to scramble over it.

In this photograph, a wooden trestle table and benches were drawn up under the shady arbour. The table was covered with a blue checked cloth and a dozen wine bottles stood amongst a clutter of plates and glasses and the debris of a Sunday lunch.

Polly was sitting at the far end of the table, a straw hat tipped back from her face. Ben sat beside her in his highchair, a winsome mass of blond curls. Alpha and Omega loomed in the foreground, two peas mugging for the camera, all stretched mouths and stuck-out tongues.

'I love this one. Don't we look sweet?'

'I think we look quite annoying.'

Katherine sat in profile, her hair casually drawn up in a way that revealed her long throat and delicate jaw. She had been beautiful, back then. She was listening with a serious face to something Jake was telling her. It was right at the beginning of Jake and Miranda, maybe even the first time she had introduced him to the group. Miranda herself was just visible, on the opposite side of the frame from the twins, a cloud of dark hair and a thin crescent of pale cheek like a new moon. Her gesticulating hand was a blur, as was the figure of little Toby Knight, caught in the act of squirming down to escape from the table. The back of Amos's head, thatched with thick hair, was turned to the camera.

The central places were taken by Colin and Stephen. They looked freakishly well turned out, in pale linen jackets and expensive shirts, and there was a suggestion of detachment about both of them. Stephen's fingers caressed the stem of his glass, Colin's eyes seemed to be on him. Selwyn had taken the picture.

Polly was pregnant. No one knew except Selwyn. She had miscarried a few days later, at thirteen weeks. The dark memory ran counter to this sunny snapshot of lunch in the country.

She also worked out that this was most probably the occasion that had marked the beginning of the break-up of the old group.

Sam and Toby Knight were boisterous boys and they had spent the whole day fighting each other and the Davies children. The twins had whined and cried and demanded attention. Amos and Selwyn had both drunk too much. Polly remembered clearly that Stephen had been fastidiously polite for the whole weekend visit, but she hadn't had a moment of Colin to herself, which was what she craved.

There was never a serious falling out, or even a real disagreement that she could remember. Selwyn and Amos had always sparred but they also colluded in the way that men did, taking each other's declarations of success and satisfaction with life at face value, in exchange for the same courtesy. What actually happened was that Miranda and Jake gradually withdrew to Mead, and Colin and Stephen lived in a way that was increasingly unfathomable to married straight people. Children or childlessness came between the four couples.

It was left to the three women and Colin to keep in touch via Christmas cards and intermittent phone calls. Then Jake died, and Stephen was murdered. Amos's fine career was abruptly halted, and Selwyn and she finally and irrevocably ran out of money. Now those who were left had come back together again, at Miranda's eloquent suggestion, to pick up the old threads and weave a new pattern.

Omega checked the screen again to see what was holding her mother's attention. 'Ah, it's the New Mead posse. Is that why you're interested in this one, Mum?'

'I suppose so. Look at us all.'

'Colin was very gorgeous in those days.'

'Yes, he was.'

'Shall I print you off a copy?' Alpha asked.

'Yes, please.'

'Matt or glossy?'

'Whatever you've got.'

The printer whirred and the bright photograph slid out of the machine. Alpha waved it in the air to dry the ink, and trimmed the margins with the kitchen scissors.

'Thank you,' Polly said.

After Omie had gone home, Alpha pulled the sofa out into a bed and made it up with clean sheets and a spare pillow from her own bed. She ran her mother a hot bath, and once Polly was pinkly installed under the duvet she brought her a

209

mug of camomile tea. This reversal of roles made them both smile.

After Alpha had withdrawn to her bedroom, Polly heard her having a long murmured telephone conversation, presumably with Jaime.

Before she fell asleep she listened, through the drone of traffic, to the fizz and crackle of the last of the November the Fifth fireworks displays. She thought about Nic, and hoped that whatever decision she made about her pregnancy would be the right one for her.

Rather than meeting at the offices of the listings magazine, Ben had suggested a little city park. Polly guessed that he quite naturally didn't want his mother turning up in her country woollies at his funky place of work, and agreed without question. She arrived early, because it had been much easier to find the place than Ben's convoluted directions had suggested. She made her way slowly under a lattice of bare branches to sit down on an empty bench. The park was a tiny triangle of paths and worn grass wedged between high walls and iron railings. Bricked into one of the walls she noticed the carved stone outlines of lancet windows, and when she half-turned she saw that the base of the wall behind her was lined with a row of weathered tombstones. The names and dates were barely legible, but she managed to decipher elegantly carved numerals, *1792*. French Revolution, she noted automatically. This scuffed space trapped between office buildings had once been the graveyard of a city church; the church itself had probably been bombed beyond repair in 1940.

Polly rested her plastic bags of shopping at her feet and sat quietly, thinking about the plague hospital that had once stood a few hundred yards from this spot, and the walls of the City of London that lay the same distance in the opposite direction. She had wandered through these streets before her children were born, when she had been researching a history of the plague. The book had had a respectable sale, but was now out of print. She knew that office blocks and shopping malls were built over plague pits all over this part of the city. Reflecting on time and history brought her thoughts back in a different direction to Mead, and to Amos's house that would eventually rise over the princess's grave. She wondered if the stolen grave goods would ever be recovered, and reflected sorrowfully that they probably would not.

An old man shuffled along inside the railings that separated the park from the road. On the benches opposite, a pair of office workers ate sandwiches from Tupperware boxes and an Asian man in a white knitted cap intently read a thick book. Polly was soothed by the peace of the tiny enclosure, where even the intermittent wail of sirens and roar of traffic were muffled. She fitted in quite nicely here, after all; with her clothes and various burdens she could easily pass as a bag lady. The idea made her laugh, and laughter was restorative. It seemed warm in the middle of the city, after Mead, where the winds off the sea constantly scoured the fields and rain lashed the lanes and paths into seams of mud. She tilted her head towards the opaque sky and let her eyes close.

'Are you ready?' a voice shouted.

Her eyes snapped open and she saw the old man standing in front of her. His clothes were a map of stains and his eyes stared out of a bush of hair and beard. A strong smell blew off him.

'I don't know. I don't really think so,' Polly admitted.

'You should be. Or you'll be sorry.' He shook his fist in the air, acting true to type and berating some invisible authority. 'Get out of here. Go on, shove off. Leave us alone, I tell you.'

Behind him, Polly saw Ben approaching. With his cycling clothes and festoons of belongings Ben fitted in here too, in the kingdom of the slightly dispossessed.

'Here's my son,' Polly said to the tramp.

'Pleased to meet you,' the old man said to Ben. 'Won't take any more of your time.' He drifted away to the Asian man, who ignored him, and the secretaries, who snapped shut their boxes and pulled their coats closer around them. 'Get ready,' he yelled at the sky.

Ben dropped his bags next to Polly's. 'Mum, you always start chatting to people. You're a properly friendly person.'

'I wasn't really chatting.'

Ben undid the bags and showed her the cardboard cups of soup insulated in corrugated sleeves, bread rolls and a plastic tub of ready-cut fruit salad. She was sure he would have forgotten about offering to bring a picnic, and she was touched that he hadn't and also ashamed of herself for doubting him. He dealt out paper napkins and plastic spoons, and ordered her to eat up before the soup got cold. From early childhood Ben always had been kind, even thoughtful in his special off-beam way. Polly thought he would make a decent father, although probably, sadly, not in partnership with Nicola.

'Good place,' she said, blowing on her first spoonful of soup.

'Yeah. I like thinking of all the people from around here who used to come to the church, long ago, you know? Like, shopkeepers and street sweepers and – what were they? – night-soil men. All their names in the parish register, right? Births and marriages, and then dead and buried here. I was wondering what would have happened to all the old dead bodies when they turned this into a park?' He nodded at the tombstones.

'They'd have been decently excavated by the contractors, examined by archaeologists, eventually given a respectful reburial somewhere else. The procedures are quite tightly regulated.'

Polly knew about this from her research into the plague sites, and also from the recent events at Mead. She had known more about the laws that governed the excavation of bodies even than Amos, but she had modestly kept this knowledge to herself.

Ben turned his familiar beam of wide-spectrum radiance upon her. He was still wearing his cycling helmet.

'I *knew* you'd be able to tell me. You always know things, Mum. I remember being so proud of you when I was little because you were really clever. Other people's mums made salads and came on school outings, but you wrote *books*.'

'Wait a minute, I made salads too, and I remember more than one class trip to see the lions of Longleat,' she laughed.

'Yeah, you were supermother.'

Ben threw a few crumbs of bread to the waiting pigeons. They were scabby, unlustrous birds, some of them with scaly fused knobs for feet. She wondered if they formed a sort of avian dispossessed, then decided as they gobbled the bread that they were very much in possession of this urban patch. There were no sparrows or starlings to be seen, and their only rivals for the territory were the beady seagulls drawn up on a white-splashed wall. The sight of them made her think of Mead yet again. Unsettlingly, it seemed to draw her back only to push her away, attracting and repelling.

'You should write another book, it would be a good way of keeping your end up,' Ben remarked.

She turned to look at him in surprise. Was her recent relegation to the margins so evident that even *Ben* was noticing it?

'What end? Do I need one of my own, do you think?'

He blinked. 'You know, I mean with Dad being so obsessive about the barn, don't tell me he isn't, and that joint set-up with all those old mates of yours, and me and the twins not being with you so much and everything. With the writing you'd have something for yourself, wouldn't you? Everyone needs that,' he said judiciously. 'Why did you stop, anyway?'

'I found it harder and harder to make the proper time for it, I suppose. I don't like half-doing things, and I was.'

She had been subsumed into Selwyn, into attending to his projects and acknowledging his glamour, answering his wide-mouthed, hot-skinned insistence that she was there, his steady right hand, always, or whenever he needed her. That was what had happened. She had been sucked into steering their ramshackle ship, and she had done it willingly, but ever since they had been at Mead she had been wondering if they were about to capsize in treacherous currents.

No. Whatever happened she and Selwyn would stay afloat. She'd see to that.

'You should think about it, Mum.'

Polly leaned against her unpredictable son, filled with affection for him. 'Listen to you, my life coach. Maybe you're right. We'll see. Anyway, I thought we'd come here to talk about you and Nic.'

'Ah.' Ben puffed out a long breath as his smile faded. 'I dunno. What can I do, Mum? Half the time I'm thinking, you know, what happens is what will happen.'

This was like him. Sometimes he was hyper-optimistic, at others drowning in gloom, and yet on occasions he could be perfectly balanced and sanguine. She put her hand over his.

'Yes,' she said gently. 'Let's take it as it comes.'

Ben nodded. He spread a fresh square of paper on her knee, opened the plastic tub and gave her a tiny wooden prong. They took turns to stab at the chunks of fruit as the pigeons lost interest and hobbled away.

'It bloody hurts,' Selwyn complained.

'Sit still.'

Miranda was changing the dressing on his head. The singed hair had been cut away from the burn. She lifted off the padding, checked for signs of infection, applied fresh antiseptic, and renewed the bandage.

'There.'

The actual injury was superficial, but a single inch to the right and the rocket could have blinded him, or worse. A sense of might-have-been stalked them both, as palpable in the room as a third person.

Selwyn watched her as she put away the first-aid box. The empty house was quiet, except for the ticking clocks and the wind in the chimneys. As she passed again behind his chair Miranda put her hand on his shoulder and Selwyn caught her fingers. Instead of breaking away she stooped and quickly kissed the top of his head, avoiding the rakish bandage. She should have moved aside then, but she couldn't help laying her cheek on the spot where she had kissed him. He took her other hand, drawing her arms down over his shoulders. She closed her eyes and buried her mouth in his hair.

They remained like that for a long moment, listening to one another's breathing.

'It's not unlimited, you know,' Selwyn said in a low voice.

Miranda knew, but she still asked 'What?'

'Time. We've got maybe twelve, fifteen more summers? Calculating on an average sort of life span? You'll have longer, being female.'

She thought of the years as a tunnel, dappled green as if made of entwined summer branches. It was a lengthy tunnel, but the distance lying behind was measurable. And the distance left to travel was much shorter than that.

'There's still a quarter of our lives left.'

'Three-quarters has gone.'

'Sel, I'm trying to cheer you up. Do cooperate. Half full's better than half empty.'

'I don't need a rallying call. I'm working out how much there is that I want to do before it's too late. There are a lot of things.'

'Do a bungee jump? Run a marathon?'

'Neither of those.'

His quietness rebuked her. She lifted her head and moved out of his reach. None of the avenues down which the conversation might have moved felt neutral enough. She wondered how long they could realistically continue to skirt around each other like this. What had seemed black and white only a month ago was now, increasingly, infinitely grey.

Selwyn sighed, tweaking his dressing to make it sit more comfortably over his temple. 'Come over and have a look at what we've done in the barn. There's been more progress.'

They walked across the yard together.

Selwyn and a plasterer had been hard at work. The downstairs space was now mostly enclosed by smooth walls from which sprouted tufts of electrical cable. One end of the big room was open, under the restored roof, all the way up to the fine beams of the barn. At the other end, under a lower ceiling, was the embryo of a kitchen. Between the two areas, a ladder rose through a hole into the upper space, which would be divided into bedrooms and bathrooms. Now enclosed by solid walls and a door that locked, Chemical Ali had given way to a proper flushing lavatory.

Miranda nodded at the ladder. 'May I look?'

He steadied it for her as she cautiously made her way upwards. The timber framing for stud walls was in place, forming notional rooms. In one of the spaces was the camp bed, with Selwyn's clothes strewn around it. Polly's were nowhere to be seen, presumably stored in the cardboard boxes stacked against the wall. A new window let into the roof slope gave an unexpected view of the copse shielding Amos's site and the rooks' nests held aloft in leafless branches.

Slowly but steadily a proper house, a home secure against the wind and weather, was emerging out of the tumbledown barn.

Miranda admired what Polly and Selwyn had done. She turned to Selwyn, who was leaning against the splintery outline of a wall.

'You're going to be happy here.'

'Am I?' His face was dark.

'You and Polly,' she said precisely.

'Polly and I seem to have reached the point where happiness is way beyond our expectations. Mutual tolerance, possibly deteriorating to mutual avoidance, that's the best we can hope for.'

Miranda didn't want to hear this – and yet she did. A knot of dread and longing was forming beneath her ribs. She stared down at the floor of salvaged boards, where Selwyn was toeing a little heap of dust and shavings.

'Long marriages . . .' she began, without knowing where the sentence was going to take her. 'Long *partnerships*, are more complicated – aren't they? – than you could begin to envisage when you enter into them, when you're full of optimism about life and airy notions about love and for ever. After thirty years the grooves of habit are worn so deep you feel interred by them. But now if you were actually to find yourself without them, without those rails, you might run off into the wilderness and perish.'

She was speaking almost wholly for herself, remembering how all the world had seemed a wilderness after Jake died. Without Polly, she was sure that Selwyn would be similarly lost. But he was impatient with her warning, and he wasn't thinking about the riddles of any experience other than his own.

'Barb, I was a crass oaf back in those days. I was so helpless, so self-absorbed, so hobbled by vanity and the fear that anyone might detect my uselessness that I made an impediment out of what was actually perfect freedom.'

'That's not how I remember it. You were very beautiful and funny and inspiring. Everyone wanted to be you or be with you.'

'I was terrified of you finding me out. I was afraid to marry you. I let you go and I let Polly choose me instead. Then I fiddled around for thirty years, wasting her life as well as my own. Polly deserved better than me. If I'd married you, I'd have driven myself harder. For you, I'd have become Prime Minister.'

'In that case, you've got me and Polly to thank that you aren't. You haven't got to deal with Afghanistan or the economy. That's something, isn't it?' She tried to make him smile, but he wouldn't. His eyes had been fixed on the pile of dust and shavings but now he lifted his head and looked straight at her.

'God help me, Barbara. How have I cocked up so badly?'

'You haven't,' she breathed.

She didn't want to have this conversation across the camp bed; it was like talking over the prone body of her friends' marriage. She made for the protruding top of the ladder and then looked down through the gaping hole at the long drop to the new cement floor. A rush of vertigo made her head swim.

'I can't climb down there.'

'Yes, you can. I'll go first.'

He descended and stopped with his shoulders sticking out of the hole.

'Come on. I'll be right below you. You can't fall.'

'I can't do it.'

'Come here.'

She edged towards him and he reached up for her hand. She took it and shuffled to the edge of the yawning hole, seeing how the ladder bounced as Selwyn shifted his weight on the rungs.

'Close your eyes,' he said. 'Put your foot here.' He grasped one ankle and placed it. Miranda heard an embarrassing whimper escaping from her own throat. Polly must climb up and down this ladder to go to bed, or just to change her socks. Blindly she shuffled the other foot on to the top rung. With her knuckles white on the uprights she opened her eyes to narrow slits and let Selwyn guide her feet down the successive rungs. At last she stood on the blessed firm ground. He cupped her face in his hands and kissed her on the mouth.

'Fear is a protean creature,' he murmured.

She refused to cling to him. 'I'm all right now. Let's go outside.'

They emerged into the yard. Miranda shook herself.

'Let's take a walk.'

Without speaking they passed out of the yard gate and took the path over wind-bitten grass to the little wood. Selwyn followed in her footsteps under the knitted trees and past the arms of dead brambles. The plateau with its belt of trees was completely deserted. The builders' cabin was padlocked, and the site caravan also. Excavated earth stood in clayey heaps, and polythene sheeting flapped in the stronger gusts. They stood and looked at the holes in the ground, and the landscape beyond. The abandoned trenches contained only brown puddles and reflections of skidding clouds.

The absence of a house was underlined by a deeper absence that soughed in the trees and flattened the colourless grass.

Miranda had no coat, and she shivered.

'I wish she had never been uncovered,' she said. She wished the ground unbroken again, and the bones still lying in peace.

Selwyn took her hands and rubbed the knuckles to chafe warmth into them.

'So do I. Two thousand years is a long time for her to have possessed a fine and private place. I'm sorry she had to be disturbed.'

Miranda completed the lines in her head. She had thought of them more than once since the princess and her treasures had been dug up and carried away from Mead.

The grave's a fine and private place,
But none I think do there embrace.

'It's done now,' she said quietly.

And what *wasn't* done, what about that?

Was it right to leave it that way, or between them should they set the sun running, as the poet believed?

Selwyn put his arm around her shoulders. 'Let's go back.'

She led the way in the other direction, along the track that would some day be Amos's drive, all the way to the house and the front door under its peeling portico. Unthinkingly, she stroked her fingers over the russet bricks. Selwyn looked up at the old glass in the windows, the spines of roses hung with sparse orange hips, the tall chimneys and ribbed tiles on the roof.

The walls held warmth and the sheltering wings kept out the wind, so they lingered comfortably outside the front door.

'Mead's full of stories,' Miranda said. 'These two wings were added to the old farmhouse as the Meads made their way up in the world. Those rooms up there were for a maid and a manservant. The last addition was by the Victorian Meadowes who stuck on this elaborate porch so they could climb out of their carriage under shelter.'

They began to make a slow circuit, skirting spiny shrubs and looking inwards instead of out. At the side of one wing was an engraved block, reading 'JM 1748'. In places the soft stone of lintels and sills was crumbling, the silica bedded in it faintly glinting. Windows were veiled with dust, and glazing bars shed layers of fading paint. They passed the back of Amos and Katherine's cottage, where the windows were polished, and came into the yard again via the gate. Selwyn latched it behind them.

'The carts were kept in your barn, then the carriage and horses, and in the end the cars. The yard man and a couple of farm workers lived in the cottages.'

'I feel suitably feudal, milady,' Selwyn grinned.

'We've just made a complete tour of everything I own,' Miranda pointed out.

'It's not a negligible possession.'

'I know that.' She linked her hand in his. 'I still feel that I'm only looking after it, for Jake.'

'And then what will happen to it?'

'I don't know,' Miranda said.

They went into the house, passing through the kitchen and into the hall. The clock struck four as they looked into the drawing room. The heavy curtains at one of the windows were still half closed, cold ashes scattered the hearth and the gloom of a winter's afternoon stalked them.

'Shall I get a fire going for you?' Selwyn asked.

Miranda didn't trust herself alone with him in front of the fire.

Their first time, thirty-odd years ago, had been one afternoon in her chill, oddly-angled bedsit, the only good feature of which had been a small open grate. As well as the fire there had been a deep-fringed pink lampshade and the scent of patchouli, marijuana, and a rancid Afghan coat.

There was something about the damp wood smoke and the filtered grey light of this afternoon that strongly reminded her of that day, and as she thought back to it the intervening time folded inwards on itself and then collapsed into nothing. Selwyn looked physically almost the same. She felt, even within her changed body, just as she had done in those days. Anything was possible.

'Come with me, I'll show you something,' she said quickly.

She led the way down a passage to a cluttered room that Jake had used as an occasional study and for storing the farm accounts and other paperwork. The walls were lined with bookshelves, some of them enclosed by old-fashioned metal library grilles. The lowest level was made up of cupboards with blistered woodgrain varnish. A table in the window and a brass reading lamp were overlaid with dust. Miranda switched on the lamp and a rising cloud made them both cough a little. She began to search through a pile of folders that were stacked on a shelf. Selwyn browsed along the bookshelves, lifting a volume here and there and blowing dust off the fore-edge before opening stained leather covers.

'Here it is,' Miranda said.

She took a sepia photograph out of a folder and laid it under the light of the lamp. Selwyn was immersed in an old manuscript book that seemed brittle enough to fall apart in his hands. He turned over bound parchment sheets covered in spidery brown script.

'But these letters are hundreds of years old,' he said wonderingly.

'They are the Mead archive. Family letters, account books, estate records. Jake was always threatening to get an expert in to sort and catalogue them. Come and look at this.'

He replaced the volume on the shelf beside its companions and peered over her shoulder.

The picture was of the yard at Mead. In the foreground was a cart loaded with hay. A horse stood in the traces, its harness garlanded with flowers. Two young girls in pinafores and straw hats, also wreathed in flowers, were perched on the back of the cart. A small group of men, one of them holding a pitchfork, solemnly gathered at the horse's head. Behind them was Selwyn's barn, the big doors propped open. Miranda pointed to the faded handwriting on the photograph's reverse. It read 'Estate picnic, August 1914. Jos. Green, d. France 1915'.

221

She turned it over again and they studied the faces from a summer's day of almost a hundred years ago.

'Which one is Jos Green?' Selwyn murmured.

'I don't know. He wasn't the only one. There are fifteen names from the estate on the First World War memorial in the church. Jake's great-uncle's is there too. It's a lot of young men, for a place the size of Meddlett.'

Selwyn stooped to examine the picture more closely. The left-hand door of the barn stood wide, and in the shadows within, the glimmering bonnet of a car was clearly visible.

'It's a Rolls-Royce. Jake's great-grandfather had a passion for them,' Miranda told him.

'A Silver Ghost,' Selwyn agreed.

It was only a picture of a long-ago rural celebration, with girls in their Sunday best and farmhands enjoying an afternoon's rest, but the photograph also captured a moment of profound change, with cars replacing horses and carts, and men about to march off to war. No wonder Miranda had wanted to show it to him. It made him look at the riddled old barn and the estate itself from a longer perspective. In that instant, his own headlong gallop of hours and days slowed and he heard the patient tread of history over these fields, stepping all the way back to the princess of the Iceni.

'You're in love with Mead, aren't you?' he said wonderingly, properly acknowledging this truth for the first time.

'I am,' she agreed.

'I am *jealous* of it. I want you to love me.'

He looked black, and Miranda laughed at him.

'You can't be jealous of a house. And I do love you.'

She put down the photograph. The shelves breathed dust and dry leather and old paper. He lifted her chin so that her face was tilted up to his.

'I'm part of Mead now,' he said. The bandage had slipped again, pushing down the outer edge of one dark eyebrow. He was wonderfully familiar to her and the connection was easy, silky, without the irritating abrasions of habit.

'Yes, you are.'

Gently he rolled up the sleeves of her jersey and kissed the inside of her wrists. The blue skin inside the crook of her arm instantly developed a million new nerve endings, all of them alive to his mouth. She wondered if she had in fact been dead for years. Cryogenically frozen until this moment. Effectively, she must have been. He undid three buttons and found more inches of skin to kiss.

The ability to resist him finally deserted her.

He lifted his head and she heard herself say, 'Don't stop now. It's too late, isn't it?'

'Where?' he muttered thickly.

'Here,' she replied. 'Now.'

The dust swirled in thicker clouds, enveloping them.

Everyone must be asleep.

Polly's back from seeing her girls, Amos from business some-where, Katherine from work.

And I can't close my eyes on the certainty that Selwyn and I have done something indelible that has already changed Mead.

Yesterday, if anyone had asked me (who would that have been? I don't discuss such things even with Polly or Katherine), I would have answered that I can perfectly well live without sex. I have done, since Jake died and even before that whilst he was ill, and I was the same person – only minus the inconven-ient flashes of heat and the illogical, embarrassing behaviour characteristic of sexual desire – that I have always been.

But then today happens.

Remarkably, as well as being imperative to begin with, it turns out to be intricate, tender, and finally exalting. The only difference from the way it was when Selwyn and I were young is that it's more resonant. Memories and experience function like extra receptors, opening little windows of pleasure related to other times and places, layering this event with bright slivers of the past and thereby increasing its intensity.

I have *existed* without sex. It's not the same as living, of course.

I suddenly understand Selwyn's sexual insistence, and its associated howl of dismay – I don't want to give up either. I don't want to grow old. I don't want to lose this wordless language of desire and satisfaction that has been ours for decades.

I'm greedy and selfish and carnal.

And temporarily I am filled with wicked delight.

Afterwards, breathless and half choking on surprised laughter as well as dust particles, Selwyn dragged a tired cushion off an armchair and we propped our heads on it. The cover was torn and a few feathers drifted in the air above us. I lay with my face turned into his shoulder and my heart gradually slowed from its wild thumping.

'How was I?' Selwyn asked. The self-parody was only partial. I remembered what he had said about fear.

I laughed some more, lying loose in his arms.

'Not bad.'

'All my own work, you know. No chemicals involved.' He examined my earlobe, frowning at close quarters. 'I'd better warn you right now, it might not always be like that. I am an old man.'

The assumption of *again* was already there. I should have pinched out the little bud there and then, hard and sharp between frosty fingers, but I was dizzy with warmth and sexual release and I only stretched out against him, my head against his chest, to hear the steady beating.

Selwyn murmured, 'And as for you, Barbara Huggett, possessor of my heart, man and boy, you are more beautiful than you have ever been and I love you.'

I know that the skin of my upper arms puckers into tiny creases when I pinch it. There are vertical seams fringing my upper lip and nets of fine wrinkles around my eyes, but just for that moment I was prepared to believe him. Through the window I could see the smoky sky, and a frame of black twigs as fine as hair.

'And I you,' I admitted.

'So what are we going to do?' he whispered.

Belatedly, I marshalled my thoughts.

'Secretly, we are going to place this afternoon's precious bead on the necklace of our lives, where it will shine brightly and uniquely. There will be no others, but that will increase the brilliance of this single gem. We won't talk about it again, but we'll both remember it.'

My head fell an inch as he sharply exhaled.

'You do talk bollocks, Mirry. Be real, can't you?'

I thought about what real meant.

In a few days, Joyce would be arriving for one of her visits. Amos and Katherine were waiting for their building project to restart. I had accepted and banked Selwyn and Polly's money for the barn, and spent some of it on repairs to the main chimneys, which otherwise would have been in imminent danger of collapse. The treasure might have been stolen, but there was still a significant archaeological site to be studied and chronicled. I was looking forward to that. It would soon be time to start making plans for Christmas. All these factors I drew up and ranged like a housewife placing storage jars on a shelf.

By contrast, sex in the afternoon with my friend's husband might be living, but it wasn't my life.

'I am real,' I said.

Selwyn sat up, gently lifting me. We shifted backwards so that we leaned against the armchair and its little nimbus of feathers.

'I am going to have to leave Polly, you know. I can't go on being her younger brother and part-time son, and that's what we've made of each other. I'm not saying I haven't colluded in my own infantilizing, and that's all the more reason why I should have the balls to end it.'

'Polly loves you. You are her life. You can't discard her after thirty years. I won't be a part of that.'

'There'll be a terrible upheaval, but it will be the right thing to do. I want to marry you. I want to live with you, wake up and fall asleep with you, from as soon as possible until one of us dies.'

'No,' I said.

He looked straight into my eyes, into my head.

'What did this afternoon mean to you?'

I glanced away. It had meant much more than I wanted him to know.

'I'm sorry. It should never have happened,' I whispered.

His fingers closed on my wrist. 'Yes it should. That's exactly my point. We haven't got much longer.'

'If we had just two more days or all eternity, Sel, it wouldn't make any difference.'

I saw the hurt and disappointment in his face. I understood something of the complicated choreography linking him and Polly, and his lament for manhood. There is a lot of the selfish wild boy in Selwyn, but that is not all or even most of what he is.

'You'll change your mind,' he said, kissing my face and neck and gently fastening the buttons he had undone.

That was how we left it.

The others came back to Mead, except for Colin, who is in America. The lights went on in the barn and the cottage and then before midnight the windows were all dark again.

I sat all evening on the sofa in front of the ashes of an unlit fire, my book closed on my knee.

NINE

Early the next morning, Miranda left the house. She put her overnight case in the boot of the car, thinking as she did so that it was weeks, possibly even months, since she had spent a night away from Mead.

She drove through a heavy sea fog that rubbed out everything more than a few feet beyond the car's windscreen. On days like this the mist damped sound as well as scenery and the world seemed fleeced in grey wool. In Meddlett the shop was only just opening for the day's business and not a soul was visible through the murk. She could just make out that the debris and black smudges of smoke damage from the Fifth had been tidied and washed away. The duck pond was a sheet of dull aluminium and the willow trees were spectres of themselves. She continued westwards out of the village, heading for the main road. She wasn't running away from home, nothing of the kind. She was simply going to collect her mother from her sheltered flat, making sure while she was there that everything was in order, perhaps having a chat over a cup of tea with the warden, and then, when Joyce was ready, bringing her back to Mead for a few days' holiday.

It would be better to leave Selwyn to himself for a while.

It was even better to be slipping temporarily out of his reach, since she already knew that she couldn't behave properly around him.

She tried not to think that outside Mead, away from the confines of the walls and the defining views and the ticking of the hall clock, she felt like a snail abruptly prised from its shell.

After a few miles the light brightened and she glimpsed a line of traffic snaking ahead of her. A minute later the fog dispersed, as if it had never been. She switched on the radio and listened to the end of the *Today* programme.

Two hours later she was parking her car in one of the marked diagonal slots outside Joyce's sheltered block. She walked up a paved path between clumps of municipally tended shrubbery and rang her mother's doorbell. After quite a long time she heard the very slow approach of slippered feet and the clinking of locks. Joyce opened the door to a narrow slit governed by a chain fastening, and peered out.

'What are *you* doing here?' she asked.

Her voice was very hoarse, and even this question made her gasp for breath and then collapse into a coughing fit. Joyce unchained the door and shuffled backwards into her tiny hallway. Miranda took her arm and guided her into the living room. Her mother seemed to weigh next to nothing. She was all sharp bones and dry, hot skin. Miranda helped her into her chair, adjusted the gas fire and drew the rug over her knees.

'I told you I was coming. Why didn't you let me know that you're not well?'

'I did.'

It was almost impossible nowadays to distinguish what Joyce had done from what she thought she had done or had completely forgotten about.

Miranda knelt down beside her, holding the thin blue wrist in her fingers. The pulse seemed very fast and fluttery. 'All right, Mum. I'm going to ring the warden and then perhaps we'll get the doctor in to have a look at you. Shall I make you a hot drink first, though?'

'I don't like those new teabags she got me.'

'We won't have them, then. What about a cup of hot milk, or cocoa?'

'Cocoa? Always reminds me of the Blitz. What are you doing here?'

Miranda smiled, with as much reassurance as she could summon. 'I've come over to see you. Didn't you want me to?'

Joyce's eyes fixed on her. They were pale and watery, set in folds of inflamed red eyelid. She coughed again, but her gaze didn't waver.

'Have you still got Selwyn living in your barn?'

She was infallible. She might be well over eighty, feverish, intermittently forgetful, but she still possessed the uncanny and almost always unwelcome knack of placing her finger precisely on the most central of her daughter's concerns. It had been the same for fifty-odd years.

Miranda nodded.

'And his wife? What's her name?'

'Polly. Of course she's there.'

Joyce shook her head. 'What kind of arrangement is that, I'd like to know? What does your husband think about it?'

'It's a practical and cooperative set-up. Jake's dead, Mum.'

'That's right. Younger than me. Never looked strong.'

'I'm going to make us a cup of tea.'

Miranda went into the kitchen and while she was waiting for the kettle to boil she rang the accommodation's warden. The warden told her she had been planning to ring this morning, and was very glad that she was already here. The doctor would be visiting Mrs Huggett later.

Out on the square of grass beneath the windows of the block Miranda saw a blackbird. It tilted its head towards her, staring sceptically out of one round eye.

She carried a tray with the teapot and two cups back into the living room. It was hot in there, with the papery smell of illness.

'Here we are.'

Joyce stared at her. 'What are you doing here?'

'I've come over to see you.'

'You've forgotten the tea cosy. That tea will be stone cold.'

*　　*　　*

229

Kieran pulled back his dreadlocks and wound them in a thin scarf. He straightened his fleece and did up the zip, then knocked on Mr Knight's door. Mr Knight opened it immediately, frowned at Kieran's site boots, and curtly indicated that he should take them off before following him into the kitchen. Mrs Knight was there and she smiled at him before pouring a welcome cup of hot coffee, and sliding over a plate of biscuits so it lay within easy reach.

The boss had told him that he was to call on Mr Knight this morning and formally notify him that AAS's investigations at the Mead dig would be complete in two more days. Nothing further of any archaeological significance had been discovered in the immediate environs of the grave, and it seemed likely therefore that it had been a high-status burial site deliberately maintained apart from any village settlement. In due course Mr Knight and the county archaeologist would be receiving copies of the AAS report on the excavation and the finds, with an evaluation of the probable importance of the now unfortunately destroyed grave site and its artefacts set in the context of the other Iron-Age civilizations of the area.

Then, after the archaeology team had finally withdrawn from the site and the county authorities had approved in writing the resumption of works, Mr Knight would be free to get his contractors back at any time.

Chris Carr had been adamant that he wouldn't come to this meeting himself. This puzzled Kieran, because usually Dr Carr insisted on speaking to clients and landowners personally. However, quite a number of things about this dig were puzzling and some of them were positively uncomfortable. He wasn't even going to speculate any further about Damon and Jessie and what they might have spilled out between them to the local lowlife, for example. The fight at the Fifth party had been bad, and in the end all he had got for suggesting that Jessie and his brother might have been implicated in the theft and violation was a couple of punches in the head. Kieran was still staying at his mother's house for safety's sake.

230

What was even worse, the fight had been broken up by none other than Mr Knight. Rather bravely, too, Kieran had to acknowledge. Damon's mate Donny Spragg probably hadn't been carrying a blade to the Meddlett Fifth bonfire and hog-roast, but then again it wasn't impossible, and the lawyer couldn't really have known either way. He'd just marched over, stood up to two much younger blokes and sent them packing. Kieran reflected that he should have been grateful for this, but the scene hadn't shown him in a very good light, not with Jessie looking on. Therefore he couldn't warm to Amos Knight. He didn't like the way he was asking questions now and making notes of Kieran's answers, probably twisting his words in some lawyer-like fashion as he did so.

Most troubling of all, though, was the loss of the wonderful grave goods of his imagination and the way that the delicate evidence of the surrounding site had been trampled to nothing.

The mere thought of that was enough almost to bring tears to his eyes.

Gloomily, Kieran reached out for one of the biscuits. It turned out to be unbelievably delicious, with dark chocolate outside and a centre filled with some kind of oozing ginger syrup. Way out of the HobNobs category. He wondered if it would be too much to help himself to another.

In the end Amos screwed the cap back on his fountain pen and stood up. Kieran thanked Katherine for the coffee and biscuits. She walked to the front door with him, and waited politely while he put his boots back on.

'Thanks Mrs Knight,' he mumbled as he stood up. 'At least you'll be able to get the building work going again. You'll be moving into your new house in no time, I should think.'

'We'll see, Kieran,' was all she said. He thought she was looking very serious today, as well as friendly and nice as she usually did.

When Katherine came back into the kitchen, Amos was already on the telephone to his builder.

'No, I am *not* willing to accept any revised schedule. You'll have to do better than that,' he snapped.

Katherine collected up the coffee cups and slotted them into the dishwasher. Standing at the sink she looked out over the rim of Miranda's garden and across open fields. A dense cloud of birds rose over the ploughland and wheeled in a lung-shaped phalanx across the whitish sky. She wondered how they achieved such precision, without some of them forgetting what they were supposed to do and colliding with the rest.

At last Amos put down his phone. He gathered up a sheaf of papers and began making rapid notes. Katherine drew out the chair opposite him and waited until he had finished scribbling.

When he looked up she said, 'Amos, I want to talk to you.'

He put the papers aside at once, with only the ghost of a sigh.

Amos's reputation required him to be good at listening to people and evaluating what they had to say. She guessed he would be expecting a short discussion about some aspect of the boys' plans, or perhaps an expressed preference for granite over the brutal-looking polished concrete he and the architect had in mind for the new kitchen. She searched for the right words with which to begin. As it stretched beyond the point of normality the silence between them seemed to hollow out and grow brittle.

'I don't want this house,' she said at last.

Amos's eyes moved from her face to the pine fronts of the holiday cottage cupboards, then back again.

'There's a delay, yes, it's unfortunate, but we won't be here for ever.'

She placed her hands on the table. The rings briefly caught her attention. Engagement, wedding, and eternity, from their twenty-fifth anniversary. Eternity was a long time.

'Not this house. The new one. I don't want to build it. I don't want to live in it. I'm sorry. I couldn't not tell you so, once I was sure of it myself.'

Now he brought his elbow up to rest on the table, one finger curled against his lips, watching her and weighing up this disclosure.

'I see,' he said deliberately. 'Once you were sure, you say? It's a radical change of mind, isn't it? May I ask what has prompted it?'

The measured nature of this response absolutely enraged her. They were discussing what would have been their future home, and she was his *wife*, not a witness making a deposition.

To stop herself from intemperately shouting at him she tried to recapture the certainty that she didn't want to build or occupy the house, as well as the deep relief at not having to, that had come to her as she sat drinking Chris's mug of tea in the bedroom of the flat in Bloomsbury.

Amos listened in attentive silence as she stumbled through a summary of her misgivings. It wasn't easy to convey to him how the very thought of the house-to-be brought on claustro-phobia, or how the architectural spaces waiting to be filled with *things* only fired up her longing to own fewer, not more, items of serious sculpture and considered furniture. Most of all she didn't want to see all this spoil, the trophies of Amos's success, heaped up on what had been the long resting place of the Iron-Age princess.

In any case Amos's career in the law hadn't been crowned with glory. She didn't actually say this. It wouldn't have helped. But it had always been in the back of her mind that a cottage somewhere, a little grey house with quiet square rooms, would have been more appropriate in the circumstances than this blinging construction of glass and turbines and eco-vanity.

Katherine finished by saying that what she really wanted was for the wind and the rain to go on playing over that acre of ground, and for the sun to be allowed to warm the grass.

'If we did build this house, you know, I'm afraid it would only bring us bad luck,' she murmured.

Even though it had turned into quite a long and impassioned speech, Katherine felt inarticulate in the face of her husband's meticulous consideration. As she too often did. Amos sat still, reversing the Mont Blanc pen between his fingers.

'Well?' she prompted.

He frowned. 'Bad luck. *Bad luck?* That's the kind of dippy nonsense Miranda would believe in. It must be catching.'

'This is nothing to do with Miranda. It's to do with *me*, and what I want.'

The glimmer of surprise in his face was more eloquent than words. It came to her that he was totally unused to hearing her express what she wanted. And she knew that she probably had herself to blame for not having been more insistent.

'So where *do* you want to live?'

'What's wrong with here?'

Amos didn't actually look around the kitchen, or out to the view through the window. He didn't need to.

'Look. There's a bloody great delay anyway. I've spoken to Rona and to McDade.' These two were their architect and the main contractor. 'He's got our team on another job, the slippery little rat. I'm going to have to look at the clauses in the contract, see how to bring him back into line. There'll be plenty of time for you and me to talk about this.'

He wasn't attaching any significance to what she had said. He had dismissed her misgivings outright, assuming that she would change her mind in time.

He was wrong, though.

Katherine stood up.

'I'm going out for a while. I need a long walk.'

There was a grove of pines leading from the road northwards in the direction of the distant beach. Katherine parked her car next to a National Trust kiosk and wound down the window. Salty air flooded in and she leaned her head back and briefly closed her eyes. Seagulls screamed overhead and an occasional raindrop pinged on the roof.

A gentle tap on the car door made her jump. She opened her eyes to see Chris.

She got out and they turned to walk down the sandy track, heading for the great bowl of space beyond the trees. Their boots crunched in sugary wet sand laced with grass. Katherine sucked in lungfuls of the clean wind, enjoying the rhythm of their steps and the way that Chris didn't fire questions at her, or find it essential to speak at all.

'Thanks for meeting me,' she said after a while.

'I'm skiving. I'm supposed to be at a site assessment in Breckland, but I sent one of the assistants instead. It feels rather good. I think I'll do it more often.'

They negotiated a narrow path through the trees, scrambled up a steep incline where the exposed tree roots were polished by passing feet, and ran down to the point where a view opened up across an immense flat beach. In the distance, grey-white breakers raced towards the shoreline. An onshore wind blew straight into their faces and they hung briefly on the balls of their feet, clothes ballooning, leaning their bodies into its resistance. Katherine reached for the anchor of Chris's hand and he reassuringly took it, rubbing his thumb in the web of skin between her thumb and forefinger.

'My girls used to love this beach when they were small. We brought them up here every summer for picnics and swimming,' he said as they began to walk.

The coarse sand was the colour of dried clay, studded with all kinds of shells. Katherine noticed the elongated blue-black envelopes of razor clams. In the distance were the stick-figures of other walkers, and their dogs scudding through tidal drainage channels. She felt a strange, thrilling release of adrenalin that made her want to run too.

He swung their linked hands, smiling at her.

'I was pleased to hear from you, Katherine, and I can't think of a better way to spend a morning, but you didn't call me just because you wanted to go for a walk, did you?'

She shook her head. 'Have you seen the plans for our house at Mead?' she began.

'I glanced at them when the archaeology brief came in for

tender from the planning department, and again when we embarked on the watching brief. It looks very magnificent.'

'It's much too magnificent. It's self-important. It feels to me like a tomb lid, pressing down on us. On me. I told Amos this morning that I don't want to live there. I don't think we should be going ahead with the building.'

Chris reflected on this.

'I'm sorry if the excavation is the reason for that?'

'It's not, or not directly. I don't want to think of our house or anyone else's towering over the princess's grave, but the reasons are more complicated than the archaeology. It's not a whim, or a capricious changing of mind. It's to do with me and Amos and our life up until now, and the way I should live in the future.'

'What did your husband say when you told him?'

Katherine smiled a little grimly. 'Nothing. That's partly it. He assumes that I will get over it, change my mind again, if he even thinks that hard. The real truth is that my opinion doesn't matter much to him.'

'I see,' Chris said quietly. 'Can you tell me any more?'

'Not right now. I will some day. For now, I'll just say that I made a decision while I was driving here. I'm going to leave him.'

He kept her hand clasped in his but he was looking ahead, at the wide curve of the beach and the low outlines of sand dunes in the far distance.

'Go on,' he said.

'I shall move out of the cottage. I'll probably go to London and live in the flat for the time being, until I find somewhere permanent.'

She was making this up as she went along and he would be able to tell this from the way the words haphazardly fell out of her.

But the more the certainty unfurled, the more certain of its rightness she became.

She recalled the elation that she had felt back in September as she and Amos drove up here in the Jaguar, the upsurge of happiness at finding herself drinking wine in the afternoon with Polly and Colin in the Griffin, and other recent moments of joy, not only in Chris's company. They were all to do with change, green tendrils of independence emerging from bare soil, nothing to do with Amos or the building work.

I am not anyone's good or chattel, she repeated. Of course not. She was still Sam and Toby's mother, and what she was contemplating would shock them as well as hurt them, but they were grown men now. If she had achieved anything, she thought, it was to have brought up sons who had never had cause to question whether they were loved, or put first. The boys would thrive, whether or not she continued to live under the same roof as their father.

The strange euphoria that had eddied around her ever since coming to Mead now found an anchor. The optimism born of it was crystallizing, taking definition in the briny wind. She felt drunk and at the same time never more sober or sure of herself. She glanced back over her shoulder at their footprints, and then forwards over a vast shining expanse of untracked sand to the sea.

'I think you've made up your mind,' Chris observed.

They stopped in the middle of the beach. Blown sand whipped around them, stinging their cheeks, forcing them to turn their backs to the waves.

'Yes, I have.'

She needed to reassure him, and she took a moment to choose her words. The simplest would also be the most honest.

'I'm so happy we met. But I want you to know that nothing that has happened between you and me has affected the decision I've made. I'd be coming to the same conclusion if I didn't know you at all.'

She half-turned into the wind, in order to look into his face.

'You don't have to worry that I might pursue you. You're not going to be involved in what will happen between Amos and me. I don't expect you to do, or even say, anything about

237

it. Well . . . except maybe as a friend. If you want to be. If you did decide to be that, I'd welcome it with all my heart.'

He was going to speak but she stopped him. 'I loved the other night, I felt like a young girl again and that's the best present you could have given me, but it's not what convinced me I need to leave my husband. That's all I wanted to say. More than enough, probably.'

She smiled, a wide smile of complete frankness that he found touching. He wound his finger around a strand of her hair that had blown across her face and caught at the corner of her mouth. He studied it for a second before tucking it inside the collar of her coat.

'Can I speak now?'

She smiled even more broadly. There were some grains of fine sand caught in her brows and eyelashes. 'Yes, you can,' she said.

'Are you saying that you want me to be your friend and no more?'

She hesitated. Physically she was longing for a different relationship with Christopher Carr, and to want someone's body was such an exciting rebirth of sensation that it was hard to ignore. She did her best, though.

'I don't know yet. There is a lot of ground that I have to cover first, and I have to do it on my own. It wouldn't be fair to Amos otherwise. After that, I don't know what will happen. I'm not even sure quite who I'll be, if I'm not Mrs Amos Knight any longer. That's the truth, Chris.'

'I understand,' he said.

He cupped her face in his hands and briefly kissed her. Then they walked on.

He added, 'I'm not afraid that you might pursue me. I don't have any experience of women doing that in any case, but it doesn't strike me as your style at all. I can't make any judgement about your marriage. How could I presume to do that? But I will tell you this. I've only just met you, but I want to go on talking to you. I want to tell you what I know and what

I believe in and hope for, and I want to hear you telling me the same things. I want to look at your face while I'm listening to you. Maybe I haven't led a very varied or exciting life, but this is the first time I've ever felt anything of the kind. If it's falling in love, if *that's* what this is, I can understand why all the world makes such a song and dance about it.'

Katherine's eyes were stinging, not just from the wind. The only other times she had heard such eloquence from Chris were when he talked about archaeology. His candour left her tongue-tied now.

He promised her, 'Whatever does happen, though, you can count on me as a friend.'

They reached the shelter of the belt of pines. They had walked a huge arc, almost to the breaking waves and then veering away again. Now they followed a path to a distant village across salt marshes dotted with sheep. Chris led the way to a little café looking over the maze of tidal creeks towards the sea defences, and when they reached it they sat on a bench at an outside table, leaning comfortably against the splintered silver-grey wood of the hut wall. They ate thick crab sandwiches and drank rapidly cooling tea while predatory gulls eyed them from their perches on tarry mooring posts. The two of them must have looked, Katherine thought, like the most companionable of settled couples, the kind who keep a National Trust handbook and a guide to local walks tucked in the glove compartment of their car.

When she had set out the other evening for her restaurant date with Chris, she had been both shocked and pleased to consider herself on the brink of adultery. The evening had maintained its double-edged promise by being serious but also skittish, flirtatious, a *date* date complete with candles and complicit waiters, and ending up with going back for a nightcap. If Toby hadn't called when he did, it was likely that she and Chris would have gone to bed together.

Today, though, the tenor between them had altered. They were sitting on their bench with the fibres of shared experience already beginning to knot them together, not yet knowing whether the final balance would favour love or friendship, but certain that it was going to be one or the other. They had moved into one another's lives and it wasn't the kind of stake that you gave up on.

It was late in life to make such a discovery. These were the kind of connections that everyone made quickly and thoughtlessly in their teens or twenties, and which were then woven into the fabric of life. Marriages or old friendships of the kind that were entrenched at Mead were almost all begun early in life. This new coming-together was so un-expected and so unlooked-for that it seemed doubly precious. There was something solid here, weighty with promise, yet also wide and free-ranging.

As they sat with their hands linked, silently watching the swirl of seawater filling the creeks, the broad skies and silent empty marshes stretching around them seemed their own country.

Miranda waited by her mother's hospital bed until Joyce finally fell asleep.

The GP, when she came, had been concerned about her breathing and the rising fever. An ambulance was called, and in the A & E department a diagnosis of pneumonia had been followed by a long wait for an in-patient bed to become free. When they finally reached it it was in a mixed ward full of mute, waxen old people and the sound of despairing coughing. Joyce held on to Miranda's hand, saying very little.

The medical staff reported that she was weak, but not in immediate danger. A mask was fixed over her face and drips were connected to her blue arms.

Once she was definitely asleep Miranda slipped away, saying to the nurses that she would collect some of her mother's belong-ings from home and bring them in for her. Back at the flat she took a tartan zipped suitcase down from the top of the wardrobe and blew a layer of dust off the lid. Guessing, she opened cupboards and found two nighties, underwear, a cracked washbag that she filled with toiletries from the bathroom. In the bottom drawer of the chest lay the cashmere cardigan jacket that Miranda had given her for her last birthday, still folded in the shop's tissue paper. She packed the fleece dressing gown that hung behind the bedroom door and collected a pair of trodden-down slippers from the rug beside the bed. She stood for a moment with these in her hands, studying the imprint of her mother's bare feet. The dark impression of heel and toes in beige fur-fabric was too intimate to be handled comfortably, just as it felt intrusive to be searching and selecting from amongst these predictable belongings. It was like going through the private possessions of a stranger who happened also to be her mother.

She put in the paperback novel – a historical romance – that was lying on the bedside table and zipped up the suitcase with a sense of relief. Everything in the flat was tidy and fairly clean, but the clothes and furniture and the few other items, from china knick-knacks to pot-bound house plants and a small row of paperbacks, all had the air of being perfunctorily assembled, as if their owner had lost interest in them as well as in the wider world. The flimsiness of this place of her mother's, a temporary perch only a few wingbeats from the end of a long flight, made Miranda feel deeply sad. Not for the first time, she vowed to overcome Joyce's blank refusals and make her come to live with her at Mead. In the cottage now occupied by Katherine and Amos, perhaps, if she refused to surrender her independence altogether.

There was nothing else here, as far as she could see, that Joyce might need for a short stay in hospital. Miranda carried the case out into the hall and made a quick check of doors and windows. She would be coming back later, to spend the night. This was where she would stay until Joyce was discharged. The houseman who admitted her had said antibiotics should bring the pneumonia under control, and if she could stay free of hospital infections she would recover quite quickly. As she glanced into the kitchen, her mobile rang. It was six o'clock. Through the lit window of the flat opposite, Miranda could see a very old woman, tottering in minute steps across the bright backdrop of her kitchen.

Glancing at the display she said, 'Katherine? Hello?'

'Yes, it's me. Where are you, Mirry?'

'At my mother's.'

She explained what had happened and why she would be away from Mead for a few days. Katherine's voice was warm with sympathy.

'No,' Miranda answered, 'thanks. Nothing you can do. Everything should be all right in the house, and Colin's back in a few days. Wait, though – you could just mention to Polly and Selwyn what's happened?'

'I'll do that. Go on. Off you go back to the hospital.'

Miranda almost rang off, but she remembered just in time to ask if Katherine had called for any reason. There was a second's silence before her reply. No, she said. Nothing important. Just hi.

They said goodbye. Miranda took the tartan suitcase out to her car.

Katherine sat in the bedroom at the cottage. What had seemed straightforward and inevitable this morning on the beach had now become dark and convoluted. She had been going to confide in Miranda, had even worked out the exact words she would use. The notion had been to confirm the reality of what she was doing by telling another person, but this was the way things happened. You got so immersed in your own concerns that you started thinking of other people almost as cardboard cut-outs to be moved about in the unfolding drama but then – chasteningly – you were reminded that they were busy on their own stage.

Katherine was fond of Joyce, and hoped that she would soon be better. She was also concerned for Miranda herself, whom she knew to be troubled by the awkwardness of her relationship with her mother. Katherine's own gentle, conventional mother had died of breast cancer ten years ago.

242

In any case, she decided now, her decision to speak to Miranda had probably only been a delaying tactic. Perhaps she had been hoping that her friend would dissuade her, tell her that she mustn't do anything of the kind – was that it?

One thing she did know: she wasn't going to approach Polly in the same way. Because there was something wrong between Polly and Selwyn, too. He was brittle and irritable with everyone, and cutting to Polly herself, whereas Polly had developed a kind of mute, imploring meekness around him that she was too clever to wear comfortably.

It isn't until you come to live in each other's pockets like this that you start to see all the cracks, Katherine thought. Miranda with her love and vivacity had convinced them that Mead would be the place where they could start to grow old, and Amos had taken the proposal and decorated it with his grand designs. She had gone along with his notions, because that was what she did, and to her surprise she had been the one who had been woken up by the change.

But it didn't look now as if they would be seeing out as much as a season of the great Mead plan together. Katherine was sorry that out of all of them she was going to be the one who began the retreat.

When she came into the cottage, having said goodbye to Chris next to their parked cars on the beach road, Amos was sitting in an armchair with the whisky decanter at his elbow. She passed by him without speaking, and he had ignored her. Separately, in the hours that she had been out, they had been moving towards the crisis. Amos was no fool. He was intuitive, in his own bull-headed way, and he'd know that today had a different dimension from any of their previous crises, serious though some of them had been. Now she could hear him moving about downstairs, banging against furniture and shouldering through doorways.

If she didn't go and confront him soon he would bring the fight upstairs to her.

She found him in the kitchen. He had shaken fresh ice out

243

of the ice tray and there were cubes melting on the floor. His face was dark red.

'Why do you have to drink so much?' she asked in exasperation.

Amos had never been a drunk. But since he had been asked either to leave his chambers or face a harassment charge – the pearl-handled revolver no-option option, as he bitterly called it – he had been starting earlier and earlier in the day.

'Because I'm fucking miserable, and it helps,' he snarled.

His pain was so obvious that she put her hand out to him, exactly as if he were one of the boys come home from school with a problem that she could solve. For all these years her role had been to soothe and comfort these three men, and now she was going to be the cause of their suffering.

Amos shook it off. 'Don't minister to me. Don't do your bloody concerned thing. I'll just get on with it, thanks.'

'All right.' She took a cloth and mopped up the melted ice. He stumbled past her into the living room and flopped into his chair. She followed, and stood in front of him. She felt slightly ill with apprehension, and self-disgust. It would have been so much easier to go upstairs to the second bedroom and climb into bed. In the morning Amos would be sober, and they could pretend that what was wrong was not significant, and nothing much would change, and so she would hold on to the life she knew instead of reaching for the one she wanted.

It was remembering the brave, determined picture of herself that she had painted for Chris that made her hold her resolve.

There is a lot of ground I have to cover. I have to do it on my own.

Oh, please. Who did she think she was? Joan of Arc?

But she *had* said it.

'Amos, I'm going to London tonight.'

'What the hell for?'

He looked at her from under thickened eyelids. He knew what was coming, but he was going to make her say it.

'I'm leaving you.'

He swirled his glass and threw down another inch of whisky. Then he laughed.

'Why? Haven't I earned enough money to keep you happy?'

She did him the favour of ignoring the question. 'Amos, you say you're miserable. Hasn't it ever crossed your mind that I might be too?'

He laughed again, with desolation cracking his face. 'If you are, we've got more in common than I thought. You seem to me as happy as a cow in clover.'

'I meant, I'm miserable being married to you.'

A tide of terrible delight was rising in Katherine. It was such a relief to utter these irrevocable words. She had never even breathed such a thing to him before.

Amos recoiled, exactly as if she had struck him. A dull flush rose from his throat to his cheeks, reddening his contused face still further. He looked down at his empty glass, then back at his wife, all the time swinging his head from side to side in a confused attempt to shake away the onset of pain. She stood very still, amazed to have reached this point so rapidly, and appalled by her capacity to hurt him. The brief delight was already dying within her.

He was groping for words, but for once his lawyerly fluency deserted him. All that came out was a howl as he bellowed at her.

'Go on then. Fuck off.'

He turned his back and blundered off to the kitchen in search of more whisky.

Katherine went upstairs and collected together a very few of her belongings. She noted, in a detached corner of her racing mind, that out of so many clothes and jewels and pairs of shoes there was nothing much she wanted to take with her. Her almost-empty overnight bag banged against her calves as she descended again.

Tumbler in hand, Amos had placed himself between her and the front door. She thought that he might physically oppose her, even lash out, but she kept walking. He stood his ground and in the end she had to push past him, keeping her face averted. He put his free hand out to restrain her, but she shook it off.

'Katherine . . .' he began as the door opened on wet darkness.

'No,' she heard herself say. A small, hard, cold snap of a monosyllable.

Then she was outside, crossing the cobbles to the yard gate. Her Audi was tucked out of sight behind Selwyn and Polly's barn, where they all parked their cars. As the gate clinked shut behind her she heard his footsteps on the slippery stone. He stumbled and slid, half-falling with a heavy crash against the stone wall.

The pain must have unleashed his rage. He began yelling after her. She caught only a few of the words.

They were obscene and ugly and jagged with despair.

Katherine reached her car, flung in the bag and collapsed into the driver's seat. She reversed too fast, spun the wheel and skidded towards the driveway, crunching the forward wheel arch against a stone gatepost at the back of the barn as she did so. The clang of metal barely registered on her. She righted the car and accelerated under the arch of bare trees, out into the lane, and away towards Meddlett and London.

Tears were pouring down her face.

Selwyn and Polly stopped work and glanced at each other. Selwyn had been varnishing wood, and the windows were open to allow fumes to escape. He rested his brush on the open tin and as he did so the crunch of Katherine's collision with the gatepost was audible from the other side of the barn.

Polly slowly descended from a stepladder. Neither of them spoke. The miasma of the Knights' scene bled in through all the cracks and chinks of the building and occupied the room with them. Selwyn took his brush to the sink and rinsed it in white spirit, then stuck it in a jar. Polly pretended to be examining her making good, but she was hoping that Selwyn would say something. Anything would have done: a murmur of concern for their friends, or one of his caustic comments about Amos, perhaps even an admission that problems took many forms and a reference to Nic's pregnancy. Predictably Selwyn had greeted that piece of news with dismay, and irritation at Ben's lack of common sense.

But the silence extended. Selwyn couldn't keep still. He walked from the sink to the alcove where his tools were stacked, back again to the sink, then to the front door, which he yanked open. He avoided looking at Polly.

Amos must have retreated to the cottage. The curtains there were drawn, and the main house was in darkness.

It was cold in the barn with the door and windows standing open. The clutter of building materials and dirty mugs and stacked planks was dispiriting. It was one thing to tackle the restoration of a wreck of a house aged thirty, full of energy and the desire to make a home for babies, but at almost sixty it was a different matter. They were too dejected and divided, Polly thought sadly. Selwyn stared at the windows of the house, as if he were willing them to blink alive with light. She watched him, but her neck and shoulders were tense with the readiness to look elsewhere as soon as he moved. He had started complaining that she was always staring at him.

'I'm going over to see if Amos is all right,' he muttered. He didn't give Polly time to answer. She folded the stepladder with a bleak clank of the metal struts and leaned it against the wall.

Amos opened the door and jerked his head to signal Selwyn inside. The television was on, turned up very loud. Selwyn shouted over it that he'd have wine, not whisky, and took the over-filled glass that Amos unsteadily handed him. They sat down in armchairs and watched Chelsea score a goal against Sheffield Wednesday.

Polly answered her phone, expecting it to be one of the twins but hoping it might be Ben with some news of Nic.

Katherine's voice was shaking.

'Where are you?' Polly asked. 'Are you all right?'

'In a lay-by. Not really. I've left him.'

'Is that for good, K?'

'Yes. I'm really sorry.'

Polly asked her why on earth she was apologizing, and Katherine muttered something about not wanting to visit their problems on everyone else at Mead. Polly advised her with a touch of grimness that she shouldn't waste too much time worrying about that.

She said quickly, 'Listen, do you want me to come down to London and keep you company for a couple of days while you sort things out?' The option became distinctly more appealing than staying in the barn.

Katherine said maybe, once she'd had some time to think, and Polly promised that she'd definitely come and would try to bring Mirry with her.

'Tell you what. We'll have a night out. Talk a lot and drink too many cocktails. It'll be like old times.'

'Miranda's why I called, really. I forgot to give you a message from her.'

Kathcrine relayed the news about Joyce and why Miranda was so unusually absent from Mead.

'Don't be so concerned about everyone else all the time,' Polly advised. 'Save your energy for yourself, for once. And drive carefully, will you?'

Chelsea won three–nil. After the post-match analysis finished they watched the opening five minutes of a documentary. Amos stared fixedly at the screen.

'Anything I can do?' Selwyn asked.

Amos shook his head.

'Is it serious?' Selwyn persisted.

'She's left me.'

'Christ. I'm sorry.'

Amos turned his head now. His eyes looked poached.

'Are you?'

248

'Yeah. Of course I am. You know.'

'I know fuck all,' Amos sighed. 'Apparently.'

They watched the programme for a few more minutes, then Selwyn stood up. He put his hand briefly on Amos's shoulder.

'I'd get some sleep now, if I were you. It may all look quite different in the morning.'

'What are you? Thought for the bloody Day?'

Selwyn shrugged and made for the door.

'Sorry. I know you're only trying to help,' Amos muttered as he went.

'That's all right. You know where we are if you need anything.'

Polly made scrambled eggs and a pot of tea. She said nothing as Selwyn came in, but piled the eggs on the buttered toast and set a plate in front of him.

'How is he?' she asked later, when they had both finished eating.

'Pissed. Angry.'

'Yes.'

'Do you think it's permanent?'

He did look at Polly now. Their eyes met across the cluttered table, and she realized with dismay crawling up her spine that her own future might not involve many more suppers or nights in the same bed as Selwyn. How had this happened, so suddenly and stealthily? Was it Miranda's fault for recapturing Selwyn's wandering attention, or her own, for not being someone different?

'Yes, I do,' she said sorrowfully.

She told him about Katherine's call. Selwyn nodded, rubbing the flat of his hand up and down the back of his head so that dust fell in a shower. The bandage over the rocket burn had become a nuisance and now he wore just a pad of lint taped to the shaved skin where bristles of hair were already poking through. He looked so rumpled and familiar and dear to her that Polly got up and kissed his cheek. He didn't respond, but nor did he push her away.

Encouraged by this she mentioned, 'I thought it was going to be Ben calling about Nicola.'

This did annoy him. He snapped, 'Ben's not a kid any more, you know. He's got to sort out his own problems.'

Polly moved away. She told him the other piece of news, that Joyce had been taken to hospital and Miranda would be staying up there with her.

At once, Selwyn's head jerked up so that he could see out of their new, tall windows to the main house.

He was searching for lights in the windows, willing them to shine. Polly saw it, and knew that he was wishing and longing for Miranda. She didn't know what Miranda's response might be, but the structure of long friendship and the foundations of the life they had planned at Mead now seemed built on quicksand.

She picked up the plates and cutlery and ferried them over to the sink. She did the washing up, using the small tasks to shield her dread. If Katherine and Amos's long marriage could implode, what did the thirty years shared with Selwyn count for?

Ben's words came back to her. *Keep your end up. Everyone needs something for themselves, Mum.* That's what he had said, hadn't he, more or less?

Everything she cared for and everything she owned, inextricably linked together, was tied up in this barn. That had been an unwise move, she now understood, and it had taken Ben, of all people, to point it out.

Sam and Toby

Like their father, the Knight boys were tall and well-built. In the tight confines of the Bloomsbury flat they gave the impression of needing to bend their necks and pin their elbows against their ribcages in order not to bump any extremities against the walls or the ceiling. Tonight this physical constraint was lent an extra dimension by their not knowing quite how to treat their mother. Going through the routines of cooking dinner, wrapped as usual in the faded Morris print apron that had seen service in several of their homes before this one, the sight of her was utterly familiar. But at the same time they had to couple this outward appearance of normality with the extraordinary fact that she had left their father, and was remaining calmly resistant to any suggestion that she might soon be ready to go back to him.

Katherine splashed wine into a sauté pan. Sam and Toby eyed her warily, holding themselves poised at the ready, as if her next move might be to play a bassoon solo or to open the window and hurl all the plates out into the street.

She opened a drawer and lifted out a sheaf of table mats.

'Sam? Could you lay?'

'Sure.'

'Are we drinking wine? Toby, what would you like?'

'Just a beer, thanks,' he mumbled.

Over her head he exchanged a glance with Sam. It was a flash of mutual incomprehension, sharpened with embarrassment.

Katherine brought the dishes to the table and placed the open bottle of red wine on the silver coaster in the centre, making sure it was equidistant between the lit candles.

The boys helped themselves to food, their mother's ever-excellent home cooking, and she poured herself a glass of wine.

'Looks good,' Sam commented, shaking out his napkin.

Katherine raised her glass to them.

The three of them had met separately, but this was the first time since the parents' separation that they had all sat down together.

'I don't know what to propose,' she said after a moment's thought.

'To our family,' Toby said, with firm emphasis.

'To us,' Katherine amended, and they drank. 'And to the future, whatever it is.'

Cutlery clinked as they settled down to eat, and through the drawn curtains muffled traffic noise seeped into the room.

'Apropos of which,' Sam began, after clearing his throat. 'We want to talk to you, Mum. Not just for us but for Dad, as well.'

Their sons had been recruited, Katherine saw, into the movement to restore the status quo. Or more probably, to be fair to Amos, hadn't been actively recruited but belonged to it naturally, because children – even adult children – wanted their parents to stay on the safe plateau of advanced middle age, preferably beaming side by side like the grey-haired bicycling couples on the back of porridge oats packets, leaving them free to enjoy their own more interesting lives. Children didn't want to find the time and energy for worrying about awkward parental upheavals. Not if they didn't have to.

The two of them kept exchanging glances. They had clearly worked out in advance what they might say to her, to cajole her back into the fold.

'Go on,' she said. Despite her intention to be attentive and

252

receptive to whatever they had to say, because she loved them, a flicker of irritation rose within her. It burned higher because she did love them so much, flesh of her flesh. She took another sip of her wine, and waited.

'Obviously it's been difficult, with the move up to Mead and the house building being delayed and the publicity about the archaeological finds, and then the shock of the robbery,' Toby offered. 'Coming on top of the problem with Dad and the chambers. No wonder you feel unsettled.'

The irritation was already fading, replaced by her instinctive wish to make everything well for them again. Her conviction wavered.

'I don't know what I do feel,' she confessed. 'It's confusing.'

Her younger son blinked. His mother was supposed to be just *there*, not to be battered by the winds of doubt or uncertainty.

How like Amos they both were. Studying their broad, flushed faces she could see their father's certainty and confidence, and sense the mass of their shared male solidarity like granite under mountain turf.

'We aren't trying to tell you what to do, Mum. We just want to know what's going on. To help, if we can. Dad's fairly distraught. I'm sure you know that.' This was Sam, always more diplomatic than his brother.

'He wants you back home,' Toby put in.

Katherine nodded.

'Well?' Toby persisted.

They were both eating quite heartily, she noticed. Her own plate lay untouched. Food had lost its importance lately, but wine was good. She cleared her throat.

'I'm not going back.'

Saying it over their own dinner table with Amos's empty chair facing her gave weight to the words. Sam reached out and put his hand over hers. A cow's lick in his hair, above the right eyebrow, forever battled with his good haircut. An ancient chickenpox scar indented his forehead near the bridge of his nose.

253

'Is it because of the other women?'

This was a bold acknowledgement. Sam and Toby both knew that their father had affairs, and Katherine knew that they knew, but they had never openly discussed it. In times of crisis the boys would put their arms around her shoulders more demonstratively than usual, and ask with extra emphasis if she needed any help with anything, but even when the threat of the harassment suit had compelled Amos to leave his chambers and initiated the whole process of removing to Mead, the subject had never been directly aired.

How English we are, she thought, and how conventional.

Even in their business suits as they were tonight, having come straight from work, her sons looked as if they ought to have a cricket bag or a pair of skis somewhere about them. They were decent, healthy, traditional men, slightly at odds with their own times. She had bred that conventional quality in them, she understood, and she felt a surge of compassion for them, as well as love. Their father was and always had been more outrageous and less forgivable.

She opened her eyes innocently wide. 'What other women?' It was an attempt to lighten the atmosphere by showing them that she wasn't afraid to joke, but they both looked so appalled that she immediately felt sorry for being clumsy. She said quickly, 'No, it's not because of that. If it were, I'd have left long ago.'

Toby leaned forwards, steepling his fingers just as his father did.

'Why, then?'

'Why did I leave, or why am I not going back?'

'Both. First one first.'

She drank some more wine. It had the effect of amplifying the rush of blood in her ears.

'I left because being at Mead with Miranda and the others gave me an idea of how I might live differently from the way I have done up to now.'

They gazed at her, striving to decipher her meaning. She sliced a small portion of food, speared it with her fork and placed it in her mouth. It tasted of nothing. She chewed and swallowed, with difficulty.

'Yet you've left Mead behind as well as Dad. Isn't that a contradiction?'

Toby's question was studiedly uninflected in tone.

'Yes, I can see what you mean. I believed in the Mead idea and I'm really sorry to be the renegade. I wish it was working out the way Miranda dreamed, and I suppose it still could. Being there made me see myself differently, though, and you can't unsee things once the light has gone on, can you?' As gently as she could she added, 'There is a completely different reason why I can't go back.'

There was a second's absolute silence. Even the traffic seemed stilled.

Neither of them would ask what the reason might be. Instead the table mats and candlestick bases seemed suddenly to become objects for close scrutiny. Her sons knew that she was about to say something they didn't want to hear and would wish to have unsaid as soon as it was uttered, but Katherine had reached the point of truth and she clung to her conviction that it was time to speak it.

Into her head came the memory of the evening in Chris's offices, when he had placed the torc about her neck and she had reached up to finger the heavy twists of metal as it lay against her skin. Some piece of alchemy had taken place and she had been transformed.

When their eyes had met and locked she hadn't glanced away, or tried to apologize. She hadn't even blushed. She had stared back at him, open as the excavated site, and leaping with life. She had been eager – greedy – and he had read that in her eyes and responded to her.

It struck her now that it was the first and only time in her life that she had felt no inhibitions.

It was at that moment that she had fallen in love with him. That was when, and that was what it was.

She was in love with Chris Carr and she wanted to be with

him. She hadn't seen him since their walk on the beach, they had only spoken briefly and inconclusively on the telephone, but now she wanted to leap out of her chair and rush to him. Under the table, out of sight, she clamped her fingers to the sides of her chair.

'I have met someone else,' she said. The drained words were hardly adequate, but to her sons she couldn't give them the proper emphasis.

Sam and Toby weren't glancing at each other now. Shocked, they looked straight back at her. They didn't want to believe what she was telling them. She was their mother, not a women's magazine feature on midlife crisis.

'Who is he?'

'Do we know him?'

'No,' she said.

'Are you,' Toby frowned, 'having an *affair* with this man?'

'You've made the assumption that it's a man,' she pointed out with a touch of mischief.

Their faces froze in horrified disbelief. She repented again.

'It is, in fact, but it might not have been. I'm not having an affair yet, but I'm not going to rule it out. A relationship with him, that is. I don't want to rule anything out. That's sort of the point. I'm being as honest as I can. Can you understand any of this, at all?'

She could see how difficult it was for them – more than difficult, positively distasteful – to make this dizzy shift in reckoning. She belonged at their father's side, and if not there then in her office at the charity, or here in the flat cooking dinner in her William Morris print National Trust apron. The admission that she had just made set up all kinds of unwelcome speculations. Their mother had a mind of her own. Their mother made calculations for herself that did not number themselves as points one and two for consideration. Their mother almost certainly *thought about sex*. They were right on that one. Sex, she acknowledged to herself, occupied quite a large proportion of her waking thoughts these days.

This struck her as funny and she laughed as her sons gaped at her.

'Does Dad know him, whoever he is?'

'Not really.' She thought she was justified in saying this. Amos had met him, that was all.

'How long has it been going on?'

Katherine held up her hand. It was not so much answering her sons' questions as recognizing the depth of disapprobation that lay behind them that was uncomfortable.

'It doesn't matter who he is and there's nothing much going on at the moment. This is just as much about Amos and me, and the new house, and, well – just the age that the two of us are.'

Sombre-faced they listened to her while she tried to explain to them why she didn't want to live in a sparkling new house built on top of the princess's vandalized burial site, and how living at Mead had made her feel vital in a way she hadn't done for many years, and finally that despite what she had just said, their parents' long marriage had been not a failure but a success.

'Do you still love Dad?' Sam wanted to know.

'Yes,' she acknowledged, because she did. You did love people, when they had been the father of your children and embedded in your life for every day of thirty years. Even though they had not always behaved well, or considerately, or even thought about you that much, except as an accessory.

Now they were looking at each other again, the immediate rictus of embarrassment having passed.

'This may be just a phase, then,' Toby murmured.

She made no response to that.

She was reflecting again on how their conventional attitudes were her legacy. Yet her own exterior didn't convey the full picture, as she was only just discovering, so by the same measure her sons' appearances might mask surprising opposite tendencies. She was gripped by a fierce longing to discover what these might be. How well did she really know them, even though she had given birth to them and fed them and finally discharged them into the adult world?

257

Maybe in time all four of them would learn to see into each other instead of merely glancing at and then past the spaces they occupied.

A wave of optimism swept through her. The room seemed brighter, her sons less censorious.

'You look happy,' Sam told her wonderingly.

After they had gone, Katherine cleared the plates and scraped her almost untouched food into the kitchen pedal bin. She blew out the candles and collected up the place mats. Her shadow fell across the polished table top.

She picked up the phone and dialled his number. He answered on the second ring.

'I want to see you,' she said. 'Is that still what you want?'

She could hear his breath in her ear. It was unbearable that he was a hundred miles away.

He said, 'Are you sure about that? When?'

'Yes, I'm sure. Tomorrow. As soon as possible. *Now.*'

Chris laughed, the sound warm inside her head. 'OK.'

Toby and Sam walked to the Tube.

'So, what do you think?' Toby asked.

'I think it's like Mum said. And Dad's given her quite a hard time, over the years, hasn't he?'

'In a way. But it hasn't all been bad.'

They had been brought up to recognize that they were privileged because of Amos's success. That had been Katherine's doing, and she had always been clear that she included herself in this.

'No, it hasn't,' Sam acknowledged.

'I had a long talk on the phone to Alph Davies. She says her parents have been pretty rocky, and even more bonkers if that's possible to imagine, since they went to live up there.'

'It's the stage they're all at. They're getting old and they don't want to. They fear age, and death. Sex is a way of not thinking about death.'

Toby shrugged. This kind of speculation was not his *métier*.

They passed under a row of lights that marked the farthest limit of the recently illuminated Oxford Street Christmas decorations. A ragged star blinked on and off in a cobweb of cables. Every Christmas of their lives so far the Knight brothers had spent with their parents.

'What will happen this year?' Toby wondered.

'Do you suppose Mum will want to be with Mr Mystery? If it comes to a choice, we'll have to be with Dad. We can't leave him on his own with a microwaved turkey feast for one, can we?'

'No, we can't do that, of course. Happy Christmas,' Toby sighed.

DECEMBER

TEN

The drive out of London reminded Katherine of the afternoon in September when she and Amos had headed for the first proper Mead weekend. She had felt a knot of excited anticipation beneath her diaphragm then too, impossible to ignore and more intense than the circumstances called for. Her sense that something major was about to happen had grown, and the effect of it was to burnish the intervening events, lending them a texture in her memory that other momentous times in her life had never acquired.

She saw again the group of teenagers swarming out of the village bus shelter to jump on Amos's Jaguar, the bar at the Griffin, the trampled grass in the shelter of the white tent as they stood on the lip of the grave and peered down at the princess's uncovered bones.

Then came the moment when Chris placed the massive gold torc around her neck, and the sequence that led from there to the walk on the beach and the point where she said to Amos, *I'm leaving you.*

The events seemed inevitable in retrospect, but whenever she thought of this last, a ripple of disbelief ran through her.

She had said it, and then she had actually done it. And now she was driving out of town at the end of a lightless December afternoon, passing over orange ribbons of elevated roads and into the slow current of motorway traffic, on her way to meet Christopher Carr once again. When they had dinner together he had joked about Manhattan or the moon, but as it turned out even a couple of nights together in rural Norfolk had been comically difficult to arrange.

It was two and a half weeks before Christmas. The boys and Amos wanted to know if she was coming home to Mead for the holiday, and she couldn't tell them because she didn't know herself. She was in the opposite corner to all the clockwork family holidays of the past.

Chris was busy. The Mead artefacts were in the hands of the Iron-Age experts, the bones were now boxed up and filed on the shelves at his offices. He had written his report on the finds that had been saved and on the loss of the remainder, and now other work had intervened. Much of it was routine, he told her, and none of it was as fascinating as the great discovery at Mead. Katherine listened intently. His work evidently absorbed him, just as Amos's had done, but Chris talked about it more generously. And when he wasn't working, his family made a series of calls on his time. In this last part of the Christmas term there were school plays and carol concerts and a disco. Then his ex-wife and her husband went shopping in New York, and while they were away his daughters came to stay with him.

'I want to see you so much,' he told her. 'This isn't very romantic, is it?'

'It is, in a way. It's ordinary life illuminated by pure amazement,' Katherine smiled.

Finally, there was a site to be assessed in Lincolnshire. Chris told her how he had grabbed the job file for himself.

'Meet me there?' he asked, sounding diffident now that the moment had come.

'Yes,' she said without hesitation.

Chris mentioned booking a hotel, perhaps in Peterborough or Spalding.

Katherine saw the room as clearly as if she were already

264

standing in it. There would be dark red Anaglypta beneath the dado, dark- and sludge-green Regency stripe above, a trouser press and a tiny kettle, a television behind shiny double doors with the laminated list of channels including an adult one, and the reek of illicit cigarettes trapped in the curtains.

An hour later he called her back and said he had found a rental cottage. The owner was happy to let it for a couple of nights off season.

'It will be a bit more homely,' Chris said. This word stayed in her head.

A home? Was this what they wanted together?

He did all this gently, with consideration for what she might want or expect, and she was appreciative. But she felt old. Long ago, with Amos and before him, just doing it had been the imperative, not making all the attached accommodations. Two people would have fallen behind a hedge or into the back of a car or under a pile of coats at a party. It was odd to have reached an age where the setting was significant. It had to be free from previous associations, and private, and appropriate to their maturity.

How unexpectedly complicated it all was.

Katherine was smiling as she peered into the traffic.

Complicated, but also exciting.

She had even bought new underwear. Lace yes, but not black. It was a sort of old rose colour, much more appropriate. Trying it on, she was surprised to see how much weight she had lost.

She reached the fen country. In the darkness on either side of the road she was aware of empty flat land seamed by dykes, and the sea like the end of the world ahead of her. There was a narrower road and a jumble of dark houses, a single white finger post suddenly rearing in the headlights. A mile or so further on the road petered out. There was a low building to one side and a square of light in a window.

The robot voice of her satnav informed her, 'You have reached your destination.'

*   *   *

The setting didn't matter so much after all, she discovered.

As soon as Chris opened the door she had a blurred impression of low ceilings and latched doors, the smell of bottled gas. But other impressions were much stronger. Hands and skin; breathing suddenly having become very difficult. A strange sensation beneath her breastbone, somewhere between a trapped hiccup and a cough, that when he stopped kissing her escaped as a bubble of pure, delighted laughter.

The stairs were very steep. He hit his head on a lintel and swore, until she put her mouth to his.

The bed, when they fell on to it, smelled damp.

Not much notice was taken of the rose-coloured lace.

The beard was a difference. But otherwise having sex with Dr Christopher Carr seemed both apt and oddly familiar, like a reprise of a soaring musical theme that she thought she had forgotten but which was in fact embedded in every cell of her body and her soul.

Afterwards they lay back, breathless and tangled up in the twist of unaired sheets. She rested her chin in the obliging hollow between his neck and shoulder.

Katherine was amused to realize that in the past half-hour she hadn't given a thought to her wrinkles, or the folds of flesh around her belly. Chris didn't appear all that much younger than she did, now they came to look candidly at each other. Bodies were admirable pieces of machinery. She was quite proud of hers, tonight, and the warmth and weight of his was welcome, separate but also comfortable, only representing a partial answer as yet to a series of questions. The full answer would no doubt come in time: if they were to have time.

His fingers knotted in her hair.

'My barbarian,' he said. That made her giggle. It would be hard to imagine anyone less barbaric than the woman she had been.

'What's funny?' he lazily asked.

'Sex, I suppose.'

266

'I know,' he breathed, rolling on to his side so he could look into her eyes. 'I know.'

Affection and regard for him swelled up in her. He was a nice man. A good man. Was that faint praise, she wondered?

'Do you know something else? I'm hungry,' she said, after a while.

'That may be a problem. There's a pub in the village, though.'

But Katherine had done just as she would if she had been on her way to the old home in Richmond, or up to Mead. The boot of her car was full of supermarket carrier bags. Once they had put their clothes on again he carried the bags in for her.

'You're a miracle,' Chris said, in genuine admiration.

The cottage wasn't furnished with Miranda's style, but there was an oven, and Katherine found pots and pans and crockery stacked in spidery cupboards. She cooked dinner, and Chris opened a bottle of wine and leaned against the sink and talked to her. The talk went on and on. They laughed, and then turned serious again. He looked at her, and she returned his stare. They were wondering, both of them, what was supposed to happen next now the first major thing had happened. But the kitchen was warm with the oven's heat and the thin curtains were drawn. This is what we do, she thought. We make a domestic scene out of this temporary shell. Even in the warmth and yellow lamplight, though, the picture was fragile, as if a single breath might whirl it away.

The next day, she went with him to the site.

He gave her a hard hat and a hi-vis waistcoat to put on over her raincoat. They tramped across a raw field where a new estate of boxy houses would eventually rise.

'If the developer doesn't go bust first, that is,' Chris said.

She watched him while he took measurements and soil samples. They were undemonstrative with each other in the presence of an architect and an engineer, but once, when no one was looking, Chris caught her hand and lightly ran his thumb over the bones of her wrist. This tiny gesture seemed to touch her as intimately as anything that had taken place between them the night before. He was a good talker, but she was learning that he was more eloquent with the unspoken. The opposite of Amos.

A thin shawl of rain came at them off the Wash.

'Are you warm enough?' he asked. He wanted her to sit in the car with the heater on but she preferred it out here, with him. It felt companionable, although – like homely – that was an odd word to come to mind.

Wasn't that what she already had, a home and a companion, and had done for the last thirty years?

On the drive back to the cottage they stopped at a café in the middle of a village. There was another long featureless street, but this place didn't seem to have the teenage population of the place where she and Amos had had tea back in September. Or maybe on a day like this everyone between thirteen and twenty was indoors, smoking and listening to their MP3s. This café wasn't organic with Victorian embellishments, like the other one. It was bleary with condensation and smelled of frying.

Katherine and Chris were eating soup. It was both salty and tasteless, with the powdery packet residue at the centre of occasional lumps.

'Don't say I don't show you the world,' Chris laughed, but he was apologizing at the same time, fearing that she might be critical of his choice although they had passed no other alternatives apart from a Chinese takeaway. Much of his life must consist of days like this, Katherine realized. Long drives to remote sites, and hasty meals taken en route. They still didn't know much about each other, even though he was now officially her lover. She was faintly oppressed by the prospect of how much separate history lay behind them, and how much they still had to discover. It was like being given a text to study in a language not her mother tongue.

Outside, a young woman in a parka came by with her child. The child was dressed in a bright red all-in-one with the hood pulled up over a knitted hat, making it impossible to guess what sex it was. It was riding a tiny tricycle, pedalling furiously but still making such slow progress that the mother kept stopping to let it get ahead by a yard before two steps brought them parallel again. They were both intent on this journey, their cold-pinched features showing a strong resemblance. Sam had owned just such a trike when he was a toddler, and the snail's-pace of days with a tiny child came vividly back to Katherine. A glance at Chris revealed that he was watching the pair too, with an expression she didn't want to fathom. Neither of them spoke until the tricycle had passed out of the frame of the café window.

With a younger woman, Chris could have a new family. He had claimed once that he didn't want to start again, but she had no way of telling whether this was the truth.

It was raining harder now, and there was still a distance to drive back to the cottage.

'Shall we go?' he asked gently.

Katherine nodded, gathering up her bag and damp raincoat.

The next morning she woke reluctantly from a sleep that seemed deeper than usual, and it took several seconds to remember where she was. Then unwillingness for the impending separation from Chris flooded through her. She pressed closer against him and he held her in his arms.

'What's wrong?'

'Sadness.'

His mouth moved against her ear. 'That's always going to be with us. It's the accumulation of experience, building up like scale inside a kettle. The more you learn, the harder it is to be thoughtlessly optimistic. We can learn to live with it, though.'

'Do we have to? Isn't there some product we can use just to fizz it away?'

'I can think of something we might try.' His hands slid over her. And for half an hour at least, it worked.

In the end, they couldn't put off getting up any longer.

Katherine knew before switching on her mobile that there would be several messages from Amos, and probably from the boys as well. Chris walked naked to the window and opened the curtains to the view of grey sky. She studied the set of his shoulders and the collar of flesh at his middle. His legs were furred with dark hair.

'I have to go home. For Christmas, at least,' she told him.

Without turning around he said, 'I know you do.'

They ate breakfast together at the pine kitchen table. Afterwards they emptied the small residue of food into a bin liner and carried it out to the wheelie bin at the side of the house. Katherine's car was where she had parked it two nights ago, with the wheels tracked sideways. Salt air had already touched the crumpled front wheel arch with rust. He put her small bag in the boot and held open the door for her. When she slid down the driver's window he leaned in and kissed her.

'After Christmas,' she promised, although she didn't know *what*.

He stood back and watched, with his hand raised, as she drove away.

The days crept by and Christmas came closer.

Katherine stayed in London, going to work and coming home each night to the Bloomsbury flat. She reorganized the charity's main donor index and devised a major appeal to be launched in the New Year, impressing her colleagues with her flood of energy. In her spare time she went Christmas shopping, not quite able to resist the guilty impulse to buy more presents than usual for her sons. Toby and Sam came to see her again, separately as well as together, and she did her best to convince them that she was all right and so would they and Amos be, given time. She knew that they were disappointed in her, although they tried hard not to be.

She spoke to Chris every day, but even so when she was not immersed in her own work she was startlingly lonely. She hadn't taken into account how the background reassurance of a long partnership fills all the waking hours.

She also talked to both Polly and Miranda, and she was pleased when they suggested coming to London to take her out.

'Yes please, let's do that,' she agreed. Being away from Mead and separated from Amos made her understand how much her affection for both her friends had deepened.

Miranda was still with Joyce. Katherine asked Polly for news about Amos, and Polly told her all she knew, which was very little. She said that he seemed to spend most of his time watching television and drinking.

One night over a bottle of wine Amos confided to Selwyn that his sons were shocked and incredulous that their parents' long marriage could shatter like this.

'What am I supposed to say to them?' Amos was at a loss for words, for possibly only the second or third time in his life.

'Maybe it hasn't shattered,' Selwyn attempted. 'Perhaps when you've both had a chance to think it over, you'll be able to patch things up.'

Amos surveyed his surroundings. The cottage was no longer polished and pin-neat. There was a strong smell, partly relating to the overflowing bin in the kitchen but more to do with unopened windows and despair.

Selwyn added, 'You should allow Katherine a bit of leeway. She'll probably come around. She's given you plenty of slack over the years, hasn't she?'

'For Christ's sake. There's a difference between taking a couple of minor diversions along the route and blowing up the whole fucking road. I always came home. I don't know about you, but I have never suggested or considered that my marriage was for anything less than life. *From this day forth*, you know. But you and Polly never actually got married, did you?'

Selwyn rested his head in his hands. It was late, he was always tired, and there were knots here that were too serious for him to risk even the gentlest attempt at unpicking. Across the yard Miranda's windows were still in darkness. He was unnerved to realize how deeply her absence was affecting him.

'No. We never said those words. What difference does it make, after three decades of sharing a life?'

'None, so it seems.' Amos shook his head and refilled his glass. He had physically shrunk. His unironed shirt collar revealed the sad folds of his neck.

Back in the barn, Selwyn related this exchange to Polly. With Miranda and Colin both away, they had become unofficial care-takers of Amos.

'You don't think he'll do anything stupid, do you?' Selwyn wondered. He tightened the jaws of a bench vice and ran his fingers over a length of planking before taking up a plane.

'If you mean shoot or poison himself, no, I don't. He might drink himself to death, but that will take a while.'

Polly had come back from the house, where she had used the washing machine in the utility room off Miranda's kitchen. Selwyn watched her place the plastic holdall that functioned as their laundry basket in a relatively undusty spot at the other end of their trestle table. She took out clean pairs of jeans and T-shirts, shook them with a sharp snap and refolded them in the air since there was nowhere clean enough to put them down. He couldn't read her expression.

'Poll?'

'What?'

'I don't know. Here.'

He stretched out a hand towards her and she hesitated for several seconds before reaching out for it. Her attention focused on the shirt hanging from her other hand.

Polly could have taken this brief connection of fingertips as an opportunity to talk, but she found herself unable to say even a word. The spectacle of Amos and Katherine loomed over her, as colossal and with as much rude impact as a film on an iMax screen. The projection was so close that the margins of the picture seemed to flicker over her own face, making her blink and want to screw up her eyes. She was afraid that if she spoke, the conversation might skid into a discussion about their own possible separation. Maybe, she thought, Selwyn was searching through the barriers for a way of introducing the subject.

After a moment he withdrew his hand. He returned to the bench and bent his shoulder to the plane. Ringlets of crisp woodshavings coiled to the floor.

By five minutes after closing time, the bar at the Griffin was almost empty. Earlier it had been crowded for the weekly quiz night, but now only the hard core of customers remained. Vin Clarke flapped a towel over the pumps and told the last half-dozen drinkers to get a move on because he had a bed to go to, even if the rest of them didn't.

Amos had been sitting alone at a small table for two hours. Having summoned up the startling amount of energy and determination necessary to get himself out of the cottage, drive to Meddlett and enter the pub, knowing that if he sat at home any longer he would go mad, he had been greeted by a couple of curt nods and a muttered, 'Evening. What'll it be?' from Vin himself. He passed the time by eavesdropping on the quiz.

The teams took it very seriously, huddling around the tables, shielding their papers with bent arms and energetically sledging their competitors. A small flame of competitiveness rekindled in Amos and he toyed with the idea of making a single-handed late entry. Once Vin began reading out the questions, he was relieved that he had not, because he couldn't answer any of them. He wasn't at all clear on who Angelina was, let alone the names of her twins, and the five original members of Liberty X were also completely unknown to him.

The night's prize (twenty pounds and a round on the house) was eventually scooped by the youngest and noisiest team, a gang of shaven-headed boys and their girlfriends.

Now the last pair of men heaved themselves off their bar

stools and lumbered to the door. Vin gave Amos a meaningful look.

'Everything all right up at the house, is it?' he asked.

Amos nodded. The evening had left him feeling like the last living representative of an about-to-be extinct species. Now he came to think about it, the entire severed, twitching, unfamiliar rump of his once-familiar life was giving off the same impression.

'Shame about that robbery. Must have left you pretty gutted,' Vin observed, with immeasurable satisfaction. 'No sign of them catching anyone, is there?'

Amos was surprised to remember that he had been so exercised about the excavation and the delay to his building project. Now the events were diminished and remote, as if he were observing them through the wrong end of a telescope. He hadn't been to the site, or even thought much about it. Why had it never occurred to him that he would derive no satisfaction from any of his plans or projects if he had to see them through alone?

Hadn't he ever considered that he might miss Katherine so much?

Even to see Selwyn and Polly together, fielding the tail ends of each other's sentences and skirting through the tricky choreography of domestic life in their barn, made him squirm with jealousy and weary outrage.

How had this happened? When exactly had his wife hatched into the cool, detached and seemingly implacable creature who barely deigned to speak to him on the telephone?

Vin shrugged. There was no useful information to be gleaned here. He turned his back and began flicking switches. The bar was plunged into semi-darkness and Amos took this as the signal to leave. In the doorway he almost collided with Jessie, who was carrying a pile of glass ashtrays.

'Hi?' she said, looking behind him.

'I'm on my own,' he told her.

'Thought you might have brought the guys from the commune to quiz night,' she grinned.

'It's not a commune,' he said automatically.

She dealt out the ashtrays and took off her apron.

'Got your car here?'

'Yes, I have.'

'Give me a lift home? It's bloody cold walking in this weather and *he* won't drive me, even though I'm staff. Of course, if you hadn't knocked me off my bike and squashed it flat I'd be able to ride home.'

'I didn't knock you off your . . .' he began. Jessie let out a hoot of laughter.

'We've done this routine already, haven't we?'

Her face was bright with mockery and as his gaze slid southwards from her smile he noticed the tendrils of the intriguing tattoo.

'Come on then,' he relented.

Outside, the cold stopped them in their tracks. Freezing air flooded into Amos's mouth and nose, prickling the membranes, and shrinking the skin on his bones. The silence was vast. Jessie tilted her head and stared up into the blue-black sky.

'Look at that,' she breathed.

The stars were luminous, chains and clouds of them, with the brightest and hardest pinned to the faint swirls of the most distant like gems on a net skirt.

Her small chin pointed upwards. 'Makes you think, doesn't it?'

The Jaguar was the only car left in the car park. Amos pointed his key fob and the lights obediently blinked at the soft *clunk* of the central locking.

'Hang on,' Jessie said. She unlatched a side door and the dog bounded out. It leaped up at her, paws planted on her chest, tongue slathering her face. '*Raff*. Get down, you silly bugger.'

As soon as Amos opened the car door the dog bounded inside, treading in the embrace of the front passenger seat as if it planned to take up residence. Jessie piled in and shouldered the animal into the back seat. She settled herself and sighed with satisfaction as Amos swung towards Mead. The

275

dog's head projected between them. It clicked its jaws and the tongue flagged out, trailing drool over the leather upholstery. The tarmac of the road, hedges and dipped branches of trees all glimmered with damp.

'I love this. It's just such a brilliant car. You must be pretty pleased with it,' Jessie murmured. She stroked the dashboard and the plump curves of the seats.

Amos felt embarrassed by her frank lust for it. 'It's just a car.'

She directed the way to a turning off the road to Mead. The headlamps lit up an overgrown gateway and a cottage beyond it. Rafferty barked once in Amos's ear. Jessie opened the door and swung her legs out.

'You can come in for a bit, if you want.'

Amos saw no reason not to. He had nothing to hurry home for. The garden was a crisped wilderness of sharp twigs and branches that stabbed at his face. He ducked to avoid them and his feet skidded on the slippery path.

Inside, there was a kitchen in a state not much more squalid than his own. A light bulb flickered and Rafferty slobbered at some leftovers in a dog bowl. Jessie made two mugs of instant coffee without offering Amos a choice. She jerked her head and he followed her across the hallway into a living room. There were music posters layered on top of ancient flowery wallpaper, and black cobwebs in the angles of the ceiling. Jessie dived at an electric fire on the hearth and switched it on. The two bars fizzed a little and then glowed, a tiny source of optimism in the icy room. The main items of furniture were two armchairs and a sofa covered in some bristly dun material.

'It's a bit shit, but it's home. Isn't it, Raff?'

The dog bounded past them, a streak of black elastic, and took one of the armchairs.

'What happened to sit, and heel? You ought to train that animal. It would be a kindness.'

'You dissin' mah dawg?' Jessie murmured, equably enough. She pressed a couple of buttons on an MP3 player and some kind of noodling, tinkling music seeped out of minute speakers.

'Have a seat,' she nodded. Amos chose the second armchair and Jessie plumped down on the sofa. They both kept their coats on. From an inner pocket she produced her Golden Virginia tin and began a complicated process of licking and gluing papers. Amos watched her, but in his mind he was transported a long way back to nights with Selwyn, and Blue Peony parties, and Miranda dancing in her tiny skirts and suede waistcoats. In his day, he had been an acknowledged master of this particular craft.

Jessie lit the twisted end and sucked in a deep lungful. She closed her eyes and blew out smoke, then extended her arm.

'You want some?'

He took the joint from her and she grinned at him over the rim of her coffee mug.

'You're all right, you know, for an old bloke. Like at the Fifth bonfire. Kieran was dead lucky you were there. Not many people would have weighed straight in like that, against Donny Spragg and Damon and that lot. You probably didn't have a clue what you were up against, did you? How's your mate, by the way, with the burn?'

Amos blinked, trying to recall. Selwyn had now discarded all the dressings. The hair on one side of his head remained shaggy, on the other side it was rakishly stubbled, bisected by a livid red scar.

'Um, he's all right.'

Jessie regarded him. 'You look pissed off tonight. What's up?'

Amos thought. A long time seemed to pass, during which his mind ranged widely over the possible answers. In the end, the simplest seemed the best choice.

'My wife left me,' he said.

Jessie sniffed, turning down the corners of her mouth in a knowing way. She reached out for the joint.

'Sorry. Why'd she do that?'

The room was losing its glacial chill. He unbuttoned his coat.

'I've no idea.' For no apparent reason, or a thousand accumulated ones, he could have said. After another extended interval he added, 'She says she doesn't want to live in the house we're building.'

This information appeared to strike some sort of a chord with Jessie.

'Do you remember at the Fifth there were people with placards? Some of them got up in woad or whatever stuff ancient tribes wore?'

For some reason quite large sections of Amos's memory now seemed to be melting or collapsing into each other, much more calamitously than the usual sporadic noun- and proper name-loss, but he did retain quite a sharp mental picture of the group of middle-aged people toting a plastic skeleton and waving home-made signs to do with honouring history. He had been sitting with this girl on a hay bale, and she had regaled him with rather good stories about Meddlett people and their doings. Now, with the same relish, she told him that there was quite a big protest movement getting up in the village about incomers desecrating local heritage and sticking up great big houses that no one wanted there. Mrs Hayes was part of it, the one who had been arrested for setting fire to her neighbour's shed, and Mrs Spragg in the shop, not Donny's ma, his aunt, and quite a lot of others. A couple of them had been in the Griffin tonight, hadn't he realized?

No, he hadn't.

And, he pointed out, if they were talking pillage, it wasn't he or anyone else he knew who had crept up in the middle of the night, hit an innocent guard over the head and robbed the locals as well as himself of the major portion of their shared heritage.

He was quite pleased with this response, in the circumstances, but Jessie dismissed it with a shake of the head. He had to realize what he was dealing with, although it was difficult for townies to understand the nuances. No one was that amazed the stuff had got nicked. It was either pikey locals or immigrants who had done it, it was what happened around here, but what everyone was really united against were Amos's sort.

Anyway, Jessie continued, quite a lot of these placard people . . .

'You mean, as distinct from the thief people?'

'Yeah, that's right.'

. . . believed that it was a mistake to have opened up the grave at all, just for some house to be built, let alone to have removed the bones from their ancient resting place and bundled them away. The stuff, gold and whatever it was, belonged to Meddlett. But people were quite superstitious, as well. There was a lot of talk about the grave-opening bringing bad luck.

'As in crop failure? Plagues of boils? The curse of Mead?'

He laughed as he took a last long toke from the joint. Smoke scorched his throat.

Jessie looked narrowly at him and then started work on a fresh construction.

'All right, you rip it as much as you like. I'm just telling you, that's what some people think. And maybe, just maybe, this business with your wife is the start. Have you thought about that? Perhaps she's superstitious too.'

The dog snored in its armchair. The room was definitely warm now.

Another eternity passed.

'You could say that the bad luck started right away, with the robbery. The security guard certainly would,' Amos mused.

'Yeah.'

They lapsed into silence again. In some way, this inconclusive talk had eased his heart. Mentioning Katherine and listening to Jessie's theory had helped to put her at a little distance. He found he could begin to contemplate an interval without her.

In fact the whole world had receded, he noticed, and his bewilderment at the events of the last few days along with it. He listened to the winding music with minute attention. It was nothing like 'Crawling King Snake', but it was all right. Jessie's head was bent, and he could see the pale skin of her scalp where the hair parted. She was very pretty. They seemed to have been talking for hours, and he was gradually overcome

279

with the desire to be closer to her. The odd tricks that time was playing made it easy to forget years. Not much had intervened, after all, since he sat in Selwyn's college rooms respectfully listening to the new Doors album and watching Miranda Huggett twining her fingers in the air. It was the same, all the same. Time and age. What did they matter? Amos slid off his chair and went to sit beside Jessie on the sofa. His arm circled her shoulders. She sighed a little, and he took this as a good sign. He began to kiss her.

Jessie lunged away from him.

'For fuck's sake,' she yelled.

The dog woke up. It leaped off the chair and came straight at him, snarling. Amos crouched, arms raised to protect himself, the blood draining from his face and flooding out of his ventricles. His heart squeezed and fluttered, apparently on thin air.

Jessie grabbed Rafferty's collar and hauled him off.

'Shit. Stop that. I'm fucking *sick* of it. Can't I just sit and have a smoke and a bit of a talk with someone, anyone, without them sticking their tongue down my throat? Even an old man like you?'

She threw down the tobacco tin. There were tears in her eyes. She looked like nothing more than a little girl having a tantrum.

Amos felt a suffocating wave of humiliation. The flare of hearty lust died, leaving him shaking. A point of sudden and absolute clarity in the midst of his peripheral confusion told him that his career as a lover of women had just ended. All those lunches, the little drinks dates, the enjoyable rituals of the chase leading to the smooth necks to be kissed and the buttons straining to be undone, all now lay behind him.

He was old.

This was where his sexual life effectively finished, in a grimy cottage at the end of a lane with an electric fire giving off its dry red glare and a tattooed girl crying with anger at him. He was old. He had no work to absorb him, no colleagues or clerk of chambers or dinners, no wife, no point. Even the dope he had just enjoyed smoking was much too strong for him. He felt an overwhelming desire to sleep, and yet his limbs twitched like a marionette's and his eyes burned in their sockets. He was old. He rolled his tongue experimentally in the dry cave of his mouth and managed to speak.

'I'm sorry. Really. I didn't mean it. No, I *did* mean it, but I wish I hadn't.'

Jessie sighed.

'All right. Forget about it. It happens all the time, right?'

To Amos's relief the dog retreated. It settled on its haunches and began licking its rear end.

'You look pretty awful,' Jessie said.

Amos slowly nodded his head. The urge to sleep was like being sucked into a swamp. He was going deeper. The ooze compressed his ribcage, making it difficult to breathe. The walk to the car, the depths of cold, the drive back to Mead, all were beyond him. Jessie was standing now, looming above him as he wilted sideways into spilled ash on the sofa cushions. She picked up a blanket from the dog's chair and folded it over him.

'I want to ask you something.'

'What?' she frowned.

'Will you show me . . . your tattoo. Please?'

She seemed very tall. Seven feet high. Her face was a long way off, solemn, as unmoving as if it were carved out of stone.

Silently she undid the buttons of her coat and let it drop. With her right hand she grasped the hem of her jersey and in one smooth movement she peeled off the top layer and several more that clung beneath. She was naked to the waistband of her jeans.

The tattoo was a fine, lacy pattern of leaves. It rose from the shadowed hollow of her waist to cover one breast, tapering away into the tendrils that showed at her throat. The density of it made the other breast look marmoreal.

Time did its expanding trick again, the membrane stretching to a taut dome, tighter and further, then collapsing with a whisper. Amos exhaled a long breath.

'Thank you. That is . . . magnificent.'

Offhandedly she bent and scraped up her clothes.

'I've been called a lot of things. Never that. Come on, Rafferty.'

The dog's molten glare as it went by him was the last thing Amos saw before the swamp closed over his head.

When he woke up there was grey light filtering through layers of window grime, which meant that it was not early. The landscape of the night's vivid dreams was temporarily more real than the confined space of Jessie's living room. He was very cold, and when he tried to sit up cramp seized his back and neck. The sofa cushions had printed themselves into his cheek, and his mouth was full of sand. He would have liked to plunge back into sleep, but he was much too uncomfortable. He began a yawn but stopped before his head split in half, then slowly levered himself off the cushions and achieved a semi-standing position. The jagged pain in his frontal lobes subsided to a dull ache. Wrapping his coat around him he plodded to the kitchen in search of a cup of tea. There was an open box of teabags on a shelf, and a half-pint carton of milk in an otherwise almost empty fridge. The window looked out on a thick tangle of bare twigs and some medium-sized evergreens, each one furred with frost. As he stood in the silence, he could just hear a car swishing past on the Meddlett road. The cold of the lino tiles struck up through his socks.

The mugful of hot tea made him feel better. A further brief exploration brought him to a downstairs bathroom, painted a clammy green colour. He rinsed his face in warm water and sleeked back his hair. When he returned to the kitchen the dog was there, licking up and crunching some sort of dry biscuit from its bowl. To his relief, it ignored him. He made himself a second mug of tea and as he drank it he heard footsteps overhead. A moment later Jessie descended the stairs. She was wearing a blue dressing gown like a child's. She looked altogether childlike, blinking and frowning at him. She seemed too young and vulnerable to be living alone in this bleak cottage.

'Well. Hi,' she muttered.

'I'm just going,' he reassured her. 'I needed a cup of tea first. Sorry if I've overstayed my welcome.'

She was opening a tin of dog food. The smell of it reached Amos and he swallowed hard. She forked chunks of brown meat into Rafferty's bowl and threw the fork into the sink.

'It's all right.'

'What are you doing today?'

The memory of her bare breasts was still with him. He was fairly sure they had featured in his dreams, but this aspect of his interest in Jessie was now muddled with another, different response. The daylight kitchen, so chilly and bare of what he would consider essentials, and the sight of her pale ankles under the childish dressing gown, made him feel protective of her and even vaguely paternal. The question was the same one he might have asked Toby or Sam at some point during a university vacation.

'Working,' Jessie said, pointedly. 'I'm on double shift again.'

She moved past him, drawing the blue edges of her dressing gown together. She was also thinking about last night's tattoo episode, he understood. Now he felt like a pervert.

'I'll let you get your breakfast,' he said. He rummaged in his coat pocket and found the car keys.

'See you, then.'

He paused. 'What *was* it we were smoking last night, by the way?'

'Something stronger than you're used to.'

He laughed at that. 'I'm not used to anything at all, not any more. Do you know how old I am?'

'Sixty?'

Amos cleared his throat. 'Well, almost,' he said.

The dog barked once, in approval, as he let himself out of the front door. He slithered down the concrete path to the parked Jaguar.

When he let himself back into the Mead cottage he noticed the bad smell immediately. He emptied the bin, threw out an arrangement of dead flowers, and sluiced away the khaki slime that had gathered in the vase. He picked up his phone and dialled Katherine, but as usual her mobile was switched to voicemail.

Katherine walked under chains of Christmas lights towards the bar where she was to meet Polly and Miranda. She passed glittering shop windows where clusters of satin and sequinned dresses turned the winter streets into the anterooms of a silent and static party, but she didn't notice any of the displays. The three of us, she was thinking. We could almost be three women friends in a feel-good film, except that by this time of our lives you'd imagine there'd be nothing much to look forward to apart from the final credits. The audience blinking hard and blowing their noses before the lights come up to reveal their tears. But now it turns out that there's a twist, and another twenty minutes of the movie yet to run.

She was so preoccupied with her thoughts that she walked right past the bar Miranda had chosen. She stopped several yards further on and retraced her steps. In the doorway she hesitated, peering into the throng. She noticed a slick waiter passing with his loaded tray of drinks and an eyebrow cocked at her as if to signal *Please, not in here. You look all wrong. Couldn't you find a nice teashop?*

In defiance of him she lifted her head and marched into the thick of the crowd, searching the room for Polly and Miranda but finding no sign of them. She was the first to arrive.

It was a stroke of luck that four young men in dishevelled suits and no ties stood up just as she reached the far corner. She ducked behind one of them and secured the vacated table. As she sat down, a different waiter removed the empty glasses and swiped his cloth over the surface. He placed a long thin menu in front of her. The table was wedged beside the Christmas tree, and the lights were flashing on and off in a migraine-inducing way, but she found that if she twisted away and stared in the opposite direction she could just about exclude it from her field of vision.

So she saw Miranda as soon as she came in through the door. Of course Miranda didn't hesitate even for a second. Several heads turned to watch her entrance, even now. Katherine waved to her, and Miranda lifted her elbows in acknowledgement. Her wrists and hands were loaded with carrier bags. She used the burden like a snowplough to open up her path through the mob.

'Here you are,' she gasped, letting fall the shopping. They hugged for a long moment, wordlessly touching cheeks, and then leaned back so they could study each other's faces.

'Here I am,' Katherine agreed.

They squeezed hands and separated. Miranda sank into a chair.

'How's Joyce?' Katherine asked quickly.

Miranda reported that Joyce was now sitting up in her hospital bed and telling anyone who passed by that before this she had never had a day's illness in her life. The doctors were sure she would be well enough to come home for Christmas, and Miranda planned to bring her straight back to Mead.

'So I took the opportunity to rush down here first, to buy presents, but mostly to see you, of course. And now that I *can* see you face to face instead of just listening on the phone, will you please tell me how you are?'

Their eyes met.

Katherine was touched and pleased that this cocktail meeting had been arranged, but she also felt awkward and quite distinctly exposed. As if she were standing up in her underwear, for the others' scrutiny.

'Let's wait until Polly gets here,' she demurred. She handed Miranda the menu to look at and they joked about the outlandish concoctions of Baileys and cinnamon and Kahlua and apple vodka. Miranda wondered if it would be completely unacceptable to order a plain gin and tonic.

'Probably. I'm going to have a Long Sloe Christmas Screw,' Katherine said.

Miranda looked startled. She wasn't sure if Katherine was joking, or making a sly allusion. She wasn't sure whether she actually knew Katherine at all.

Katherine reassured her. 'I really am going to. It's got sloe gin instead of vodka, and cranberry instead of orange. Don't you love that?'

They looked up as Polly leaned over them.

'I'll have the same. With a sprig of mistletoe, if possible.'

She manoeuvred with difficulty into the confined space between the table and the flashing tree. She greeted Miranda with the lightest touch on her shoulder, then kissed Katherine, who had stood up to make room. Just as Miranda had done, Polly held her warmly and then studied her face. Katherine suffered this, understanding that her two friends were concerned for her and needed to reassure themselves that she was neither deeply miserable nor mad.

'You look all right,' Polly judged, after the scrutiny.

'*I* am. How does Amos seem?'

Polly reached for one of Katherine's hands and gripped it.

'He's hurt. And so are you, I should think. It's the most painful thing that could happen.'

Miranda twisted sideways and found herself studying the tree and the plastic crystals suspended from fir branches to mimic icicles. The lights chased up and down the branches, ripples of red and purple and blue.

'But that doesn't mean you shouldn't have done it,' Polly murmured.

The waiter came and took their order. Miranda used the opportunity to collect herself, and turned to face Polly again. This was the first time they had seen each other face to face in almost two weeks, since Polly had left Mead to visit her children in London and the afternoon in Jake's study had intervened.

When the drinks arrived, Katherine lifted her glass. It was decorated with a plastic sprig of holly.

'Here's to you both. Friends in need.'

'Here's to the wives,' Polly responded.

They took a sip apiece and sat back.

'I'm so sorry to sabotage everything. Your great scheme for Mead, Miranda,' Katherine began. 'Before we moved, Amos and I, I'd have said we were fine together. Not wonderful, I couldn't have claimed that. Which of us could? I'm not asking you to tell me,' she added hastily. 'But I thought we were all right, otherwise for all our sakes I wouldn't have risked selling up and coming to Mead. Anyway, you know Amos.'

They knew him very well. Polly nodded and Miranda twisted the holly sprig in the ruby-red depths of her drink.

'After we came to live at Mead, our marriage changed. Or probably it would be more accurate to say that *I* changed.'

'Changed how?' Polly asked, raising an eyebrow.

Katherine tried to explain. She had no sisters or daughters and it didn't come easily, this opening up her most private feelings to other women, even to Miranda and Polly.

The other two listened, leaning forwards. Louder music had now started up and the noise level in the bar was rising, making it an effort for them to hear Katherine's low voice.

She said that at Mead she had found her courage. Living there, she had fallen under a different influence. She said this seriously but glancing from one to the other, knowing that they would challenge her.

Polly did. 'And whose influence would that be?'

'I could say of the place itself. The spirit of it. Like falling under a spell.'

The princess was in all their thoughts, but they masked with smiles the idea that Katherine might be touched by her spirit. Miranda's sceptical merriment was less pronounced than Polly's, however. It wouldn't have taken much to make her believe.

Katherine concluded, 'Or I could just say that being closer to all of you finally opened my eyes. I stopped making the compromises that being Amos's wife involves and decided to get a life of my own.'

287

'And have you?' This was Polly again.

She sighed. 'I've hurt Amos, I've deeply upset our boys. I wouldn't call wreaking such havoc a positive move, exactly. But it's early days.'

The confession was unpractised but as honest as she could make it. Miranda had been twiddling her holly sprig, but now she lifted her head.

'Is there someone else involved in all this? I don't mean one of Amos's. I mean for you?'

Polly had begun a laugh at this question, but it died away.

Two pairs of eyes fixed on Katherine, one astonished and the other unreadable. The floor now reverberated with the pounding music, and the lights chased each other in faster pulses.

'There is! Tell us who it is,' Miranda demanded.

Katherine enjoyed the moment of suspense. The other two sat on the edges of their chairs.

'Christopher Carr.'

Their jaws dropped.

'The archaeologist?'

'Yes, him.'

Clapping her hands Polly cried, 'Well, that's good. Really good. The older you get, the better you'll look to him.'

There was a beat of one second and then laughter exploded between them.

Miranda fell back in her chair, shaking with pure joy. With her face alight she looked twenty again. Polly's features squeezed up into the noodle lady's series of slanting lines and Katherine laughed too, thinking how good and nourishing it was to be with them both. Miranda's theory of friendship was right, and her own musings as she walked from her office to the bar hadn't been so far wrong.

Husbands, marriages, children, lovers, all these came and went. What you were left with was friends.

Their waiter saw them and was encouraged. This trio of sombre-looking old women were now acting like everyone else. Amazing, really, what just one drink could do.

'Same again, ladies, is it?' he called.

'Oh, yes please,' Katherine sighed.

Miranda dried her eyes with a folded cocktail napkin. Two girls wearing novelty reindeer antlers perched next to their table.

'I want to hear more. Do tell us. Polly?'

But Polly's broad face now made an arrangement of circles. Deaf to everything else, she was staring at someone across the room.

A girl was standing in three-quarters profile, listening without much of a show of interest to a boy who was commanding the attention of their group. When she shifted her weight it became obvious that she was about six months pregnant. Her tight black top was stretched over a prominent bump.

'It's her. There she is,' Polly cried.

Katherine and Miranda turned their heads, not knowing who they were looking for.

For her size, Polly could move fast. She sprang out of her chair, almost colliding with the waiter. Reaching the girl's side she grabbed her wrist and held it in an iron grip.

'Nicola? Nic, what are you doing here?'

Nicola blushed dark red, then looked for a means of escape.

Polly blocked the way. 'No, you don't. You don't have to run off. I just want to talk to you.'

Nicola now shook a curtain of hair across her eyes.

'Why?' she muttered.

The other people hesitated, trying to gauge what was going on.

'OK, Nic?' the leader of the boys asked.

'Yeah.'

Still holding her arm, Polly moved to cut her off from her friends.

'Just give me five minutes. Please?' she begged, putting her mouth close to the girl's ear so she didn't have to shout over the infernal music.

'What for?'

Polly took her other arm, turning her towards the door.

'Come on. Come with me.' She shuffled backwards, towing Nic with her so they looked like a pair of clumsy dancers.

'Hey, stop that,' Nic's defender shouted. A dozen other people were now turning to stare at them.

'It's all right. It's cool,' Nic sighed over her shoulder. And to Polly, 'Let's go outside. Can't hear yourself think in this place anyway.'

They emerged into the street and took up a position amongst the hardy smokers. Cold made a dark, damp shimmer on the pavement. Nic immediately began to shiver and Polly peeled off her thick cardigan and draped it over her shoulders. The girl stared at the ground and Polly chafed her hands, trying to rub some warmth and reason into her.

'What is it you want, then?' Nic demanded.

Polly wanted to know a hundred different things, but she made a start with, 'Where have you been?'

She shrugged. 'Around.'

'Have you thought about Ben?' Knowing how desperate he had been, Polly couldn't believe the girl had not.

'A bit, yeah.'

'He thinks you probably had a termination.'

Nic winced. 'He would. Well, I haven't had an *abortion*. I'm going to have my baby.'

Polly let one of her hands go, but she held the other wrist like a handcuff. She put a finger to Nic's jaw and turned her face so that she could look into it.

'It's your baby, yes,' she murmured. 'It is also Ben's. And it's my grandchild, too. You're not alone in this, you know, if you don't want to be. I'll help you, so will Ben's dad.'

Nic met her gaze. Polly knew that this was not going to be easy. The handful of times she had met this girl she had noticed how she observed their family with quiet, faintly eager curiosity, as if all the Davieses belonged to a species she had never before encountered at close quarters.

'Where are you living, Nic?'

'With a mate.'

290

'Have you got enough money?'

The girl was shivering violently enough to shake her teeth loose.

'No.'

'Come back inside,' Polly begged. She put an arm around her shoulders and tried to steer her, but Nic stood her ground.

'Let me help you,' Polly pleaded.

Then without warning Nic's face crumpled and she began to cry.

Now Katherine emerged into the street. She saw Polly and Nic and came uncertainly towards them.

'We were just wondering if everything's all right?'

'This is Ben's girlfriend, Nicola. Ex-girlfriend, perhaps I should say.'

Katherine's glance downwards took in the situation. She frowned in concern. 'You can't stand out here, it's much too cold.'

Nic was weeping now without restraint, and one on either side they tried to hug her.

'Don't you want to go inside, back to your friends?' Polly cajoled.

The girl shook her head, tears glinting on her cheeks. 'I don't really know them. Someone asked me to come for a drink, I turned up. It's Christmas.'

Katherine caught Polly's eye. She took charge of matters.

'All right. I'll tell you what we're going to do. We'll get our coats, collect Miranda, and take a taxi back to the flat. We'll get warm, have something to eat, and then we'll talk.'

Twenty minutes later they were there. Nic was placed in a corner of the sofa. Miranda extracted a pair of baby-blue cashmere socks from her mounds of Christmas shopping and put them on the girl's icy feet. Polly brought her hot lemon and honey with a teaspoon of whisky, and Katherine made omelettes.

Nic stopped shivering and then her tears dried up. Her nose and eyelids were red and shiny but she looked better.

'I'm sorry . . .' she sniffed, but they stopped her.

They ate in their armchairs with plates balanced on their laps. Nic was quiet but the other three chatted and joked to make her feel comfortable. Katherine felt the glow in the room, and smiled.

Nic refused any further offers of help, though. At the end of the evening she insisted that she would go back to her friend's flat and not spend the night at Katherine's, although both she and Polly begged her to stay. She exchanged mobile numbers with Polly and promised, yeah, that she would keep in touch.

Polly went out to see her into the taxi.

'I don't want to put pressure on you. I think I can under-stand why you don't want to involve Ben, although I wish you would,' Polly had said, as lightly and humbly as she could. She folded a twenty pound note into Nic's hand for the fare. 'But it's my grandchild, as well as your baby. I just want to make sure that everything is all right for you both.'

'Of course,' Nic replied. 'I hear what you're saying, Polly. Honestly.' She leaned forwards and told the cab driver, 'Kilburn, please,' without being any more specific than that.

After she had gone, Polly helped Katherine and Miranda carry the dishes out to the kitchen.

Katherine smiled at her, 'Thanks, *Granny*.' Polly's face made the series of circles again. 'I know. How incredible.'

Miranda reached up on tiptoe and put glasses away in a cupboard.

What you were left with was friends, Katherine thought.

And also, it now seemed, the possibility of grandchildren.

ELEVEN

Frost was rare at Mead, but now a covering of white rime stole the last remnants of colour from fields and branches. The world was reduced and refined to shades of silver, grey and graphite, appearing flat at a distance but under closer scrutiny revealing every twig and stone within a carapace of diamond brilliants. The sun rose in a brief flare of vermilion and set barely seven hours later between bars of lead and amethyst. Deserted and unvisited, the excavation trenches gaped at the sky and the puddles in the bottom froze as solid as the coins that had been taken from them.

Each successive morning the new glass in the barn windows bloomed with frost flowers. Polly heaped all their spare clothes as well as layers of covers on the bed. To work she and Selwyn wore gloves with the fingers cut off at the knuckles, doggedly continuing with the sawing and sanding that would eventually seal the place against the blades of frost. When they spoke, to confer about some aspect of the job in hand, their breath hung between them in billowing plumes.

From her mother's flat, Miranda telephoned Polly and asked her to ask Selwyn if he would light fires in the main house to keep the place as warm as possible. He did as he was told, and thin spirals of smoke drifted from the old chimneys before dispersing into the cavernous cold.

All this time Selwyn was uncharacteristically quiet. Covertly observing him, Polly saw how he tried harder than ever to immerse himself in the work. His hands were busy and his shoulders hunched over the tools, but sometimes he would look up and let his gaze wander to the new windows and the view across the frostbound yard to Miranda's house, where the fires glowed in empty rooms.

'Joyce will be out of hospital any minute,' Polly said, when the silence between them seemed to have lasted for days. 'I wonder when Miranda will be bringing her back here?'

Selwyn didn't look up. 'I wouldn't know. You're the one who saw her in London, and you've spoken to her at least twice since then.'

I wish I'd seen her. I wish she would come back to Mead.

Was that the unspoken rider, Polly wondered? Or was she being unfair to him? It was possible that Selwyn's longing for Miranda was nothing more than a jealous creation of her own imagination, born out of her deepening feelings of pointlessness and isolation. Miranda herself gave no indication that anything was going on. During the evening in the bar, and afterwards at Katherine's flat, she had seemed a little quieter, perhaps more thoughtful than usual, but otherwise she was as warm as always and equally affectionate to Polly and to Katherine.

But Miranda was an actress, wasn't she?

Polly also stared out of the barn windows at the silent frost. At what point, exactly, had their new home stopped offering even the possibility of homeliness and become a cage instead? Amos's curtains were often closed at two o'clock in the afternoon, yet every light could be on at four in the morning as he blearily insisted on turning night into day. Katherine was presumably with her archaeologist. Polly remembered how Katherine had blushed and glowed when she confessed to her affair, and enviously wondered at the transformation that being in love could effect.

Miranda's Mead experiment seemed to be ending in failure.

Friendship turned out not to be the enduring force of her theory after all, but to be subsidiary to coupledom – either the pursuit of it, or the mourning for its loss.

How *ordinary* of us all, Polly thought. Disappointment swelled in her, and in that instant she felt a closer bond with Miranda than with Selwyn. She also ached for the balm of Colin's company. At least he had promised her, and Miranda too, that he would be back in a day or so, and would stay at Mead for Christmas. Polly guessed that Christmas, as it often did, might draw several truths to the surface.

One afternoon, when they both happened to be in Miranda's house at the same time, although they had been separately occupied with laundry and fire-laying, Selwyn came to the utility room to search Polly out.

'I want to show you something. Come and see,' he smiled.

He leaned against the door frame with his arms folded, thin and shaggy-haired, and apart from the lines in his face he looked exactly as he had done thirty years ago. She was so surprised, and so happy with this overture, that her heart leaped with love inside her.

She followed him down a passage to a room at the other end of the house that she had never been into before. Selwyn quickly kicked apart the remnants of an old fire and made a tripod of dry logs. He struck a match and a flame licked upwards. As soon as the fire caught, he took Polly's hand and drew her across to the bookshelves.

At one end, protected by a grille still backed by tatters of cloth, she saw row upon row of ancient brown book spines. She opened the door and picked out one of the oldest-looking volumes, handling its disintegrating binding with the utmost care. Dust forced her to swallow a sneeze.

These books must have stood untouched for generations. She turned the pages with mounting eagerness, entirely forgetting Selwyn.

When she glanced up again, the fire was blazing.

He rubbed his hands on his trousers.

'I knew you'd be interested,' he said, nodding at the shelves and the clouded cupboards.

It suddenly dawned on Polly that he was making her an offer, sliding some unfamiliar currency across a divide, but she wasn't sure if it was legal tender and whether it related to a trade in which she had any inclination to be involved.

In confusion she glanced down again at the book in her hand, and the loops and strokes of barely decipherable handwriting. She picked out a column of figures: *3 guineas; seven shillings and eight pence; 16 shillings*. On the next page was a list of materials, *3 yards linsey for winter cape Joshua, 5 yards ribbon, to gown trimming*.

She was looking at a book of household accounts. There was no date, only a month, August. She turned to the flyleaf and saw written there Mead House, 1714. The month and also the year of the death of Queen Anne.

Replacing the volume, she drew out another at random.

The hand here was different, much smaller and more crabbed, and the words were abbreviated to the point where they were almost in code. She gave up the attempt to decipher the first paragraph and slipped it back into its place, her interference betrayed by a broad smear in the shelf dust. The cupboard beneath the shelves, when she stooped to peer inside, revealed a tier of boxes. Some of the boxes sagged under the pressure of others and the corners had split open, showing the tantalizing strata of more papers. She slid one box out of the stack and lifted out the top layers of yellow parchment. These were letters. She unfolded one from its thick creases and read, *This day Madam, Your obdt. Svt, Thos. Mead-Howe.*

Polly's heart hammered a rising cadence. It was beating so hard it felt like a foot kicking her ribs from within. When she was able to look up she saw Selwyn leaning over the fire, one arm stretched along the mantelpiece. He was gazing down into the flames, absorbed in his thoughts, and he jumped at the sound of her voice.

'Sel? How did you know about these books? All the letters?'

'Miranda showed me.'

Of course.

'She said Jake was always planning to get an expert in to catalogue them. He put it off just too long.'

'Have you ever heard of the Paston Letters?' Polly asked.

Selwyn read a good deal, but his interests didn't correspond with Polly's.

'Um. Yes, I think so. I couldn't tell you any more than that, though.'

'Those letters are the earliest surviving private correspondence of an English landed family. I'm not saying these records compare, they're not nearly as old for one thing, but they look significant to me.'

Selwyn was staring at her, surprised by the passion of her interest even though he had planned the introduction. 'I can see that. Do you think Jake knew?'

Polly ran her finger over the nearest row of spines.

'He must have done. He was such a private man, though. Cataloguers or researchers might have been too much of an invasion.' She tilted her head, letting her eyes travel upwards. 'The stories. Just think of all the *stories* there are here.'

'I thought you would be interested,' Selwyn repeated, with satisfaction. His eyes were twin sparks but she couldn't read his expression. Her conviction deepened that he had brought her to look at this hidden library as the opening bid in some unspoken transaction. But she knew him so well: Selwyn was not a subtle man, nor was he a schemer. His probable thought had only been that she needed something, some food for the mind, exactly the same judgement that Ben had made, and old papers were the kind of thing that appealed to her. The simplicity of this calculation deeply touched her.

'You were right,' she murmured.

After dinner that same evening Selwyn fell asleep in his armchair, his head a little askew and a snore catching in his throat. Only a few months ago he would have derided such elderly behaviour, but now he was physically exhausted. Polly snatched up the telephone at the first ring so that he wouldn't be disturbed. The caller was Colin.

'Welcome back,' she cried in delight. 'Where are you? How was it?'

'I'm in a cab from the airport. It was freezing cold over there.'

She laughed. 'Wait till you get up here. It's Siberian.'

'That's what I'm afraid of. Poll, have you done your Christmas shopping?'

Polly had decided that she was going to have to buy her presents locally. She hadn't achieved a single purchase on the recent trip to London to see Katherine, and time was against her.

'What do you think? No.'

He crowed with glee. 'So forget the cold and the DIY for a couple of days. There's been a flood in my block, so I've booked a suite in a gorgeous hotel in Mayfair. Come down in the morning, stay for a couple of days and we'll shop and eat and pamper ourselves. Just the two of us? What d'you say?'

In the years when he lived with Stephen, Colin had made a point of avoiding Christmas. Usually they went on holiday to Bali or Vietnam, escaping the cycle of parties and glitter with which those people who didn't have families or the benefit of belief embraced the season's rituals. Because both Polly and Miranda had pleaded with him to be there, he was going to spend this Christmas at Mead. But he reckoned that two days in London was what he needed first. The only element of the annual mix which he really did enjoy was the shopping. He loved the crowds and the build-up of retail pressure and the extravagance of the displays, and he wasn't going to miss out on that entirely.

'Col, thank you, but I can't afford it,' was Polly's automatic response.

'It's my treat, and you can't refuse,' he told her. 'Please? I want you to so much.'

298

'So do I,' she said in a rush. 'Let me ask Selwyn.'

When he woke up, Selwyn rubbed his jaw and yawned. 'Why not?' he muttered.

Why not, Polly mutely echoed. She was quite well aware that self-denial was not always a gift to other people.

Bountiful hot water gushed from the taps of the hotel bathroom. Steam rose and silvered the mirrored walls.

Polly ruffled the piles of soft white towels, opened the complimentary jars of creams and sniffed them, smoothing lotion into her winter-chapped hands. Colin cleared a swathe of mirror so they could examine their faces. Her reflection glowed at his.

'Look at me,' she cried. 'I'm not wearing a jumper. I can put my hand down here, like this, and hey presto, it's not covered in muck. I can run a hot bath, or even two if I feel like it. You can't imagine what a joy this is, Col. Thank you.'

She swaddled herself in the white towelling bathrobe.

'Everything is so clean and shiny. I love it. You're very generous.'

'Why generous, since I'm getting exactly what I want?' he grinned.

It wasn't generosity, he knew that much. He had more than enough money. Coming back to Mead, as he had been doing for the past three months, had given him more of a sense of home than he had known for a long time. It was Polly who was the kernel of that homeliness, and he wanted to make some return to her.

He was increasingly aware that there were invisible triangulations between Polly and Miranda and Selwyn, and he believed it would be good for his old friend to have a change of scene and some looking-after for a day or two.

'Look at me,' she sighed. Gingerly she held up a hank of her hair between two fingers, then let it fall again.

'You need a haircut and a manicure, that's all. See?' He drew back the offending hair and tilted her face. 'You know, Poll, to me you don't look one bit like a grandmother.'

She had told him about the chance encounter with Nic in

the bar, and how she and Miranda and Katherine had taken her back to the Knights' Bloomsbury flat for supper and the solidarity of women.

Since then Polly had dialled the mobile number several times a day, but never got beyond the voicemail service. She was forced to admit that Nic had conclusively vanished again.

'I'm going to *be* a grandmother soon enough,' she said now to Colin. 'If Nic will let me be, that is.'

A knock on the door turned out to be room service, with a silver ice bucket and a bottle of champagne.

'We'll drink this, then we're going out to dinner,' Colin told her.

They stood at the window with their drinks, gazing down into Park Lane. The trees were ethereal clouds of tiny fairy-lights, backed by the glowing river of evening traffic. Beyond that lay the massy darkness of the park. Polly breathed in Colin's scent of clean shirt and citrus cologne. She went on sipping champagne and silently admiring the view with him at her side, like an old couple who no longer need to converse because each already knows what the other is thinking. Two trees with their roots entwined, bending away from the wind, Polly thought. Mercurial, demanding Selwyn never made her feel like a tree. Life with him could be nourishing, or famishing, but it was never tranquil. She needed him physically and mentally, like needing a fix, but there was never peace.

It didn't take more than a single glass of alcohol these days to make her knees melt. She half-closed her eyes and the moving lights became a glittering snake.

'I'm so happy,' she sighed.

She meant it lightly, but it came to her that the simplicity of being here with Colin was as near to real happiness as she could hope to come these days.

'What's Selwyn doing with himself while you are away?' Colin asked. His thoughts seemed to follow the route that hers had taken.

'What he's always doing. It doesn't matter that Amos is out

of the race to get a habitable home at Mead, it doesn't even matter that there never really was a race. Selwyn has created this imaginary challenge for himself, and he's going to be the winner even though there isn't another competitor in the field. By December the twenty-fourth I can guarantee you that all the bedrooms will have glass in the windows, there'll be at least one functioning bathroom and a log fire burning, the children will come for Christmas, Sel will be the paterfamilias and that will be QED from him.'

'Is that so?'

Polly's mouth curved. 'The barn will be habitable, yes. I expect Alph and Omie to come, although Alph's got this new boyfriend she seems to have fallen in love with. Omie's Tom goes to Ireland, to his own parents. Ben's never predictable. Especially as he's so distraught about Nic.'

It seemed to Colin that the dramas of Davies family life continued, as always.

'*Why* is Christmas so important?' he wondered. 'Miranda wants me to help her to decorate the house. We have to start by going into the woods to cut sheaves of ivy and mistletoe, apparently. She wants there to be a Boxing Night party. The guests confirmed so far are her, me and Joyce.'

Miranda had telephoned each of them to say that Joyce was definitely going to be discharged from hospital the next day, and they planned to come straight home to Mead.

Polly's features narrowed to slits as she laughed.

'Are we Davieses invited?'

'Expected, I'd say.'

They talked about how Miranda was eager to create a big, sprawling, boisterous family Christmas. It would symbolize the new Mead, and she was determined that this was how it should be because Jake had never wanted such a thing, and because she had no children of her own, and because she was so anxious for her great experiment not to break up into the fragments of splintering families before it had properly got under way.

'That's what I mean about Christmas,' Colin groaned. 'It

301

bears far too much weight on its knock-kneed, tinselly little legs. It isn't too late for you and me to just skip away to Goa together, you know.'

Polly shook her head. 'Can't do that. And I like Christmas just the way it is, quarrels and family dramas and all.'

Was that strictly true, this year? Perhaps not. A sense of foreboding fluttered beneath her diaphragm.

Quickly she added, 'Anyway, Katherine's the one likely to be shedding responsibility for the familial turkey and trimmings and slipping off with another man. We can't all do it.'

Swearing him to secrecy, she had told Colin about Katherine and her archaeologist. He hadn't been all that surprised.

'Where would they go? Looking at ruins somewhere?'

'K and Mirry and I will do the ruins jokes for ourselves, thank you,' Polly retorted.

'All right. Amos will be with us, won't he?'

'Yes. I don't know where else he would go.'

It was strange how quickly the ability to direct and determine seemed to have oozed out of Amos. He had become an almost pathetic figure. 'I suppose Sam and Toby will rally round?'

'I expect they will do absolutely the decent thing,' Colin agreed.

Polly was still smiling vaguely at the dazzle of lights. 'No doubt Miranda will organize us all.'

Colin drew in a breath as if to say something, but then he changed his mind. Instead he took the empty glass from her and put it aside.

'Come on. The table's booked. What are you going to wear?'

She made a dismal face.

'My old black thing.'

'Tomorrow. Shopping,' he said, slicing a crisp shape in the air from her shoulders to her hips.

It was the middle of the next morning when they reached Selfridges. In Colin's wake Polly zigzagged through the mobs on the overheated ground floor, breathing in walls of perfume as thick as stone slabs and blinking through her hangover at the glitter of lights and mirrors. In Colin's company, her appetite kindled by his, she was invigorated by the infinity of choice. With a credit card in her purse any of these necklaces or face creams or jangly handbags could be hers, and the bills would come another day.

They stopped at a counter where Colin showed her the eye cream that he insisted on using himself. Examining his face as he demonstrated, she saw how losing weight had sculpted his cheekbones. Rimmed with tiny white dots of cream his dark eyes looked luminous and certainly quite free of surrounding wrinkles. He tapped the cream into his skin, using the very tips of his fingers.

Polly paid what seemed an extortionate price for a tiny pot of this elixir, and they headed for the escalator. In the men's department she enlisted his help in finding a designer T-shirt that Ben wouldn't dismiss as too gay.

She held one up for his approval. 'What about this one?'

'I'd wear it.'

'Good.'

'But Poll, I'm gay.'

Polly's mobile rang. She glanced at the number and then dropped everything.

She gabbled, 'Hello? Hello? Yes, I'm here. What is it? Listen to me, just tell me where you are. Wait, that's only around the corner . . .'

Colin let his attention wander. Across the aisle an assistant in a tight black shirt was folding cashmere sweaters. Colin returned his half-smile but Polly shook him by the arm, summoning him back to earth.

'We've got to go down to the café on the ground floor. Never mind the T-shirt. That was Nic.'

The café was crowded but they squirmed into a booth by a table covered with dirty crockery. There was a view down a shallow flight of stairs over a sea of heads. Everyone seemed to know where they were going. Nobody tripped or collided with anyone else, the tide just flowed to the refrain of piped Christmas carols. Then they both spotted the lone exception. One person stumbled towards them, creating a miniature whirlpool of turbulence in the steady current. She clawed her loose coat around her as passing heads turned to glance at her streaming face.

Polly bounced up out of her seat and dashed to meet her.

Nic was sobbing and incoherent. Between them, they guided her into a chair. Polly murmured reassurances and fed tissues into her hand while Colin managed to attract the attention of a waitress. He ordered tea, water, buttered toast.

'Is it the baby?' Polly whispered. Her face had gone grey under her make-up. 'Nic? Tell me, is something wrong with the baby?'

The girl gasped and coughed, wadding up the tissues and pressing them into her eyes.

'No. Except for me. I'm what's wrong. Look at me. What kind of a mother will *I* be?'

Polly relaxed a little. She hugged the shuddering girl.

'A good one. Of course you will. We'll all help you.'

The tea and toast arrived with surprising speed. Colin poured a cup, laid a buttered slice close to Nic's clenched fist.

'Shall I leave you with her?' he murmured.

No, stay, Polly signalled. If Nic made another dash for it, it would be easier if there were two of them in pursuit.

'Drink some tea,' she said firmly. 'You're all right here, with us. When you're ready, tell us what's happened. It won't be anything we can't handle.'

It took two cups of tea and most of the toast before they were able to piece together the story.

As part of her beauty therapy training Nicola had been on a week's placement at an urban spa only two streets away from where they were now sitting. She had been giving a reflexology treatment to a woman who was also pregnant. As Nic described it, the customer had been a rich bitch. There were so many diamonds in her rings she couldn't have lifted a finger even if she'd tried. Every item of clothing a look-at-me label. Bag worth two grand, which was more money than Nic had seen in three months. Complaining non-stop about how tired and uncomfortable she was. Sighing and fidgeting and prodding her BlackBerry.

'Made me feel really crap. Said I was clumsy. Didn't like a single thing I did for her.'

Then there had been a moment when Nic applied more pressure than was perhaps necessary to the arch of the customer's pedicured foot. The woman jumped straight in the air and then started screaming her head off.

'For God's sake. What are you trying to do?'

Nic said she was only trying to release her *qi*; the customer exclaimed that she was massacring it.

Nic's supervisor dashed in, the customer complained about being given a student to work on her, in her condition, and the spa manageress had to be called to placate her.

'The manageress told me to go and sit in the staff room, and she'd come and see me,' Nic said. She had gone in there to wait and caught sight of herself in the mirror.

'I thought, I'm pregnant too. The only difference between us is she's got plenty of money and everyone's running around looking after her, while I'm bending over her feet and I've got nowhere to turn and I'm a useless therapist and how am I ever going to look after this baby?'

Nic had collected her coat and walked out of the spa without a word to anyone. Then she had found herself standing alone in the street. At that moment the only person she could think of to call had been Ben's mother.

'Thank God you did. It's such a piece of luck I was right here,' Polly said.

Nic blew her nose. 'What were you doing?'

'Christmas shopping.'

Nic's eyes instantly refilled with tears. A couple of fat drops rolled down her cheeks. 'Mary's Boy Child' arranged for the pan pipes drifted over their heads. Colin moved her cup so he could take her hand.

'It's the best time of year if you're happy and with the people you love, and if you're alone or hurting it's the very worst. I've personally never been able to see the point of reflexology, by the way. It wouldn't be my desert island treatment.'

Nic turned her head, and looked properly at him for the first time since Polly had made the introductions.

Polly said afterwards that it was like seeing someone recognizing a long-lost sibling, or understanding how to solve a quadratic equation after never having been able to do even basic maths. Nic just fell into adoration with Colin.

Polly would have been jealous, if she hadn't understood exactly why any woman would be drawn to him.

Nic said slowly, 'You're right. Thanks for the toast. I was starving.' She blotted the tears, and folded an arm protectively across her bump. 'Which treatment *would* you choose, actually?'

He gave the question proper consideration.

'Shiatsu.'

Later, when it became clear that Nic had no intention of ever going back to the spa, and was only temporarily lodging with friends on their sofa bed in the flat in Kilburn, they conferred about what was to be done. The result was that Polly telephoned the course organizer, and gave herself some authority to speak for Nic by introducing herself as the mother of Nic's boyfriend. Nic shook her head and spluttered *no*, but Polly held up her hand to silence her. It was finally agreed that under the circumstances Nic should take some time out, and come back to resume her coursework in the New Year.

'Ben and I split. It's totally finished,' Nic snapped.

'I know that. But you've got to help us to help you,' Polly said.

Colin interceded. He pointed out that so far the only purchase they had managed was one small pot of Eve Lom eye cream. He said that he would take Nic back to the hotel and let Polly get on with buying her presents. Anxiety leaped up in Polly at the thought of allowing the girl out of her sight again, but it was clear to Colin that Nic couldn't be coerced or captured.

'If you don't mind spending the afternoon hanging out with me, that is?' he said casually to Nic.

It was evident that she had no objection.

'Buy that T-shirt for Ben,' Colin advised as Polly departed.

Room service brought up another pot of tea with a plate of tiny triangle sandwiches and miniature mince pies. While they talked, Nic devoured everything. Colin suspected that she hadn't been taking proper care of herself.

'Why are you all on your own like this, Nic? Where's your own family? Is there anyone you can rely on?'

Her exact words, as he repeated them later to Polly, were that she didn't want to rely on anyone, because no one was reliable, were they? Why place unreal expectations on the world?

Her mother was up in Liverpool, living with a boyfriend Nic didn't like. She had left home at seventeen, to escape his predecessor, and there hadn't been much communication since then between mother and daughter.

'Does she know about the baby?' Colin asked.

Nic shrugged. 'No.'

'Have you got any siblings?'

'I had a younger brother. He was killed in a motorbike accident on the M56. He was on the pillion when he and his mate went straight under a truck.'

'That's very hard for you, Nic.'

She pushed the crumbs of the last mince pie into a heap in the centre of her plate.

'Have you known anyone who was killed?'

'Yes, I have.'

'Well, then,' she said. Her shoulders lost some of their rigidity. Colin lifted his arm an inch, and Nic slid a little closer to him.

'So this will be your mother's first grandchild. Don't you think that will be important to her? You already know how much it means to Polly.'

307

She exhaled sharply. 'My mother had me when she was sixteen,' she said, as if this explained volumes. It told Colin enough for the time being.

He asked her about Ben, and why she had chosen to keep the baby but not the boyfriend.

'I thought about having an abortion but I decided it was the wrong thing to do. Even my mother didn't have one, which means I'm here now, doesn't it? But as it is I'll have the baby and myself to look after. I don't need to add a third person to that list, do I?'

Knowing Ben Davies, Colin had to concede that this was a reasonable standpoint. In fact, Nic might currently be vulnerable and she might be neglecting herself physically, but she struck him as fundamentally a strong and determined young woman. Polly was quite lucky with the mother of her grandchild-to-be.

At the end of the afternoon, her arms stretched under a load of bright yellow and shiny purple carrier bags, Polly reached the suite again. Nic was lying on the sofa with her bare feet in Colin's lap, fast asleep in front of *Breakfast at Tiffany's* on the film channel.

'She's never seen it,' he said in astonishment.

He lifted the girl's feet and replaced them on a cushion. They left her to sleep and went into Polly's bedroom. As soon as she came in, Colin had seen her anxiety dissolve into relief that Nic was still there. In time Alpha and Omega would have their babies, of course they would, but Polly was fixed on this one with such tenacity probably because it was Ben's, her hopeless, charming and favourite child's, and Nic's evasiveness only increased her resolution.

This was the future, he realized, with a sense of satisfaction. If Nic was going to stay afloat the child would probably need a grandmother, and for Polly a grandchild would be a welcome anchor.

Polly listened to Colin's account of their conversation.

'Ben'll grow up. He'll have to.'

308

She looked straight at Colin, defying him to mention Selwyn in the context of perpetual adolescence.

'What do you want to do?' he asked instead.

'I want to take her home with us.'

Of course, Colin thought. For Christmas, Madonna and child. But this had been his thinking too – for a couple of weeks at least, he and Polly could look after this girl between them, and then maybe she would accept some longer-term help that would mean the baby could stay within Polly's orbit. The barn was hardly the place to take a pregnant woman, though, even one who had until today been sleeping on a sofa bed in Kilburn. Besides, Ben might well also be at the barn and Nic wouldn't want to be forced into such proximity with him. What Ben's response might be to the arrangement would be for Polly to deal with.

'Do you think she'd come?' Polly mused.

'Let's try asking her if she'd like to stay with me and Miranda, at the house.'

'Really? Would you do that for her?'

'We'll have to ask Mirry.'

They called her up.

'Yes,' Miranda said without a second's hesitation, as they had both known she would. 'The more the merrier, I say.'

When Nic woke up she looked disorientated, and then relief softened her face.

'How long have I been asleep?'

'About an hour,' Colin told her.

'I'm really sorry. I'd better go, hadn't I?'

'You don't have to. There's two beds in my room, or I can share Colin's room, or one of us can sleep out here,' Polly said. Her eagerness for the girl to stay was so naked Colin could hardly look at her. Don't crowd her, he wanted to say. Let her come to the decisions herself.

Nic's eyes slid to Colin.

'I dunno,' she murmured awkwardly.

Polly and Colin had tickets that evening for a sold-out new

play that Polly was eager to see. Polly offered to take Nic along in Colin's place, but the girl dismissed this idea with a short laugh.

'Theatre? No thanks. I need to pee too often.'

'But . . .' Polly said, then stopped herself. Colin handed Nic the room service menu, the TV remote, a white bathrobe.

'It's lovely here,' the girl sighed. 'I can't quite believe it.'

'See you later, then,' he said.

Suddenly it was Nic who looked anxious. 'What time will you be back?' she wanted to know.

In the taxi, Colin told Polly that if it was offered in the right way, Nic would be glad of their help. And as far as that evening went, he was proved right. When they got back to the hotel, Nic was a small, sleeping huddle under the covers of the second bed in Polly's room.

I am so happy to be home.

Mead absorbs me and I feel that I never want to leave again, not for any reason that I could imagine. The old walls and the creaking stairs envelop me like a second skin, and the scent of cold stone, dust, wood ash and mould is as dear as a lover's perfume. I love this place, even though it's full of uncertainties. I am angry that there is no progress in the hunt for the princess's treasure; as the time passes with no news the robbery feels more and more like a violation. I am torn between desire for Selwyn and guilt towards Polly, by sympathy for Amos and surprise about Katherine, and by a growing anxiety that I have brought discord instead of harmony to my friends and my house. But even so, in spite of all this, my spirits soar just because I am here.

We'll have Christmas together, all of us. It will be a happy time, and I know that perspectives can change within days, even hours. Maybe the new Mead will succeed after all, and become the real Mead.

Already my quiet house is no longer quiet at all. My mother is physically frail and sometimes her mind is confused, but she is tough within. I've inherited that toughness, too, I realize. Joyce plays her radio at full volume because that's the only way she can hear it, and shouts to me even when I'm briefly out of the room.

'Barbara? I heard them giving a nice recipe for piccalilli. It said you could get it off the BBC website. You could ask Selwyn to show you how to do that. Do you know you've left that pan on the stove? Aren't you afraid of the house burning down?'

Amos comes across and sits in the kitchen, positioning himself across the table from Joyce, and they watch as I ice the Christmas cake I made last month, and cut pastry circlets for mince pies. Amos confides, when Joyce is upstairs, that Katherine still isn't answering her phone. She told him she was going away for a couple of days, what did I think that meant?

I assume that Katherine is with the bearded archaeologist, but I know little more than what she confided to Polly and me in the cocktail bar. She has turned out to be the darkest of dark horses, although when I think back over the time since she and Amos arrived at Mead I'm aware that she has acquired a glow, a positively sexy sheen, that I never saw in her before.

'I don't know,' I have to say. 'You've got to let her do what she wants, and hope that she decides to come back in the end.'

'I want her to.'

'I know you do.'

You can't always get what you want. I feel sorry for Amos. Katherine has put me in a difficult position, but I can hardly criticize. My own behaviour is far worse than hers.

What has possessed us all?

Whenever I speak to Polly I can hear a note in her voice that's the equivalent of a chill breeze on a summer's day, just ruffling the surface of still water. She's too astute and perceptive not to have picked up the changed nuance between Selwyn and me, but she can't know – can she? – what happened that afternoon.

It was just once. It was wrong, and it was a shocking betrayal of Polly's friendship, and it will never, ever happen again.

But it was also wonderful. I can't erase the memory, and I wouldn't even if I could. I keep coming back to it, in my mind and in my dreams.

And then there's Selwyn himself. Even when he's not actually in the house I can hear fusillades of drilling or hammering out in the barn, until the noise abruptly stops and seconds later he's back here, bringing with him a blast of cold air and adrenaline. He grins at me, all red mouth and unshaven face, before sitting down knee to knee with Joyce to get warm in front of the range. He flirts with her as well as teasing, taking her Sudoku puzzle out of her knotty hands and filling in half the numbers for her. Then he says that she deserves a drink, and goes in search of the bottle of Baileys he has put aside just for her.

'Here's to you and me,' he says, clinking his glass against hers.

'Merry Christmas,' Joyce answers, although she is usually less of an enthusiast for the season even than Colin. It's mostly thanks to Selwyn that she has been so cheerful since I brought her back here.

The telephone rings a lot, adding to the noise. Polly and Colin want to bring Ben's pregnant ex-girlfriend to Mead for Christmas. I tell them yes, of course she must come, while Selwyn semaphores at me, '*What? Polly's mad.*'

Sam and Toby Knight call too, if they can't reach their father at the cottage. I usually pick up the phone, and tell whichever one it happens to be that Amos is here with me, yes, and he seems all right, and reassure them that Mead is going to be home to everyone for Christmas this year. I am more and more excited by the prospect. As well as the big Christmas tree that stands in the hall, Selwyn has brought in another for the kitchen. We decorated it together, under Joyce's orders.

'It needs more tinsel. Load it on. I can't be doing with your so-called good taste, Barbara. It's plain dim.'

I found some more strands, not too tarnished, in a box in the cupboard under the stairs. The resiny scent of the two trees floods the house.

We are sitting in the kitchen again, Selwyn and Amos and my mother and me, as the thin light of day seeps away into twilight. It is almost the shortest day of the year. The four of us make a strange family. Joyce is nodding in her chair, Amos is reading, and I can feel Selwyn's eyes on me. The two of us are in a state of suspense, waiting for I don't know what. I do know that I love him and I push the certainly aside, brutally and deliberately, out into the darkness.

Headlights sweep an arc beyond the yard gate, and a moment later I open the back door to the vicar. He rubs his hands, blinking in the light and nodding affably. He doesn't often call at the house, mostly because I haven't encouraged him to. Of course he's picked up that the household doesn't consist of just unresponsive me any longer, but is now lively with people and interesting activity. As if to underline this the phone rings yet again. It's Omie, asking to speak to her father. The vicar sits down with us while I take a batch of mince pies out of the hot oven. He wants to know whether he'll be seeing us all at the Christmas services.

'I'll be at midnight communion,' Amos says, unexpectedly. 'I always like that one.'

'Tea, vicar?' Selwyn asks, coming back from the phone.

'If you're doing your parish visits, this is probably about your fifteenth mince pie of the day,' I apologize, but he takes one anyway.

It turns out that he is actually here to speak to Amos.

'How can I help you, vicar?' Amos asks, with a flicker of his old, silky courtroom manner.

The vicar clears his throat and brushes pastry from his lapel. The Meddlett Princess people have enlisted his help. The torc and shield are out of reach, for the time being at least, although there is talk of staging a protest at the museum to demand that the treasure be returned to the village. He says that there is a strong current of feeling locally that the princess herself ought to be brought home, to be reburied in her proper resting place at Mead.

313

'Whereabouts, exactly?' Amos wonders.

'Well . . . I suppose, I imagine, somewhere close to the original grave site. I know of course that your house will be built over the grave itself . . .'

'I've heard mention of the idea,' Amos continues. Probably in the Griffin, I think. Apparently Amos has taken to going there in the evenings. He has joked about integration and how one or two of the friendliest patrons no longer actually turn their backs on him. Then he adds abruptly, 'The fact is, I don't know if the house will even be built.'

Selwyn and I turn to stare at him. This is the first we have heard of it. There is a silence, prickly with embarrassment.

'Who is this?' Joyce suddenly wants to know. The vicar was introduced to her fifteen minutes ago, but she has had one of her forgetful moments. He reminds her, and they shake hands all over again.

'Never a one for church, my daughter,' Joyce puts in.

The vicar turns back to Amos. 'I'm sorry if I've put my foot in it by asking. If there's anything I can do to help, either in pastoral or spiritual matters, you can always find me at the vicarage.'

'Thank you. I'll remember that.'

After he's gone, Joyce dozes off again. Selwyn has been too generous with the Baileys.

'I didn't know you'd decided not to go ahead,' I venture to Amos.

He jumps up, scattering newspapers and sending his book flying.

'I don't want the bloody house if I can't have Katherine there with me. What am I supposed to do with the place?'

He swings away from us and blunders out into the darkness. We see the lights in the cottage flick on. Selwyn doesn't say anything, let alone try to make a joke of it. Joyce sleeps soundly through all of this.

I wash up the teacups, dry the teapot and put it back on the dresser shelf, then store the remaining mince pies in an airtight box in the larder. These won't last long with the Knight boys and all the Davieses and Ben's girlfriend here. I'll make another batch tomorrow, I decide. These small decisions help to keep at bay a rising tide of dismay. There will be no glass and steel house on the violated site. The community is breaking up, piece by piece, before it has even properly established itself.

I don't know even what the next days will bring, let alone another year.

Selwyn has taken to following me through the house. I tell him not to do it, intending never to be alone with him, even for one minute. But how are you supposed to make convincing an order that is the opposite of what you really want?

After I have helped Joyce up to bed, I'm sitting in Jake's old study. Selwyn told me as soon as I came home that he had shown the old letters and estate records to Polly. I expressed mild surprise and he said defensively, 'Why not? Are they so private? I thought it would interest her, and I was quite right.'

She must have spent hours in here. Some of the books and papers are set out in orderly rows, under notes and dates in her familiar handwriting. The room is cold without a fire lit, and I pull my layers of cardigans tighter. Now, precisely on cue, Selwyn appears in the doorway. He closes it behind him and then leans against it. He looks tired.

'I want to talk to you,' he says.

'Go on.'

'I want to leave her.'

I am appalled by his flat certainty. Genuinely, to the core of my being. I manage to stammer, 'No. Not because of me, or to be with me. I won't have that, or you.'

He marches at me, grasps me by the elbows, kisses me as if that will work in a way that words don't. He is so warm, vital, and as our bodies fuse together I feel rather than think the words, *I saw you first, you were mine first and Polly has had you all these years, don't we deserve our time together now?*

But I have known his intention, haven't I, ever since that snatched afternoon? Maybe, even, the possibility has been in the back of my mind from the beginning, when the great plan for the new Mead was first conceived? Where Selwyn is concerned my capacity for self-delusion, deception and denial is apparently limitless. I shrivel within myself in shame and confusion.

'I'm going to do it anyway. After Christmas. I can't stand living like this.'

I shout at him now, 'Can't you see what's in front of your eyes?'

I gesture through the thick wall, towards Amos's cottage. 'The misery these things cause?'

He comes to me again, takes me in his arms, rests his face against mine. 'There are levels of misery, Barb. Trust me, won't you?'

We're standing there, locked together, when the door suddenly opens. We jump apart like criminals and I see Joyce standing there in her dressing gown.

She has only been in bed for an hour, but probably isn't aware of that.

She says plaintively, 'Barbara, have you seen my book? I want to read. I can't find my book anywhere.'

There's no doubt she has seen us. I can't attempt an explanation, or an excuse, and now none of us will know when or how a reference to this little scene will spill out of her. I go to her and take her arm, leading her out of the room.

'Let's see if we can find it,' I say.

CHRISTMAS

TWELVE

Meddlett church and its land are familiar in all seasons, but I love this stark midwinter version. In the very depths of the year, the world seems spun out of threads of black and white. The massive yew by the churchyard gate is a black shape snipped out of a pearl-white sky, the tower stands like a flint bulwark against the wind, and the ranks of gravestones are set in steely grass that holds only the vaguest memory of green. There are flowers on some of the graves, but cold has nipped the glow out of the petals.

My breath smokes ahead of me as I cross the path leading from the south door and head for the Meadowe plot. I have made a little wreath of ivy and holly from the Mead woods, as I do each year, and I place it against the simple headstone that marks Jake's grave. Then I rest my hand on the shoulder of stone, rubbing the coating of loose grit and lichen with my fingertips as if to coax it into life. I'm telling Jake in a word-less rush of a confession that time has looped and doubled on itself, that I love Selwyn but I can't allow him to turn his back on his marriage, and I'm not sure how at our age we can resist the turbulence that threatens us all.

A temporary peace descends, at least.

Christmas is nearly here. It's not taking shape in quite the way I had planned and imagined, because no one seems to know quite who will be coming, and if they do appear what frame of mind they will be in or how they will all respond to each other. It's probably a good thing that I can't influence any of this, because in my eagerness to have it turn out well I might try to over-choreograph everything. The uncertainty is novel, after all the Christmases that Jake and I spent here together when our routine never varied. He liked to dip into the new books that were all the presents he ever wanted, to open up one of his bottles of good claret so that it had plenty of time to breathe, and then drink it quietly with our dinner.

This year I'm enchanted by the way that all the previously empty rooms of the house are warm and lamplit, and that when I look into them I don't know if I am going to come across Joyce and Amos watching television and grumbling at cross-purposes about declining standards in broadcasting, or Nic watching *YouTube* on Colin's laptop while he tapes swathes of fir branches to a mantelpiece. In Jake's study I will almost certainly find Polly poring over old letters with her bifocals pushed down her nose and a scarf wound around her throat for warmth. If she is there I back out, nodding generalized approval and smiling vaguely. It's not easy to behave normally in Polly's company, what with the broad undertow of guilt about my behaviour and specific anxiety about what Joyce saw the other evening. My mother hasn't come out with any mention of it yet, but I can't be sure she won't.

Since she came back from London with Colin, bringing the pregnant girl, Nic, with them, Polly has seemed her usual generous self. She is touchingly solicitous over Nic, and she was admiring of the results of Selwyn's last huge efforts to finish off the barn. But I know that she is watching him, and me. I can feel her eyes on my back, observing and assessing.

Back in the kitchen I might find Selwyn himself, paging restlessly through my newspaper and thawing out after a bout of sawing in the yard. The floors of reclaimed wood have been laid throughout the barn and so Polly has decreed that from now on the messiest work has to be done outside. I think she is surprised by the way he meekly complies with her orders. His eyes follow me over the top of the paper as I move between the larder and the oven. We are all watching one another.

My ungloved fingers have gone numb. I clap them to get the blood flowing and as I turn from the grave I see Nic threading her way between the headstones. She asked if she could come with me in the car to the village, and tactfully she went in to take a look at the church while I came across to Jake. She's wearing a bright red short coat, blue woolly tights and a plum-coloured knitted hat, and the brilliance of this get-up bleeds into the surrounding air so that she seems enveloped by a sort of fuzzy electrical field. She stops beside me, head on one side and a hand resting on her bump as she studies the inscription on the headstone. It gives just his name and dates.

'You must have been lonely after he died.'

'I was, a little,' I admit.

And so the plan was conceived to bring my old friends up here to Mead. It's only since they arrived that I have been able to assess how cut off Jake and I had become, and now they are here I so much want them to stay. I think again with a twist of apprehension that this Christmas celebration will be an interval of peace before whatever seismic upheavals the new year must bring. Knowing this makes the prospect seem even more precious to me.

'Didn't you want to have kids?' she wonders.

She's an unusual girl, this Nic. Her bluntness seems almost deliberate, as if she has made a decision not to be the tactful type, but she can also be outstandingly kind. She'll sit for an hour and more and massage my mother's swollen feet and ankles, and the other day she gave her a pedicure complete with a start-ling fluorescent polish that Joyce is inordinately pleased with.

'Have a look at my feet,' she keeps calling out to the milkman or the window cleaner or whoever else drops in to wish us the compliments of the season. Their wheels used barely to stop turning on the gravel before they were off again, but lately the household has become much more interesting to them and, like the vicar, they tend to linger in the hope of a chat and, no doubt, some gossip to circulate in the village.

Nic adoringly tracks Colin around the house. Luckily Selwyn has stopped doing it with me, now Polly is back from London, or we would look like the participants in some complicated game. She spent hours with him while they sprayed winter foliage with silver paint to twist into decorations, asking him endless questions about New York and which celebrities he has met. They exchange names I've never heard of. But she's sensitive enough to leave him alone when she guesses he might be getting tired of her, or just tired.

'Children didn't happen,' I tell her.

'Hm,' she says, rubbing her belly.

Nic has already said that she never really considered a termination because, as she put it, her own mother had kept her in the days when she had much less going for her. Mind you, she hadn't done a lot for her since that time, she sniffed, but the gift of life and all that, you can't deny it.

'You have to admire our Nic,' Colin said in private to me, and I rather do.

She wanders a couple of steps to the next headstones, which belong to Jake's father and mother, and his grandparents lie next to them. The Meadowes were not a prolific clan in the last century; Jake and his father were both only children. Nic reads all the names, and then tilts her head to take in the other burial plots and the fine tower of the church. She rocks on her heels and coughs a cloud into the icy air.

'All your family, all in one place,' she says in wonderment. 'I mean, roots like this, must make you feel special.'

'It's my husband's family. Joyce is all there is of mine,' I remind her.

'Your mum's great. She's not like a real old person. I know what you mean, though. I used to feel dead envious of Ben because he had his sisters and a mum and dad and they were all really close, and into looking after each other. Polly's so kind and sort of reliable without being judgemental, isn't she?

322

She's the kind of mum you'd go for if you could buy a pattern and knit yourself one. Maybe that's why Ben's pretty hopeless, though. He's never had to sort things out for himself, has he?'

'I don't know about that,' I say, diplomatically.

Nic sighs. 'I'd quite like my kid to have a family.'

'But it will do, won't it? Its grandmother could hardly be more eager for it.'

'Yeah. But, you know. You can't rely too much on other people. I've basically got to do it myself. At the end of the day Ben is Polly's son, and me and Ben – that's never going to happen, trust me. I'm dreading him getting here, to be honest. It's been so peaceful and lovely the last couple of days, just hanging out with you and Colin and Polly, and as soon as he arrives there's going to be all the drama.' She's shivering now, and glumly chewing her lower lip as she stares at Jake's grandparents' grave.

'It might not be so bad. You're in the house with me and Colin, Ben's in the barn with his family. We'll make it all right, between us.' I take her arm. 'Come on, you're getting cold. Did you see the memorial in the church?'

'No.'

'It's a good one. Let's go and look.'

The dim interior is scented with dusty hassocks, spilled wax from the children's Christingle service, and a large Christmas tree. The same nativity scene is put out every year, a circle of carved wooden animals surrounding a plaster Mary and Joseph and a swaddled plaster Christ child in a straw manger. The memorial tablet is on the south wall, so Nic and I pass behind the pews and down the side aisle to reach it.

I told Selwyn about this, when I showed him the 1914 photograph with the estate workers and the young girls gathered in the sunlight in front of the barn, and Jake's great-grandfather's Silver Ghost just visible in the shadows within. An emblematic moment of change, history itself changing gear.

Selwyn claimed that I am in love with Mead, and he was jealous. I told him he couldn't be jealous of a house, and we agreed that anyway he was part of it now.

Then he kissed the inside of my wrists, first one and then the other, and I knew I had been frozen until that very minute. Now I'm melted, and running away in all directions.

Nic is studying the carving of the memorial. There are no lachrymose angels or stone poppies. At the head of the tablet in bas-relief there is an old wagon, piled high with hay, and a pair of pitchforks bracket the names of the fifteen Meddlett dead. At the foot there is a lusty-looking bull, complete with a fine pair of horns. It is a rural tribute to men who never came home to the fields, and it always makes me feel sorrowful and at the same time uplifted.

'Second Lieutenant George Edwin Anstruther Meadowe,' Nic reads.

'That was my husband's great-uncle, his grandfather's younger brother.'

'He was twenty. That's younger than me.'

'Yes. Some of them were hardly more than children, look.'

There are three Coopers, and no fewer than four Greens, presumably brothers, or – as I always hope, for the mothers' sake – perhaps only cousins.

Nic lifts her head, jams her hands deep into the pockets of her red coat. She mutters, 'We've just got to get on with it, all of us, haven't we? At least we're alive for now.'

I can only agree with that.

After we have finished in the church we leave the car where it is and walk on up to the green, passing the pond with the row of ducks hesitating under the willow fronds like guests waiting to be introduced. There are coloured lightbulbs draping the front of the Griffin, and several of the houses have American-style Christmas wreaths adorning the front doors. The village looks picturesque, and Nic is impressed.

'It's like a film set, this place. You know, Richard Curtis. Someone comes over from America and falls in love.'

'I know the film you mean.'

We reach the shop, and prominently taped in the window next to an invitation to all to join the 5K Family Fun Run on

Boxing Day is a Meddlett Princess poster. Nic stops to read it. She has been taking an interest in our Iron-Age history since Colin told her about the find.

'They're so right. The treasure ought to stay where it was dug up. It should all be laid out in a museum right here, and then tourists would come and that would be good for the village and the shop and everything. Or maybe up at Mead? What about that? You could have the museum, and a virtual tour of the settlement, and – oh, souvenirs and teas. It's a business opportunity. I'll stay and be your car park attendant.'

These are not new ideas. Laughing, I explain to her that I don't disagree with the protesters' demands, but the remaining archaeological finds belong to the Crown and will probably be bought eventually by whichever museum can afford to acquire them, and the burial site itself doesn't belong to me any longer, but to Amos.

And I also note that Nic may be joking, but still the idea that she would like to stay on up here is taking shape within her.

We progress inside the shop.

There is a queue at the post office counter and Mrs Spragg is behind the till. I say good morning to her and exchange nods with the other people I know. I collect Colin's copy of the *Guardian* and put some cartons of milk and a bag of onions and some other supplies we need into a wire basket. Nic is buying chocolate and *heat* magazine. Someone shuffles and then stops in front of me.

'Morning, Mrs Meadowe.'

I look up, and after a mental rummage I place the young man. He's the archaeologist from the site, the serious one who made the discovery on that first morning. A long while ago.

'Hello,' I smile at him. I can't remember his name, though. 'Not working today?'

'I'll be starting on a site near Norwich straight after Christmas. I've got a couple of days off now. How's everything up at the house? Has Mr Knight's building work started again?'

'Not yet.'

325

Nic comes up beside me. In her blaze of clashing colours and with her emphatic eyeliner she stands out like an urban beacon alongside everyone else's olive-green padded country jackets and dun corduroys.

'Hi?' she chirps.

'This is Nicola. And Nic, this is . . .'

'Kieran,' he promptly helps me. He's a nice, polite boy.

I tell Nic that it was Kieran who first saw the princess's bones as the digger blades cut into the earth and who called an immediate halt to the work. I remember the silence that fell, and Amos's protestations, and later, the moment when we looked down into the trench and saw the skull filled with earth and the fragile bowl of her pelvis exposed to view after two thousand years.

Nic says how amazing, and Kieran mumbles about it being his job and therefore what he's trained to do, and if only the rest of the burial goods hadn't been stolen, the discovery would have been something really magnificent.

'It makes me mad just thinking about it,' he almost spits. His vehemence brings to mind his boss, the equally passionate Dr Carr, and then I automatically think of Katherine, and it's a second or two before I realize that the other customers are listening. There is that suspension of activity that people display when they don't want to be seen eavesdropping, but can't continue their business and concentrate on other people's at the same time. Stan Cooper, the builder who came to repoint the Mead brickwork for me, is standing with his back to us pretending to examine the newspaper headlines, and Mrs Spragg is holding a tub of margarine motionless over the till scanner. The postmistress is openly staring from behind her rampart of glass, and the queue is frozen.

Anger at the loss and despoilment rises in me again.

Do this Kieran and Christopher Carr think they have a monopoly on such feelings? Mead is mine and all its history, and I hate the violation as passionately as the archaeologists or the villagers do. But in the silent shop the fury quickly seeps away, replaced by the same discomfort that I always have here, an outsider denied the gift of anonymity. It's mostly my own fault that I don't fit in in Meddlett, but knowing this doesn't make it any easier to deal with.

'Me too,' I say crisply.

Now Kieran looks uncomfortable too, and I'm sorry for that.

'I know it's just as much your loss and there's nothing you can do about restoring the grave goods, Mrs Meadowe. I should try to be more philosophical, shouldn't I?'

Nic rocks on her heels with her eyes resting on Kieran. Her short red coat has ridden up even further in front, where the bump sticks out, and there is an unfeasible length of bright blue leg on display. Stan Cooper picks up a copy of the *East Anglia Times*, Mrs Spragg swoops the marge over the till reader, and the postmistress serves the next customer in line. Someone pops their head in from outside and asks how much the bundles of kindling are.

Nic and I pay for our shopping and emerge again with Kieran on our heels.

'Everyone was having a good old listen, weren't they?' she says.

'I know. You have to get used to that.'

'There are secrets and no secrets in places like Meddlett,' Kieran observes. 'Nice to see you, Mrs Meadowe. Say hello to Mrs Knight from me. See you around,' he adds, this last to Nic, whilst trying not to let his gaze drop below her chin.

'Yeah, probably,' she calls after him.

Nic and I walk back to the car. On the drive home she says, 'That shop was something else. I don't know anything about the country, do I?'

'Except from Richard Curtis films.'

'I've lived in cities my whole life and even I know that must be all bollocks. Sorry.' She pats her belly, and I get the impression she's apologizing for her language to the baby as much as to me.

As I swing the car past the back of the barn, I see that

Katherine's car is parked beside Amos's Jag. The front wheel arch is buckled and rusting. I knew from Amos that she was probably coming back today, but still I feel concern at the difficulty this return must present for the two of them. Nic and I carry our shopping in through the yard gate and I'm looking to see which lights are on in the three houses. There is a ring of damp sawdust on the cobbles to show where Selwyn has recently been at work, but I can't hear anything except the rooks in the trees of the copse.

It's beginning, I think. The New Mead Christmas, and God bless us every one.

In the cottage Katherine unpacked the dozen bags of shopping that Sam had carried in for her from the car. They had driven up from London together, and Toby would arrive later. Unwrapping packages and stowing them in the fridge and cupboards recalled the same sequences as performed at the other holiday cottage with Chris. Then and now she had bought the same tea and the same wholemeal bread as she always did, thus staunchly maintaining brand loyalty in the process of betraying her husband. She felt miserably confused.

But you *had* left him, she reminded herself. It wasn't a betrayal in the strictest sense.

She was back today by negotiation, out of loyalty to her family, because it was Christmas. The oddness of her situation made her wonder if her life was really just measured out by supermarket trips, and meals prepared for men and for sons and for friends of her sons, and therefore did it actually matter which men were involved just as long as the beef was rare and the pastry crisp?

'Mum?' Sam was standing by the fridge. He was looking at her as if he feared she might be slightly mad. She had laughed out loud, she realized.

'It's all right,' she told him.

The sink was stained and the plughole clogged with some kind of greasy debris. The floor felt both sticky and gritty underfoot, and the table was covered with a mass of news-papers and coffee cups and empty glasses. Amos didn't have much experience of cleaning up after himself, but she thought the state of chaos he had allowed their home to descend into was a deliberate underlining of her dereliction.

He came in now, bearing the linen that she had sent him upstairs to collect off the bed. One glance into their room had settled the uncertainty that had gnawed at her, all the way from London and for days before that.

She wasn't going to share a bed, or even a room with him.

It seemed impossible, but in the eighteen days since she had left the cottage, apparently he hadn't thought of changing the sheets. Out of such omissions, she realized, came finality.

Amos was a womanizer and he drank too much, he was overbearing and deficient in sensibility, but those faults were embedded in him, the man she knew, and because they were familiar to her she could perhaps have gone on trying to over-look them. Just as, in his turn, he probably tried to overlook her no doubt comparable failings. Yet although he had begged and begged her to come back to Mead, not to desert him and the boys at Christmas because they all loved and needed her, he hadn't thought enough about her and about her known pref-erences to have welcomed her back to a clean house.

There was only one spare twin bedroom in the cottage, in which the boys would be sleeping. She would have to ask Miranda for a bed in the house. Katherine longed for Miranda's company right now, and Polly's. When she looked out and saw Miranda crossing the yard with Nic, she had to stop herself from running out after them.

Amos stood helplessly with the sheets spilling out of his arms.

She directed him to the washing machine, and told him which cycle to use. The remaining jars and packets were put away in the proper places, then she swept up the spilled sugar and swilled out the sink. Sam slid away to watch television, but Amos still hovered in the kitchen. In the past, or in a parallel world, she would have had a meal under way by now.

'I'm going across to see Miranda,' Katherine said.

His face fell. 'What for?'

'I'm going to ask if she'll give me a bed.'

'But . . .'

She went to him, put her hands on his arms. It would be easier to capitulate and do what he wanted, but knowing this gave her the determination not to concede the ground already gained. She felt a little surprised at how hardhearted she could find it in herself to be.

'Amos? I've come back for Christmas because you asked me to, and because I know the boys want me to be here, and because I don't want just to discard our family. But you and me' – as she said it she felt his bodily warmth through his sleeves and the palms of her hands, an engine completely separate from her own – 'we're not the same as we were, and it would be a mistake to pretend otherwise.'

He cleared his throat. 'This is very humiliating, making your withdrawal from me so public. Is that what you intend? It's understandable, as an act of retaliation for what has gone before. What I don't understand is why you have left it until now.'

'I left when I did, and I haven't come back as a wife, only as a mother. Surely you don't have to feel humiliated, Amos? You're among friends here.'

He gave a gusty sigh. 'All right. Toby said he'd be getting here about eight, depending on the traffic out of town. Shall I, ah, Sam and I, start putting some dinner together?'

It was one of those questions that expect an answer in the negative.

'Good idea,' Katherine smiled at him.

She paused outside their front door. Smoke rose from the chimneys on all three sides and there were lights in most of the windows. Sheets had been tacked at the new windows upstairs in the barn, presumably to offer the twins some privacy once they arrived. In spite of the proximity she had the impression of three redoubts, with the Knights and the Davieses respectively holed up within theirs, the pains and pleasures of other people's families and lives as ever opaque to outsiders.

Miranda's theory, that families were only a temporary intervention whereas friends should last for ever, seemed not be to holding up particularly well.

Miranda herself, of course, had neither husband nor children, so her theory wasn't subject to personal testing.

It was cold. She hurried on to Miranda's kitchen door.

The kitchen was bright, steamy with warmth and the smells of cooking. Joyce and Colin and Nic were all there, variously occupied, and there was music playing quite loudly. It was a noticeably harmonious scene. Katherine went straight across to Joyce, who was in her chair beside the range. She told her how glad she was to see her, and how well she was looking, both of which were true.

'Have you seen my feet?' Joyce demanded.

She extricated them from her slippers and stretched them out for Katherine to admire. Ten bright orange toenails decorated bunioned blue-white toes.

'Beautiful.'

Joyce pointed, adding quite loudly, 'She did them. Very nice young girl, not what you'd expect. I can't remember her name.'

'Nic,' Nic laughed from the table.

Katherine said to Nic how good it was to see her at Mead, then hugged Colin and in answer to his murmured question said yes, she was all right so far.

Miranda came in. A draught knifed in from the passage and she latched the door quickly behind her. She placed three bottles of wine on the dresser, which left her arms free to hold out to Katherine.

'You're here. Come on, there's a fire in the drawing room. Let's go and sit in there.' She said more loudly, 'You'll be all right here, Mum, with Colin.'

'I'll be all right, will I? Where are you going?' Joyce was confused, but not distressed.

There was a huge tree in the dim hall, lights shimmering,

wrapped presents laid out beneath. Colin's would be the ones dressed with wired bows and sprays of crystal beads. There was indeed a fire in the drawing room – fresh logs crackled and showers of red sparks were sucked up the chimney. An immense garland of silver-sprayed evergreens swagged the stone mantel. Miranda laughed as Katherine pointed to it.

'I know. Col and Nic spent two days on it. They've been having a lovely time.'

'You seem to be orchestrating it all brilliantly. As always,' Katherine said. Miranda looked uncertain. 'I don't know. I . . . K, it's so good you're back. Let's sit down.'

They took opposite ends of the battered Knole sofa. Close to the fire it was warm but, as always at Mead, the chill lurking in the corners was only temporarily held off. Katherine kicked off her shoes and drew her feet up amongst the velvet cushions. Miranda burrowed for them and rubbed hard.

'Poor cold thing. You've got too used to London central heating. That's better. Now then. Tell me how you are?'

Katherine hesitated. It didn't get any easier to confide. It seemed disloyal to Amos to be talking about their marriage, even to Miranda.

'Where's Polly?'

Miranda's head came up quite sharply. 'Why?'

'I just wondered. I wanted to tell her too. You know, the three of us. You were both so generous about coming to see me in London. It meant a lot to me,' Katherine said.

'We're friends. That's what matters, K, friendship is the absolute. It's the solid gold bar in the safe.' Miranda's face was shadowed, but she added, 'The twins and Ben will be here any minute, I expect Polly's waiting for them.'

With her fingernail Katherine scraped at a blob of wax on one of the cushions.

'Mirry, can I stay in one of the rooms upstairs? Just over Christmas, you know. After that I'm going back to London.'

There was no need to spell out anything more.

'Of course,' Miranda said gently. 'It's final, then?'

Katherine nodded. 'Yes. Our marriage is over. I'm confused and guilty, angry with Amos and astonished at myself, unable to sleep, anxious about what it means for Chris, and as madly in love as a teenager. I don't know whether to cry or sing or run away and hide, but I do know that much.'

Miranda had to smile. 'That seems straightforward, at least.'

'I'm sorry, Mirry. I'm really so sorry to let you down. I know how much you wanted this Mead experiment to work.'

Miranda reached for her hand. 'At this stage of life you think you have everything stitched up, don't you? Then love comes along and rips every seam.'

'At my age,' Katherine muttered.

'At our age,' Miranda echoed, very softly.

Katherine had only instinct to go on, but a question that until now had been floating in her mind was snagged and held by gossamer threads of conviction.

Their eyes met. 'What's going to happen?' she breathed. 'To all of us?'

Miranda's head fell back. 'God knows. Nothing at all in my case. Bar of gold in the safe, eh? Let's have our seasonal revels and forget ourselves.'

The door leading from the yard banged open. Colin, Joyce and Nic turned to see who was there. Framed in the doorway, wintry air sweeping in with him, stood Ben. His hair was completely hidden by a grubby knitted beehive hat. His beard had been reduced to a patchy goateee, and various scarves and messenger bags trailed from his coathanger shoulders. His eyes went straight to Nic.

'I love you,' he shouted as if the room were empty but for her.

Everyone gaped at him.

'Why did you run away? Did you mean to break my heart? Was that the idea?'

Colin lifted one hand to his eyes. Joyce leaned forward in her chair, peering with interest at everyone in turn. Nic sighed as Ben bounded across the kitchen and dropped to his knees beside her. One of his bags slid to the front and threatened to choke him. Batting it away, he stretched his arms wide and rested his ear against Nic's jumper.

'You look so *pregnant*.'

'Yeah? What did you expect?'

'Who is this?' Joyce demanded.

'Ben, please try not to be such a dork,' Nic said, with some restraint. 'Get up, will you?'

'Doesn't he know about shutting a door behind him, whoever he is?'

Colin got up and closed it. Ben was still kneeling at Nic's feet, head on her belly and eyes shut, his face wreathed in a beatific smile.

'He's my baby's father,' Nic told Joyce.

'Is he? You mean this is Selwyn's boy? He looks more like a tramp. Why do all young people dress like refugees nowadays?'

'I just want to *be* the father,' Ben mumbled. 'I want to do what's right.'

'You've done all that's required so far,' Colin put in. Nic grinned at him as she pushed Ben away.

'If you don't get up, Ben, I'm going to kick you.'

He rocked back on to his heels. 'Say what you like. I'm going to stand by you, Nic. You can count on me.'

'Right now I'm counting on you to stand *up*.'

Ben bounced to his feet, sending his accoutrements flying.

He beamed. 'I'm just so happy to see you, Nic. And so pleased you feel you can be here, for Christmas with me and my mum and dad, and everyone . . .' The realization that there were other people in the room now dawned on him. He flew to Joyce and reminded her that the last time they had met had been when he was twelve, and towards Colin he directed his warm, absolutely disarming smile. Even with the misshapen hat and goatee, he was a good-looking boy.

'I'm sorry guys, that was really rude. Only, this is just such an amazing moment, I can hardly believe it. Nic, you're actually *here*.'

Now there was a knock on the back door and a girl's head appeared.

'Hi? Can we come in?'

It was the twins, pretty and long-legged, consciously differentiated in their presentation but still as alike as their own reflections. Unlike their brother, they had evidently taken the time to go to the barn and deposit their luggage. There were more greetings and exclamations. Nic was briefly enveloped by them.

'Crewe Station,' Joyce grumbled. 'Is it going to be in and out like this all Christmas?'

Alph and Omie wanted to know where Miranda was? Polly said would everyone come over and have a drink right now? Now that they were all here, they wanted to christen the barn really properly?

Their sentences often ended on a rising inflection.

On cue, Miranda appeared with Katherine. She clapped her hands and kissed all the newcomers. She looked bright-eyed, even slightly feverish.

They streamed out into the yard, light from the open door splashing the cobbles. Headlights swung briefly over the old flint walls as another car drew up. Toby Knight loomed out of the darkness and joined the tail end of the procession into the barn.

Polly stood at the door and welcomed them all in.

She had decorated a fifteen-foot tree that almost scraped the huge cross-beams. The vast open fireplace held what looked like half a blazing tree trunk, and on the newly laid stone hearth stood Selwyn, arms outstretched, glowing with triumph. The backdrop of leaping flames made him appear even more demonic than usual.

The floors were laid, even though there were no skirtings. The walls were solid against the weather, although they were raw plaster. Upstairs the bedrooms all had doors even though the mattresses were laid on bare boards. In *two* bathrooms as well as in the kitchen, hot water lavishly gushed from the taps. Selwyn had done what he had set out to do, as Polly had always known he would. It was a serious achievement, and through the hubbub she smiled her admiration at him. He gave her a wink in return.

Ben gazed about him. 'Hey, Dad. Wow. Not bad.'

Amos crossed the room. He held out his hand.

He said, 'Well done. It all looks wonderful tonight.'

Selwyn shook, grinning at this generosity. 'Thanks, Amos. I'm not going to say I wish we were doing this in your glass palace instead of my old barn, because – well, that would be a lie, wouldn't it? But next Christmas, trust me, we'll be round at yours.'

They shook, and everyone applauded. No one whispered about where *yours* might be, if it was not to be the glass palace in the meadow.

Joyce was placed in the only armchair, as the Davies children hurried around with glasses and bottles. Polly took her place beside Selwyn. Everyone else drew into a semicircle around the hearth.

Selwyn lifted his glass. Uncharacteristically, Polly noticed, he seemed to be taking the trouble to choose his words. A flicker of foreboding darkened the room's brilliance and in spite of herself she glanced at Miranda. Miranda's gaze seemed to be directed into the heart of the fire.

He said, 'Here we all are. I don't believe in speeches, as you know.'

There were various catcalls but he raised his voice over them.

'It's taken us a while to get here, to Miranda's pastures old. Forty years, as a matter of fact. A blink of an eye, you might say, to an Iceni princess, but a long time to all of us. Let's drink a toast to history.'

They began a low obedient murmur, but Polly linked her arm through Selwyn's and firmly drew him closer to her.

Alpha and Omie squeezed each other's hands.

Polly hesitated and in the crackling silence the huge log fell an inch, sending a rush of sparks up the chimney. She said in her warm voice, 'None of us knows what tomorrow will bring, let alone next year. But for tonight, we know who and where we are, and that's with friends. This is the toast. *Here's to us.*'

'Here's to us,' they shouted back to her, filling the barn with a roar. As Polly lifted her glass she saw that Nic's eyes were shiny with tears. She slipped away from Selwyn's side and went to her.

'What's wrong?'

She gulped. 'Nothing at all. It's more that everything's all right, for now. I'm not used to it, am I?'

Polly drew her hand under Nic's arm and connected her to the circle. On Nic's other side Colin murmured, 'Polly's right, you know. *Us* is a good notion. Hang on to that, if you can.'

It was Christmas Eve.

No one at Mead had made a definite suggestion; it was more that a plan had evolved from Amos's expressed intention to go to the midnight service in Meddlett. Toby and Sam said at once that they would go with him, and both having had girlfriends from good county families they insisted to everyone else that it was traditional to go to the village pub before heading to the church. Selwyn instantly declared that now it was sounding more like his kind of evening and he would come along too.

Polly reminded him that they used always to go when their children were small.

'I remember, Mum. I loved it,' Ben dreamily sighed. 'Being up so late, so excited I couldn't breathe, looking into the starry sky for a glimpse of the reindeer. I'm definitely up for it. Nic, are you coming?'

She had fixed him with a glare. 'Round our way it was the night for getting legless on rum and black down some club, then feeling so bad all Christmas Day you couldn't eat your dinner. It didn't matter anyway, because your mum had forgotten to take the plastic bag of insides out of the turkey when she stuck it in the oven. It's not going to be like that for my kid. So yeah, I'll do church. Why not?'

In the end, by ten o'clock, everyone from all three houses had decided they would come.

Joyce wore a fur coat that had belonged to Jake's mother. It came down to her ankles, and gave her a marsupial appearance. She topped it off with a knitted hat not totally dissimilar to Ben's, and as she tottered with him out to the waiting car Polly thought they looked like the old and young of some sub-polar tribe. She nudged Selwyn and pointed it out to him.

Selwyn had drunk a lot at dinner. Amos had drunk and eaten well too, gesturing with his fork and describing how he took statins to control his cholesterol level. When the time came to leave, Polly and Katherine manoeuvred the two men into the passenger seats of their cars and took over the driving themselves.

Polly saw Ben trying to corner Nic, but Nic skipped into Colin's passenger seat as the twins folded themselves into the back. Alph and Omie were wearing little berets and high ankle boots that crunched on the gravel, and together they were a sharp reminder of urban worlds a long way from the crumbling exterior of Mead. Polly was proud of all three of them tonight, even Ben.

Selwyn leaned across Polly and pressed the horn.

'Let's get going,' he shouted, baring his teeth.

The cars set off in a convoy. The curve of the driveway, the trees, and after a few seconds the house itself, were all invisible as the cars headed into a thick mist from the sea. In the lead, Polly hunched forwards and peered into the depths. The beams of the headlamps bounced back at her off a curtain of fog. She was glad that she was driving because otherwise the rolling motion would have made her feel sick. Ben's head craned over from the back seat.

'What's this fog thing? It's meant to be all frosty and starry,' he complained in her ear.

Selwyn wound down his window and stuck his head out. Damp air scented with salt and leaf mould instantly filled the car.

'. . . Then one foggy Christmas Eve, Santa came to say,' he

338

bawled into the night. Colin braked hard to avoid hitting Polly's bumper and happily sang back at the dim red glow of her tail lights. The three girls laughed and joined in, Omie improvising a passable descant line. The four cars edged between the stone gateposts and headed for Meddlett, the chorus of 'Rudolph the Red-nosed Reindeer' drifting raucously into the soundless fog, with Toby and Sam slapping at the side panels of the Jaguar as accompaniment.

The Griffin was packed. Beside the door was another 5K Fun Run poster. Sam and Toby pointed it out to each other.

'Got to be done, eh?'

'Bloody hell, Tobe, Boxing Day? Are you mad?'

'Come on, I'll beat you both,' Selwyn shouted.

'We'll see about *that*.'

'Oh please, don't,' Polly begged him.

At one end of the bar a band was sending their special version of 'Jingle Bell Rock' booming through the amps, the bleached singer lost in being his equally special version of Billy Idol. Behind the bar, framed by fairylights flashing in complicated sequence, Vin Clarke sweated under a foil banner wishing A Merry Christmas to All Our Customers. Amos led the way through the crowd, greeting by name a surprising number of the crimson faces that swam up out of the throng. When Alph and Omie took off their hats they attracted a lot of attention from the boys crammed in next to the band. Nic stayed glued to Colin's side. Miranda came in last, imagining she was shielded by the broad backs of the Knight boys. Vin, however, spotted her at once.

'Evening, Mrs Meadowe. What a pleasure, and on Christmas Eve,' he bawled.

'Jingle Bell Rock' ended on a ragged chord. In a momentary hush a voice cried out, 'What have you done with our princess?'

A space opened, leaving the Mead arrivals in the centre.

Amos wheeled around. 'I've told you, Stan. And if I've anything to do with it, she'll be coming back to rest. That's a promise.'

'Where's her treasure?' another voice called.

Amos was easily up to this amateur cross-examination. 'Your guess is as good as mine. Or perhaps better.'

There was a rustle and a rippling shove, the circle threatening to close in on them. From just behind her Polly heard a woman murmur, 'She never comes down the village because she don't like the way her old man used to be friendly with some people round here.'

'Old Jake Meadowe never strayed once he was married to her,' someone else insisted.

Polly looked, but all she could see was a row of backs. That was what villages were like, as she knew perfectly well. Gossip had a half-life of approximately twenty-five years.

You could listen to it, or choose not to.

The band was already into the next number. Most of the Griffin's patrons were more interested in getting another drink before last orders than in the dim provocations of archaeology.

Miranda said, 'Good evening, Vin. Merry Christmas.'

A large man heaved himself off the corner bar stool and half-lifted Joyce into his place. He patted her fur shoulder and she gave him a frown.

'Who are you? You're not my cousin's husband? He's not as bald as you.'

'I'm Roy, my love. Merry Christmas.'

Amos was buying drinks for anyone whose glass was empty, which turned out to be most of the crowd. Polly was impressed and amused that he had discovered how to work the pub to his advantage. Miranda was standing quietly, a little apart from the rest of the party.

If the whisper she had heard contained any truth, Polly thought, it would explain why Miranda kept out of Meddlett. Then her gaze travelled on and she saw Selwyn looking at Miranda too. His smile for her alone was tender, without any piratical gleam.

Polly turned away. She let Toby lead her into the dancing.

Jessie pushed through from the kitchen and dumped two full plates on the nearest table.

340

'That's your lot. Kitchen's closed,' she yelled. 'Back again?' she asked Amos as she passed.

Ben was dancing with Alpha. His spidery arms and legs shot out in different directions, attracting sniggers from some of the onlookers, but he was oblivious to them. Omie and Sam Knight joined in, followed by Selwyn, who drew Miranda by the wrist. In the end the Mead people were absorbed into the Griffin festivities without too much difficulty.

Nic had refused to dance with Ben. She was standing a little to one side while Colin made sure that Joyce had the right drink.

'I don't dance either,' a voice said in her ear.

'Actually I can dance all night, but I'm not going to, not at getting on for seven months gone,' Nic retorted.

The man looked stricken. 'No, of course not. I didn't mean you should be. Sorry, I don't really know what I meant. Is that your husband dancing there?'

Nic exploded with laughter at the idea of being married to Toby Knight.

'I haven't got a husband. I'm going to be a single parent. It's Kieran, isn't it?'

'Yes.' He looked pleased.

Four or five men including Stan Cooper and Joyce's new friend Roy pushed their way out past the dancers. Vin rang the brass bell behind the bar and called time over the band's finale of 'I Wish it Could Be Christmas Every Day'. After a little while, through the hubbub and the stamping and singing, Polly heard a different clamour. It was the church bells, ringing out for midnight service.

The streetlamps were no more than pale smudges in the murk. The bells were muffled and damped but they rang on, drawing a stream of people from the pub and the cottages to the looming bulk of the church. The congregation filed in, coughing and whispering and sobering up, insistent fingers of fog following them in and melting away beneath the soaring roof. Within the body of the church the bells were insistent and a glimpse of the shirt-sleeved ringers and the rising striped sallies connected the peals.

The Mead group filled two pews on the south side. Polly reached out for and grasped Selwyn's hand. Miranda tilted her head towards the war memorial. Nic's baby kicked hard against the stretched skin of her belly. It was listening to the ringing, she thought.

The vicar came up the aisle as the bells chased each other down and were stilled. The congregation shuffled to its feet with the first chord from the organ. A small boy with an old-fashioned parting in his hair appeared on the chancel steps. He composed himself, after a quick glance at the large woman in the front pew who was evidently his mother, and in a pure soprano began to sing 'It Came Upon A Midnight Clear'.

Standing between her husband and her son, Polly found that there were tears in her eyes.

Once the pub had emptied out, Jessie cleaned up in the bar. It had been a long, hard day's work and she was tired. Vin was clicking off the lights as she finally took off her apron and replaced it with her coat. Tomorrow at least was a day's rest, because the Griffin wouldn't reopen until Boxing Night. Geza kissed her on the cheek and wished her a happy Christmas as he loped off towards his caravan. She called after him that she would be eating her Christmas dinner at her mum's tomorrow afternoon, but he could come to hers after that.

'I will sleep and sleep, that will be the best present for me,' he called back. 'And I will see you after I wake up.'

Jessie made her way through the dense murk to the shed. She unlatched it and Rafferty burst out. His paws hit her shoulders and his wet tongue flagged her cheek before he bounded off.

'*Rafferty!*'

The last verse of 'Hark the Herald Angels' thundered to a close and the organist crashed out a major chord before picking himself up and trickling into a voluntary. The congregation began a surge for the west door, beaming and glowing with goodwill and conferred sanctity. Joyce had fallen asleep during the communion, her knitted hat askew, and once awakened she was confused and querulous. Colin and Miranda helped her to her feet and Amos led the Mead party from their pews. At the door the vicar wished each of them a happy and blessed Christmas, and they streamed out into the fogbound churchyard.

There was a knot of people chatting at the lychgate, where the great yew was no more than a patch of darker darkness. Amos passed by them, affably nodding goodnight. He had told Miranda that he would walk ahead and collect the car, so Joyce wouldn't have to make the return trip to the Griffin car park. He heard Omie and Alph laughing and chattering with Sam and Toby just behind him. Amos walked fast, keeping to the narrow pavement that hugged the flint wall of the churchyard. Damp glistened on the flecks of quartz and he realized in a split second that there was a car coming, travelling much too fast, the headlamps twin cones of light breaking through the swirling murk. He pressed instinctively against the wall but there was something else moving, a black streak that intersected with the light cones. There came a screech of brakes that failed to muffle a small, sickening thud. The black streak instantly became a bundle, rising and then falling through the air in a smooth arc. The car accelerated, diminished into a brief glow of red tail-lights, and then was swallowed up.

Amos heard a voice, a rising scream. He started running to where the black bundle had landed yards away at the kerbside. He knelt down, but Jessie was there before him. She flung herself over the dog's wet, bloodied body.

'Rafferty, Rafferty,' the girl crooned his name as she lifted and cradled the animal in her arms.

Amos saw that the dog's eyes were dulled. There was no doubt that Rafferty had been killed by the impact.

THIRTEEN

Geza pushed between the overgrown shrubs blocking the concrete path to the front door of Jessie's place.

He had telephoned his mother in Kosice, but otherwise he had spent most of Christmas Day asleep in the frowsy capsule of his caravan. Now it was dark again and as he made his way through the village most of the curtains were already closed, leaving only a few lamplit tableaux of families gathered around their tables or televisions for him to spy on. The overnight fog had broken up, but the brackish smell of it seemed to linger still.

There were no lights showing in Jessie's dilapidated cottage. He banged quite hard and then rattled the letterbox before listening to the silence that followed. A car swept along the road behind him, the headlights briefly lighting up the thatch of spiny twigs that hooded the door. He waited and listened again before trampling through the undergrowth to peer in through the front window, cupping his hands to his eyes as he did so. There was only darkness within.

Geza frowned. She wasn't here. This was unlike Jessie, who was surprisingly reliable, given the way she looked and talked. She must have decided to stay longer at her mother's, even though she had insisted to him that just enough time to exchange a gift and eat Christmas dinner would be plenty for both of them. He hesitated, becoming more aware of how hungry he was. He did enough cooking six nights a week not to want to bother with it for himself, but in his bag were two steaks and a bottle of nice wine, French, good stuff. That was what he had promised Jessie, who complained that her mother could burn water. Now he would have to go back to the caravan to cook and eat their meal on his own. He retraced his steps down the cracked path and turned back along the Meddlett road. No more cars came by. In the village, by the time he reached it once more, all the curtains were drawn.

In the barn, Polly embarked on the washing up. Selwyn and the three children were setting up a game of Pictionary, automatically Ben's favourite because it was the game he was best at.

'You're going to be a father, Benj, not the baby yourself. You'll have to get used to not getting your own way every single time,' Omie tartly observed. She had wanted Trivial Pursuit.

Selwyn flashily shuffled and cut the deck of cards.

'Come, my children. Let's play, and no bickering. Christmas Night is a time for wholesome family fun. Poll, aren't you going to join in?'

'No,' she said. Polly hated most games, seeing them as a waste of good reading time.

'All right, then. Ready . . . go,' Selwyn said, upending the egg timer.

Alph scribbled furiously as Ben scratched hooked fingers in his hair.

'Alps? Wait . . . armadillo? Erm, iguana? What's that supposed to be coming out of its mouth? Bad breath? Is that the word? Halitosis?'

'Minute's up,' Omie and Selwyn called.

'It's a *dragon*, you loser,' Alph sighed.

'You're the loser. What kind of a dragon is that?'

Polly reflected that Ben was still only a child himself, and it was impossible to imagine him taking on the responsibility for a baby. Luckily Nic was different. Polly was glad they had been able to persuade her to come up to Mead for the holiday, even though Nic had politely but firmly made it clear that she would prefer to spend today with Colin and Miranda rather than with Ben in the embrace of his family. She was even right about that, in a way; it had been good to have this interval, one day of it, just for Selwyn and Ben and the twins. All day long, Selwyn had been bearishly genial, intent on the four of them, as assiduous as if he were playing the role of father and husband for some hidden camera. Even so, though she deplored herself for being easily mollified, Polly felt happy in the glow of his attention.

Polly was determined that when the time came she and Selwyn together would make sure that Nic and this first grand-child got whatever they needed. If it was money, it would somehow be found. If it was love – Polly briefly rested her bulk against the sink, staring out into the blackness of the woods that sheltered the burial site – there was plenty of that, and some to spare.

At the table Omie's phone beeped a text message signal. She groped for it with the hand that wasn't drawing. Ben flung himself back in his chair.

'How many times has Tom texted you today?'

'Lots, thank you.'

'I know! Weather,' Selwyn shouted in triumph, with twenty seconds to spare. 'Well done, Omie. We're way ahead.'

Polly put away a pile of plates. 'Anyone hungry again?'

They all groaned.

Polly left them to the game. The fire was banked up so high and glowing on Selwyn's vast hearth that the room actually felt stuffy. That was a first.

She put on a coat over the vast, multi-striped, multi-coloured, exuberant chunk of mohairy knitwear that had been Selwyn's gift to her, and slipped out into the yard. The stillness descended, cooling her hot cheeks. She could hear the creak of a rising breeze in the branches, and knew that it would chase away the last pockets of fog. There was even a single star showing over the square shoulder of Mead's tallest chimney. She walked through the gate and took a few steps along the path that led to the wood, but then slowed and hesitated. She knew what she really wanted to do. Why not? Everyone else was occupied. She turned back again.

The idea that was steadily taking shape in her mind was a big one, and she was grateful and intrigued by the way that it occupied more and more of her thoughts. I must have been so mentally disengaged, she reflected. What did I think about?

The kitchen of the main house was deserted, although there were pans and dishes and the signs everywhere of a large meal prepared and served. The remnants of Colin's extravagant present wrappings spilled out of a bin liner, jumbled up with more humble crimson or Christmassy prints. The dining room was empty too, the table scattered with nutshells and the debris of crackers. It was a sweet thought, the idea of her grand-child's mother pulling crackers with Colin and Joyce. With Miranda, too.

Polly walked along the passage that led to Jake's study. From the drawing room she could hear the television, turned up loud for Joyce's benefit. She opened the study door and clicked on the light. In the grate lay a pile of grey ashes, but Polly hardly noticed that the room was cold. She pulled her coat more closely over the billows of knitwear, and took from an old box at the back of the shelves a bundle of letters. They were all in brittle brown envelopes, addressed in black handwriting to Mr and Mrs G. H. Meadowe and stamped with a crimson triangle enclosing a crown and the words 'Passed by Censor'. Very carefully, so as not to crack it along the folds, she took a sheet of lined paper out of the top envelope and settled down to read.

Miranda didn't want to move. It was warm and comfortable on the sofa. Beside her Colin was watching television and Nic was curled up on the other side of him. In the armchair next to the fire, Joyce had fallen asleep again. She dipped in and out of her dozes, often resuming her monologue from five minutes or half an hour earlier without being aware of any

347

interval. Her cough was almost gone, and with Colin's teasing and Nic's treatments she had acquired a haphazard sparkle. Colin was in good spirits too. His decorations and extravagant gifts to each of them and his ironically camp spun-sugar or savoury-torte elaborations on Miranda's straightforward cooking had all been a big success.

'This food,' Nic had said thoughtfully as she dipped her spoon, 'makes me want to write a poem.'

'You should have done this years ago,' Joyce said to her daughter, over the Christmas pudding.

'Done what?'

'Had a family.'

Colin and Nic smiled. They were all used by now to Joyce's tangential pronouncements. Whether Joyce was confused about whose daughter Nic might be, or was mixing up Colin with Jake, there was somehow a zigzag of truth in what she meant to say. Colin silently raised his glass to Miranda, and Nic followed suit.

It had been a remarkably happy day, Miranda thought.

'Are you asleep?' Colin murmured now. 'Nic is. She's like a puppy that's overeaten.'

'No, I am not. But I might as well be. Why are we watching *The Vicar of Dibley*?'

'Because it's Christmas Night. And I fancy Hugo.'

'What's this? You told me you didn't fancy anyone these days.'

'I know. I find I suddenly do. Rather good, isn't it?'

Desire *was* good, Miranda thought. But – unless attached to television actors, made safe by sheer distance – at this time of life it came shot through with so much danger and discomfort that it was more like an affliction.

She slid away from Colin and stood up.

Christmas was almost over. The holiday had been a barrier between herself and Selwyn and the future, and now that barrier was slowly lifting on a landscape that seemed to contain all their small figures, heading in uncertain groups towards an unfamiliar horizon.

She piled two unnecessary logs on the fire. The fir garlands on the mantelpiece were beginning to droop and spill their needles.

'Where are you going?' Colin lazily asked, his eyes still on the television.

'I'll be back,' she said.

The kitchen was a mess. She began the washing up, thinking mundane thoughts. There was Boxing Day's big dinner to consider. Dinner for everyone at Mead; the Knight boys were leaving the day after tomorrow for a ski trip, Alph and Omie were returning to their boyfriends. Most of the cooking was done already, thanks to Colin. A huge ham was resting in the larder, the fat honey-glazed and carved into diamonds studded with cloves. There were sweet and earthy root vegetables to be roasted, a pair of sharp lemon tarts to offset all the richness, a whole Stilton. People would be hungry. Sam, Toby and Alpha were all determined to enter the village charity run. Selwyn was making claims on it too. There had been talk of everyone else walking to Lockington, where the route would finish, to greet their runners as they came in.

At the end of the afternoon once the daylight had gone there would be candles lit, glasses filled, the gathering at the table. Afterwards they might even play charades, Miranda thought. She bent her head over the sink, scrubbing hard at the pan that had held the turkey.

Polly stood in the doorway. With her back turned, Miranda could have passed for a girl in her twenties. She was dressed in a wide-necked short top that fell off her shoulders, a full skirt of some pinkish diaphanous stuff sprinkled with sequins, thick ribbed tights and her well-worn cowboy boots. As always, Polly noted, Miranda's ensemble was theatrical, but it fell somewhere on the right side of fancy dress.

Miranda must have felt watched because she spun from the sink.

'Polly, it's you.' There was a catch in her voice.

'I'm sorry, lurking about your house, tonight of all nights. I don't mean to intrude.'

349

'What? It's not an intrusion at all.' Miranda's voice was warm, she had recovered from her surprise. 'Is everything all right?'

Polly nodded. 'They're playing a game.'

'Highly commendable. It's telly, across here.'

'Mirry, can we talk?' It was crucial to ask Miranda, Polly acknowledged, before the idea took such a firm hold of her that she would be unable to let go.

Miranda dropped the pan scrubber into the bowl of greasy water. Slowly she peeled off the washing-up gloves. Her heart seemed to leap into her throat.

'Of course. That's an amazing coat of many colours. Would you like a drink?'

Polly compressed her lips. 'God, no. Thanks, though.'

They sat down at opposite sides of the table. Miranda piled up plates, sweeping debris away from underneath. From the pantry, she could hear the shudder of the fridge motor starting up.

'I should have asked before . . .' Polly began.

Miranda waited, the same feverish brightness in her eyes.

'. . . but the more I got involved, the more superstitious I felt. I had to go on reading, in case I was overestimating it all. Then I saw this.'

Polly unfolded a sheet of lined paper. She was about to smooth it out on the table but the surface was too greasy and sticky. She held it awkwardly in midair, not quite handing it over.

'What is it?' Miranda asked in bewilderment.

'A letter. From Jake's great-uncle, in France. Christmas 1915.'

The shelves and cupboards of Jake's study held a jumbled cache of letters, diaries, account books, estate papers, bills and farm records that went back almost two hundred and fifty years, that was what Polly had discovered. They were mixed up, incomplete, some of them barely legible, others in a language almost forgotten. But none of that daunted her. She was a historian, and a trained researcher. As she had burrowed deeper into the records, her conviction grew that here was a story that had been waiting generations for her to arrive and unravel.

It was the story of an English house, not a great aristocratic

350

residence, not even a country manor house, but a small estate and a farm building that grew with a family's fortunes and changed with the changing times. She had found a bill of sale dated 1759 for a pair of plough horses, the record of a daughter's dowry at her marriage in 1820, love letters from Mr Edwin Meadowe to his sweetheart before he married her in the 1850s, bills from Victorian tradesmen in Meddlett, folded up and stuffed away, quite possibly never paid. Edited, annotated, properly arranged, Polly was certain that all this material could make a sensational book.

A sensational book meant money, of course, and the Davieses seriously needed funds.

But Polly was also aware that Mead was Miranda's house. The Meadowes were her family even if only by marriage, and she was the last to bear the name. Nothing more could be done with any of the records without Miranda's consent, and Polly knew just how jealously Miranda guarded her privacy and her husband's legacy.

Then two days ago she had uncovered the box of First World War letters, written from France by Second Lieutenant George Meadowe to his parents and elder brother at home.

Miranda looked bewildered. 'A letter? I don't know where I've put my glasses. Is it important?'

Polly faltered, 'Yes. Well, not this instant, of course . . .'

'Read it to me,' Miranda said quietly.

Polly pushed her own glasses up to the bridge of her nose.

My dear Governor, Muth and Eddy,

Well, we had our Xmas day, the best we could do, because it rained like Hades and the men and horses were sliding like poor amphibians through the mud. We had our company service at 11.30, the men somehow under shelter in a barn, the padre did it very nicely, and we sang 'While Shepherds Watched' and other favourites. Sergeant Gillings has a very fine bass, it was touching to hear such a man giving voice to the familiar words, but I have to

*confess that I felt more than a tremor of longing to be
with you all, listening to the Governor reading St Matthew
in church and afterwards Muth complimenting the Misses
Cooper on their new tippets before returning to the warm
fire at Mead. After service we had our Christmas dinner,
there was ham and plum pudding so we did very well, and
all the time the Boche less than a mile away and ourselves
within range of the damned field guns. They have been
quiet today, for which we thank God or the generals. Then
there was more singing, this time the men inclined not to
carols but less suitable songs, however it being Christmas I
did not feel it right to reprimand them. So now the day is
ended, I hope and pray that there has been some cheer for
you and that Muth especially has not felt my absence too
keenly. It will not be for ever, my dear beloved family, and
until then my love to you all,*

   Georgie

As Polly finished reading and refolded the sheet of paper,
Miranda looked towards the window, and the yard and the
outbuildings invisible beyond it.

'I've never seen that one,' she said.

'There's a box full of them.'

'Jake was always saying he would sort out the family papers.
I'm glad you're doing it, Poll, he would have been grateful. I
think that must have been George Meadowe's last Christmas.'

Polly nodded. In the same box she had found the pale buff-
coloured Post Office Telegraph message, dated six months later
and beginning with the terrible words, 'Deeply regret inform
you'.

Miranda added, 'I do know that George was the late, unexpected baby of the family, fifteen years younger than his only
brother, who was Jake's grandfather. Edward, Eddy, had what
was probably rheumatic fever as a child. He was always a semi-
invalid, and he couldn't have hoped to go to France. Naturally
their parents were deeply proud of their strong, heroic second

son. It was ironic, wasn't it, that it was Edward after all who lived on finally to marry and father a boy of his own?'

Polly nodded. The threads of all these stories woven around Mead tugged so insistently at her that she almost lost her balance. A historian's giddy omnipotence briefly possessed her and she speculated on how thrilling it would be if she could just find the evidence and follow it back further and further, digging deeper into the past until she arrived at the princess of the Iceni herself, not just her sad uncovered bones, but the real woman, long before the time of any Christian festival, dressed in her leather cloak and protected by her great shield, heading her tiny army out of the settlement under the sketched-out margins of Amos's house.

That would be a narrative trajectory.

When she came back to earth it was with a sense of fragility – Miranda's, her own and Selwyn's, and the rest of them who were temporarily anchored at Mead this Christmas – as against the absolutely steady continuum of life itself.

Polly had not concerned herself much with the taboo about mentioning age, or the threat of the ten-pound box. If she thought about it at all it was to reflect that Amos and Selwyn went on far too much about getting old, and it was men in their vanity and vulnerability who were more concerned with ageing than any woman could be.

But now it came to her. The magnificence of the continuum itself was the best corrective to fears of enfeeblement and death.

Miranda was still sitting opposite her. She was resting her chin on one hand, half-turned to stare into the square of blackness beyond the kitchen window.

Polly began, rotating the letter in her fingers as she spoke, 'I was going to ask you, how would it be if I were to catalogue the Mead papers properly, perhaps with a view to arranging them for publication?'

Miranda lifted her head from her hand. Polly could clearly see the inward reckoning she was making: Miranda was nobody's fool. Polly bit the inside of her lip as she waited, and then winced from the pain. She wanted *so much* to write this book. Nothing had stirred her so deeply since – well – perhaps since Ben was born.

'You want to write a book about Mead and Jake's family?'

'Yes.'

There was a silence.

'I'd have to think about it. Is that all right?' Miranda lightly said.

Her smile was open, and warm with their long friendship, but Polly knew suddenly and for certain that there were quicksands between them that no one had even ventured upon. Not yet.

All she could do was nod in acquiescence, shielding her passion as discreetly as she could manage.

'Of course. It's only the vaguest idea. I might not even be able to interest a publisher in the end,' she said.

Nic came in. She held her arms akimbo, palms of her hands pressed to her belly. She was flushed and tousled from sleep, half yawning and half smiling. She wasn't ordinarily a pretty girl, but with the glow of pregnancy and relaxation on her she looked beautiful.

'Can I make a cup of tea, Miranda? This baby is kicking so hard you can probably see it from over there.'

Polly stood up and went to her. When Nic guided her hand to it, she distinctly felt the pressure of a tiny heel against her fingers.

Here then was the continuum, made flesh beside her.

The race start line was on Meddlett green.

A trestle table had been set up and a sizeable crowd of runners milled in front of it, registering their names and collecting their race numbers from officials. The more serious ones performed stretches or ran up and down the road in mysterious spurts. Whole families turned up to compete. Friends and supporters muffled in scarves and hats crowded on either side of a tape stretched beneath a 'St Andrew's Church Tower Appeal' banner.

'This is all right,' Toby approved.

He, Sam and Alpha were in lycra running tights with reflector flashes down the sides, and they had brought safety pins to attach the numbers to their vests. All three of them were regular runners, although Alpha protested she wasn't fit at all and probably wouldn't even get around the course.

'Yeah, right,' Omie mocked, who knew her sister better than that.

Selwyn wore khaki shorts over a pair of Polly's leggings, and his all-purpose trainers were decorated with paint splatters.

He passed his number across his chest as though it might attach itself by suction.

'What am I supposed to do with this?'

The others each donated one of their pins, and Alpha patiently secured the number for him. Selwyn at once set off on a circuit of the duck pond, arms and legs pumping, sending the ducks scattering for shelter under the willows. Children stared at him. He drew a round of applause and catcalls from the teenagers wheeling on their bikes in front of the Griffin. The vicar and his wife passed through the crowd with trays of mince pies, wishing everyone good luck. There was an atmosphere of rising hilarity as more runners turned up, these later arrivals mostly plump, wearing comedy costumes or noticeably hung over. Compared with a huge man decked in a tulle ballet skirt, Selwyn began to look like a serious contender. Soon the joke entrants outnumbered the serious contestants, whose sinewy legs and self-absorbed warm-ups now suggested overkill.

Everyone from Mead had come to see off their runners except Joyce, who said she wasn't interested in a whole lot of people dashing about like schoolkids in the freezing cold, and Polly who offered to stay behind and keep her company. The box of half-read letters was calling to her, and she declared that Selwyn was absurd to insist on running five kilometres in the wake of three children in their twenties.

Colin got out his camera. Selwyn posed between Sam and Toby, with Alpha in front of her father. Selwyn circled her with his long arms and beamed over her shoulder. The bare willows and the pond made a pretty backdrop. Miranda stood watching them. Several people in the crowd said 'Hello, again' to her, with the unspoken rider that it was a surprise to see her in the village twice in as many days.

Nic stood out in her red coat. One of the lean figures in running kit dropped back from the keen contingent who were pressing up to the tape for an advantageous start position. Alpha, Toby and Sam were now amongst them.

'Hi again,' Kieran said to Nic.

'Hello.' Her face was pink, probably from the wind. 'You look pretty fit. Are you going to win?'

'I don't think so. But wish me luck anyway.'

'Three minutes,' the vicar boomed through a megaphone, looking as if he were presiding over a 1950s school sports day. There was a general stripping off of fleeces and gloves.

Standing beside Amos, Katherine was reminded of all the afternoons of the boys' school days when she had turned up to football matches and track events. There was even the same smell of fresh mud and open Thermoses. Amos had been a less regular supporter in terms of physical presence, although to do him justice he had always been proud of his sons' sporting achievements. She reached up to touch the necklace he had presented her with yesterday. It was weighty, massive with the implication of money spent, and it felt like a shackle. She had the urge to tear it off. He saw the gesture and she knew he read her thoughts, and was waiting with his lawyer's precision to see whether she would do it or not.

Suddenly, like equals rather than adversaries, they smiled at each other. Katherine lowered her hand.

Amos was brutal in his way, but sometimes his care for other people surprised her. On Christmas Eve he had fetched a blanket, wrapped the dog's broken body in it and placed it in the boot of the car. He had waited with the distraught girl until it became clear that the car and its driver had vanished into the fog, and then he had led her away and driven her home.

Amos would be all right. Toby and Sam would be all right too, she realized. She felt dizzy at the prospect of freedom.

'One minute,' the vicar called.

Two people stood at each end of the tape, waiting to lift it. The runners formed a broad column, singlets and lycra at the front, children and ballerinas and a single defiant Elvis at the back. There was a rowdy attempt from the crowd to count down the seconds. Toby had his forefinger to the button of his stopwatch.

'On your MARKS,' shouted the vicar. 'And . . . GO.'

The tape broke, there was a cheer, and the front runners streaked away. The rest of the field jostled over the start line and the ragged column poured towards a lane at the far end of the village. The finish line, via woodland tracks and bridle paths, lay in the grounds of Lockington Hall.

'Go, Kieran,' Nic shouted and clapped her hands as he passed. He looked back over his shoulder at her and almost tripped.

'Who was that?' Ben jealously frowned.

'Kieran,' Nic said.

Colin snapped the runners as they went by the post. Selwyn raced by, already at full stretch, his arms windmilling and his mouth open in a wild smile for the picture.

The spectators watched until the last runners turned the bend of the lane and headed for a belt of dense woodland blanketing the same low ridge that sheltered Mead. Then the groups started to break up, some heading for home, others regretting the fact that the Griffin was closed. With the rest of the Mead contingent following her, Miranda led the way to the short-cut that would take the walkers across to Lockington. Only Amos said he wouldn't come.

He turned aside to where he had parked the Jaguar, in the same spot near the church as on Christmas Eve. He drove back along the Mead road as far as the gate to Jessie's cottage, and then pulled in on to the verge.

No one answered his knocking, and, like Geza he moved to the window and peered inside. But unlike Geza, he went on to the back door of the cottage. On the way he pushed open the door of a tumbledown outhouse. The body of the dog still lay there, wrapped in the lap rug that – he now remembered – had last been used in the summer for a Glyndebourne picnic.

Amos didn't even knock at the back door. He put his shoulder against the flaking paintwork and shoved hard. The screws holding a small bolt on the inside immediately pulled loose, and the door scraped open.

'Jessie?' he shouted as he stepped inside. There was no response, but a hint of warmth in the clammy interior air indicated that she had recently been there.

He shouted louder. 'Jessie?'

He went through the kitchen into the living room, which was empty and looked just as it had done on the night he had slept on the sofa. The bathroom was also empty. He knocked on the closed bedroom door.

'Are you there? Come on, where are you?'

Fearful now, Amos turned the handle.

The curtains were drawn, but they were thin and let in the greyish light. There was someone lying in the bed, completely covered by the bedclothes. One step took him to the bedside. He stretched out his hand and touched the body. It was warm and breathing.

In a lower voice he said, 'Jessie, come on.' He peeled back a corner of the covers and saw her tangled hair and an expanse of bare neck. He put out his hand very gently and touched her shoulder. 'You can't lie here like this,' he said.

She rolled further away, out of his reach. 'Why not?' she asked in a voice that was hoarse with crying.

'I've come to help you bury the dog,' he said.

She was too cried-out even to sob.

Amos went into the kitchen, boiled the kettle and made two mugs of tea. There was milk in the fridge, but it was sour. He took the black tea into the bedroom, put the mugs on the stool beside the bed and sat down on the edge of the mattress.

'Go away,' she croaked.

'I'm not going to go away, so you might as well sit up and drink some of this tea while it's hot.'

It looked for a moment as if she wouldn't respond, but then she slowly uncoiled and pushed herself into a sitting position. Her eyes were so swollen she could hardly open them. Amos put the mug into her hand and left her to drink it. He rinsed out a flannel in the bathroom, brought it back to her with some cold water in a bowl. Then he said he would give her ten minutes to get dressed. He drank his own tea in the living room, revisiting the skunk episode and, with an extra twist of guilt, his memories of the tattoo.

After a while he heard Jessie moving about. Some more minutes passed and she appeared fully dressed in the doorway. She kept her face turned away.

'Do you want to bury him in the garden?' he asked.

'No. This place is nowhere.'

'What about at your mother's place?'

'God. No.'

'Where, then?'

'There's a walk he used to like. Over the ridge. By where you knocked me off the bike.'

'I didn't . . .' he began automatically, and then stopped. 'All right, we can go up there. I've brought a spade. Is there anyone else who should come with us? What about your ex-boyfriend?'

'What about him?' she snapped. That was better, Amos thought, with some relief. 'Bloody Damon's got enough to think about. Didn't you know?'

'Know what?' he asked.

She picked up her coat and pulled it on. 'I don't want anyone there, right? Can we just go and *do* this?'

'That's what I've come for,' he said, with restraint.

Jessie insisted that she would carry Rafferty's body herself. She laid the bundle of rug gently in the boot of the Jaguar once more. Amos drove to the spot and he took the spade while Jessie carried the dog. The path up through gaunt trees was steep and he was soon out of breath, but she trudged upwards under the heavy burden without slowing or looking back. At last she stopped in a small clearing. The slope of land gave a view to the south. Mead was beneath them and to the left, and the tower of Meddlett church and, in the distance, the grey outline of what Amos now knew to be Lockington Hall could both be seen.

The race would be over by now, for all but the slowest or most outlandishly-dressed runners.

'Here,' Jessie pointed. She lowered the bundle to the ground, and knelt beside it, her hand patting the stained plaid. 'Here we are, Raff.'

Amos turned aside from the sight. He began to dig. Mercifully, the earth was quite soft. Even so, after five or six minutes' work he was bathed in sweat. He could just hear the gnat's whine of model aircraft circling somewhere in the drained sky.

Even taking turns, a surprising amount of time and effort was required to dig a hole big enough, especially as deeper down the earth was a tangle of stubborn roots. At last, Jessie nodded. She threw aside the spade. Amos had assumed that she would bury the animal in the blanket, but she was having none of that. She turned back the covering to expose the dog's body. The fur was dull and matted and the side of its head clotted with blood. It looked very, very dead indeed. Jessie scooped it up and hugged it in her arms. Then she knelt and, finally, lay flat on her belly in order to place the animal as gently as possible at the bottom of the hole.

'Go away,' she ordered.

He stumbled fifty yards down the path and waited. The model aeroplane noise had stopped. Now all he could hear was the intermittent cawing of rooks.

Jessie came down the path. She was carrying the folded blanket and the spade. The single look she gave him indicated that he was not to say a word.

A gaggle of panting runners pounded along the track beside a ribbon of woodland. The going was rough here and their legs or ballet skirts were thick with mire. An open gate and a stencilled sign marked the 4-km point and a small band of supporters had gathered to clap and cheer encouragement as each runner passed through. Selwyn was dismayed to find himself back here with the fancy-dress contingent, whilst Alpha and the two boys were presumably celebrating on the right side of the finish line. At the gateway he sucked in a couple of gulps of air, and it was lucky for the well-meaning lady in the green padded coat who exhorted him to keep going because he was so nearly there, that he had no breath to spare for any words.

The track unrolled across a field and entered parkland. Selwyn saw but was too weary to speculate about three men busily making their way in the opposite direction, away from Lockington and into the thick belt of trees.

Seven and a half minutes later, he was summoning his very last reserves to manage a semi-sprint across the finish line on the lawns in front of the house. Miranda and the others clapped him home. Toby, Sam and Alpha were already zipped up in fleeces, their faces radiant with adrenaline and fresh air. Selwyn folded at the hips, his head hanging and hands resting on his knees.

'Enough,' he gasped.

The three men fanned out as soon as they reached the margin of trees. They began combing through the undergrowth.

'About here, I reckon?' one of them shouted.

'No, further to the left it'll be. I saw 'er come down.'

'More likely to be caught in the branches up there, that's what usually happens,' called the third.

They plodded up and down through dense thickets of brush and bramble, searching for the lost model plane.

'I can't go back and tell my Tina it's gone on my first bloomin' day out,' the youngest of the three said.

'We'll find 'er,' the others insisted.

It was the youngest who stopped beside the thickest sprawl of bramble. He prodded with a stick, which met sudden resistance. Forgetting for a moment the lost plane, he shouldered into the damp mass of prickles. Beneath the vicious spines there was a slab of crumbling concrete.

'Look at this.'

The others came to his side.

'Old wartime pillbox, isn't it?'

'I never knew this was 'ere, Ken, did you?'

On the far side, away from the edge of the wood, the leaves and branches appeared slightly trodden down. The pillbox entrance gaped darkness, lopsided from the partial collapse of the structure.

'Don't go inside, the whole bloody lot'll come down on your head. What'd we tell Tina then?'

Too late; the youngest was already inside. The other two, peering up into the branches in search of the model plane, heard him call out.

'Now what?' Ken sighed. 'Liam? What you got there?'

Liam came out backwards. He was dragging an Adidas sports holdall by the handles. It was clean and dry, not even dusty. They gathered around as he unzipped it. There was a moment's silence.

'Load of scrap,' Ken said.

There was a rough jumble of misshapen plates, cups blackened with age and earth, objects less easy to identify because they seemed fused together almost as if melted. Two or three green metal discs fell and clinked to the ground as Liam lifted out the topmost plate. A scrape at the rim of the plate with his thumbnail, and grey metal appeared.

He murmured, 'It's not scrap at all, mate. I know what this lot must be.'

They fell silent then, understanding what they had found, with the bag held between them and the ancient coins scattered over the wet earth.

FOURTEEN

'Not in the least,' Selwyn insisted when Polly asked if his legs were hurting. But when he got up from his chair he moved as if every step drilled his thigh bones deeper into his knee joints.

'Not at all. I could quite easily have run back again,' he elaborated.

The Davies and Knight children had adopted the barn as their preferred gathering place, and the five of them and Nic were polishing off a substantial lunch after the race. Polly saw Alpha's grimace of amused disbelief and flashed her a warning glance. Sam and Alpha had both put in good times in the Fun Run, and Toby had come in second overall and was proudly displaying the medal around his neck. Delighted with this performance the three of them were already making plans to enter a bigger race in the New Year. This coalition had the effect of driving Omie and Nic into an anti-hearty alliance, and to seal it the two of them were planning to spend the afternoon watching television and eating chocolates. Ben hovered as close to Nic as he could, although she gave him little encouragement.

Selwyn scowled. His genial paterfamilias performance had lasted only for Christmas Day itself. The sprawling children and their banter were irritating him and he made no attempt to pretend otherwise.

'I'm going to have a sleep,' he announced, shuffling towards the stairs.

Polly was startled. He had never taken an afternoon nap in his entire life, even in the throes of the worst hangover after the wildest party. She asked if he would like her to bring him some tea, but he replied that all he wanted was an hour's peace and quiet. What she most wanted was to leave the children downstairs and go up to lie beside him, but the time in their relationship when she could easily have suggested such a thing seemed to have slipped into history. She wondered bleakly how they would ever recover their old closeness.

The truth was that they knew each other too well to be intimate, that was one of the sad secrets the old kept from the young. Intimacy belonged to lovers and newcomers, lasting until the abrasion of time rubbed away the glamour of it. In the end it faded and disappeared altogether, and familiarity was all that was left.

Polly realized that Omie and Alph were both looking at her. She gave them a smile ripe with normality.

'Ben,' she called, 'I need some fresh air. Won't you come for a quick walk with me?'

Ben grumbled that she should have come on the morning's excursion across the fields to Lockington, if fresh air was what she wanted. As far as he was concerned two walks in one day would be major overkill.

Nic looked up. 'If Polly would like a walk you should go with her,' she told Ben.

'Don't you want me to stay with you?'

'No. I'll be fine here, thanks.'

It was clear even to Ben that there was no point in argument. He pulled on his knitted beehive and followed Polly out into the raw, smoky twilight of mid-afternoon. They took the path through the wood and on past Amos's site, where the deserted excavation with its torn remnants of polythene coverings and the contractor's trampled markings struck a note of absolute desolation. Once they were out on to the Meddlett road, however, the bracing air flooded into Polly's lungs and her spirits soared. As they turned up the hillside she stuck her arm through Ben's and hugged it against her side.

'I love you, Mum,' he murmured, as he often did.

'Do you remember when we had that picnic lunch in the park near your work?' she asked.

'Um, yeah.'

'And you told me I should write another book?'

'That's right, I do remember.'

'You're very clever, and I wanted to say thank you. I didn't think much about it at the time, but the suggestion must have been working away in the back of my mind. When Dad showed me a whole room full of records and letters belonging to Mead, and I started reading through them, the thought was already there inside me because you had planted it. I want to edit those papers, put them into a narrative and write a history of this place. It would make a wonderful book, Ben, a miniature of English rural history, if only I could do it justice.'

Even during the rush and work of Christmas Day, her thoughts had kept turning to her project and the speculation about whether Miranda would give her blessing. She had wanted to tell Ben where his suggestion was leading her, and this was the first opportunity.

'Course you'll do it justice,' he replied. 'Sounds brilliant.'

They were panting as the incline steepened. Polly stopped to catch her breath, looking back at the unfolding view.

'It's not quite that simple.'

'No?'

Polly knew her son could only properly handle one train of thought at a time, and now his attention was plainly elsewhere.

'It's up to Miranda. The papers belong to her.'

'She'll be all right with it.'

'How do you know?'

Ben was gazing with melancholy longing in the direction of Mead, and Nic.

'She wants to keep you sweet, doesn't she?'

A gust of wind rattled in the trees and Polly shivered.

'What do you mean?'

Ben might be unworldly, but he could sometimes be intuitive in a way that his more down-to-earth sisters were not. Had Ben noticed a connection between Miranda and Selwyn, as a result of which she herself had to be propitiated? She felt cold with foreboding.

'Uh, I guess with her wanting you and Dad, you know, to go on living up here and keeping her company and all that.'

Polly breathed again. Ben only meant that Miranda wanted to defend the Mead community. She drew his arm closer and they walked on uphill.

'I hope so,' she smiled. 'I'm so in love with the idea of my book.'

Ben was absorbed in his own thoughts.

'Is it Nic?' Polly asked gently.

He gave a gusty sigh.

'She's being totally impossible.'

Polly put her own concerns aside. 'Let's talk about it.'

Ben needed no encouragement. Why wouldn't Nic recognize how much he cared about her, how much he wanted their baby now he had got used to the idea, how good they would be together if only she would let him back in? He waved his arms in the air to emphasize his questions, walking backwards so he could look Polly in the eye at the same time.

She said, 'Darling, don't keep insisting to her what you want and what you'll do. You can only show her what you mean over time, by being it and doing it.'

He gave her his sweetest, most unfocused smile.

'How weird. That's exactly what Nic says herself.'

Polly sighed. 'So are you going to try it?'

At the top of the hill where there was a view over to Meddlett they passed within a few feet of a patch of freshly dug earth, but neither of them noticed it.

'Mum, you don't understand. I *love* her.'

Polly's patience was wearing thin. She wanted to shout at him, what do you know about love? What do you know about time, and the protracted measures of loving another human being – not just the impatience of desire, but the pathos of its absence?

She answered these questions for herself. Ben knew nothing yet because he was barely out of childhood and such knowledge came only when you got old, when love was mostly past so you could see it for the obstinate business it really was.

'Wait and see what happens. Help her in whatever way you can.'

Ben ran a few steps down the hill, swung around and punched his fists in the air.

'I'm going to write, get my column, make some cash, prove to her that I can buy what she needs. Her *and* the baby,' he added, remembering.

That wasn't the sort of help that had been uppermost in Polly's mind, but she agreed that it would be a good start.

Miranda had invited them all for six-thirty on Boxing Night. Amos and Katherine were the last to head for Miranda's house, bringing Jessie with them.

Amos had been out most of the afternoon, and whilst the boys were over at the barn, Katherine took the opportunity to pack some of her clothes. She folded blouses and skirts and put them into a suitcase, not bothering to deliberate over the selection. It was more a symbolic gesture of withdrawal than needing extra clothes to wear in London. Her phone beeped a text alert but she left it for a few minutes, expecting the message to be an update on his whereabouts from Amos. At the start of the race this morning he told her that he was going to help the young girl whose dog had been so horribly run over on Christmas Eve, and Katherine wondered whether Jessie was going to be the next object of his attentions. She was good-looking enough. Then she had remembered that it didn't matter to her whether the girl was or was not Amos's current target.

When she did look at the text, she saw that it was from Chris. She searched on the dressing table for her glasses. Catching sight of herself in the mirror, she noticed the reflection of her fond smile.

Am I a fool? she wondered.

Miracle! Police found yr treasure. On way to check it out. Big secret 4 now.

Katherine's smile broadened. But it's not my treasure, she thought, or Amos's.

Happy for you & archaeology. Already have all trsure I need tho' x K

When Amos did call, it was to ask whether he should bring Jessie back with him. He had helped her to bury the dog, she was all on her own in a bleak cottage, and it was Christmas.

'Of course you must bring her back. But you'll have to ask Mirry, won't you?'

'Mirry will say, the more the merrier.'

When Jessie arrived, her muddy boot prints tracking Amos into the cottage, Katherine led her into the kitchen and Jessie sat down, looking at her with frank curiosity. Amos had told her that his wife had left home, so it was obviously intriguing to find the same wife ensconced here. Katherine gave her tea and Christmas cake.

'I am so sorry about your dog.'

The girl looked straight back at her. Whatever Amos's intentions might be, it was evident on Jessie's part that she wasn't going to be one of his acquisitions.

'Thanks,' Jessie said. Her expression indicated that the quaint marital arrangements of old people were a legitimate focus for speculation, but her own losses were private.

Katherine was amused. She could see why Amos was interested. She chatted to the girl about Meddlett and her job at the Griffin, and Jessie made a noticeable effort to respond with questions of her own, recognizing that a polite conversational code was being observed.

'Do you like it in Meddlett? I mean, it must be a real pain, not being able to get your house built, with the princess being dug up and all that?'

Amos had opted for whisky rather than tea. He broke in now.

'Katherine's ambivalent. She likes Meddlett all right, but she's decided she doesn't want to have the new house built, or to live in this one with me. So it's a bit of a conundrum.'

'Yeah?' was all Jessie said. She gave Amos the briefest glance and it was Katherine's impression that her husband subsided.

She continued to Katherine, 'What kind of dinner is this going to be? It's very kind of you to ask me, don't get me wrong, but I'm not sure what I'm doing here, really.' Then she grinned. 'Curiosity, I expect you're thinking.'

Katherine smiled back at her. Self-reliant Jessie made a sort of counterpoint to Nic, not that Nic wasn't strong in her own way, and the Davies girls were like the other two corners of a square. It was going to be an interesting evening.

'You're very welcome. Ours might seem an odd set-up, but people, families, make allowances at Christmas, don't they?'

Jessie raised her eyebrows a fraction, suggesting that her own standards were more exacting.

'There'll be nobody you won't recognize. We were all in the Griffin on Christmas Eve. There's my two sons . . .'

'*Our* two sons,' Amos corrected.

'. . . Polly and Selwyn's three children with Ben's ex-girlfriend Nicola, who is pregnant, and of course Miranda, and Colin, and Miranda's mother.'

'Quite a big party. Will I be OK like this?' Jessie hitched a couple of layers of clothing over her shoulders.

Katherine considered. In fact Jessie looked rather as if she'd dug the dog's grave without a spade. 'You are welcome to have a bath, if you'd like to,' she said tactfully.

Jessie put back her head and laughed heartily. Amos gave Katherine a surprised, admiring look.

* * *

'Barbara.'

Selwyn's voice was urgent and Miranda thought he must have been lying in ambush, poised like a statue amongst the coats in the passage. This comical image started up a snort of laughter, but his hand covered her mouth. His other arm circled her waist and dragged her into the folds of gardening clothes. In the darkness a row of Wellington boots toppled over like dominoes. It was in this corridor, in exactly this spot, that he had kissed her on the night they all arrived at Mead. Miranda wriggled and tried to break free. The house was full of lights and music and people, just as she wished it to be. Someone might come crashing through here at any minute.

She twisted her head, murmuring, 'Let me go.'

'Kiss me.'

'Sel, stop it.' But she did kiss him. Her hands cupped his face, drawing him closer even as she struggled to get away from him – one kiss representing all the contradictions of their love affair. She felt the fast pulse that beat beneath his jawbone.

'Barb, I want you to know. Tomorrow I'm going to tell Polly that I'm leaving her. I'm going to do it while the children are all here, no misunderstandings, no contradictions.'

She stepped back. A coat fell off a peg and flopped over her feet.

'Don't do that.'

Her voice was sharp and much too loud.

'Shhh. You won't make me change my mind. I can't live like this, with you and without you.'

'Don't be so selfish.'

'Call it whatever you like.' She could see the breadth of his smile, reckless, certain.

'If you leave her you are on your own. Don't think you can count on me.'

It was his turn to laugh.

'But I have always counted on you, Barbara Huggett.'

* * *

370

Nic washed and set Joyce's hair. She teased out the thin white curls, covering up the naked pink scalp as best she could.

'Where's my daughter?' Joyce wanted to know.

Nic explained again that Miranda was downstairs with Colin finishing off the last preparations for the party. Conversations with Joyce could be quite soothing if you ruled out the expectation that they might lead anywhere or cover any new ground.

'What's your name, again? I keep forgetting it.'

'Nic. Short for Nicola.'

'I'd have guessed that bit. No more frizzing out, please. You'll have me looking like a golliwog.'

'I'll do your make-up, then. There's this nice coral lipstick. It'll suit you.'

When they were both ready they surveyed themselves in the wardrobe mirror. Nic turned sideways and examined her distended silhouette.

'Look at me. I'm so fat. I used to look, you know, quite all right, and now I'm gross.'

Joyce shifted her upper set of teeth with the side of her tongue in the probing gesture she always made when she was about to deliver a rebuke.

'I never heard such rubbish. I only wish I was your age, back before Barbara was born. If I had my time again, I can tell you. You don't know what you've got until it's gone, my girl.'

'Can you remember it? Being young, I mean. I don't mean to be rude,' she added hastily, not wanting to suggest that it was a long time ago or that Joyce was in any way forgetful.

Joyce's face unexpectedly softened and brightened. 'Oh yes, I do remember,' she insisted. 'We had some lovely times. I was a machinist, we used to make all our own clothes. Full skirts, yards of material if you could get hold of it, proper corsetry underneath, not like women nowadays who seem always to be sagging in trousers and no support at all. We'd go dancing on a Saturday night, and you'd be as happy as a queen if you got a man who was a good dancer.'

'That sounds wonderful.'

371

Nic tucked Joyce's arm under hers and they descended the stairs. The old oak boards creaked underfoot, and the Christmas tree shimmered in the dimness. There was restrained jazz playing in the drawing room, obviously chosen by Colin. A sharp blast of cold air indicated that the back door was standing open, then Miranda hurried out from the recess behind the stairs just as Omie appeared from the other direction. Omie was wearing very high strappy heels and a tiny skirt.

'Look at you,' Miranda called.

'She'll catch her death,' Joyce observed.

They gathered in the drawing room. Everyone was dressed up, Polly noted. She had ironed a shirt for Selwyn, and pulled her own best blue dress out of the storage box where it had languished for months. Selwyn had headed across from the barn before she was ready, muttering about helping Colin with the drink, but he was nowhere to be seen when she arrived in the twins' wake. There was plenty of laughter rising above the music, and more congratulations for the runners, but she also sensed a prickle of unease in the air. Miranda herself spun at the centre of the room, laughing and welcoming them all as though she could hold them to her ideal of Mead by the force of willpower alone.

But the wilting fir boughs were a reminder that the Christmas interlude was almost over. Tomorrow people would start spinning off on their separate trajectories. Except for Joyce, they were all talking faster and louder, as if they knew they were being swept along on a tumbling current. Polly became increasingly aware of pressure, a sensation as difficult to ignore as an imbalance in the inner ear, except that she couldn't swallow or yawn it away. She took a glass of champagne and drank it quickly, telling herself to lighten up. It was the year's end, that was all, a time that demanded both summings up and looking ahead.

Apart from Selwyn, Amos and Katherine were the last to appear, shepherding Jessie with them. The girl's eyes travelled over the room, taking in the folds of velvet and heavy gilded picture frames. She was welcomed by everyone, particularly warmly by Sam and Toby. She had taken off one or two of the outer layers

372

of garments, and the upper tendrils of her tattoo were enticingly visible. Colin gave her a quick nod of welcome and reassurance.

'Hi, I'm Ben,' Ben called, bounding up to her like a huge dog looking for a pat on the head.

'Hi.' Jessie's lips didn't move.

Omie and Alph moved to her side. Polly was pleased to see their natural friendliness. They were brimming with sympathy for Jessie.

'Are you all right? We didn't know what to do. It was so awful, you poor thing.'

'That driver ought to go to prison. Will you be able to find out who it was?'

Colin was threading between the groups, a bottle of champagne in hand. Polly slid past Jessie and the twins to reach Miranda's side. Miranda's cheeks were flushed and her eyes were very bright.

'You look lovely, Poll.'

'So do you.'

They were both watching the door as Selwyn came in.

Omie was still talking to Jessie, but she caught her father's hand as he passed.

'Hey, my dad,' she said fondly, and kissed his cheek.

'It's Raff's company I miss,' Jessie was saying. 'Dogs are mostly nicer than people, aren't they?'

Joyce had been standing near the fire, supporting some of her weight on the back of an armchair. Now she made an unsteady turn and looked straight at Selwyn.

'Here you are. Where have you been all this time?'

Polly saw how his gaze slid straight to Miranda. She was sure that he tried not to, but he simply couldn't stop himself. That's where he had been, with Miranda. She had to swallow hard and keep the smile pinned to her face.

Joyce didn't wait for an answer.

'Barbara, here's your husband at last,' she called.

Miranda said in a bright voice quite unlike her usual one, 'He's not my husband, Mum. Jake's dead. Selwyn is married to Polly, you know that.'

Joyce completed her rotation. Her best shoes were firmly planted on the scarred rug, her backdrop was now the cheery log fire and fir branches. Her face clouded and she frowned.

'But I saw you. What were you doing?'

The various conversations faltered one by one. Joyce's words dropped like a pebble into a pond of silence. Polly sensed that Alph and Omie were gazing towards her, their bright faces shadowed with dismay.

Miranda's lips moved but she didn't produce any words. Logs crackling and the mellow trickles of jazz were the only sounds. Polly took three steps to reach Selwyn's side. Her legs were shaking and it seemed a long way to travel.

'Joyce is confused,' Polly murmured to him. 'Tell her again who's who.'

Selwyn said too loudly, too jovially, 'Joyce, I'm not *Jake*, am I? I'm just Barb's old friend. And you know Polly, we've been together for twenty-something years.'

Joyce took exception to his words. Maybe Selwyn spoke too slowly, as if to a child. Maybe she clutched at the certainties she did have, suspecting how fugitive they were. Her mouth narrowed to a thin line and a spark of cunning defiance glinted in her eyes. She was enjoying the attention of the whole room.

'That's not what I *saw*,' she almost shouted.

Polly knew with absolute certainty that whatever it was that Joyce had seen, she must under no circumstances be allowed to describe it. But she was frozen to the spot. Speech, movement, any attempt at damage containment – all were beyond her.

But mercifully, as if they had been choreographed, Miranda and Colin and Katherine flowed into action. Miranda went to her mother and took her hand, murmuring reassurance and drawing her to a chair. Katherine picked up a dish of canapés and offered them around the group. Colin took a place beside Polly as Selwyn abruptly peeled away.

'Is it me, or is it hot in here?' Polly asked him. The lower half of her face was still smiling but it felt stiff, like a mask.

'It's hot,' he said.

Omie and Alph set up a counter-diversion, demanding that the music be changed for something decent. Ben said he would put on the compilation mix that he had made for Nic's Christmas present. Nic and Jessie were left to exchange the baffled glance of outsiders to a group who knew something awkward had just happened but couldn't define what it was.

Selwyn was left isolated by all this activity. He shook his head, perhaps to clear it. Then he gathered himself up, standing upright as if he had come to a decision. He walked to the middle of the room, looking for a place where everyone would see and hear him.

Polly followed him with her eyes, inwardly crying *No*.

Amos came to the rescue now. He planted himself in front of Selwyn, cutting him off from the rest of the gathering and murmuring something in his ear.

Ben's choice of music, Jay-Z, blared out of the speakers.

'Ben, that's bloody awful,' yelled Toby.

Joyce began telling Nic and whoever else would listen that music had been music in her day, nothing like this racket. Miranda and Polly were only five feet apart.

Selwyn and Amos might have been squaring up to each other, just like in the old days, but Selwyn's shoulders sagged and he turned aside.

He looked suddenly tired and old.

Alph and Omie gamely drew Katherine's attention to the bangle they had given Polly for Christmas, and Miranda leaned over to admire it too. Shock and rising anxiety competed in the pit of Polly's stomach, making her wonder if she might be sick. She stretched out her arm, the slippery blue sleeve falling back from her elbow.

'Isn't it pretty?' she managed to say.

Katherine fingered her gold necklace from Amos. The women talked about jewellery until Colin announced that dinner was ready.

Gratefully they surged across the hall to the dining room. It was lit only by candles, and the gentle glow hid the worn patches in the rugs and tattered slits in the curtains. Reflections of the points of flame were multiplied by the age-spotted mirrors, the polished table and sideboard gleamed with silver, each place setting had its platoon of glasses and triple rank of cutlery. Colin and Miranda had spent a happy afternoon opening cupboards and bringing out what passed for finery at Mead. None of it was precious, but it had the harmony of belonging to this place.

Catching sight of Jessie's face, Amos winked at her.

She muttered out of the corner of her mouth as she passed by him, 'Oi feel a proper yokel, oi du.'

Sam Knight drew out her chair for her, indicating the place cards. Instead of names Colin had drawn passable cartoons of everyone, but he had hurriedly done Jessie's from memory as Miranda was laying the extra setting. It was flattering and inaccurate, making her look both sweet and simple.

'Is this actually what I'm like?' Jessie muttered to Colin. She had already downed three glasses of champagne.

'Not really,' he grinned.

Polly found her seat. Colin's cartoon made her appear benign, like a beaming earth mother. She still felt slightly sick and the nape of her neck prickled with sweat. She made herself breathe evenly as she looked down the avenue of faces.

Miranda was at the head of the table, Colin at the other end.

This was the Christmas celebration Miranda had planned, the emblem of the Mead renewal, with old friends and families and welcome guests gathered together under one roof. Polly knew Miranda wasn't going to let it all fly apart, tonight or in the future.

But Joyce's words still hammered in her head. *But I saw you.* What had she seen?

Selwyn was placed towards Colin's end of the table. He pointed a cracker at Jessie and she grabbed it and pulled. The contents scattered over the cloth. Miranda picked up her fork and tapped it against her glass. Thirteen pairs of eyes immediately turned to her. Polly had to admire her sheer determination to make a success of the party. And then she thought, but I can pursue what *I* want just as energetically. I want to stay with Selwyn, I want to research the book.

I want Miranda's vision for Mead, therefore, almost as much as she does.

Miranda was saying, 'I'm so pleased and happy that we're all here tonight. I want to make the first toast, too. I think we should drink to . . .'

She paused, theatrically.

'. . . Jessie. Because if she hadn't been brave enough to join us, I've just realized we would have been thirteen at table tonight.'

She smiled through the candlelight and raised her glass, and everyone else followed suit.

Jessie actually blushed.

'Cheers,' she mumbled.

It was a good dinner. Selwyn collected himself, summoning up a great burst of energy and manic humour. To all of them who had known him in the old days, not just Polly, the original Selwyn magically reappeared at the table. As he always had done, he dominated their circle and there were hoots of laughter as he retold and embroidered familiar stories.

He pointed another cracker like a magic wand, conjuring up their shared memories.

'Remember, Col?'

Colin's thin face was bright with amusement. 'Remember what? If I could, I probably wasn't there.'

'The bridge?'

Long ago when they were students, Miranda and Polly, Selwyn and Colin and Amos had all got drunk and stoned. That wasn't remarkable, but on this particular night they had jumped one by one off a high bridge into the river. In spite of his denial, even at this distance Colin could indeed remember the sensation of being in the air, not falling but flying. The shouts and splashes all around him belonged to another dimension, unrelated to his flawless trajectory. He had felt utterly calm and perfectly certain of himself, and it was so unlike his normal state of mind that he had never forgotten it. Then he had hit the water and, a millisecond later, the river bed.

'Exactly how drunk were you, Dad?' Ben wondered.

'Epically,' Selwyn said.

'Really, Dad? You must have been, like, totally *wiiild* when you were young.'

Selwyn majestically turned to his son. 'My dear boy, just be aware, everything you think you know best, we discovered in the first place.'

Alpha tilted her lovely face to her father, taking up the tease. 'Go on, tell us again about Grosvenor Square.'

Sam was enjoying this too. He leaned forwards to Amos. 'And Ho, Ho, Ho Chi Minh, eh Dad?' Sam and Toby were both known to be politically right wing in their views. Amos held up his hand.

'You may mock. This is your allotted role. But Selwyn is right.'

Alph and Omie and Toby waggled V-signs in the air. 'Peeeeace, man,' they drawled. Jessie sniggered and Amos raised an eyebrow at her.

Selwyn rested his elbow on the table and massaged the purple-red rocket scar at the side of his head.

In the last hour he had grown back into himself. Now he seemed larger and more animated than any of the rest of them, as if there were volumes more blood running in his veins, and richer air inflating his lungs. For forty years, through his own reversals, even through the quite long intervals when the couples had grown apart, each of them would have acknowledged that he had been and always would be the leader of their small group. Now he commanded the attention of his old friends, their children and the guests. Looking on, Polly felt her heart swell with love for him and pride at his importance to all of them.

Now he rose up and demanded, 'Listen. What do you think you know, you kids? Sex? Began in 1963. Music? What do I need to tell you? You're still listening to it. Recreational drugs? Our invention. Political activism? Our generation's trademark.

Social anarchy? Check. Art? Culture? Fashion? Look what we started. And *admire*.'

The room was ecstatically divided now. Polly applauded, pounding her hands together as Miranda and Katherine joined in.

'Blame it on the Boomers,' jeered the young ones.

Joyce cupped a hand behind her ear. 'What? What are they all saying?'

Selwyn roared, 'What have you given us, you X-ers? The bloody internet. *YouTube*.'

A tinny jangle of music sounded. It was surprisingly insistent and it went on and on. Selwyn looked around to see what was interrupting his moment.

Jessie jumped, almost knocking over her glass.

'Sorry, God, sorry. My phone.'

Sam steadied the glass with one hand, with the other he reached for her bag and handed it over.

'Nice ringtone,' he grinned.

Jessie stabbed at the buttons. She turned aside in her chair and hissed into the phone, 'What do you *want*?'

She listened and then replied, 'Yeah, well, where do you think I am?'

The noisy talk at the table rippled on. Jessie listened more intently, pressing her finger to one ear. After a few more muttered remarks she snapped the phone shut and tossed it into her bag. She sat upright, squaring her shoulders against the high carved back of her chair.

'This is interesting,' she announced. 'Guess what?'

She was brimming with news, happily half-drunk, delighted to be the one who could pass on a juicy piece of information.

'What?' Selwyn rejoined.

'They've got the treasure back.'

Miranda gasped. She clapped her hands agian, this time in sheer delight.

'Our treasure? The *Mead* treasure?'

Amos looked first at Katherine, to see her reaction. It was several seconds before he turned to Jessie.

'Them?' he queried softly.

'Yeah. The police. The fabulous stolen treasure of Mead was found this morning by three of those model plane guys, hidden in a ruined pillbox in Lockington woods. I know the place, we used to have a den in there when we were little, but no one ever goes near it now. Kids nowadays have got better stuff to do than make dens, I reckon.'

'And that was the police on the phone, was it, to notify you personally?'

Jessie cocked her head at him.

'Nope. It was Damon. He'd, um, already heard on the grapevine that the cops were on the track of it. Blokes who nicked the stuff must have got nervous and stashed it up there for a bit.'

'Your ex-boyfriend is remarkably well-informed,' Amos remarked.

Miranda called out, 'Is he sure? Are they sure? It's wonderful, if they're right.'

Jessie's delight was fading. It occurred to her that perhaps she shouldn't give too much away.

'Damon heard the gossip. You know what Meddlett's like. The news is all over the Griffin tonight, you can imagine how they're all gabbing away. Glad it's my night off. Apparently they've got the archaeologists in now, checking the authenticity. Probably the police'll tell you in the morning.'

Amos was expressionless. 'I'll hope for that,' he said.

Jessie was aware that her story had somehow misfired. Whatever Kieran might choose to believe, the actual truth was that she didn't know whether Damon had found out any more than she had originally mentioned to him, back when she was quite missing him after they had split, or whether he had then been involved with the theft.

She had her suspicions, though.

Red in the face, she blurted out, 'Uh, maybe Damon has got it all wrong anyway. He's had a few drinks, by the sound of it.'

'I hope it is true,' Omie sighed. 'I love to think of all the treasure being safe in one place again, not taken off and sold all over the world to rich people.'

A general move away from the table began as people carried plates through to the kitchen. Selwyn was put out that the centre of attention had shifted elsewhere, Polly went to him and laid her cheek against his head, where the red scar puckered his skin.

'I love you,' she murmured.

Selwyn didn't answer, but she thought he nodded.

Katherine took a tray of glasses and tried to duck away, but Amos caught up with her. He took the tray and roughly deposited it on the oak sideboard in the hall. The lights of the Christmas tree twinkled behind them.

'You knew, didn't you?'

Katherine stared at the stone floor, the curled edges of a rug, the scatter of fallen tree needles at her feet.

She had forgotten to look surprised at Jessie's news, and Amos was far too sharp, too forensic, not to have noticed. However much whisky he put away he saw what he chose to notice, and his choice – after so long, ironically since she didn't welcome it – now fell on her. She could almost hear the ticking of his formidable mind as he scrutinized her.

'*How* did you know?' he persisted.

When she didn't answer, he nodded slowly.

'Ah, I see. Of course. Well, I suppose I'm hardly in a position to complain. Your choice of a lover is unusual, if it is who I think it is, but that's your business. The difference between us is that I never went as far as to deny our marriage, or to back out of it because of any of my liaisons. I always honoured you as my wife.'

Katherine raised her eyes. 'Do you call that *honour*?'

He took in a breath.

Mutual pain now separated them as precisely as any of their differences.

This hurts so much, Katherine thought. She felt blinded, hobbled by it.

'Mum?' Toby called.

Her son – no, both her sons – were hovering at the foot of

381

the stairs. They stared at their parents and the shining tree, a distortion of the happy family Christmas tableau.

She sidestepped her husband and crossed to the boys. She put an arm around each waist.

'I'm so sorry,' she whispered. Then she went quickly on into the kitchen.

From somewhere Miranda's voice called, 'Charades?'

Polly was scraping plates into the compost bin. Her face shone with sweat and when she glanced down she saw a dark grease stain on the sloping shelf of her blue silk bodice.

Seeing Katherine's face she asked, 'Are you all right?'

'I'm not sure.'

They regarded each other, battered but not extinguished. Ben was now calling for charades too, his voice echoing through the house.

'What about you?' Katherine asked. Joyce's words were still in her head, so she could imagine how clearly they must sound for Polly.

Polly rotated the bangle on her wrist, forwards and backwards.

'I'll carry on,' she said at last. Feet were running up and down the stairs, a pair of stilettos clicked in the hall and a door slammed. Music briefly blared. 'Let's go and play charades. It's as good a metaphor as any, don't you think?'

Briefly, they clasped hands.

Jessie hovered near the back of the drawing room. The big sofa with folding arms and fat tassels had been pushed back and a tatty old rug or two rolled away to leave a space of bare floorboards. She had never played charades in her life, and had only the most approximate idea of what the game involved. It was the kind of thing you puzzled over in old-fashioned novels, or maybe read in articles in dentists' waiting-room magazines about the Royal Family at Sandringham. In fact apart from Pass the Parcel at one or two birthdays she had been to when she was seven, the only indoor game she could remember participating

382

in was Spin the Bottle, and having to kiss Kenny Carson as a result of it. Yet all these people knew exactly what they were doing, as if they had spent half their lives playing party games. Jessie wondered if by noticing this divide she had stumbled on a really quick and effective way of determining whether or not you were posh.

Names were written on slips of paper and then pulled out of Ben's woolly hat to make two teams. The one Jessie was on withdrew across the draughty hall to the dining room. There were puddles of wax on the table, nutshells and satsuma peel scattered everywhere. Sam Knight put a piece of paper and a pencil in her hand and told her to write down a film or a book or a song title, or a quotation if she felt like it.

Her mind went blank. She screwed up her concentration to the point of pain and wrote *One Flew Over the Cuckoo's Nest*. Apparently that was good enough, because a minute later they were back in front of the fire. Selwyn and Miranda and the rest of the other team were waiting, drawn up in front of the fender like a row of migrating birds.

The hat was held out once more. Selwyn rolled up his sleeve and rotated his wrist over the opening.

'I'm going first,' he announced. With a magician's flourish he extracted a piece of paper and unfolded it. Toby clicked one of six buttons on his all-purpose heavy-duty mountaineer's and deep-sea-diver's watch.

'Go!'

At once Selwyn's arms and hands flew around. He held up fingers and mugged at his team. At once everyone started yelling.

'Film. Six words. Second word. One syllable.'

Jessie stared. What on earth was all this?

Selwyn drew himself up. Balancing on the balls of his feet on the fender bar he filled his lungs with air. His chest visibly expanded. His face was flushed and his hair stood up in a stiff crest. Then he extended his arms, lifting and stretching them away from his shoulders. His fingers drooped like wing feathers as his elbows rose and fell in a slow arc. He closed his eyes, transformed from a starling into an elegant raptor.

'Bird?'

'Crow?'

Selwyn's eyes snapped open. He glared as he launched himself off the fender, gliding and swooping. Miranda and Ben and the twins shouted bird names.

Amos barked, 'Flight?'

Selwyn whirled around. He stabbed a finger at Amos and beckoned.

Miranda and Polly knelt side by side on the floor, shouting words. They were both absorbed in the game.

Selwyn jabbed his thumb over his shoulder, silently exhorting them. His eyes suddenly widened, staring at nothing, the whites showing.

'Are you hitchhiking?' Joyce shouted.

'Mum, you're on the other team,' Miranda called.

Selwyn's shoulders jerked.

He had been poised, like a puppet held by invisible strings. Now his head tipped back, his jaw hanging open. His knees buckled beneath him. They watched, their shouts and laughter frozen in their mouths. Selwyn dropped like a ruined tree. His head smashed against the corner of the fender.

Omega's voice rose in a thin scream.

There was a rush of people, scrambling from their seats. Selwyn lay without moving, his face turning a dark, contused crimson.

'Is he still acting?' Joyce wanted to know.

Polly knelt beside his body. She laid her head to his chest, her mouth shaped to a cry but no sound coming out of it. They were trying to loosen his clothes. She heard confused voices crying out for air, water, a telephone.

This has been the longest night I have ever lived through.

I can see Selwyn lying on the floor. I am staring down at the fingers of his left hand as they uncurl, slowly and tenderly, as if he is letting go of something deeply precious.

I know for certain that he is already dead.

Yet for what seemed like an hour, Toby and Sam and Colin took it in turns to kneel at Selwyn's side, blowing air into his stopped lungs and compressing his chest with cruel thumps of their hands. Counting the breaths, willing a tremor into him, watching for a flicker in his darkened face.

Polly knelt there too, with her head bowed and Selwyn's hand folded between hers. She was whispering encouragement and endearments to him. Their children looked on, drawn into a huddle, silent and white-faced.

The paramedics came running into the room with their cases of implements and coiled wires. They worked on him, but even as I prayed I knew with the detached, dry kernel of myself that they wouldn't get him back.

Selwyn was carried out of my house on a stretcher. Polly went with him in the ambulance and Colin drove the three children after it. The rest of us sat anyhow. The kettle was put on and tea was made, then left undrunk. Eventually Joyce fell asleep amongst the cushions on the drawing-room sofa. I tucked a rug over her shoulders and folded it beneath her feet. Amos and Katherine waited, not speaking to each other. Their boys murmured in a corner of the kitchen. Jessie and Nic sat together, awkwardly holding hands.

The telephone rang at last, splitting the silence, and I snatched it up.

'Col?' I said.

He told me that Selwyn was dead on arrival. The time of death had been given at approximately ten-thirty p.m., when we were playing charades in front of the fire as if we had all our lives ahead of us.

The doctors had told them that the heart attack was so huge he would probably have known nothing about it.

I heard myself whisper, 'I see. Yes, I see.'

I remember thinking, this means Sel won't be able to get the barn properly finished. He'll be angry about that.

Colin said he would be bringing Polly and the three children back home to Mead. He wanted me to be there when they arrived, but he thought it might be best if everyone else withdrew.

I put down the phone. There was no need to say anything. Katherine came and we held each other for a moment.

I was grateful to Amos for taking charge. He told Sam and Toby that they should go back to the cottage. If there was anything they could do, he forestalled them, he would come and collect them. He said that he would drive Jessie home. She picked up her coat and they went off into the night. I filled a row of hot-water bottles, then wondered futilely if I should make some sand-wiches. The kitchen was messy with the debris of dinner. Did I have enough food in the house for the next days?

Nic slid away to bed, her face blotted with tears. Katherine and I woke up my mother and between us we helped her upstairs. I broke the news as she sat on her bed.

'Who'd have thought I'd outlive him?' she kept saying. Her hands on our arms were knotty and dry as dead leaves.

When Joyce was asleep Katherine and I waited together. We washed glasses, rinsed and dried them and put them away, moving around each other, hardly exchanging a word. Shock silenced us.

At last we saw the lights of Colin's car sweep over the field grass beyond the yard gate. I went out into the dark and held open the gate. They came slowly, in bewilderment, letting Colin and me lead them into the barn. After the long weeks of chill in there I was struck by the warmth lingering in the big room. Colin found the switches and lights blazed. Selwyn's jumper lay discarded on a chair. Polly picked it up and held it to her face.

The two girls clung together. They were deadly pale, their eyes ringed with smudged mascara and puffy with tears. Ben made them sit down and brought them a small glass of brandy apiece. His shapeless face had taken on firm, sombre contours.

'Drink this up,' he ordered, and they did as they were told. Omie's teeth clinked against the rim of the glass and she coughed helplessly. Ben stroked her shoulder until she caught her breath.

Polly was sitting at the table, her hands spread flat in front of her. I covered her left one with mine and our rings grated.

'Would you rather Katherine be here with you?' I whispered.
She shook her head. 'Stay with me. Stay with us.'
Colin nodded at me over her head.

Polly and I sat there for hours and hours. Colin went quietly away, and it was Ben who saw his exhausted sisters to bed. He came back again to check on his mother and me, then rolled himself in a blanket and stretched out on cushions laid in front of the fireplace.

'Remember Katherine and Amos's wedding?' Polly whispered to me.

'I remember.'

Selwyn was Amos's best man. I was done up in the Ossie Clark dress in which I had planned to marry Selwyn, even though Polly and Selwyn were an acknowledged couple by this time. A self-absorbed and strikingly careless gesture, I thought, in shame at myself. I began a mumbling apology, but Polly dismissed it.

'Do you remember Selwyn's speech?'

'No, I don't think I do.'

'He read out that poem by Robert Herrick.

> Then be not coy, but use your time;
> And while ye may, go marry:
> For having once but lost your prime,
> You may for ever tarry.'

She recited it in a low voice, then smiled at me.

'He found that himself. Is that surprising? I don't think it was. Selwyn believed in marriage, even though we never did it ourselves. I suppose it was me who didn't want to, not him. He was a traditional man, beneath it all.'

'He was. He was a believer in one's prime, too, and in not tarrying.'

The impatient, surging, hot-blooded essence of him seemed to rise up and fill the whole room. His son was breathing evenly on his mattress of cushions. I curled up inside myself, the first intimations of loss stabbing through shock's anaesthesia.

'We loved each other, you know,' Polly said.

'Yes.'

Tell her, I ordered myself. Grief and guilt goaded me beyond reason. My mouth opened and out came the first words.

'Polly, I have to tell you something. I won't know how to deserve your friendship if I don't tell you.'

She turned to look full into my face.

'No,' she said.

That was all, one cold dry monosyllable, but it was as explicit as if written on a page for me to read.

Don't try to absolve yourself by confessing. Don't damage Selwyn's memory for me. Keep what you know to yourself, and live with the knowledge of it.

We held each other's eyes. Her eyelid twitched with weariness, but I was the one who looked away.

'It's nothing,' I murmured.

We sat on together until it was almost morning.

Polly pulled Selwyn's jumper around her shoulders but she was still shivering. I asked her if she would like to lie down in her bed for an hour or two, and she said that she would.

Now, in my own bedroom, I lean my forehead against the cold window glass and stare outside. There is grey in the sky between the trees, and the striking of the Meddlett church clock is just a reverberation in the chilly air.

'I love you,' I say aloud to Selwyn.

Another secret to add to the legions that each of us hides in our hearts.

FEBRUARY

FIFTEEN

The strip lights hummed as they walked down the avenue of bones, past the metal racks stacked with boxes labelled *Hum F, complete*. Chris held open the door to his office and Katherine followed him inside. Severe air conditioning lent the air the sterile tang that she remembered from her first visit, when he had placed the torc around her neck and astonished her by saying, 'I so much wanted to do that.'

She put her fingers to her throat, remembering the ornament's cold weight.

'Where is it now?' she asked.

'With the Iron-Age metals experts, undergoing XRF.'

She raised her eyebrows. His work jargon was becoming a joke between them.

'X-ray fluorescence. To determine the metal content. And other tests. None of this happens quickly. The pieces have a long history, it takes time to unravel it.'

They touched hands. It was still remarkable to them that their lives had somehow tilted together. Sometimes Katherine woke in the night and reached out to make sure that he was there, that it was really Dr Christopher Carr breathing beside her, only to discover that he too was awake and reassuring himself that she was with him. In spite of everything that had happened in the last weeks, Selwyn's death and the end of her marriage, she didn't think that there was any other time in her life when she had felt so vitally in the place and the moment. This, she finally understood, was probably what being in love meant. The condition withstood even the harshest external circumstances.

'Show me the new finds?' she asked.

He unlocked the safe. This time he lifted out a tier of plain cardboard boxes. Inside the largest lay a series of polythene pouches. One by one Chris unwrapped metal ornaments and laid them on a piece of folded cloth for her inspection. They were dirty and corroded, crusted greenish-black with verdigris. They looked less glamorous than the torc and shield, but Katherine had learned enough from Chris by this time to understand how important they were. He pointed to each object in turn.

'Amber and metal alloy brooch, two more brooches and the chain to link them together, two decorative hair tresses, and a pair of gold earrings.'

'She must have looked very fine, don't you think, dressed up in all her glory?'

'To primitive people she would have appeared no less than a goddess.'

From the second box he produced the iron wristlets that protected her arms from the fierce recoil of her bowstring, and a scatter of sharp flint arrowheads. She had been a true warrior.

'What's in there?' Katherine pointed to the third and smallest box.

She had heard much about this last of the finds retrieved from the sports holdall. The newspapers after the recovery had all shown pictures, and Chris had appeared on the local news again to discuss it. But hardly anyone except the police and archaeologists had seen the real thing as yet.

Chris lifted out a cocoon of cloth, and gently peeled back the layers to reveal it.

The gold cup was crumpled at one side, but it was still magnificent.

It lay heavy in her hands, shining because the pure metal did not corrode. The body was decoratively ridged and the rim incised with a scroll pattern. The handle was a ribbed curve of gold, fastened to the body of the vessel with leaf-shaped rivets. Chris showed her how the cup would have been hammered from a sheet of soft metal formed into shape over a block of wood. For a piece so old, he said, the workmanship was extraordinary. She traced her fingertips over the rim, imagining where the princess would have touched it with her lips. This physical link made her seem almost present in the room with them. Then she touched the smooth rounded base. The cup wouldn't have stood up on its own.

'Why is it like that?' she asked.

'It wasn't made to be set aside. It would have been too significant. So the child slaughtered and buried with her might well have been her cup-bearer, because she would have needed to take him as well as the cup itself with her on her journey into the afterlife.'

'But you don't know for sure?'

Chris shook his head.

'In my world we don't know many things for certain. And because the site was so badly disturbed by the looters, we lost all the context. But still, to have recovered these pieces at all goes a long way to compensate for that.'

It did compensate. He was so enchanted by this Iron-Age treasure, and the depth of his passion for it made him lovable in her eyes.

'Tell me what you do know?'

The work by David the osteologist and others on the two sets of bones was complete, and the skeletons were boxed up in the repository.

Chris returned the cup and the ornaments to their places in the safe.

'She was somewhere in her thirties. She was tall, about five foot six inches, and fairly well nourished on a mixed diet of grains and a little meat. Her teeth were bad, and she would have suffered from toothache. We don't know what she died of, though. There are no specific skeletal indications. It could have been pneumonia, tetanus, a tumour, an aneurysm or even poisoning. We shall never know.'

In her mind's eye Katherine saw the burial ground, and the views over the pastures. She realized that she no longer even thought of it as theirs, hers and Amos's, let alone as a site for the futuristic house. Their plan belonged to a different time, as conclusively as the princess herself.

'There is this, too,' Chris said. Against the wall were two covered crates. In one, bagged up, lay several clumps of earth thickly studded with metal discs. In the other were sherds of dark brown grooved pottery. It was a hoard of Icenian coins, and the remains of the jars that had contained them.

He detached a single coin from the mass and held it out.

'Face-Horse,' she murmured, examining the faint outline of a human profile and remembering the other time she had seen the design, back in the Mead woods on the day of the robbery. He stood back in admiration.

'Would you like to join my team?'

'Maybe,' she laughed.

'There's one thing we haven't come across before.'

They picked out and examined some of the slivers of pottery. Chris said that from the materials and the rudimentary incised decorations it was clear that they were pre-Iron Age, perhaps even as early as Neolithic. Katherine looked up at him in surprise.

'But the coins they stored belong to the same period as the princess herself?'

He nodded. He thought that the jars must have been buried or hidden amongst rocks by much earlier peoples, and then discovered and incorporated by the Iceni into their own rituals. The ground seemed to slide from under Katherine's feet again. She peered into further, even more remote layers of prehistory.

She said, 'For thousands of years, different peoples have been living and hunting and eating and drinking, growing their crops, hiding their treasures, dying and being buried, just on that one patch of ground.'

'The more I study it, the more I realize what a rich site it is,' Chris answered.

'Does Miranda know about the pottery?'

She was thinking how interested Miranda would be in this latest discovery from her beloved Mead. She could almost hear her saying, 'If only Jake were here. He would have loved this.' She still talked about Jake as if he were only temporarily absent, but of Selwyn she spoke hardly at all.

'Only you and I and my team know, as yet, and we haven't had time to do any detailed examination because the police took so long to release the artefacts. So I haven't said anything to Mrs Meadowe or your husband, but they will be able to read everything when I submit my report.'

Your husband. Chris didn't like to call him Amos. Katherine knew it was because he was pained and embarrassed to think of the hurt he had caused him, and this distress gave rise to an odd formality. She had tried to tell Chris: You didn't cause the end of my marriage, Amos and I did. I made the decision. He didn't really accept her assurance, though. He was a very good man, she thought once more. A reticent but decent, moral man.

'I don't know what Amos intends,' she said now.

In the six weeks since Selwyn's death, following the first terrible days and the funeral, Amos hadn't mentioned the new house at all. In the abandoned trenches the churned-up earth formed hard crests and then softened again with the winter cycle of frost and thaw. Like Miranda and Polly, Amos had fallen into a limbo at Mead. Without Selwyn amongst them, it was as if the dynamo that had lately powered the place had run down and stopped.

Katherine put the pieces of ancient pot back into the crate.

'Let's go home,' she said to Chris.

Home was no longer the cottage at Mead, and now the separation from Amos was final she felt uncomfortable in

395

the Bloomsbury flat. If she had a home at all in those glazed, grieving weeks of January, it was Chris's terraced house near the city ring road. From the front bedroom windows the dirty white-bronze glare of the motorway lights was clearly visible, but the back was quiet, with a view of tall trees.

'Make yourself comfortable,' he said to her, often.

Chris liked to cook, she discovered. He clipped recipes from the colour supplements and picked up ingredients on the way home from work. Katherine sometimes lay on his sofa with a glass of wine, watching him through the open door of the kitchen as he stirred a wok. This experience, she wonderingly told him, was as exotic for her as a journey to Tibet.

Quite often they ate sitting on the sofa too; refilling each other's glasses and talking across whatever was on television. Katherine realized how pleased she was to have withdrawn from the world of table mats, and crystal glasses that were too good to be put in the dishwasher. After their meal she would lazily postpone the washing up, stretching out instead with her feet in his lap.

He said once, 'This is all anyone wants, you know. Anyone who isn't a power-crazed megalomaniac, that is. Parties, date restaurants, singles bars, internet sites – they all exist ultimately to enable people to find just one other person to lie on the sofa and drink wine with.'

'Wearing tracksuit bottoms,' she said, indicating hers.

'Of course.'

'Where does sex fit in?'

Chris grinned. 'Oh, somewhere on the menu. It's not the ultimate driver, though. It's a big mistake to make it that.'

'We only think that because we're old.'

'Age has its benefits, then,' he answered. 'Hindsight being one of them.'

Tonight she drew the curtains and lit the coal-effect fire. There was a good smell of frying garlic. She looked into the kitchen.

'Do I have time to speak to Polly?'

'Yep.'

Katherine tried to call her every day. Sometimes Polly was calm, almost troublingly so. At others she sounded unhinged, as though grief rampaged through her and sabotaged all the structures of her being.

She confessed once, 'I'm scared, Katherine. I wake up at three a.m. and remember all over again, and I have to stuff the sheet in my mouth to stop myself screaming. I'm frightened that if I do scream I'll sound to myself like a lost person. But I don't know how I'm going to live without him. How will I do it? Can you tell me? I don't know anything, and I used to think I knew so much. I thought I'd made a watertight contract with my life. How mistaken can you be?'

Katherine tried to soothe her. 'It will get better. You won't always feel this bad. Shall I come and be with you? I could come right now, Poll.'

Polly's voice rose. 'No, I can't bear to see you. Amos didn't go and die, you had the luxury of deciding you didn't want him, and now you're in love with someone else.'

'I know. It's unfair,' Katherine said humbly.

Polly had even been angry with Colin. In the first days after Selwyn died she couldn't sleep or eat and her old friend had tried to persuade her that she must swallow some food and then take a sleeping pill. He even held out a spoon to her, as if she were a tiny child. She swatted his hand away and the food spilled on his clothes, and she had wept with the hollowness of pure desolation.

'Stop it, Polly,' he pleaded.

She rounded on him.

'You don't know what it's like. Why couldn't it have been me who died? Why is it me who is left behind?'

Knowing the selfishness of grief, he tried to reason with her.

'I do know what you're feeling. Stephen died. He was murdered, remember?'

She put her head in her hands. 'I'm so sorry. But you and he, you weren't living together then, you'd split up months before.'

397

Colin said, 'I still loved him more than any person in the world. Except maybe for you, Polly.'

Her head snapped back. He saw that her face was contorted with anger.

'Why is it you who is here, and not Selwyn?'

Not long after that Colin had gathered himself up and taken a job in America, telling Katherine that he was making it harder for Polly just by being at Mead.

'I'm so sorry,' Polly cried now to Katherine. 'I'm ashamed of myself. I'm sorry to be so horrible, and so weak at the same time.'

'You're neither of those things. It's grief. Is Mirry there?'

'Miranda?'

The tone of Polly's voice made Katherine say quickly, 'What about the twins, or Ben? When it's bad, why don't you call them?'

'Because when it's bad I don't want them to know how bad it can be. I want to try to protect them from that.'

Katherine didn't say so, but she was reassured to hear this. The maternal instinct was still strong. It would take time, she thought, but in the end Polly would recover from her loss.

Tonight there was no answer from the barn, and Polly's mobile was switched off. Katherine went back to the kitchen and stood behind Chris at the stove. Slowly she inclined her head until it rested against the breadth of his back.

In the barn Polly was surrounded by memories: Selwyn wielding a sledgehammer in a thick cloud of plaster dust, Selwyn crouched under the tarpaulin with rain spilling from the porous roof, Selwyn baring his teeth in a saurian smile on Christmas Eve as he welcomed everyone into the firelit room. Wherever Polly looked, there were pieces of him.

Alpha had printed Colin's photograph of him flying past the start line of the Meddlett Fun Run on the last day of his life, and it was pinned to the wall next to the sink. But even if she were to go to some remote place where he had never set foot, she knew that her head would still be clamorous with his absence. In any case she couldn't run away because she didn't have enough money. Characteristically, Selwyn had left their financial affairs in worse shape than she might have predicted.

The three children had stayed on with her for a few days following the funeral. She was comforted by the solid weight of their bodies pressing against hers, and the smell of their skin, which now seemed hardly to have changed from babyhood. Alph and Omie suffered long bouts of crying and Polly held them as they wept, stroking their hair as she had done when they were little girls. Alph talked a lot on the telephone to Jaime. He was a doctor, her family now learned. He had offered to come up to Mead and do whatever he could to help, as had Omie's Tom, but for now the Davieses clung to each other. It was too much to see anyone.

Ben was the one most changed by his father's death. He might easily have chosen to be prostrated by it, but instead he moved quietly between the three women, trying on the new role of man of the house. He did his best to second-guess their needs, lighting the fires and bringing his mother cups of tea that she didn't have the heart to tell him she didn't want.

After ten days the twins had to go back to work. Ben stayed a little longer, until he heard that there was an opening on the magazine for a regular weekly film review.

'Go on. Dad would want you to do it,' Polly insisted.

Promising that he would come back at weekends, or at least whenever he didn't have a movie to check out, Ben caught the coach back to London.

Nic stayed on at Mead until everyone returned from the funeral in Somerset, but then she told Polly and Miranda separately how grateful she was for their hospitality and announced that she was moving on.

Polly didn't even know how to take this news.

'I need you to tell me exactly where you'll be living in London,' she attempted.

Nic sat close beside her.

'I'm not going back to London.'

'Please, Nic. Don't run off again,' Polly begged. Nic's heart twisted at the sight of her exhausted face and the purple pouches under her eyes.

'I'm not going to run anywhere. Jessie needs a lodger, she asked me if I wanted the room. I'm moving in with her until after the baby's born.'

Polly was too extinguished even to be surprised by this. All she could think of were obstacles.

'What about your course? You need to finish it off, you need to be able to support yourself and . . .'

'I can do the course work at a college up here. There's sure to be somewhere nearby. In the meantime I'll work for myself. You know, waxes and pedicures and that, locally. Card in the shop window, cash in hand. I'm good at what I do, and word will get around in a place like this. I'll make enough money. I don't need much.'

Polly thought about it. In the desolate landscape, a tiny light winked and began to glimmer.

'You'll be here? You and the baby? In Meddlett?'

'That's the general idea. I know I shouldn't be asking this right now, but maybe you could help me with looking after the baby sometimes, while I'm working?'

Polly's eyes narrowed to horizontal slits, her cheeks rounded into apples and her lips curved to show her teeth. For the first time in long days, she was smiling.

'Oh Nic, of course I will. I'll be here. We'll make it all right for him.'

'Him?'

'Oh yes, it's a boy. I'm certain of it.'

By the time February came, Polly was on her own in the barn. The beams creaked and the roof shivered in the gales. She took a bitter, comradely pleasure in the harshness of the weather. Sometimes she shook her fist at the dark grey whirling skies. Do what you want. Do your worst, she cried.

The telephone rang a good deal. When she didn't feel like speaking to anyone she let the machine pick up and listened to the disembodied voice of one or other of her children or friends leaving a loving message. She was grateful for the net that proved able to hold her, but she was also detached from the outside world. She let the waves of anger and loss and fear wash over her, and she sluiced backwards and forwards with them like seaweed in the tide.

Katherine called her every day. Polly could hear the gulps in her voice as she tried to soften the high note of her own pure, humming happiness and offer instead the murmur of concerned sympathy.

'I'm all right,' Polly claimed. When a different admission forced its way out Katherine soothed her as best she could.

Every evening she gazed out at the yellow squares of lighted windows in the cottage across the yard, and in the main house. They usually blinked off early, leaving an outline of deeper blackness. It occurred to her that she and Amos and Miranda were like castaways on three adjacent islands, separated by a tidal race. But she also knew that this impression was distorted. In fact the other two regularly made the short crossing to her island, bringing supplies, news from the distant world, and the possibility of a condition other than solitude.

Amos came over to roost in Selwyn's chair beside the over-sized hearth. Firewood burned away to powdery ash with frightening speed, and then Polly would have to make yet another trip out to replenish the log basket. Amos propped his socked feet on a stool and drank the whisky he invariably brought with him. He was looking less well scrubbed and tailored these days. His shirts were left unironed and his trousers could have stood a visit to the drycleaners. He was usually disappointed to find that there was no more chance of a wifely hot supper in the barn than there was in the cottage. Polly had no appetite at all, and subsisted on cheese sandwiches and occasional boiled eggs. The waistbands of her skirts grew noticeably looser.

'It's the death diet,' she said mordantly to Katherine.

401

Amos talked about the past. He reminisced about university, and his own attempts in the intervening years to jump out from Selwyn's long shadow. 'I never did manage it, did I? Now he's gone, I'm more aware than ever of the difference in our relative stature.'

Polly listened with a dulled ear. Her own memories marched with her, most vividly in the endless insomniac nights.

'Selwyn didn't think of you as being in his shadow. You're the one who was a success in life,' she said.

Amos described how he was becoming quite an accepted face in the village. He regularly ate dinner at the Griffin, and was making the transition from eavesdropper to contributor in the bar conversations.

'That Slovakian chef they've got there, Geza, he's not that bad. Food's quite decent.'

'Is it?' she murmured. The flames leaped as another log hissed and settled. Talk was more of an effort than she felt capable of making, and Amos knew it. He rambled on, seamless in whisky.

'This notion about locals not welcoming incomers, you know, it's partly true, and why should people be overjoyed at strangers buying up the houses and cutting them out of their own community?'

It was interesting to hear Amos, of all people, using a word like community. Polly angled her head towards him.

'But it's not that difficult to break through. It's been harder for me than it would be for most, just because I happen to own the land where the princess was dug up, although Jessie's probably put a word in for me.'

Polly raised her eyebrows by a hair's-breadth. Amos laughed, slightly abashed. 'It's not what you think. I'm not making a play for her. But I do think she is interesting.'

'Yes,' Polly agreed. She was listening with more than half an ear now. Amos waved his whisky glass.

'I'd like to help her out. Maybe you and I could, you know, think of a way. An appropriate way. As I was saying, I've been

402

talking to people. Vin Clarke, the local builder, the guy who farms next door to Mead, one or two others. Their roots are right here, even more than Miranda's. The princess belongs to this land, bones and her cup and torc and coins and all. It's not just the soap-dodgers, those placard people, who think so. Most people in Meddlett do.'

Amos was lonely, and disconcerted, and he was spending more time in the pub. He picked up ideas, and endearingly latched on to them as though they were brand new. Shaken out of herself in spite of everything, Polly looked at him with affection.

'So what do you want to do?'

His shoulders sagged. 'Christ. I've no real idea. Get the bones and the treasure and the land reunited in some way.' Words suddenly burst out. 'I don't know what I want to do. I feel so clapped out and pointless, Poll. I've no reason to, I'm not ill. Colin's got bloody prostate cancer, Jake and Stephen and dear, inspiring, unique Selwyn have all gone and died on us, whereas I'm all right. I should be grateful, shouldn't I? But for the first time in my life I can't work out what I'm doing or where I want to be.'

The neck of the bottle rattled against the tumbler. He caught himself.

'I'm sorry. Shouldn't be visiting this on you, of all people.'

'Go ahead. In a way it's helpful.'

Amos was on his feet now, two fingers of Glenmorangie slopping in the glass.

'We're all old.'

Their eyes fell, simultaneously, on the fines box. It stood amongst books and CD cases on a set of makeshift shelves that Selwyn had constructed from planks and blocks of wood. Stuck to the side was a label on which Miranda had printed DON'T MENTION THE O WORD. Amos picked it up and turned it over. The lid fell off and five- and ten-pound notes fluttered out and drifted to the floor. He knelt down, grimacing at the twinges in his knees as he counted the money.

'Two hundred and twenty quid in used fives and tens, and an extra fiver. Where did that come from? Did someone half-mention feeling as old as bloody Methuselah? Or did they say they only felt half his age?'

Suddenly, Polly was laughing. She felt lighter than she had done for weeks.

'I think that was Joyce. The rest of us agreed that she was more entitled to complain about feeling ancient than us Boomers, so Mirry stuck in a fiver for her.'

Amos stuffed the money back in the box and replaced the lid.

'It's good to see you laugh again. We're never going snow-boarding in St Anton, are we? What shall we do with the cash?'

Polly thought about it.

'Why don't we give it to Nic, to buy a pram?'

He sat back on his heels. 'Ah, that's a good idea. One of those pneumatic all-terrain beauties you see these days. A futuristic vehicle for the new generation.'

Amos wasn't inclined to sit down any longer. He paced the length of the room and back again. Then he stopped in front of her, hands in pockets, forehead corrugated.

'I have made one decision. I'm definitely not going to build the house.'

She thought of the solar panels and thermal insulating glass and ground source heat pump, and all the proud technology he had described in such loving detail to whoever would listen.

'Oh, Amos. All those plans.'

'Yes. Plans are just that.'

'Where will you live?'

He shrugged. 'Somewhere here, near you and Mirry, if you'll let me. It occurs to me – late in the day, I know, as Katherine would no doubt agree – that bricks and mortar, glass and steel, whatever, don't matter at all. The only value on earth is in your friends and the people you care about.'

'Oh, Amos,' she said again. Coming from him, this statement of the obvious had the impact of pure revelation.

He said, 'I am going to give the site back to the princess, so that she can come home to rest.'

Polly closed her eyes for a second. The sensation of lightness stayed with her.

The next evening Miranda came across to the barn, having telephoned first to check if this would be all right. She never arrived unannounced, and Polly appreciated her tact. She brought a shopping basket with her, and unpacked a pot of home-made soup, a fresh loaf, some cheese and an apple pie. She didn't ask what needed to be done, just went ahead and did it. Polly sat by the fire, drinking the glass of red wine that Miranda put in her hand.

The microwave pinged.

'Eat this,' Miranda ordered.

The hot soup tasted good. Polly dipped a chunk of warm bread into her bowl.

'May I talk to you?' Miranda asked, after a few mouthfuls.

Polly hesitated.

'That depends. No confessions. Don't say anything that either of us might wish unsaid.'

Miranda reddened slightly. Polly's voice was gentle, as ever, but there was an underlying note of warning.

'I won't.'

'Thank you. We've been friends for so many years, and we'll go on being friends, won't we?'

Polly stretched her hand across the table, touched her fingers to Miranda's. After a second, in which they both listened to the wind howling off the sea and battering the chimneys, Miranda looked up.

'Because Sel is dead,' Polly said sadly.

'I know.' Miranda let the ambiguity of the flat acknowledgement shield them both. Her face was pinched with misery and her eyes heavy from lack of sleep.

Polly tapped her hand and smiled encouragement, the touch of steel melting away. 'Go on, then.'

'All right. You asked me if you could work on Jake's family papers, and I said I'd think about it. Now I have thought, and I want you to go ahead. Whatever you'd like to do with the material, it's yours. If there's a book to be written about the history of Mead, I couldn't imagine a better person to tackle it.'

Polly spooned up the last mouthful of soup, then wiped the bowl clean with a twist of brown bread. For weeks she had hardly thought about the boxes of folded letters, the ledgers and account books and farm records, and the hours that she had already spent perched on a rickety chair in Jake's old study.

Her face changed.

'Thank you. No, wait . . . that sounds inadequate. I don't think you can imagine how much of a difference it will make, to have that work to do.'

Nic was living only a mile away, waiting for the baby to be born. Now, after all, here was a book to be pieced together out of the Meadowe papers. Suddenly it seemed that all over the plain of darkness there were tiny lights glimmering.

They clinked their glasses, still wary of each other, but fired up by shared optimism. Miranda chopped herself a wedge of cheese and pushed the plate across to Polly.

'So Amos is not going to build the wonder house after all,' Miranda remarked. He had told her that he planned to give the site to Meddlett, and wanted to find a way between them to hammer out the rights of access. She had reminded him that as far as legal matters went he was the lawyer, not her.

'Can it be done?' Polly asked.

'I don't see why not,' she said.

'Wouldn't you mind?'

Miranda had thought hard about it, remembering the home-made placards and posters. Amos was right, she decided. If people wanted to come to visit the burial site, if they wanted to connect to the princess and her history by stepping on the same ground and looking out at the same sweep of pasture, then what reason could she put forward for denying them?

'No. I wanted people at Mead. It's one way of doing it, isn't it?'

She didn't try to explain to Polly – not tonight, but maybe she would in time – that this act of propitiation was one way of making peace with herself.

'Will there be a Visitors' Centre?'

Miranda saw that Polly was gently teasing her. It was heartening that her old friend was able to forget herself to this extent.

'Possibly. And a tearoom and a toilet block. Who knows what Amos will be able to pull off?'

'Who knows,' Polly echoed.

The following day, Polly went to work. She put on her thickest skirt and leggings, a fleece and a pair of fingerless mittens, and crossed the yard to the main house. She felt weak, as if she had been ill for a long time, and there was a pain in her hip that was becoming familiar, but the icy air flooding into her lungs delivered an invigorating kick. Joyce was reading the newspaper in her chair beside the kitchen range. She peered over her spectacles at Polly.

'Could you come back at some other time?' she asked.

From deep in the house came the sound of hoovering. It was Miranda's way to bring her feelings under control by throwing herself into diversionary activities, and housework was the current favourite. The kitchen looked unusually tidy, and the old red tiles had been washed and waxed.

'It's Polly, Joyce. How are you today?'

Joyce studied her. 'What happened to you?'

'I survived.' It was a thin, low-voltage smile that accompanied the acknowledgement, but it was still a smile.

She went on through the house and ensconced herself in Jake's old study. On the table beneath the window she set up her lined notebooks and pencils, her vintage laptop computer and an index card box. The window panes were silvered with condensation, and the frame of bare, tangled twigs contained a misty landscape distorted by water droplets. She stared out

407

for a few moments, then drew a bundle of papers towards her. She began rereading the letters that Jake Meadowe's great-uncle had written home from the Front.

The Griffin was busy.

Part of Amos's plan for the evening related to this being Jessie's night off. He was sitting at the table in the window where Colin had first seen her arguing with Damon, and he was engaged in a debate with Stan the builder and a shifting cast of other people who all had views on what should happen to the Meddlett Princess and her regalia. Geza's sweating visage occasionally appeared between the strands of kitchen curtain. Vin Clarke's second waitress shuffled in with two plates of lamb pilaff and dispensed them to waiting customers. Amos had already eaten his pork with prunes.

'You own all that gold now, don't you?' an oblong man in biker's leathers said.

Patiently Amos explained the law yet again. The inquest at the court of the coroner for the district had recently declared that the find did indeed qualify as treasure, but there was still a long way to go. He embarked on his practised account of how the cup and the torc and the rest would now have to go before a treasure valuation committee, after the archaeologists and scientists had completed their reports and valuations, and only then would their value in monetary terms begin to emerge. The local and national museums would look to their budgets and bid to acquire the objects, whilst the exhibition and collections experts would want all the items to be displayed together in order to tell a coherent story. Somewhere down the line, a reward would be paid out.

The crowd listened to all this with moderate good humour, only Vin muttering about how much the lawyer liked the sound of his own voice, same as all his kind. Big, bald Roy sat massively in his special corner beside the bar, nodding in agreement.

'The normal procedure is for the money to be split between the landowner and the finder,' Amos said, as he had done several dozen times before. 'It'll be a decent sum, but not a fortune.'

'Depends how you define fortune, doesn't it?' someone muttered. 'Strikes me it wouldn't be the same amount for me as it would be for you, not at all.'

There was a shuffle and some elbowing at the bar. A figure emerged from the throng, nudged forwards by the other drinkers. Amos looked across and saw that it was Kieran. He waved to him, and asked, 'Why did you leave me to do all the explaining? You know much more than I do.'

'Doesn't sound like it,' Kieran countered.

Someone else said to him, 'You were the finder, mate, weren't you? So you'll be getting the other half of the cash, eh?'

Kieran's sensitive skin flared. 'The company will, not me. I'll get a bit of a bonus, maybe, if I'm a good boy.'

He came over to stand in front of Amos.

'It's a decent thing you're doing, making the site over to Meddlett,' he began.

Amos raised an eyebrow. 'Thank you.' Remembering something, he glanced at his watch.

Roy's wife was with him tonight. She was a broad-hipped woman who wore her grey hair in a plaited crown. In a flash of recollection Amos recognized her as one of the people who had dressed up in makeshift prehistoric costume on the Fifth of November. He had even pointed her out to Selwyn.

Roy's wife pressed her hands together with an expression of transcendent joy on her face.

'Return the princess to her resting place, and peace will be restored to Meddlett.'

Amos looked hard at her. 'Right,' he said.

The churchwarden and president of the bowls club chipped in, 'I reckon the vicar would favour that.'

A slabby man in a car coat put his head around the door into the bar. Amos jumped up at the sight of him.

'I've got to go,' he told the assembly importantly. 'But I've had the same thought. Leave it with me.'

A couple of boys gestured behind his back as he made his way out in the wake of the slab man, but the chorus of good-nights was mostly unironic.

Kieran finished his pint in two gulps and tailed the two men out into the car park.

Amos and the other man were standing at the rear of a small white van. The back doors were open and they were both leaning inside. Kieran had been intending to pursue Amos further about the grave site, but now curiosity drew him on.

A cardboard box with holes punched in the sides was opened, and the man put his hand inside. He drew out a small, squirming black shape that emitted tiny yipping noises. Amos took the puppy into his arms, and under the nearest light he examined the little creature's eyes and ears and paws.

'Pride of the litter. You saw that when you picked 'im out,' the man said.

Amos returned the puppy to the box and transferred the box from the van to the passenger seat of the Jaguar. A small sheaf of notes was counted into the van driver's hand, he and Amos shook on the deal, and the doors slammed. Once the van had reversed away, Kieran stepped out of the shadows. Amos was about to climb into his own car.

'I can guess who that puppy's intended for.'

'I expect you can. I'm on my way over there now to surprise her.'

Kieran didn't miss a beat. 'Is it all right if I come with you?'

Amos looked distinctly unwilling.

'I'd like to see her face when you lift him out,' Kieran pleaded.

Amos sighed. 'There's safety in numbers, I suppose. You can back me up if she hates the very idea of a new dog.'

Before Amos could change his mind, Kieran hopped into the passenger seat, balancing the puppy box on his knees. The Jaguar slid out of the Griffin car park, turned along the side of the green and headed past the church towards Mead. The puppy snuffled and scratched in its bed within the box.

'How's work?' Amos inquired pleasantly.

'All right, thanks. We're pretty quiet at the moment, as it happens.'

'Your boss must be pleased to have some time to spare.'

Kieran was embarrassed. Fortunately it was dark enough in the car for his red face to be hidden.

Amos said, 'It's all right. I'm not quite the first person to lose his wife to a younger man.'

'I don't know what to say. He's a decent bloke.'

'Katherine wouldn't be with him if he were not,' Amos observed. There was no further discussion. Kieran was forming the impression that Amos Knight was quite a decent bloke himself, contrary to all the outward signs.

The car stopped at the overgrown gateway. Blanketed by darkness, the cottage looked quite welcoming, with its lights shining from behind closed curtains.

This impression was soon dispelled, however. Jessie yanked the door open in response to Amos's knock. She stood outlined by the glare from the overhead bulb.

'It's my night off. Can't the Griffin manage without me?'

'Nice to see you too, Jessie. May we come in?'

She considered the proposal. 'I suppose. And him as well?'

Kieran slipped into the narrow hallway. He peered eagerly over Jessie's shoulder.

The living room now looked liked one half of its old self, with half of an entirely different room grafted on to it. Music posters were still tacked on top of the grubby wallpaper, but the one over the mantelpiece had been replaced by a large and intricate thangka painting in strong tones of blue and green. The sofa and armchair were draped with throws, there were cushions in jewel colours, and a large jar in one corner was filled with an artistic arrangement of twisted willow twigs and catkin branches. The antique electric fire had been replaced with a slightly larger, more modern one, and in front of it stood an old crate covered with a cloth for a coffee table. A clutch of mother and baby magazines and a battered Penelope Leach book were fanned out on it. Scented candles burned on the hearth.

411

In the midst of this sat Nic. She was knitting.

'Hi. Hi, Kieran,' she said, looking pleased to see him. He slid across and perched beside her on the sofa.

'It was a girls' night in,' Jessie said. 'I suppose you want a coffee or something now you're here?'

Amos held the box in his arms.

'I've got something for you.'

He knelt down, placed the box on the floor and removed the lid. Immediately there was a frantic burst of the high-pitched yipping. Jessie's hands flew up to her mouth.

'Oh my God,' she whispered.

Amos reached in and lifted out the puppy. Its black feet splayed as it steadied itself on the hearth rug. It checked its surroundings, then it trotted over to Jessie and sniffed at her foot.

Jessie crouched down and Nic rolled her bulk off the sofa. Both girls knelt at puppy eye-level, melting with instant adoration.

'Is he mine? Is he for me?' Jessie cried.

'He is yours. He's a black Labrador pup, fully certified, vet-approved, and of a rather good pedigree.'

She scooped the creature up in her arms, rapturous as a small child on her birthday. The puppy yipped, then licked her face.

Kieran watched this scene, finding to his surprise that he needed to blink. Surreptitiously he reached for Nic's hand, and held it. She didn't pull away.

'You want to keep him, then?' Amos asked.

'Don't be stupid. Of course I do,' Jessie said, with her face buried in the puppy's black fur.

Jessie and Nic

The kitchen window ran with condensation. The air was thick with steam and the smell of frying bacon. Jessie sat hunched at the small table, chewing her bacon sandwich and reading a thick paperback. Her tobacco tin, a packet of Rizlas and a saucer for an ashtray were placed close at hand.

Nic shuffled slowly out of her boxroom and steadied herself against the kitchen door. Her gaze travelled over the sink, complete with greasy frying pan immersed in a bowl of cold water, spattered gas stove, and the floor patched with newspapers to catch the puppy's accidents. The dog was under the table, delightedly tussling with an old shoe. Jessie had named him Gulliver.

'This place is really minging,' Nic sighed.

Jessie didn't look up. 'You're right.'

'Is there any tea?'

'In the pot. How do you feel?'

Nic made a face, which Jessie didn't see.

'What are you reading?'

'*The Magic Mountain.*'

'. . . Mushroom?'

'Does being ten months pregnant affect your hearing?'

Nic flopped down on the only other chair. She wrapped her fingers around her mug of tea and stared at the dim grey sky beyond the window. Her back ached, and most of the rest of her body as well. She had had a fortnight of solid telephoning and beseeching to do but she wasn't bad at that, and now she had matters straight. It was much easier dealing with the system up here than in London. Sometimes people in the benefits office or the hospital appointments system even had time to speak politely to you, and the GP that Miranda had sent her to see was an old-fashioned family doctor, like in an Agatha Christie. He wore a suit with a waistcoat, and called her 'dear', which was about as different as it was possible to be from Gina, the harassed and therefore largely unsympathetic inner-city practitioner she used to work for. Nic had seen the Meddlett midwife as many times in the last three weeks as she had managed in the whole of the previous five months in London.

One afternoon Amos and Polly had come to the cottage bearing a pile of baby supplies. There were tiny snow-white babygros and vests and blankets and great bales of disposable nappies.

'The ante-natal trolley-dash, is it?' Jessie dryly asked.

Looking around the cottage Polly seemed both deferential and eager, but she tried to hide her eagerness in case Nic thought she was being intrusive. She insisted that Amos had paid for everything, except for the pram, which had mostly been bought out of the proceeds of some old people's swear-box system over at Mead that the girls didn't quite understand. The pram had fat rubber tyres and suspension as elaborate as Amos's car, and the padded body of it lifted out to become a rocking cradle in which the baby could sleep. Amos demonstrated all the mechanisms to Nic.

Nic also had a crib, bought very cheaply from a young mother in Meddlett to whom she had been introduced by the midwife, and she had knitted a small pyramid of clothes in rainbow stripes that Omie Davies had enthused over. She had been quite pleased with the arrangements she had made for her baby, and at first she felt belittled by this casual largesse of Amos's. Did he think she was a charity case, and therefore was Polly of the same opinion?

Then she looked across at Jessie, who was lounging in the doorway watching the unloading of the baby kit. Jessie wore skinny jeans and her unpregnant, undistended breasts, embellished with the tattoo, showed perkily under her open shirt. She was perfectly in command of herself and her appeal and the whole situation, but Nic wouldn't have changed places with her.

Jessie wasn't having a baby, and she was.

Nic read the warning that Jessie signalled her. It was, more or less, *He means well. Don't have a go at him.*

She was right, too, Nic judged.

She thanked both of them for their generosity, and she was rewarded by a soft, shining smile from Polly, and Amos's hearty insistence that if she needed anything else, she or Jessie were just to let him know. Polly also made her promise that as soon as labour started, she would call. She would stay with her, and drive her to the hospital when the time came.

'That's good. Don't count on me, I'll be crap at all that obstetric stuff,' Jessie said sternly when they had gone.

Nic wrote down the various numbers at Mead and pinned them in a prominent place on the kitchen wall. She added Kieran's number, too. He had insisted that he could drive her, any time she wanted, it didn't matter if it was the middle of the night, he'd be glad to help out.

Jessie gave her a long look.

'I can't believe you fancy him. You do, don't you?'

Nic went red. She felt in such a turmoil of hormones and uncertainty and anticipation, she didn't even know what it would be like to fancy anyone.

'Kieran's all right. You're just biased against his family.'

'Too right I am. Damon's turning into a mental case. What he gets up to, you wouldn't believe. Eh, Gully?' She shook her head, sombre with the responsibility of inside information. The puppy squirmed and twisted in Jessie's arms.

'Kieran is Damon's brother, not his keeper,' Nic snapped.

* * *

Nic poured herself another cup of tea. Jessie would be leaving quite soon for morning opening time at the Griffin, and a long day with no company lay ahead. She wanted to talk.

'What's the book about, then?' she asked.

'A TB sanatorium,' Jessie muttered, turning a page.

'Cheerful. Why did you pick that?'

She could have supplied the answer, but she wanted to hear what Jessie would say.

'Amos recommended it.'

'Of course. Do you always do what he tells you?'

Jessie reached for her tin. She took a whiskery pinch of tobacco, made a roll-up and leaned back in her chair. Nic had already tried to suggest that smoking in the house would be bad for the baby, but Jessie had merely replied that she wasn't smoking in Nic's room, was she? And if Nic preferred a non-smoking, puppy-free household, she could go and find one. That was how Jessie was, but it was hard to quarrel with her because she was so matter-of-fact. Nic had never had a friend like Jessie before.

'No, I don't always. But he knows more than most of the people I come across in the bloody Griffin. I'd be a fool not to listen to what he says, wouldn't I? And it's a good book, as it turns out.'

Nic had already pointed out to Jessie that Amos was fascinated by her. And so were both of his sons, judging by the way they had looked at her at Christmas. Jessie only shrugged.

'He hasn't mixed in the real world much, has he?'

'He's rich . . .' Nic began.

'And so old.'

'Has he tried it on?'

Jessie laughed. 'Just the once. It ended up with him saying he wanted to look at my tatt, so I gave him a flash of it.' Then she turned serious. 'It was quite touching, in a way. He was grateful, not really sleazy. I ended up liking him, but not in that way. Nor those posh sons of his, either. Amos says I should be applying for uni. If I choose law, he knows some people

416

who would help. They really like to give places to members of the underclass. Looks good in the statistics, I suppose.'

Nic stared at her. That would be three or four years at least of going back to school, with a huge debt to pay off at the end of it. The beauty school course had been bad enough.

'Great,' she said.

Jessie stubbed out her rollie in the ash-grey saucer. The sight made Nic feel suddenly very sick. She stood up, steadying herself against the corner of the table. There was a *ping* as her waters broke. Amniotic fluid ran down her legs and splashed on the floor.

'What's happening? Are you going to be all right?' Jessie wailed.

'This is it,' Nic said.

The puppy trotted over and licked at the puddle between her feet.

Colin

It was one of those New York days of withering cold when any skin left exposed to the wind stings in protest and then turns numb. The production of *Manon Lescaut* for which Colin had designed the set and costumes had previewed satisfactorily, and would open in three days' time. It had been an interesting job, working with a director he admired. He had just walked across to Central Park with the director's assistant, a woman who had lately become a friend, and they had parted company at a fork in the path where she headed across to the East Side and he turned north towards the bird-dotted waters of the reservoir. The trees were reduced to scribbles of twig and branch, their great boles a patchwork of tattered bark, as if the winter had defeated them and the sap would never rise again. He found himself nodding to the nearest one, a gesture of physical solidarity.

A few walkers and runners appeared between the trees. Ahead of Colin were a young couple deep in conversation and a tall distinguished-looking black man in a dark overcoat. A girl ran past, pink earmuffs over her head, her feet in silver trainers pounding steadily on the path. Puffs of breath clouded in front of her. A fur-coated mother and a child in a snow-suit came in the opposite direction, the child solemnly trundling a wheeled dog. Colin noted the features and dress of each person, conscious of how he would appear if any of the passers-by had chosen to pay the same degree of attention to him. They would see a thin, somewhat abstracted man of late middle-age, a little too precise in the arrangement of his silk-lined cashmere scarf and the exact width of his overcoat lapels. Disliking this bloodless picture, Colin immediately stuck his hands into the pockets of his coat and tried to loosen himself into a slouch. This didn't please him either. He knew that he thought too much about himself, and had too little beyond work and working relationships and New York arts to occupy his mind.

He was a sad old man, he reflected, not as brave about being ill as he would wish, and lonely again even though he had stimulating work and a wide circle of acquaintances. Even Melanie, the director's assistant, talked more than she listened.

He had only himself to blame for this, of course. To ask questions of other people rather than confiding in them betrayed an absence of trust and a fear of intimacy.

The only place where he felt properly at home was at Mead, with Polly and the others, yet still he resisted every temptation to speak or even to think of the place as his home. He was protecting himself, as always since parting from Stephen, from the possibility of caring too much or settling too comfortably in any place with anyone.

But he did think *about* Mead, all the time, and now the decades of memories shared with Selwyn, and the last months they had spent there together, seemed as vivid and precious as anything else in his life.

Walking under the bare trees of Central Park, Colin felt severely homesick for the old house and the views over ancient land, as well as for Polly's company, and his friends who were still alive.

In the pocket of his overcoat was a beach pebble, and he turned it over and over as he pondered. It was viciously cold out here and he wished he had a hat with him. He took one hand out of his pocket and drew his collar and the folds of scarf closer up to his chin.

419

There was a barely audible *swoosh* and a disturbance in the air at his shoulder. A rollerblader swept past, missing Colin's arm by a mere inch. Colin raised the arm in a gesture that was half defence and half retaliation. He was still holding the pebble, and it slipped between his gloved fingers and spun to the ground.

There was another *swoosh* as a second rollerblader came up behind him. This time there was a scrunch of grit beneath the rubber front stops as he came to a dead halt.

'You dropped something,' the skater called. He stooped down, reached between his splayed boots and picked up the pebble. The man took the time to examine it thoroughly before handing it over.

'Keepsake, huh?' he asked.

The stone was a chunk of quartz that he and Stephen had picked up when they were walking together on Brighton beach, way back at the beginning of their time together. Colin had remarked on the stone's very rough heart-shape, and Stephen had taken it to a gemstone cutter who had cut and polished it. Stephen had later presented the cloudy heart to him, with a little speech about not having a heart of stone.

After Stephen was murdered, Colin almost always carried it with him. It wasn't a talisman, exactly. But he liked to keep it at hand.

'Yes.' He took the heart and dropped it into his pocket. 'Thanks.'

The first rollerblader had vanished. This one wore tight lycra leggings, a black Puffa and a knitted beanie. He seemed supernaturally tall, perched on top of his skates. He studied Colin from a height.

'Pretty cold today,' he said.

Colin agreed.

'Which way you heading?'

'I'm just taking a walk.'

The man was young, somewhere in his early twenties. He had a wide mouth, the upper lip as full as the lower, with prominently defined margins to both that made Colin think of a piece of primitive sculpture. His large nose sloped to his forehead with no indentation at the bridge. It wasn't easy to place his accent.

'I'll roll along with you,' he said in a companionable way. Colin began walking, and the man swooped ahead, executed a turn and sped back to his side. He was a graceful mover.

'You British?'

'Yes. Where are you from?'

It was a long time since Colin had made one of these connections. He took a certain amount of care to avoid the possibility, even. But he had not forgotten how they went, and the old flare of anticipation ran through him all over again. How optimistic the spirit is, he thought, even though the body is otherwise.

The skater said, 'I am from Brazil. My family is in Rio. My name is Carlos.'

They moved on, the man slicing ahead, making a leg change, curving backwards to Colin's side again. Colin fell into this rhythm until they passed a line of benches, all of them empty.

'Is it too cold to sit for a few minutes?' Carlos asked.

They turned aside from the path.

They were talking about Carlos's unrewarding job as a barista and his forthcoming audition for a modern dance company, when Colin's BlackBerry alerted him to a message. He apologized for the interruption and checked the screen.

Nic's baby boy born 6.07 p.m., named Leo Selwyn. All well xxxxx granny

Colin crowed aloud, threw the phone up and snatched it out of the air again.

He stared at the picture Polly had sent. It showed a tiny tomato-faced infant swaddled in a white blanket and held tightly in a pair of young arms.

How important this baby was. He had no real link with Nic

beyond his liking for her and her somewhat surprising attach-
ment to him, but he felt a sudden surge of protective love for
Selwyn's newborn namesake that was almost as strong as for
a child of his own unrealized child.

'Good news?' Carlos asked.

'My dearest friend has a new grandson.'

Carlos peered at the photograph. His thigh briefly touched
Colin's as he leaned inwards. 'Hey. That calls for a celebration.'

Colin thumbed a reply to Polly.

*Best granny in the world. Kiss to Nic and the baby. Back
very soon, Cx*

He hesitated for a second and then moved the cursor over
to *back*. He deleted the word and replaced it with *home*. He
realized that he was smiling.

'Do you want to uh, go somewhere?' Carlos asked when
Colin slipped the phone back into his overcoat pocket and
heard it clink against the stone. Carlos ran his blades experimentally forwards and backwards and then rocked his boots
so the wheels spun free.

'I can't do anything,' Colin said.

The words were a denial, though. He could do things.

He was thinking of the windows of FAO Schwarz, the drive
from London up to Mead, Leo Selwyn asleep in his hospital
crib. He saw Polly's round face and heard Miranda's hoot of
laughter. He wanted to see them all, but before that, right now,
he wanted a glass of champagne – several glasses – and some
company, maybe a bar, a place and scenery that he understood,
and the touch and taste of another person's skin. It was as if
the lowering sky had split clean open, and a bright shaft of
strong sunlight struck through.

Carlos lazily smiled back at him.

'There are ways and means, man.'

422

SPRING

SIXTEEN

March came and then April, the last week of April bringing a green bloom to the countryside as Polly absorbed herself in sheaves of letters and creaking account books.

The more she read, the more deeply she was drawn out of her own life and into another world. Far from being a confined space, Jake's study now became the entrance to a colonnade of years, each one marked off by summer in the fields, harvest, the Fifth procession, then Advent and Christmas, Lent and Easter, and the recorded dates of ploughing and sowing and rabbit shooting and occasional hunting. Polly noted the bills for the twice-yearly visits of the piano tuner, the chimney sweep and the knife-grinder. A horse-drawn mower was used to cut what had then been wide lawns, the horse's hooves wrapped in sacking so they would not mark the green velvet grass. In one Victorian account book, neatly itemized, she found the total expenditure for a grand dinner for county neighbours at which Lord Lockington and his lady had been entertained just after their marriage.

These were Mead's glory days. After this the account books and farm records grew scrappy, as the head of the family turned to gambling to meet his debts. There were no more bouts of ambitious entertaining recorded.

These estate records had been kept by successive generations of Meadowe men, farmers and lately gentry. Their wives and daughters were glimpsed only through mentions of glazing to 'Mary's glass house' or the purchase of a pony, 'Amelia's tenth birthday'. For generation after generation these women had kept house, given birth to children and brought up families, playing their part on the estate as it grew and then declined again, but the last chatelaine before Miranda, Jake's mother, Gwen, was the only one to have left anything like a first-person account of herself. Dating from the Second World War, it was no more than a worn notebook filled with irregular scribbled jottings.

Jake's father had been away in the services, like most of the men in the county. So far Polly had found only two or three letters from him, interleaved between the pages of the notebook. They were written from London and mentioned 'this outfit' and 'liaison work', but they were rather formal, unlike his late uncle's loving missives from the trenches in France. It was Gwen's garden diary that Polly found totally absorbing. She had evidently been a plantswoman. There were lists of plants, *Helleborus n., Ilex argentea, M. grandiflora*, references to pruning roses and dividing clumps of bergenia, and to planting 250 narcissi bulbs in a single afternoon. 'My dear bit of garden,' she wrote in the spring of 1940. But the country was at war, and food had to be grown in place of flowers. Without confiding even a line of complaint to her diary, Gwen Meadowe grubbed up her perennials and scented shrubs and planted potatoes and onions in their place, helped by one old man from Meddlett and a series of land girls who were billeted with her. Gwen wrote pithily about these various Doras and Eileens, describing one Molly as 'a very trouble-some girl. But a merry, likeable nuisance'.

Polly looked up after she read this, and thoughtfully stretched the cramps out of her neck. She felt a distinct and growing kinship with Gwen in her solitary pursuits, and this historical Mead with its desecrated gardens grew more real than the version that actually sheltered her.

426

Satisfaction, even a muted version of happiness, was transforming Polly. To be absorbed in work like this, to realize that a whole afternoon had passed without numbering the hours, was a pleasure she hadn't known for a long time. Selwyn was gone and the pain of losing him shifted inside her like a cumbersome load, but today the weight of it didn't quite crush the breath out of her.

Outside, the rose branches that framed the window were covered with tender green and bronze leaves, and sprays of unopened buds nodded in the wind. Perhaps this very climber was one of those tended by Gwen Meadowe, who had been quietly relieved to note in her garden diary that there was no food crop that could usefully be grown in its place.

Polly knew how she was going to start her book. It would begin in 1945, with the estate and village VE Day celebrations held in the barn where she now lived, and it would work backwards from Gwen to her mother-in-law, who had been chauffeured through the narrow lanes in the Silver Ghost that had once been garaged in the same barn. Perhaps that Mrs Meadowe of the Great War would have written letters to her son at the Front in what was now Miranda's drawing room, and in the same room her husband's grandmother might have worked out the dinner menu to impress Lord and Lady Lockington and the rest of the county grandees.

Polly would trace the history of the house by telling its story backwards, through the decades of two or three centuries, as far as these records and whatever others she could unearth would allow her to go. The perspective was a long one. She puffed out her cheeks in awe just in contemplating it, but at the same time a distinct thrill ran through her.

There was a patch of blue sky visible above the trees.

She stood up, easing her painful hip. She wanted to talk to Miranda.

She picked her way through the ordered avenues of her research documents and walked through the quiet house. The drawing-room door stood slightly ajar.

'That you, Poll?' Miranda called out.

Joyce was asleep on the Knole sofa, her back and head propped on a pile of cushions. Her jaw had dropped open and she snored lightly. She had grown very frail lately, and increasingly forgetful. Sometimes in a lucid moment she announced that she must get back to her own place because she had had quite enough of being in Miranda's house, draughty old pile. But she soon forgot the intention. Nobody had any real expectation that she would be able to live on her own again.

Miranda was reading, curled up in an armchair. She looked smaller, a quieter and more watchful version of the bright spirit she had been. The room was scented with cold wood smoke and white lilac in a huge vase that stood on a side table.

I have been attending very thoroughly to my own grief, Polly realized, but I haven't given much consideration to Miranda, who loved him too.

Affection and sympathy for her friend touched her heart.

'Have you been working all this time?' Miranda wondered.

Polly nodded. She went over to the grand piano in the corner of the room and lifted the lid. She played a few notes, very softly. They keys were yellow and split and the instrument was badly out of tune.

When she looked up she saw how intently Miranda was watching her.

'I love this place,' Polly said.

Miranda's face softened, and then broke into a brilliant smile.

'Do you? Do you really?' She was deeply pleased by this.

'I do. Shall we go outside? It's such a beautiful afternoon.'

The two women went through the kitchen and out into the courtyard. Grass and weed seedlings were sprouting between the cobbles and Miranda stooped to uproot a few tufts. The warmth of spring sunshine lingered between the old walls.

Amos had recently moved out of the cottage.

Almost as soon as he had finally decided not to go ahead with his building project at Mead, a house in Meddlett had come up for sale. It was a compact Georgian house that stood

428

back from the green, separated from the road by a low wall but with a good view of the duck pond and the willows and the front of the Griffin, and he had bought it and moved in within what seemed a matter of days. Amos had always been decisive, and in practical matters whatever he chose to focus on usually came about. He was now busy with the campaign for the Meddlett Princess, and the beginnings of involvement in village politics.

'He'll be on the parish council next,' Miranda joked as she and Polly passed the door of the cottage. Katherine's pots of herbs were putting out tiny furls of leaf.

'He told me he was thinking of standing.'

'Hah.'

The prospect seemed less ludicrous than it would have done six months ago. They agreed that Amos would probably make quite a useful councillor.

'When's Katherine coming?' Polly asked.

'Tomorrow. She's collecting the last of her things.'

Amos had envisaged that his withdrawal from the cottage would give Katherine the freedom to come and go comfortably at Mead, but it was turning out that she came up less and less often.

'I have to keep up with my job, now I'm a single woman,' she told Polly and Miranda, only half-joking. She had begun looking for a flat of her own to buy in London, somewhere near where her boys lived. Most of the rest of her time was spent with Chris, in his house near the city ring road.

Colin said that he might take over the cottage from Amos and Katherine, if Miranda would let him.

They passed out of the gate, damp long grass swishing around their ankles as they followed the line of the building. Polly studied the flint walls, bowed in places, the soft orangey-red brick, the chimney stacks outlined against the fading sky. A line of crows headed for the trees. What she had told Miranda was true. With Gwen Meadowe and her predecessors for company as well as Miranda herself, Mead felt like a home of

Polly's own, a home for the person she would have to become in the next passage of her life.

The front of the house glowed with the last of the sun. A bench stood against one wall and they sat down together.

'You and me, Colin, and Joyce,' Polly counted. 'It's not what you planned for your new Mead, is it?'

Miranda's head tipped back. She studied the old guttering, and the protruding mess of what looked like a bird's nest lodged in the hopper.

'Plans have a way of turning out to be useless,' she said at last. 'But I still believe in planning.'

They sat contemplating the view for another minute before Miranda asked, 'You are going to stay, aren't you? I know the way a death can affect the way you feel about a place. When Jake died, I found I loved Mead even more. I can see him everywhere I look. But maybe that's painful for you in the barn. Selwyn worked too hard at it, didn't he? There was so much of him, an excess of the person. It overflowed into what he did. Maybe you're lonely . . .' Her voice trailed off and she looked away, across the flowerbed towards the curve of the drive.

Polly told her firmly, 'I'm not so very lonely. I'm not going to leave, either. The barn is my home.'

Miranda was still watching the bird's nest. In a light voice she said, 'That's good.'

'Did you know your mother-in-law, Mirry?'

'Gwen? Not well. She was already very old and in a nursing home when I married Jake.'

'I've found her wartime diary. It's about her garden here, and growing vegetables. It's not full of personal detail, but she shines out of it. I'm thinking of using her as the starting point for the book, if that's all right with you?'

As always when she talked about her work, Polly was aware of the gulf between the flatness of the described outline and the excitement within her. The anticipation of writing was like keeping a big secret, one that it would be damaging to spill however much she might be tempted.

430

Miranda was a voracious reader but she had never written a book. She would have no idea of this creative tension.

'Of course it's all right with me. It sounds interesting. Are you ready to start?'

The air was rapidly cooling as the sun set. Polly wrapped her multi-coloured Christmas cardigan more tightly around her.

'I'll write two or three chapters and an outline. Then I'll try it on my agent. I've got to make some money, I can't do it just for love. There's Leo to think of, apart from anything else.'

Polly had come alive again. She was leaning forward with anticipation, her eyes wide open, looking into next week.

It wasn't just the book project that had revivified her.

She regularly saw Nic and Leo, and the baby was often left in her care at the barn while Nic did a massage or pedicure. Her own three children were recovering from the shock of losing their father. Alph's boyfriend, the South American doctor, had at last been introduced and was turning out to be everything Alph needed. Omie was illustrating a new series of children's books about a cat contortionist. Even Ben was beginning to accept that he and Nic were not destined to live happily ever after. He showed a decent level of interest in his baby son, but paternity wasn't the full three-act drama he might have been expected to make of it.

Polly put one arm around Miranda's thin shoulders.

'I am so glad to be here. Thank you for sharing Mead with me.'

'I am glad too,' Miranda answered.

It was growing cold now.

'I should go in and see if Joyce is all right,' Miranda said.

They went in through the front door. The radio was playing, extremely loudly, the only way Joyce could listen to it.

'Is it really all right to borrow your car again?' Nic wondered.

Polly took the baby from her. She put her mouth to the tiny ear and whispered baby-nonsense into it.

Nic sighed, 'He was a demon last night. He was awake from ten past two until half past four.'

431

'Maybe he was hungry?'

'He can't *always* be hungry. But in case he is while I'm away, there's a full bottle in the bag. I should go, Polly. It's a new client, and she sounds minted. I could do with a recommendation to some of her smart friends, those ones with houses up on the coast that are worth half a million.'

Polly handed her the car keys. 'Go on, then. Don't be late for Madam Minted.'

Nic returned a weary smile. She hadn't anticipated quite how hard it was going to be, looking after Leo on her own whilst trying to please her first couple of clients and sell herself to new ones, even though Polly was so good to her and Leo was easy compared with some of the babies she saw at the clinic. Kieran kept offering to help out too, but she was afraid that if she just let him, all the props of survival determination that held her up would collapse and she and Leo would be submerged in dependency. She was prickly towards Kieran as a result, but he refused to be discouraged and so she was coming to count on his constancy anyway.

There was no way out of this, she had to acknowledge.

'Why do you need a way out of everything?' Jessie frowned. 'It's not difficult, is it? He fancies you, inexplicably you fancy him back. You're both free. Straightforward, or what?'

That might have been the way, before Leo, but not now. She had to be careful for both of them. Of course Jessie had nothing to do but put in her shifts at the Griffin, and the rest of her time she could spend sleeping or smoking dope or pretending to talk about philosophy with Amos Knight.

Kierkegaard, that was what she was reading now.

Nic sighed for the lazy days of pre-motherhood, gone for ever, and then worked up a warm but professional smile as she drove to the client's house.

Polly took Leo out for a walk in the turbo pram. Her hip didn't hurt too much today.

When she leaned over to look at him she saw that his dark blue eyes were wide open, fixed on the branches and clouds as they slid overhead. It was hard to separate now from then, a generation ago, when she had walked the twins down country lanes in Somerset. It felt as though the only difference apart from her ageing bones was Leo's tranquil nature, whereas the twins had operated a 24-hour rota. If one was asleep, she remembered, the other was awake and screaming.

How Selwyn would have loved this new baby, once he had held him in his arms.

Damn *you*, Selwyn. Why did you have to go, and miss everything?

She was walking back down the driveway to Mead when she heard a car. She stood aside as Katherine lowered the window and beamed out.

'Hello, Granny,' she called.

'Come over to the barn right now,' Polly ordered.

Katherine and Miranda passed the baby between them. He reclined on one lap and then the other, enjoying the attention.

Katherine said, 'It must be wonderful being that age, don't you think? All you ever see is huge melon smiles, looming over you.'

'I'm not so sure Nic's always smiling,' Polly said. 'I'd forgotten all about how relentless living with a baby can be.'

Katherine couldn't help glancing at Miranda, and Miranda returned her look.

'Yes, I do wish I'd had a child,' she said with simple candour. 'Do you think all childless women imagine their might-have-been children, waiting in the wings somewhere but never hearing the cue to take the stage? I'd give anything for a grandchild now, to see him growing up at Mead the way Jake did. But all the same, I'm trying not to be jealous of you two. You'll have to share yours. I should think there will be plenty to go around, in a few years' time.'

It was the only time either of them had ever heard her say even this much about having no children of her own. Miranda leaned down and pressed her nose against the baby's boneless button one, and the short wings of grey hair swung forward to hide her face. There was less hectic rush and sparkle to Miranda these days, and she took more time over what she said.

'There won't always only be just *you* to admire, Leo Selwyn,' she whispered.

Polly made tea, and then they agreed that it wasn't too early for a glass of wine. She warmed the bottle of milk for Leo, and Katherine fed him. He fell asleep after taking half of it, a bubble of milky drool swelling between his lips.

The new angle of the sinking sun threw different shafts of light across the room, probing the corners where floorboards didn't meet the wall and the angles under the stairs where left-over planks were propped against bare plaster, already gathering their own layers of dust. The barn was just as Selwyn had left it, and whilst it had looked good enough in the candlelight at Christmas, the citric glare of a spring day showed up all the rough edges. Polly had made no changes since the day he died. Some day she might, she told herself, but in the meantime she was settling into the fabric of the place just as it stood, laying down her own tender nacre in the abrasive new shell. In a way, Polly thought, she and Miranda might be domestic opposites but they both lived like molluscs within the pre-existing confines of their houses.

Katherine felt the difference between herself and her two friends particularly sharply today.

Coming back here to Mead was a reminder of how a predictable life could change in a mere six months. The shell she had occupied back in September had smashed, leaving her exposed to the tides. She was in no doubt that she was in love with Chris Carr, but loving a divorced man with two daughters was a series of questions, not an answer. The days and nights that they spent together made them both happy, but these were hours that had to be set aside from two lives based in two different cities, revolving around two different jobs, and partly forfeit to four children and two ex-spouses. Every week was different. Every day, even. She was surprised to realize what a creature of routine she had once been, and how much store she had set upon order in her life with Amos. Nowadays even the simplest processes, like getting dressed or cooking a proper dinner, had become fraught with difficulty. The shoes or belt vital to complete an outfit were always in London or still at Mead, and however hard she looked in the cupboards of whichever kitchen she was in, there were no vanilla pods or fenugreek.

'This is how life is,' Chris murmured to her.

They stood in each other's arms, and he rocked her on the hearth rug beside their joined reflection in the mantelpiece mirror. He was a sanguine, optimistic, organized person compared with her. Sometimes she felt frightened by her own rampaging disorder. Who *was* she, nowadays, who had once been Katherine Knight?

She had tried to make friends with his two girls. She was surprised by her own surprise at discovering that they had pierced ears, and wore pale pink hooded tops and big white trainers with grey marl leggings. They hadn't responded to her friendly overtures with any enthusiasm, and she knew within the first half-hour that she had struck the wrong note with them.

'I'm afraid they haven't taken to me,' she said to Chris.

'Yes, they have. You've got to remember they're loyal to their mum, and as far as they're concerned you take up my attention, which should rightfully be theirs.'

'I understand that. But they don't like me.'

'Yes, they do. They think you're a bit posh, that's all.'

She stared at him, swallowing a hiccup of dismay. 'Is that better than too old for you, do you think?'

Chris laughed. 'Neither objection, if that's what they are, matters in the least. They'll come around. We have the right to our own lives, Kath.'

He was the only person who had ever called her Kath. The only one she had ever allowed to do so.

* * *

435

Polly poured each of them a second glass of wine. The baby obligingly slept.

'What about you, K?' she prompted.

Katherine looked from one to the other. Polly managed her loss, talking about it when she could and keeping quiet when she couldn't bear it. Katherine loved her and admired her bravery. But Miranda, she thought, had almost the harder time.

Compared with her friends' lives, her own happiness seemed intemperate, too vivid and insistent, as if at any minute it might explode inside her.

With precise, quiet articulation she told them, 'I am fine. Everything has changed so much, but I wouldn't change it back again.'

They waited, looking at her.

'I love him,' she explained. 'I don't know how it has happened, but I do.'

'Lucky you,' Polly said, in her brisk way.

The pressure of their different circumstances seemed to ease as they all laughed.

'Here we are then, the three of us,' Miranda said. 'After all these years.'

Colin helped Katherine to take down a pair of English water-colours that had hung in the small hallway of the cottage. Amos had given them to her one Christmas. They sealed them in bubble-wrap and placed them beside the front door with a suitcase and a couple of packing cases. They worked quickly, without saying much, and were relieved when the job was done and Katherine's belongings had been trans-ferred to her car.

Stripped back to its holiday-rental bareness the place echoed as they closed doors and clicked off lights. Katherine was reminded of the fenland cottage where she had stayed with Chris that first time, and without warning found herself blushing. Colin glanced at her with amused speculation. He had woken up again to sexual nuance, Carlos in New York had done that much for him, and he saw that Katherine's sheen suited her.

There was no such thing as too old, he acknowledged. Only too sad, or too afraid, or too lacking in self-belief.

'Are you happy, K?' he asked.

'I believe I am,' she said. 'But I feel guilty about it.'

'Don't,' he advised.

They were in the kitchen, confronted by the blameless pine cupboard fronts and furniture.

'Are you really going to live here?' she asked him.

'I know what you're thinking. It's not really gay enough, is it?'

Colin had thought hard about it. If Miranda would sell the place to him, he would have an investment at Mead that would draw him back and help to keep him anchored here. It wasn't to do with money or property, but with physical commitment to a place and people.

'I can change things, of course. Rip out the pine, bring in the granite and my Basquiat.'

The places he had lived in since breaking up with Stephen had been just the sort of settings you would expect for a gay, middle-aged set designer. He saw them now as superficially glamorous but fundamentally un-homely, and he was not at all sentimental about leaving the current one. Nothing could be more different than this little house attached to Mead in its landscape of fields and copses, with Polly living opposite and Miranda next door. He had asked himself if this was a final camouflage act, another way of hiding rather than of coming home at last, but he knew that he could conceal himself from just about anyone anywhere in the world, except from his oldest friends, who were right here.

'We'll see, won't we?' he said.

Katherine glanced at her watch. 'I've got to go, Col.'

Chris was waiting for her.

Colin walked with her to her car. She didn't look back.

'Have you seen Amos's new place?' he asked, putting the last of her boxes into the boot.

'I have.'

'What did you think?'

Katherine got in and started the engine.

'Needs a woman's touch,' she said.

Amos was too busy even to find a builder to improve the Georgian house, let alone worry about soft furnishings. There was a series of meetings to negotiate, with a variety of people and organizations ranging from the parish council, English Heritage and the county planning authorities, to the vicar of Meddlett and his own wife's lover. But Amos was single-minded. He reported back after each session to Vin Clarke and the customers in the Griffin, Roy's wife whose name was Patricia, Mrs Spragg in the shop, and anyone else in Meddlett who was interested or had an issue, which turned out to be most of the population.

At a public meeting held in the sports pavilion he said, 'We're not talking the curse of crop failure or foot and mouth if we don't bring the princess home, of course not, let's not be super-stitious, although I have heard such things mentioned. It's a matter of doing the proper thing by her, according her the respect her position and her history deserves.

'It was my excavations that disturbed her rest, and although we as a community as well as the archaeologists and pre-historians have all benefited from a great discovery, I take responsibility for that original disturbance. That's why I'm standing here in front of you this evening.'

There were various murmurings in response to this, not all approving, but Amos took disapprobation in his stride.

'This is an occasion for Meddlett, present-day modern Meddlett, to show the county and indeed the whole country what we can do. We should make it a solemn day but a splendid one.'

'What does that mean, exactly?' someone called.

'Fundraising, mate, as per,' someone else shouted back.

'I believe we shall get some funds for the purpose from the

county archaeologist's department, and I will also be supporting the event personally,' Amos purred.

'You can afford it, can't you?' said the same heckler.

The meeting broke up on a positive note, however. To the general approval of the village, there would be a Meddlett Princess Day in June.

Amos relayed this news to Jessie when she called at his house at the end of her shift. Jessie seemed to prefer to spend her time at his place. Not that he objected to that, particularly. Gulliver busily sniffed around the margins of the kitchen.

'This is my dream house, you know. I'd never even been inside before you bought it,' she sighed. 'Hey, Gully. Oh God. Sorry, Amos.'

'Use this.' He threw her the kitchen roll. 'What's wrong with your own home these days?'

'Bloody Kieran and Nic, sitting on the sofa with cups of cocoa, watching romantic DVDs and having a bit of a kiss when I'm not looking, that's what. It's like living in an old folks' home,' she complained.

'That's not my impression of how old people's homes are run.'

'So it's not like that up at Mead, eh?' Her smile could take on a flicker of gleeful cruelty.

'Not at all.' He laughed back, in spite of himself. Jessie was always good company. He went on telling her about Princess Day, and the more elaborate plans that he was beginning to formulate.

'One thing I'd like to know,' he concluded.

'What's that?'

'Who was it who stole the treasure?'

Her eyes widened. 'Why do you think *I'd* have any idea?'

'Damon?' Amos suggested.

His own theory was that Jessie had told Damon about the find, and Damon had then passed on the information, for a consideration. But he had no way of knowing this for certain and Jessie was much too smart to let on. He hoped she wouldn't, in any case.

439

What Amos did know, because the police had told him so, was that a likely set of suspects had been identified, but by the time their premises were raided, just before Christmas, there was no sign of any of the stolen goods. None of the recovered items had borne any trace of a fingerprint, or any evidence that would link the suspects to them. Amos was also fully aware that unless a new lead should present itself, police time was too valuable to be expended on a hunt for thieves of goods that had all been found, or even for the attackers of a guard who was now fully recovered and back at work.

'Why Damon?' Jessie wondered, glancing up from a prolonged examination of her Golden Virginia packet.

'All right, let me put this another way. If I were able to persuade the authorities to let us put the treasure on temporary public display at Mead, what's the likelihood of persons you may or may not know mounting an all-guns-blazing assault on the treasure for a second time, and whacking another innocent security officer over the head in the process?'

She thought about this. 'How would I know? But my guess would be, people around here are such losers, if there was, like, proper security, they wouldn't be able to do anything much, would they?'

'I see. Good,' Amos answered.

He would go ahead and make the arrangements.

The white surplices of the clergy fluttered in the June breeze, a string quartet stopped playing and the expectant crowd fell silent. The only sound was the calling of wood pigeons in the tall trees and the creak of canvas from the marquees.

Miranda watched a small procession making its way from a line of vehicles drawn up at the margin of the field, where the wood opened up to the broad plateau and its view of pastureland. The bishop's chaplain bearing the crozier led the column, followed by the bishop himself in cope and mitre, the vicar of Meddlett, and then Kieran and Christopher Carr, both dressed in dark suits and ties. The archaeologists each carried a casket woven from willow branches. Behind them walked more county officials, one wearing a mayoral chain, and bringing up the rear of the procession came the Meddlett Brownie pack, with the tallest two children carrying the poles of the St Andrew's church banner. A local television camera crew, a radio team, a group of press photographers and the accompanying journalists moved alongside the official procession, jockeying for the best angle. Behind Miranda the crowd of onlookers pressed forwards to the white ropes that marked off a square of ground and a deep trench. Joyce's wheelchair was positioned at centre front, and Miranda moved her slightly so she maintained the best view.

Patches of shadow swept over the fields and then sunlight blazed again. Cabbage white butterflies wove exuberant patterns over campion and oxeye daisies in the long grass.

The Meddlett church choir was drawn up inside the rope square. When the bishop and his retinue reached the edge of the trench, the choir mistress lifted her hand and the string quartet's violinist drew out the note.

Miranda smiled to think that the form this brief service was to take had caused more debate than any other aspect of Amos's glorious Princess Day celebration plans. It was a pre-Christian interment, one faction declared. The opposition insisted that there must be a religious aspect to it, the bishop could hardly be asked to preside over a pagan ceremony.

In the end, the bishop himself had settled the matter. He had a keen interest in archaeology. There would be a single hymn, a short and wholly ecumenical prayer, and then the committal.

The choir sang, *And did those feet in ancient time, walk upon England's mountains green.* Miranda heard her mother's quavering soprano as the crowd joined in, more than three hundred people raising their voices to the summer air. Looking along the line she saw Amos singing lustily, flanked by his sons. Nic carried her baby in a sling against her chest and sang, with her eyes on Kieran. Alpha Davies slipped her hand with the new diamond on the third finger through Jaime's arm, Jessie somehow sang without moving her lips, Polly and Katherine stood shoulder to shoulder singing, and the hymn rolled out over the decorated marquee and faded away into the grass-scented breeze.

Miranda found that there were tears in her eyes.

Till we have built Jerusalem, in England's green and pleasant land.

She thought that she had never loved Mead as much as she did today.

The crowd shuffled, settling into silence once again. Overhead, a plane stitched a white thread against the blue sky.

'Dear friends,' the bishop began.

After the prayer, Kieran and Chris fitted broad green ribbons into slots in the two wicker caskets. The musicians played a piece of Elgar as the ancient bones of the princess and her cup-bearer were lowered back into the ground. The smallest Brownie came forward and dropped two white roses after them.

The final role was Miranda's own. She stepped forward to the very edge of the pit, dug a spade into the mound of earth, and shovelled it on top of the bones. At once, as if in collective relief, the crowd gave a great sigh. Someone at the back clapped their hands and the applause was instantly taken up, dying away only as the gravedigger from Meddlett churchyard took the spade from Miranda, and soil thudded down to cover the remains once more.

'We can all rest easy now she has come home,' Roy's wife sobbed to Amos. Amos patted her arm, already regretting his own insistence that there would be no alcohol served at the celebration party. Miranda caught his eye, and winked at him.

The media crews were heading for the smaller marquee outside which stood two policemen and several uniformed private security guards. The people streamed away from the burial place, hesitating between the choice of tea or a close-up of the actual Mead treasure.

With Ben and Toby's help, Miranda and Polly half-steered and half-carried Joyce's wheelchair towards the marquee.

'Where are we going? What's happening now?' Joyce cried. Miranda leaned down to her.

'We're going to look at the princess's treasure, brought back to Mead in all its glory.'

Only Colin loitered behind, one hand in his pocket, apparently watching the gravedigger.

When he was sure that no one was looking, he took a few quick steps to the edge of the half-filled grave. Then he withdrew his hand and let fall a heart-shaped piece of quartz into the loose earth. A moment later it was covered. Colin bent his head in what might have been a salute, then walked away between the daisies and the spires of sorrel.

Joyce's wheelchair was borne into the tent in the wake of the bishop's party. Cameras flashed and the news crews pressed after them.

'I feel like royalty myself,' Joyce said.

Miranda wheeled her into place, then stood at her side. Glancing down she saw her mother's tiny, veined hand resting on the arm of the chair. She reached down and clasped it.

The entire Mead treasure was laid out on a series of stepped display stands draped in black velvet. There were no ropes or protective panels. The glory of the princess's regalia lay there, close enough to touch, as if it belonged inside this tent in a field of dappled summer sunshine. The pure, soft gold of the torc and the cup was sumptuous. The huge shield, the hair and cloak adornments, bracelets and wrist protectors and everything down to the last silver coin from the hoard had been cleaned. The precious metal glittered in the camera flashes. This simplicity and immediacy of access had been Amos's idea, and he had fought hard for it. He had brought in the guards for protection, but had instructed them to stay in the background as far as possible.

Amos himself looked on in modest self-effacement as the VIPs were given a tour by the director of the county museum.

'Magnificent,' pronounced the bishop, peering over his spectacles. 'Quite magnificent.'

Joyce's white head nodded.

'I'm glad I lasted long enough to see this. I did better than Jake and Selwyn, didn't I?'

'You did,' Miranda agreed, still holding her hand. Jake was there, she was sure of it, but Selwyn's absence was an ache in her bones. She missed him deeply at this moment, and she knew she would miss him in the same way tomorrow and every day to come. But, she told herself, you're not the only one and you are not alone. Polly was here, and Colin, and Katherine and Amos, and it was the same for all of them. Selwyn would not come back, but they had all shared him.

Chris was in the bishop's retinue. Katherine waited for him near the marquee entrance with the two girls.

'You must be feeling proud of your dad,' she said to them.

Daisy nodded unwillingly. Gemma only jerked her chin.

'It's just a load of old stuff, isn't it?' she sighed. She dismissed her father's passion and expertise without a flicker of mercy.

Looking beyond her shoulder, at a loss for what to say, Katherine caught sight of Jessie. She was standing alone in the middle of the field, smoking and staring into the distance, the picture of detachment. Gulliver squatted next to her bare ankles. It was the age, she understood. The conformity of youth reassured her but the depth of their ennui also struck her as funny, set as it was against the day's reverencing of the joint gods of history and treasure. Had she ever been as mulish herself? She didn't think so, unfortunately. She would probably have been a better person now if she had been. All she could remember was her eagerness to please.

Katherine laughed. Chris's girls only stared at her.

'It *is* just a load of old stuff,' Katherine agreed.

The VIP party emerged, blinking and looking suitably impressed. They were steered towards the tea marquee, and the queue of ordinary visitors that was by now snaking a long way across the grass began to move into the display area. The

Carr girls backed away and Katherine found Amos at her shoulder.

'Well done,' she said, composing herself.

He eyed her. 'Do you mean that?'

'Yes,' she told him. She was proud of what he had done here, where the idea of their house had once dominated.

It was a beautiful day. There was stately music playing, and the smell of grass in the air. Crowds of happy people were eating strawberries and chocolate cake and cucumber sandwiches, talking amongst themselves about prehistoric gold as they strolled to the edge of the plateau to look at the view that the princess of the Iceni would also have known.

Ben Davies, hatless, passed in front of them, carrying Leo in his arms. 'My son,' he explained to Gemma Carr. Not far away Alpha in her white dress already looked bridal, swinging her hand in Jaime's as Jaime chatted to Colin. Nic and Kieran sat down on the grass, beside Leo's empty pram. Nic's narrowed eyes followed Ben's circuit with the baby.

'Thank you,' Amos said.

He began telling her about his intentions to get funding for a permanent display space in Meddlett itself, so the collection could be brought back and put on show every summer. He wanted to make sure it would stay in the county for the remainder of the year. He mentioned plans for a study centre, maybe even a recreation of the tribal village using contemporary materials and techniques, with an on-site classroom for the use of local schools.

Gazing through the crowds to the roped-off square of the filled grave, Katherine heard his voice rather than what he said. In time the turf would be replaced, and all the signs of the excavations for their foundations and of the burial site itself would be obliterated. The place would be as it had always been.

She saw the image of their house that had never materialized, trembling like a mirage over the grass, and then as silently as a soap bubble it burst and was gone.

She put her hand on Amos's arm.

He seemed to stiffen, as if only now remembering their circumstances. 'I'd better get over to the tea tent and make sure everyone's being looked after.'

'Of course,' she said gently.

Sam came across in his father's wake.

'You OK, Mum?'

'Fine.'

'Dad's becoming quite the local figure, isn't he?'

'He'll do local figure just as well as he's always done everything.'

'Yes. Shall I get you some strawberries?'

'I'll come with you,' she said.

In the evening of Princess Day, there was a village barbecue. It was held on the village green and there were to be absolutely no fireworks, by order of the parish council.

Once Amos had overseen the safe removal of the treasure by security van, he went to the party with Colin. The twins and their boyfriends and Ben and the Knight boys went with them. Nic had gone home with the baby, Jessie was working at the Griffin, and the three women said they had had enough of Meddlett celebrations for one day.

In the summer twilight, it was a benign event. People sat on folding chairs and ate barbecued food, and as darkness crept up, lanterns hanging from the branches around the duck pond were reflected in the rippling water. There was none of the threatening crackle and smoke of November the Fifth. The lanes leading away from the green were quiet, the gardens and hedges starred with the ghostly bloom of white roses.

The young people had disappeared into the hubbub inside the pub. Colin and Amos sat outside on a hay bale, drinking beer. Bats swooped overhead, missing the tangle of telephone lines. Colin was thinking of the evening back in September, when he had dawdled in the bar in order to put off the moment of arrival at Mead, and Jessie had spilled a drink into his shoes.

Amos interrupted his thoughts. 'You missed the Fifth, didn't you?'

'Yes I did.'

Selwyn's face had been blackened with cork, and he and Amos had run down the lane opposite, firecrackers exploding around their ankles. Over at the far side of the pond the Meddlett Princess people had waved their placards, and at the end of the evening Jessie had told Amos stories about strangers he had in the intervening months come to know. And then Selwyn had loomed out of the darkness, his head tragically bandaged.

Amos swallowed the last of his pint. 'Christ, I miss him,' he said.

'We all do,' Colin acknowledged. 'But you and he were such necessary adversaries, as well as friends.'

'We were. Necessary adversaries, that's just what we were. Life is pallid without him, isn't it?'

They sat for a while longer. As the rush in the pub quietened down and people began to leave the green, a number of them saying goodnight to Amos as they passed, Jessie and Geza came out. Jessie bumped down on the hay bale, a mass of boredom and irritation, while Geza hovered in the shadow behind her.

'I can't stand that pub,' she snarled, to no one in particular.

'Get out of there, then,' Amos advised.

'I am doing my best, aren't I?' she snapped back.

Colin looked up, and Jessie remembered her companion.

'Oh. You two don't know each other yet do you? Colin, Geza. Geza, Colin.'

They shook hands.

'Good evening Colin,' Geza said, very formally. 'I am pleased to meet you.'

The day had been exhausting for Joyce. Miranda helped her out of the wheelchair and up the stairs, negotiating a single tread at a time. Before long, she thought, if she were not to become a prisoner, her mother would need a ground-floor

447

bedroom, and a bathroom would probably have to be put in next to it. She ran through in her mind the possible ways of doing the work, and the likely cost of it. Once they reached the bedroom she lowered her mother into a chair and knelt down to unroll Joyce's stockings. Her shinbones stuck out as sharply as blades, the fragile skin blotched with yellow and purple bruises.

Joyce looked anxiously around her room. She seemed surprised to find herself there.

'Where is my . . . where is my . . .' she groped despairingly for the word.

'Here it is,' Miranda said. She put Joyce's fleecy dressing gown over her shoulders. 'Are you warm enough?' The windows stood open on the purple night and a pale moth spiralled towards the bedside light.

'All those people. Who were they, do you think? Such a crowd, and I don't know that that music was at all suitable for a funeral, you know.'

'It wasn't quite a funeral. A homecoming, I heard one of the campaigners calling it. I'm glad it all happened. Amos did very well, I think.'

'A homecoming? Is that what they're calling death these days?'

Joyce had forgotten what the occasion had been; she seemed to wander more and more often in the confused thickets of her own mind. Sometimes she came out into a clearing, then got lost again in a place where words and entire days and people she had known slipped out of reach in the untracked jungle.

Miranda turned back the covers and helped her into bed. Joyce lay back against the pillows, a sigh of relief puffing out of her.

'Here's your book.' Miranda put the large print volume within reach. 'Goodnight, Mum.' She bent down to kiss her.

'Night night,' Joyce said, like a child. And then, as Miranda reached the door, 'Barbara? Where's my book?'

It was still warm in the courtyard. The heaviness of the air suggested that there might be thunder coming. Miranda found Polly and Katherine sitting out at a rickety metal table under the scented tendrils of a climbing jasmine. She took the chair that was waiting for her and sat down.

Then, in the fragrant dusk, she noticed Polly's face. She was glowing with half-contained excitement.

'I've got some news,' Polly announced.

Miranda thought it must be Alpha and another grandchild on the way. But when she asked if that was it Polly shook her head, pretending to be annoyed.

'Please. Do you mind? Grandchildren are not my sole interest, you know.'

Miranda and Katherine both smiled back at her.

'Come on then. Don't keep us in suspense,' Miranda ordered.

Polly's face settled into its noodle-lady lines again.

'I wanted to tell you two first, before anyone else. I had a call this morning from my agent. We've had an offer from a publisher. They're going to take my book.'

Delighted, Miranda clapped her hands. 'But that's wonderful, wonderful news. Well done, Poll.'

Polly leaned across the table, all her features slanting in upward lines.

'Wait until I tell you what the deal is.'

She named the sum that was offered, drawing out the syllables in proud emphasis.

'I can live on that for three whole years. Longer, even, if I'm careful. So I shall have all that time to research and write. I can go right back into the history of Mead.' She broke off, and her gaze travelled over the line of darkened windows, the old brickwork and the chimneys outlined against the fading sky. Miranda's eyes followed hers, and the history of the house seemed to march past them both, drawing them together and folding them in its long progression.

'I was so sure it would make a good book, and now I know it will,' Polly breathed.

Katherine leaned forward and took both their hands.

'Do you think she's asleep again?' she asked.

Polly lifted her head. 'Joyce?'

'I meant the princess.'

'Yes, I think she is,' Miranda said.

In the rustling quiet they each pursued the notion of peace having returned, settling around Mead and the fields like a long summer.

The reality of what such peace might bring was different for each of them, and they were wary of talking about it. Instead, they let their linked hands make a circle of three. Without words they acknowledged memory and superstition and the necessity of connection.

Beneath their wrists the table was dusty with pollen.

Miranda

I can't any longer count on sleep. Some nights it withholds its blessing altogether, on others it moodily withdraws after two or three hours. I've learned not to be angry about insomnia. What would be the point?

This morning, the day after Princess Day, I woke up and lay in the darkness. I was thinking about Selwyn, as I often do in these empty small hours, remembering how we were when we were young. I spend so much time with Joyce, and I know how her memories now escape from her; I keep mine alive deliberately, exercising the muscle while it is still mine to command. I bring to mind faces and dates and sequences of events, clothes and names and smells and views. This time I had been recalling the initial full cast rehearsal for *The Tempest*, held in a stuffy gym hall where we perched on a circle of stacking chairs, our copies of the play held on our knees. The day I saw Selwyn for the first time.

There were dust motes floating in the shafts of sunshine coming in through high windows, the lines of a badminton court painted on the floor, a choir rehearsing in a room nearby.

I was pleased with my role as leading lady, and not much interested in the actors taking minor parts. We read through most of the play, and afterwards went to the pub. Selwyn was wearing a tight orange jumper, maroon trousers with exaggerated flares.

He told me casually that I had read well but a little too fast, and I responded with some prickly observation about the relative importance of Miranda and Trinculo and what that indicated about our talents as actors. He laughed at me, and in the end I joined in. I certainly deserved his mockery.

In those days, important discoveries were made quickly and easily. By the end of that same evening I was taking it for granted that from now on Selwyn Davies and I would be significant to each other.

At nineteen, the discovery of love, friendships, any new experiences, seemed not just possible, but distinctly glorious. Forty years later life feels more like a ramshackle piece of machinery, pulling you along with it, tangling you in the spokes of its dilemmas, merriment and agony spilling out as it trundles towards the horizon.

It takes persistence to convince yourself that anything is or ever could be touched with glory.

'But you are persistent, Barb,' I hear Selwyn say in answer to that.

I don't know what made me suddenly get out of bed and go to the window. At first I could only see the pearly pre-dawn light just washing the horizon, and the heavy darkness of clouds overhead. It must have rained torrents in the night, because the cobbles were glimmering with water and moisture seemed to flood the air. Maybe it was the rain or even thunder that had woken me. Then a movement of something white caught my eye. I leaned forward over the broad windowsill, and saw that the pale flutter was Polly's nightdress showing under a long cardigan. She was standing a little way from the open door of the barn, her feet in wellingtons, holding up a box in front of her.

My first thought was that she must be sleepwalking. I pulled on my own dressing gown and ran down the stairs. By the time I had struggled into boots and dashed outside, she had gone. I ran to the door of the barn and looked inside, wanting to call her name, but some folk memory was warning me that sleepwalkers shouldn't be abruptly woken. Then I saw her again. She was on the other side of the yard gate, looking back at me. The light was getting stronger. Her eyes were open, and I realized she was fully conscious.

'Polly?'

'Come on,' she called to me. When I reached her side I saw that she was smiling, and the breadth of that smile coupled with sleep-tangled hair and assortment of day and night clothes made me afraid for her.

'What are you doing?'

She held up the plain carton.

'Come with me. Let's do it together.'

I realized then what was in the box. It was the ashes.

'I don't want any more ceremony and sorrow and the children's tears. Let's you and me go and do it.'

'Now? Are you sure?' I asked, ridiculously.

Polly was already running, swishing through the grass, wobbling in her loose wellies. I started after her.

We plunged into the wood. Drops of water rained down on us, wet grass soaked our clothes, mud slithered underfoot. It seemed hot, almost steamy, and the jungly depth of the forest scent, loam and soaking vegetation and earth, came close to choking me. A minute later we burst out into the open. The eastern sky was streaked with broad ribbons of pink and lemon cloud.

The two marquees were standing empty, flat shapes in the dim light. Panting for breath, Polly tore the lid off the box and threw it aside. She dipped her fist and came up with a handful of ashes. Then she spun in an exuberant circle, and flung an arc of dust against the sky.

'Here,' she said to me.

I copied her, plunging my hand into the box, and another handful of Selwyn's ashes sprayed into the air, pattering over the grass and wildflowers.

The wildness of the moment took hold of us both. We began

running fast, and then faster, bumping into each other as we took it in turns to dig into the contents of the box and broadcast them, tripping over hummocks and trampling the daisies, jumping over clumps of dock, clumsy on our feet, our wet clothes flapping around our knees and our breath ragged with exertion. The zigzag path that Polly took brought us finally to the white ropes that still enclosed the bare earth of the burial site.

Her hand dropped to her side. With the rope at her ankles she turned the now-empty box upside down, and then let it fall. She bent over and rested her hands on her knees, sucking in air. The sky was lightening with every minute.

I was getting my own breath back. A little way from where I stood I could see a faint rime of dust clouding some leaves. With the first stirring of a breeze, it would disappear.

Selwyn was gone, but yet he seemed close to us. He was here after all, near at hand, just as Jake had been at the burial yesterday.

Polly knelt and touched a corner of the ground inside the ropes.

When she stood up again she turned in the opposite direction, with her back to me, and bent her head.

Even so I looked away. Tears burned my eyes.

With a sudden flash of green and gold, the sun came up. The grass was instantly gilded, and the trees, and the grey canvas of the deserted marquees turned to rosy pink.

Polly touched my arm. She looked chilled, but calm again.

'Thank you for doing this with me,' she whispered.

'Let's go home,' I said.

She picked up the empty box, and we searched the grass for the discarded lid. Afterwards we walked back through the copse, to the gate in the yard wall. I opened it for her and she passed through. We were both shivering, our sweaty and rain-damp clothes sticking to cold skin.

'I am going to bed now,' Polly said simply.

We had both been lying awake. Perhaps sleep would come more easily to both of us, after yesterday and this morning.

I watched her go inside, and then came into my own house. I left my wellies in the passage behind the stairs, under the line of empty coats and dented hats hanging from the pegs, and walked barefoot up to my bedroom.

Mead seems very lovely in the light of this summer morning. If I listen hard enough, I can hear the place breathe.

I rest my forehead against the cold windowpane. I am thinking about magic, and *The Tempest*. Lack of sleep has stretched my imagination, making it swell and sway, then break loose and drift like a bubble. I can see the princess crossing the meadow in her gold necklace, dressed in skins, with her red-brown hair bound in twisted ropes, her cup-bearer pacing at her heels.

Then, from across the fields I hear the bell of Meddlett church strike six, and I am anchored again.